# THE WORST ADMIRAL IN THE STAR CLUSTER

DUMB LUCK AND DEAD HEROES
BOOK 9

SKYLER RAMIREZ

eBook ISBN: 978-1-964457-76-5

Paperback ISBN: 978-1-964457-77-2

Hardcover ISBN: 978-1-964457-78-9

Printed in the United States of America

Published by Persephone Entertainment Inc.

Texas, USA

## PRAISE FOR THE WORST SHIP IN THE FLEET

If you like stories of heroes in need of redemption, this is the story for you. ...by the end, you will definitely want to read more.

TAMMY RUGGLES, READER VIEWS

...filled with humor, heartbreak, and mystery... an exhilarating interstellar adventure you won't want to end.

PIKASHO DEKA, READERS' FAVORITE

Brad's story can serve as a message of hope...

ABRAHAM OZO, ONLINEBOOKCLUB.ORG

## PRAISE FOR ROGUE AGENT

If you enjoy watching films like Black Widow, Wonder Woman, and Hanna, you will love reading Rogue Agent.

ALIJA TURKOVIC, READERS' FAVORITE

## PRAISE FOR THE GALAXY'S WORST MERCENARIES

...an altogether refreshing take on a journey through space.

KIRKUS REVIEWS

...maintained a fast pace and was full of unexpected twists with no dull moments.

ISABELLA HARRIS, READERS' FAVORITE

# CONTENTS

# DUMB LUCK & DEAD HEROES TIMELINE

## *The Brad Mendoza Chronicles*
*(Brad Mendoza's Backstory)*

*Saving the Academy* (short story)

*Bells & Bullets* (short story)

*Death Patrol* (short story)

*Siege at Jalisco* (short story)

## A Star Nation in Peril
(Heather Kilgore's Origin)

**Rogue Agent**

**Suicide Mission**

**Assassin's Flight**

THE WORST SHIP IN THE FLEET

THE WORST SPIES IN THE SECTOR

THE WORST PIRATE HUNTERS IN THE FRINGE

THE WORST RESCUERS IN THE REPUBLIC

THE WORST DETECTIVES IN THE FEDERATION

## DUMB LUCK AND DEAD HEROES (PHASE 1)
(BRAD MENDOZA & JESSICA LIN)

# AND CHRONOLOGICAL READING ORDER

## The Galaxy's Worst Mercenaries

(The Adventures of Billy Firebrand)

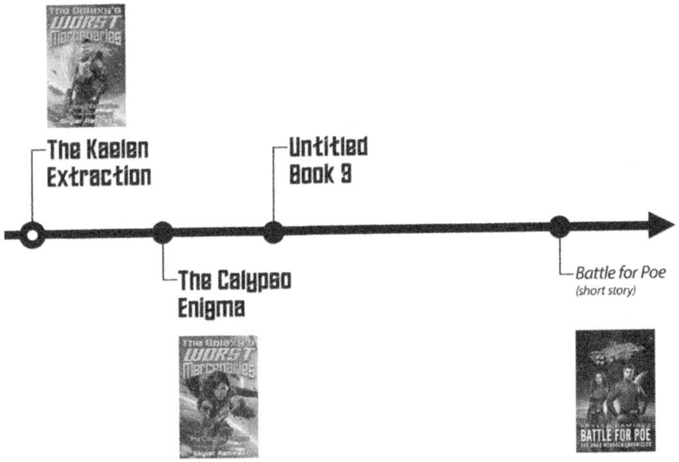


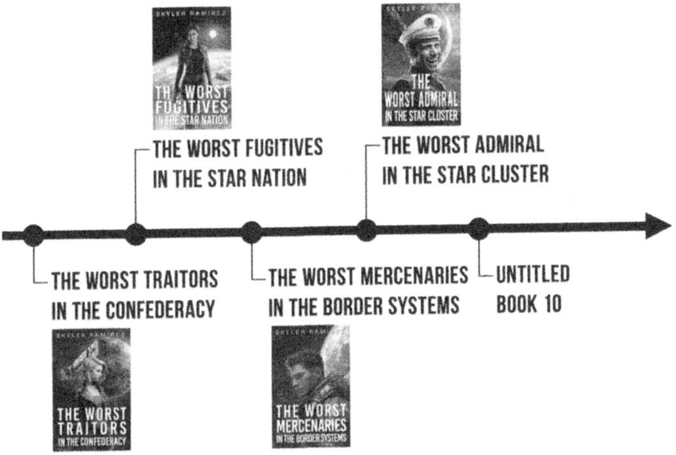

# WHAT'S HAPPENED UP TO NOW

I thought my readers might benefit from a brief recap of everything that's happened up until this point. Feel free to skip this part and go straight to Chapter One if you feel you remember most of the storyline from the first six books. Otherwise, I hope this helps. Warning: Tons of spoilers here if you haven't read the books before this one.

## BOOK ONE: THE WORST SHIP IN THE FLEET

After making an impossible decision in the line of duty that killed 504 civilians at Bellerophon, Brad Mendoza has hit rock bottom. He's drunk and recently divorced, and he feels he has nothing left to live for. But he's still a captain in the Royal Promethean Navy, and he was cleared of any actual wrongdoing. Because the admiralty can't kick him out of the Navy, they decide to force him to quit by sending him to the backwater system of Gerson to take command of the worst ship in the fleet: HMS *Persephone*.

Brad can immediately tell something is off when he arrives to take command of *Persephone*. On his first day, an enlisted man, Petty Officer Nedrin Jacobs, talks down to him and practically threatens him. Then, he meets Lieutenant Commander Jessica Lin, his new executive officer (XO), with whom he is immediately smitten. However, Jessica appears to have secrets of her own, and Brad surmises she might be in a relationship with Jacobs.

After a confrontation with Jacobs and another with Jessica, Brad learns, to his horror, that there is, in fact, a relationship, but that it's not consensual. He further learns that *Persephone's* former captain, Clancy Jessup, was also assaulting Jessica. Despite his efforts, she refuses to talk about it or condemn the two men. Just as Brad is resolved to learn the details and take action anyway, they encounter an enemy ship from the Koratan Confederacy sneaking about in Gerson's outer system.

Outgunned, outmatched, and with a blown engine, *Persephone* has nowhere to run. Brad enlists the help of his crew, especially Jessica, to devise a daring plan. They pretend to have a high-level government agent on board (a member of the King's Cross), betting that the Koratans will prefer to capture the agent alive versus destroying the ship outright.

They lure the Koratans in close and plan to self-destruct *Persephone* to destroy the enemy ship. Brad offers to be the one to stay behind and blow up *Persephone,* sending the rest of the crew out on escape pods first. He loads a message into one of the escape pods with video proof that Jacobs and Jessup have been assaulting Jessica, hoping to at least get justice for his XO before his death.

However, at the last minute, one of his officers knocks him out and takes Brad's place, destroying *Persephone* and the Koratan ship.

Brad awakens later in his escape pod to Jessica's frantic calls. The entire crew is rescued shortly thereafter and taken back to Gerson Station. There, Brad encounters a real high-level agent of the Promethean government, assassin and Agent of the King's Cross Heather Kilgore. She informs him that the Koratans were in the system to find an extremely valuable and recently discovered deposit of stellarium, a metal used to make impregnable warships. She then reveals that Nedrin Jacobs is the King's nephew and that the King will likely order Brad's and Jessica's deaths to cover up the scandal that will result from Brad's message.

Taking pity on the two officers, Kilgore arranges for them to fake their deaths from injuries supposedly sustained in the battle and then gives them a ship on which to make their escape.

## BOOK TWO: THE WORST SPIES IN THE SECTOR

Brad and Jessica flee Gerson on their new light freighter, *Wanderer*. At Jessica's insistence, Brad gets sober, and they start looking for work to pay for their new lives on the run. But when they attempt to secure a paid cargo to haul, bureaucracy gets in the way, and they end up having to take a job from a sketchy man named Owen Thompson, who is traveling with several 'friends'.

En route to the Fiori system to pick up Owen's cargo, Brad and Jessica get to know each other better, and Brad admits to himself that he's fallen in love with his former XO. But he believes she'll never feel the same. Meanwhile, Owen and his friends are scheming against them, and they take over *Wanderer*, putting an explosive implant into Jessica's head so that Brad will do their bidding.

They force Brad and Jessica to help them locate a defector from the Promethean Navy on the Rishi Paradise Casino Orbital. Owen claims the deserter has valuable intelligence his employers want and that they need Brad to use his intimate knowledge of the Navy to help them locate their man. Brad and Jessica reluctantly agree but have little luck at first.

Finally, Jessica manages to find their target, George Peterson. Brad pretends to be an agent of the Promethean Security Service (ProSec) and forces George to take them to an abandoned asteroid mining facility where he's hidden the intel he stole.

The intel George Peterson stole ends up being the exact coordinates to the stellarium deposit in Gerson, which he plans to sell to the Koratans. Once they are at the asteroid and have recovered the intel drive, Owen tries to kill Brad and take the coordinates. Through skill and a lot of luck, Brad manages to kill Tucker, Owen's enforcer, and then Owen himself.

At that point, Heather Kilgore arrives to recover the intel from Brad, revealing that she hired Owen and suggested he use Brad and Jessica to help find the coordinates. Brad is angry but focuses on saving Jessica. He boards *Wanderer* again and finds that Jessica has already somehow subdued Owen's two other soldiers. They convince one of them, Harris, to disable the explosive implant in her head. Harris then decides to join their crew, and they leave the final mercenary, Jules, alone to die on the asteroid's surface.

While flying out of the Fiori system, *Wanderer* is stopped and boarded by a Leeward Republic battlecruiser, *Dauntless,* which is carrying Jessica's estranged father.

## BOOK THREE: THE WORST PIRATE HUNTERS IN THE FRINGE

While Jessica has a meeting on *Dauntless* with her father, Brad is interrogated in a friendly fashion by Admiral Walters of the Leeward Republic, who unsuccessfully tries to learn from him what the Promethean King is hiding at Gerson. Before she releases Brad and Jessica, she convinces them to take on a mission to save a small, independent planet, Carter's World, from a pirate siege. She introduces them to Kayla Carter, daughter of the planet's president, who offers to lead them back to her home and pay for their help.

Desperate for money, Brad and Jessica agree. En route to Carter's World, Kayla starts to flirt with Brad, making advances that he rebuffs at first. But he hears Jessica say something that makes it nearly certain she will never return his feelings. Distraught, he starts to succumb little by little to Kayla's flirtations.

When they arrive in Carter's System, the pirates are waiting and almost capture them. Only some fancy flying through the atmosphere of a gas giant allows them to escape. Kayla guides them to Carter's World, where they land at her father's farm out in the countryside, away from the eyes of pirate spies. There, they meet her father, President Carter, and members of his government.

Brad agrees to train the Carter's World militia to attack the pirate base, using weapons given to them by Admiral Walters. During the week of training, Kayla continues to make advances toward Brad, but he rebuffs her again, realizing that he's still very much in love with Jessica.

Training complete, Brad and Jessica take the militia members, President Carter, and Kayla to the pirates' asteroid base. There, they confront the pirate boss, Poulter, and kill him and his crew. Afterward, they split the spoils of war with President Carter, giving him much of the pirates' stolen loot and keeping for themselves a small warship, which they name *Persephone II*.

As Jessica and Harris fly *Persephone II* out of the system and Brad flies *Wanderer* to ferry Kayla, her father, and their people back to the planet, Brad is having second thoughts about the entire mission. Suspecting there's more to things than meets the eye, he calls the planet and discovers that the real President Carter is there and doesn't have a daughter named Kayla. He's about to call Jessica and warn her when Kayla intervenes, revealing herself as a mercenary hired by unnamed forces to get the stellarium coordinates from Brad. He learns that the mission against Poulter's pirates was both a way to gain Brad's trust and a way for Kayla's organization to use him to take out an increasingly annoying ally in the process.

Kayla takes Brad prisoner, and he watches helplessly as a bomb she planted on *Persephone II* explodes, supposedly killing Jessica and Harris.

But Harris discovers the bomb just in time, and Jessica manages to get it into the airlock to jettison it. However, the bomb explodes before she can shut the hatch, and the ship is damaged while Jessica is badly burned and almost killed.

## BOOK FOUR: THE WORST RESCUERS IN THE REPUBLIC

Kayla tortures Brad for the stellarium coordinates, believing he memorized them from George Peterson's intel. Meanwhile, the real President Carter, grateful for the removal of the pirate threat, agrees to help Jessica go after Kayla and save Brad. He patches up *Persephone II* and provides her with a crew from his now-defunct system patrol fleet.

Jessica leaves the planet with her new ship and crew but has little idea where to start looking for Brad. She decides to head back to the Fiori system to confront her father there, suspecting he had something to do with Kayla kidnapping Brad.

In the Fiori system, Jessica hires Gunnery Sergeant Quinn Boyd and his team of mercenary soldiers. They help her storm Skytran Orbital, making it to her father's executive office and confronting him there. We learn that Jessica's father once betrayed her, using her to get valuable Promethean intel for the Leeward Republic, resulting in the deaths of 57 members of the Promethean Navy. Jessica has never forgiven herself, and Nedrin Jacobs and Clancy Jessup used knowledge of the event to blackmail and assault her on *Persephone*.

Jessica also confronts her father about Brad's kidnapping, and he admits to working with Kayla in return for part of the windfall from the stellarium deposit. Under duress, he gives her a comm code and a dead drop location in the Kate's Hope system to make contact with Kayla.

Taking her ship and crew, Jessica flies to Kate's Hope, but a stakeout of the dead drop location yields nothing. About to give up, she encounters an odd woman named Hayley Uvalde, who claims to be an intelligence officer for hire. Uvalde uses the comm code to trace Kayla to the Capaldi system.

Meanwhile, Brad has been barely holding up under weeks of Kayla's relentless torture. He finally gives her a set of fake coordinates for the stellarium, and when she sends a ship to Gerson to investigate, it's followed back to Capaldi by Agent of the King's Cross Heather Kilgore. But Kilgore's ship is captured by pirates allied with Kayla before she can rescue Brad, and she joins Brad as Kayla's captive.

They soon learn that Kayla's employers are officers of the Jutzen Collective, a star nation of neo-Nazis who want the stellarium to build an unstoppable fleet of conquest. The Jutzens provide Kayla with a truth serum, which she uses to enhance the interrogation of Brad and Kilgore.

Jessica and her crew take *Persephone II* to Capaldi, but they're ambushed by the same pirates who captured Kilgore. They narrowly escape and destroy the pirate ship. But then, they encounter a Jutzen battleship, whose admiral tells Jessica that Brad is already dead and warns her to leave the system.

Uvalde finds the exact coordinates of the station where Kayla is holding Brad. Escaping the Jutzens, Jessica and her crew fly to the coordinates and undertake a daring space jump to assault the station and rescue Brad. They find him and Heather Kilgore alive but learn that Kilgore gave up the stellarium coordinates under the influence of the truth serum.

During the rescue, still under the influence of the Nazi truth serum, Brad confesses his love for Jessica. He's overjoyed when she reveals that she loves him back.

The Jutzens, intent on not letting Brad, Jessica, or Kilgore escape, come to the station to chase them. Once again, the scrappy crew of *Persephone II* manages to outwit the enemy, but the ship is too damaged to continue, and they take escape pods down to the system's inhabited planet. The Jutzens pick up Kayla's pod and then leave the system to take the coordinates back to their fleet.

On the surface of Christos, Uvalde finds where Kayla stashed *Wanderer*. Some of the Carter's World crew decide to stay with Brad and Jessica, as do Quinn Boyd and Hayley Uvalde. Together, they set off in *Wanderer* to build lives as both mercenaries and legitimate freight haulers. But on their first stop back at Kate's Hope, they encounter Brad's ex-wife, Carla, who has an urgent mission for them.

## BOOK FIVE: THE WORST DETECTIVES IN THE FEDERATION

Carla hires Brad and Jessica to find a missing Promethean Navy task force, Task Force 32. Her new boyfriend, Horace Clarington, was with TF32 when it disappeared at the opposite end of Promethean space. Somehow, Clarington managed to get a cryptic message out to Carla asking for Brad's help and suggesting he find Admiral Ricardo Jimenez, an old quasi-friend of Brad's and an officer in the Koratan Navy.

They travel to Hudson, a contested planet claimed by both Prometheus and Koratas, taking cargo with them and almost getting captured by poachers and then by pirates in the process. When they finally arrive at Hudson, they find an ex-cop named Timothy Gentry, recommended to them by Heather Kilgore. He agrees, for a large fee, to help them find and question Ricardo Jimenez.

After escaping a kidnapping and assassination attempt by an unknown agent, Brad and Jessica, with Gentry's help, finally find Jimenez at a high-stakes underground poker game. Brad makes contact, but ProSec is also there to see what Jimenez knows about TF32. In the ensuing chaos, Jimenez is shot by a hidden sniper and dies, but not before confessing to Brad that he knows where TF32 is being hidden in the XB-411 system.

Captured again, this time by ProSec agent Kat Henderson, Brad's old XO, our heroes barely escape yet another assassination attempt. This time the danger comes from a traitorous member of Kat's own team. Capturing one of the traitor's colleagues, they learn that the Jutzens are behind everything, planning to use the ships of TF32 to attack Koratan ships in the Hudson system, with the goal of starting a shooting war between Prometheus and Koratas. By doing so, they hope to force the King to leave Gerson and the stellarium deposit undefended.

Unable to convince the arrogant Promethean admiral at Hudson to believe their circumstantial intelligence, Kat Henderson enlists Brad, Jessica, and their crew to help her take a top-secret stealth ship, HMS *Vampire,* to XB-411 to gather the proof she needs. At XB-411, they search for days and finally find both the ships of TF32 and a massive Jutzen dreadnought, the *Bismark.*

Our heroes sneak onboard *Bismark* and rescue the small number of surviving crew of TF32, leading them to freedom. At great cost of life, they manage to steal back one of TF32's destroyers, HMS *Bainbridge,* to use in their escape. Before they leave, they set off a nuclear bomb inside *Bismark* that destroys the Jutzen ship, but not before it manages to shoot down *Vampire* with Jessica on board.

Luckily, Brad is able to rescue Jessica and the others with her before they run out of air. They take *Bainbridge* back to Hudson, but the Jutzen-crewed ships of TF32 beat them there. Brad, Jessica, and the rescued Promethean officers of TF32 arrive at Hudson expecting to find a war broken out. However, in their absence, Carla managed to call in favors owed to her and Brad from Duke Laraby Garrison of Kipling, the Promethean Federation's second most powerful man behind the King. Duke Garrison and his fleet destroy the ships of TF32 before the Jutzens can carry out their attack, stopping the war before it starts.

When Brad and Jessica arrive at Huston Station, the Navy attempts to arrest them, but Duke Garrison intervenes and arranges for them escape *and* take *Bainbridge* with them. In return, he asks Brad to undertake a mission to rescue his little sister, Larissa Garrison, who he believes has been kidnapped by revolutionaries and taken into Koratan space. Brad and Jessica agree and leave Hudson with their crew on board *Bainbridge*.

A few days into their journey, however, they learn that Hayley Uvalde is a traitor, secretly working as an agent for the Koratan Confederate Guard, an organization of deadly assassins and spies.

## BOOK SIX: THE WORST TRAITORS IN THE CONFEDERACY

Brad and Jessica continue their mission to rescue Larissa Garrison in Koratan space, but they worry about what to do with the knowledge of Hayley Uvalde's betrayal. Knowing they will need all the help they can get, they set out in search of Quinn Boyd's old team, who took a mission at his direction in Koratan space.

Finding that Boyd's team inadvertently took a job for Koratan drug lords, Brad and team interrupt a high-level meeting of crime bosses on Santa Maria Station. They are briefly taken captive, but Hayley Uvalde reveals her true colors and takes out the cartel soldiers, allowing Brad, Jessica, Boyd, and his old team to escape on *Bainbridge*. They leave the station listening to a litany of threats from Baron Dexter Hornsby, a well-known Promethean mob boss who was part of the meeting they interrupted.

Shortly thereafter, *Bainbridge* is disabled by a ship of the Koratan Confederate Guard. Nido, Hayley's old boss, boards their ship and offers to pay them a substantial amount if they are successful in removing Larissa Garrison from Koratan space. She believe the girl is there to foment more rebellion within both star nations and is willing to share her exact location. The only catch is that Nido insists that Brad and Jessica have to keep Hayley with them, despite also revealing that Hayley suffers from multiple personalities, including a ruthless assassin named Lola.

Along the way, Brad and Jessica pick up more crew in the Santo Domingo system, including two teenage twins, Tina and Sam DeJong, whom they save from pirates. *Bainbridge* must then play a game of cat and mouse with a Koratan Navy destroyer before finally arriving at the Serenidad system, where they expect to find Larissa Garrison.

Brad, Jessica, and a troublemaking Tina DeJong infiltrate the fortress Larissa is being held in by crashing a charity auction there. Searching the manor house, they find Larissa, who claims to be there against her will. But on their way out, Tina disappears, and the rest narrowly evade capture by stealing an antique car, a 1964 ½ Ford Mustang from Earth, worth billions of credits.

Brad drives the Mustang with Jessica and Larissa to where Quinn Boyd and team can pick them up. Jessica and Larissa get to safety, but Brad stays in the car to draw off pursuit so they can escape. He crashes the priceless car and is taken back to the manor house as a prisoner.

There, he discovers that Laraby and Larissa's mother, Duchess Charlotte, is behind the efforts to gain Koratan support to depose King Charles. Charlotte hates Brad for twice before foiling her plans while he was still in the Navy (outlined in *The Brad Mendoza Chronicles*) and promises to torture and kill him. But he escapes when Tina DeJong, still hiding in the manor house, pops out of an air vent and leads him to where Hayley Uvalde has infiltrated the compound to rescue them.

Hayley, operating as her ruthless Lola persona, mows through the manor house's guards to get Brad and Tina to safety. She leads them to a safe house to await the rest of their crew. There, they are ambushed by Nido and other Confederate Guard agents, who confess to manipulating Brad for their own purposes and must now kill him to cover their tracks. In the scuffle, Hayley, Brad, and Tina are all knocked out and taken prisoner, but not before Hayley fights her own organization attempting to save Brad.

However, when Brad, Hayley, and Tina wake up, they find that they've been rescued by the personal security detail of none other than Koratan President Nanette Fournier. Fournier confides in them that she has been fighting traitorous elements in her own government, including Nido and her colleagues. She thanks them for exposing both Duchess Charlotte, who died resisting arrest, and Nido, and grants them safe passage out of Koratan space.

Meanwhile, Jessica is back on *Bainbridge* and must use strategy and cunning to defeat two Koratan warships loyal to Duchess Charlotte. After the battle, she returns to the planet, threatening to bombard it if Brad, Tina, and Hayley are not returned to her. With the cooperation of President Fournier, she picks up her three lost friends and they leave the system together on *Bainbridge.*

Halfway back to the border with Promethean space, Larissa Garrison reveals her true colors, betraying them and calling in support from Baron Dexter Hornsby, one of her mother's sponsors and financiers. Hornsby ambushes *Bainbridge* in the Helgatha system, where a third of the crew dies in the ensuing battle against his boarding forces. Only Hayley, acting as her Lola persona, manages to save the day by killing enough of Hornsby's soldiers to scare them into retreat.

Now aware that Larissa was a fully willing participant in her mother's treason, Brad and Jessica decide to return her to her brother, Duke Garrison, anyway. They deliver the rebellious teenager to agents of the duke and then proceed to a shipyard in the independent Jewel system to get *Bainbridge's* damages from the fight with Hornsby repaired. On the way, Jessica proposes marriage to Brad, and he naturally (and very ecstatically) accepts.

While waiting for their ship to get fixed, Brad, Jessica, and the crew take a well-deserved vacation at an all-inclusive luxury resort on Jewel's surface. All is perfect until Jessica gets a mysterious call and must leave abruptly without telling Brad.

## BOOK SEVEN: THE WORST FUGITIVES IN THE STAR NATION

While vacationing at a luxury resort on Jewel, Jessica receives a cryptic message that makes her abruptly depart, leaving a confused Brad behind. Shortly thereafter, Promethean Naval Intelligence Agent Jake Traeger shows up on Jewel, using threats against Jessica's safety to force Brad and the crew to help him hunt down the crime boss, Baron Dexter Hornsby. Brad is given command of the Q-ship *Odysseus,* a warship cleverly disguised as a civilian bulk freighter.

Meanwhile, Jessica finds herself held captive and interrogated by Naval Intelligence Agent Jethro Jensen, her former fiancé, on Lightman Station. There, she quickly discovers that Jethro intends to turn her and Brad over to the King for trial, even if Brad manages to capture Hornsby.

Commanding the *Odysseus*, Brad and his crew track Hornsby across the Independent Systems. Harris discovers Hornsby's unique encryption schemas, leading them to the revelation that the faux baron is manufacturing weapon components for the Jutzen Collective to start a war against Prometheus. Brad decides they must steal Hornsby's shipment to disrupt his plans and draw the crime boss out of hiding, leading them to ambush his vessel and board his factory station in the Zepha system. In the fighting, Traeger seemingly betrays Brad and allows Hornsby to capture him.

On Lightman, Jessica is still held hostage by Jethro, but that ends when a mysterious bounty hunter in black kills her ex-fiancé and almost captures her as well. Jessica evades the bounty hunter with the help of an old friend, Jetta, and they enlist a smuggler named Val to get them off the station. But in the process, Val's ship is damaged, and they crash land on the desert planet Wake, where Val dies and Jessica and Jetta are left stranded awaiting the bounty hunter.

Back in Zepha, Brad's plan comes together. After seemingly betraying him, Traeger drops off Quinn Boyd, Drake Forbes, Edgar Kluth, Hayley Uvalde, and Harris to infiltrate Hornsby's station and rescue Brad, capturing the baron in the process. There, they discover that the 'weapons' Hornsby is manufacturing for the Jutzens are actually specialized jump drives that can use unstable jump points to get around a system's defenses. Brad and Traeger figure out that the Jutzens plan to use them to attack Gerson from behind the defending Promethean fleet stationed there.

Desperate to save Jessica, Brad tricks Traeger, using

Harris's hacking skills to take total control of Odysseus. He and his crew take the Q-ship back to Promethean space, picking up Jessica's distress call from Wake.

But before they can arrive, the bounty hunter tracks Jessica and Jetta to Wake and into an underground cave system there. Playing a deadly game of cat and mouse in the caverns, the bounty hunter reveals her identity: Kayla Carter, the same woman who captured and tortured Brad and almost killed Jessica in *The Worst Pirate Hunters in the Fringe*. Kayla subsequently reveals that she's been hired by Nedrin Jacobs, the King's nephew and the man who repeatedly assaulted Jessica on *Persephone*, to find and kill her to keep her from ever testifying against him. In a close fight, Jessica kills Kayla and escapes the cave system with Jetta.

Brad arrives on Wake and rescues Jessica and Jetta from the surface. But before they can leave the system, they're ambushed by ships from the Corinthian System Patrol, sent by Jacobs and commanded by Captain Clancy Jessup, the other man who assaulted Jessica on *Persephone*. In the battle that follows, Brad and Jessica defeat Jessup with the help of their own destroyer, *Bainbridge*, which arrives in the nick of time. Unfortunately, Brad is trapped in a battle-damaged fighter that spins out of control across the system.

In a strange series of events, Brad is rescued by none other than his fictional hero, Billy Firebrand, who turns out to be very real. Billy convinces Brad and Jessica to come with him to the Reynolds system, where Leeward Republic Admiral Walters is waiting with a job for them. Then he punches Brad in the face for being an annoying fanboy.

## BOOK EIGHT: THE WORST MERCENARIES IN THE BORDER SYSTEMS

After the events of book seven, Billy Firebrand Jr. leads Brad and Jessica to a secret meeting with Princess Anne Worthington, heir to the Throne of the Federated Systems of Prometheus. Anne is planning a coup against her mentally unstable father, King Charles. She needs Brad and his ship to carry a message and a negotiator to seek the help of President Nanette Fournier of the Koratan Confederacy.

To ensure Brad takes the mission, Anne threatens to implicate Brad and Jessica in the coup and then forces them to take along her negotiator, Theresa Evers (one of Brad's ex-girlfriends).

On the way to find President Fournier in the Quito system (just inside the Koratan border), Brad, Jessica, and the crew of *Bainbridge* stumble upon a ship hit by slavers in the Edmonton system, further turning Brad against King Charles as he sees the fruits of the monarch's failing government.

When they finally arrive at Quito, they find President Fournier's fleet destroyed there by rebel elements of the Koratan Navy. To find out what happened to Fournier, they rescue several survivors from the president's escort fleet, battling the enemy rebel forces in the process.

As they escape with the survivors, *Bainbridge* is heavily damaged, so Brad and Jessica take her to a nearby civilian shipyard, where they force the shipyard owner to divert resources to fix their ship.

The Koratan survivors rescued at Quito reveal that a rebel warship kidnapped Fournier during the battle and took her away from the system. Brad and Jessica 'borrow' a luxury yacht from the shipyard to chase after Fournier and her captors.

Using every strategy available to them (Brad flirting with an amourous system patrol commander, Jessica bribing a fuel depot attendant with peanut butter, etc.), they find Fournier's trail and track her to the Torreón system.

There, they discover the system is firmly under rebel control. Tricking the rebels, during which Brad almost dies on a spacewalk, they continue to follow Fournier's trail to a hidden underground rebel base on the planet, built in old subway tunnels and stations.

They infiltrate the base, save President Fournier, and confront the rebel leader, who turns out to be Oswaldo Heraldo Hernandez Guadalupe, one of the villains from book six (Brad crashed Hernandez's classic mustang in that book, if you recall).

Chasing Hernandez through the underground tunnels, they find a manufacturing facility where the rebels are building phase torpedoes, designed for planetary bombardment.

Hernandez dies after a final fight with Brad, but not before making it clear that there is someone above him in a grand conspiracy of which the Koratan rebellion is merely a part.

On their way out of the system, Brad, Jessica, and President Fournier encounter an incoming Koratan fleet, which turns out to be loyal Navy forces also looking for Fournier. To show gratitude for rescuing their president, the Koratans fix *Bainbridge,* making her even better than new. Theresa Evers uses the time to attempt to negotiate Koratan help for Princess Anne's coup against King Charles, but President Fournier balks at taking out a fellow head of state.

However, before negotiations conclude, intelligence arrives that the Jutzen forces have sacked Prometheus itself, killing King Charles and taking over nearly a third of the Federation. And they used phase torpedoes to do it, the same type Brad found in Hernandez's underground manufacturing facility.

With this new information, President Fournier and her fleet accompany Brad and his crew back to Promethean space to meet with the newly crowned Queen Anne. Anne and Fournier negotiate a mutual support pact, while Jessica surprises Brad with a wedding on board Anne's flagship.

Anne promotes Brad to vice admiral and Jessica to captain and begs them to stay and help the war effort, but they refuse, still stinging from her earlier extortion and betrayal. Instead, they decide to go back to Edmonton and try to find the slavers who raided the derelict ship they found there earlier in the book.

All this brings us to the beginning of book nine, The Worst Admiral in the Star Cluster, where Brad and Jessica are just beginning their mission to find the slavers operating in Edmonton.

## A SUPER IMPORTANT LIST OF PEOPLE WHO WANT BRAD DEAD

Wow, that was a lot! I mean, seriously, what more could possibly happen to Brad and Jessica at this point? In reality, quite a bit more. Because there are many, *many* people in the galaxy who still want Brad Mendoza dead. In fact, I thought it might be helpful to compile a non-exhaustive list of everyone who wants to kill Brad:

1. Fleet Admiral Terrence Oliphant
2. Captain Wainwright
3. Petty Officer Nedrin Jacobs
4. Commander Clancy Jessup (deceased)
5. King Charles of Prometheus (deceased)
6. Approximately 4,328 members of the Koratan Confederate Navy
7. Owen Thompson's third cousin, twice removed on his mother's side
8. Kayla 'Carter' (deceased)
9. Vizeadmiral Heinrich of the Jutzen Collective Navy (along with all his Nazi friends)
10. Several poachers on the planet Jocelyn
11. Admiral Christoph Turly

12. 'Baron' Dexter Hornsby
13. Agent Nido of the Koratan Confederate Guard (deceased)
14. Oswaldo Heraldo Hernandez Guadalupe (because Brad crashed his priceless Mustang, which frankly infuriates me as well) (deceased)
15. Duchess Charlotte Garrison (deceased)
16. Larissa Garrison
17. A concessions vendor at the Royal King William Memorial Stadium, home of the Promethean Navy Knights (very much alive and plotting his revenge)

# BRAD & JESSICA'S CREW

Here's a helpful reminder of the members of Brad & Jessica's crew, as constituted at the beginning of book nine.

## CREW OF THE MV *BAINBRIDGE*

**Vice Admiral Brad Mendoza** (M) – Everyone's favorite idiot.
**Captain Jessica Lin** (F) – Brad's XO and better half. Seriously, she's more like 7/8s of this relationship, if we're being honest.
**Lieutenant Commander Francis Illian** (M) – Tactical Officer. Joined the crew from Carter's World initially just to help Jessica save Brad in *The Worst Rescuers in the Republic,* but he's stuck around ever since. Likes to shoot at other ships and date unstable assassins with multiple personalities (Hayley Uvalde). Otherwise, a pretty boring guy.
**Lieutenant Commander Kelly O'Malley** (M) – Chief Engineer. Was with Brad and Jessica in the beginning on the original HMS *Persephone* in *The Worst Ship in the Fleet*. Rejoined the crew in Hudson after the events of *The Worst Detectives in*

*the Federation*. Everyone likes Kelly. If you happen not to like him, you may be the problem.

**Lieutenant Hayley Uvalde (aka Agent Sparrow)** (F) – Intelligence Officer and undercover member of the Koratan Confederate Guard. Has multiple personalities, and we're never quite sure which one is going to show up or what color her hair is going to be. But extremely good at her job. Favorite pastimes include toppling planetary governments, ruthless assassinations, and making her boyfriend (Francis Illian) uncomfortable in public settings. Joined the crew in *The Worst Rescuers in the Republic.*

**Petty Officer Harris** (M) – Who knows? One day, he's a makeup and disguise expert. The next, he's a tailor sewing extra pockets on Brad's uniform. Sometimes, he's an incredibly talented hacker. But always introverted and generally a bad dresser. Joined the crew at the end of *The Worst Spies in the Sector.*

**Karen O'Malley** (F) – Ship's Cook and Kelly's wife. The only person on the crew who can order anyone around, even Brad. At least if he wants dinner.

**Lieutenant Laia Gammon** (F) – Sensor Officer. Was part of Jamie Durkin's crew, which all joined Brad and Jessica during *The Worst Traitors in the Confederacy*. Enjoys long walks on the beach and designating sensor contacts for Brad to shoot at.

**Petty Officer Toshi Ishii** (M) – Engineer. Also formerly part of Jamie Durkin's crew.

**Spacer 1st Class Pilar Moya** (F) – Engineer's Mate. Also formerly part of Jamie Durkin's crew. Currently babysitting Tina and Sam Dejong as they fly around in *Wanderer* looking for shipping contracts.

**Doctor Damien Bean** (M) – Ship's Medical Officer. A mad scientist type who joined the crew to escape the law during the events of *The Worst Traitors in the Confederacy.*

**Spacer 3rd Class Tina DeJong** (F) – Engineer's Mate. Seven-

teen-year-old girl rescued from pirates by Brad and Jessica during the events of *The Worst Traitors in the Confederacy*. Likes to hide in air vents and listen to other people's private conversations. Currently on detached duty on *Wanderer*.
**Spacer 3rd Class Sam DeJong** (M) – Helmsman. Tina's 16-year-old brother. Can't really fit in air vents like his sister. Currently on detached duty on *Wanderer*.
**Jetta** (F) - Jessica's really chatty and annoying friend from Lightman Station. She's an engineer, but Kelly makes her work the night shift and avoids her at all cost. Trust me, you would too.

## SHOOTERS

**Gunnery Sergeant Quinn Boyd** (M) – Gunny. Joined the crew to help Jessica rescue Brad during the events of *The Worst Rescuers in the Republic.* Big, scary ex-Marine, but really a teddy bear once you get to know him. I mean, don't you just want Gunny Boyd to give you a warm hug… right after he vanquishes your foes?
**Corporal Heddy Rodriguez** (F) – Gunny Boyd's original number two. Don't get on her bad side. Trust me on that. My ribs are still healing.
**Private Drake Forbes** (M) – Original member of Gunny Boyd's team. Has a secret crush on Jessica, but you didn't hear that from me.
**Private Daren Beck** (M) – Also originally part of Jamie Durkin's crew. Likes checkers over chess.

## KORATAN NAVY TRANSPLANTS

During the events of *The Worst Mercenaries in the Border Systems*, Brad and Jessica enlisted the help of several Koratan

Navy officers. Some of them, with President Fournier's blessing, chose to stay on *Bainbridge* as part of a detached duty (or the galaxy's weirdest exchange program). They include:

**Lieutenant Gio Vargas** (M) - Engineering
**Petty Officer Marcos Juarez** (M) - Engineering
**Spacer 1st Class Paulina Encarnacion** (F) - Engineering
**Ensign Diana Rodrigo** (F) - Tactical
**Spacer 2nd Class Ricardo Lopez** (M) - Tactical (Gunner's Mate)
**Chief Petty Officer Manual 'Manny' Cortes** (M) - Helm
**Spacer 1st Class Malina Martinez** (F) - Helm/Shuttle Pilot
**Spacer 1st Class Herman Estes** (M) - Deck Crew
**Marine Corporal Eliza Johnson** (F) - Shooter

# PART ONE
# THE HUNT

# ONE
# DARING ESCAPE

## BRAD MENDOZA

"What's the matter with you, boy? You some kinda idiot or somethin'?"

I sigh, reaching one hand up to massage the bridge of my nose, where a migraine has been rapidly forming since I started this conversation. Across the chipped counter in the Edmonton Station administration waiting room, the low-level clerk scowls at me with the same look my grandfather used to give me when he caught me trying to sneak a horse out of the barn for a late-night ride in my underwear.

"For the last time, Administrator Hollins," I say in my best long-suffering tone, "we're here trying to track down a slave ship that hit a freighter transiting the Edmonton system five weeks ago. It's as simple as that."

He grunts. "And I'm tellin' you, boy, that we ain't had no slavers here for as long as I can remember!"

"I beg to differ. In fact, I'm the one who called in the report about the derelict freighter they hit. It was clearly the work of slavers, not just normal pirates."

He frowns at me and checks something on his console again. "You said you're the ones called it in?"

"I did say that."

"Hmmm. Says here our system patrol found no evidence of no slavers."

I sigh, my headache getting worse. "Double negative aside, sir, all the male crewmembers were lined up and shot execution style, and all the women were missing, so . . ."

Administrator Hollins scowls some more at his console. "Wait here." He's gone before I can tell him I have no desire to do so.

Rubbing the bridge of my nose again, I look around the small waiting room with its drab carpet and Formica counters. Except for me and my bodyguard, there's no one else here right now, at least until the terribly unhelpful administrator comes back.

My first sign he's not planning on returning is when the outer door crashes open and two figures in security uniforms burst in, weapons drawn and pointed right at me.

"Freeze!" the first one, practically a boy, calls in a voice still breaking from late puberty. "You're under arrest."

With yet another sigh, I slowly raise my hands above my head. Momentarily, I wish I were wearing my new admiral's uniform, or *any* uniform for that matter, instead of the civilian garb I insisted on donning in its place. I had my reasons, and they made sense at the time, but not so much now that I'm staring down the barrels of two pistols.

The boy with the gun looks supremely relieved when I raise my hands. But his triumph is foiled when I point with one finger and the flick of a raised wrist toward my bodyguard. "What about her? Is she under arrest, too?"

He takes his eyes completely off me and looks over at the smiling form of Hayley Uvalde, lounging in one of the waiting room's chairs and looking about as innocent as can be. Her hair is bright purple today, and she's purposely sitting way back on the chair so her legs can swing underneath it like she's a kid at a park.

"Oh . . ." the boy says, hesitating. "Is she with you?"

Rolling my eyes, I nod.

"Then you're under arrest too!" he says, far too loudly for the enclosed space. He swings his gun over to point at Hayley.

His partner, a harried-looking, middle-aged woman who at least seems to have a modicum of sense, is already pointing her gun at Hayley, and has been since we walked in. "Colton," she chides, and he looks back at her in confusion.

"Oh . . . sorry, boss," the boy says, realizing that neither of their guns is covering me right now and quickly switching his back to point at my face.

Fun.

"What is this all about?" I ask, looking past the boy at his older partner, who's clearly the one in charge.

"Suspicion of piracy," the woman says matter-of-factly.

"Really? I mean, I've done a lot of things, but never piracy. On what grounds do you suspect me of it?"

"Did you file an anonymous report about a derelict freighter in the outer system five weeks ago?"

I nod. "That's why I'm here; I'm trying to track down whoever took that ship out. By the way, they were definitely slavers, *not* pirates."

"Well," she says, still sounding like she doesn't really care, "since you're now the only person we've found with a connection of any kind to that ship, we're taking you in for questioning."

There are days when I just want to scream into a pillow.

But a quick check of the reception area reveals no helpful pillows to accommodate me. I take a deep breath, keeping my eyes on the uniformed woman, trying very hard to ignore her young partner's gun, which is still shaking.

"Did you miss the part," I ask, "where I'm here looking for information on the ship and the people who hit it so that I can go *chase* them?"

"We only have your word for that," the boy says before his boss can reply, causing her to scowl at the back of his head.

I shrug at him as best I can with my arms still held above my head. "You also only have my word that I'm the guy who called in the freighter's position and status. So either I'm telling the truth about calling it in and therefore about being here looking for more information so I can *help* the people kidnapped from it, or I'm a liar and you can't trust me when I say that I actually called it in. Either way, don't you think it might make sense to put that gun down before you shoot me by accident?"

The boy looks monumentally confused. He takes his eyes off me entirely to look back at his partner, who just seems tired and annoyed now.

"Besides," I add with a smile in her direction, "your boy here forgot to turn off his pistol's safety."

Her annoyed look turns into a hard glare at him, which he has the misfortune of catching when he takes his eyes off me again to give her a guilty look. As he does so, he starts to fumble with the gun, trying to feel his way to disengaging the safety. I take one big step to the right to lessen the chances he kills me by accident.

Maybe I should have stood my ground. Once Jess finds out I took this little foray to the station without first waking her up to tell her, being shot by this stupid kid might pale in comparison.

It's not my fault. First off, for all of her beauty, grace, and extreme poise while awake, I've quickly learned that my new wife bears a disconcerting number of similarities to a Visalian crocodile when she's woken up before the appointed time. Second, I knew that if I told her, she would have tried to stop me. And I *needed* to get off the ship and stretch my legs.

"Sir, you're just going to have to come with us to the station security office," the woman says when she's finally done lecturing the boy through a series of facial expressions and gestures with her free hand. "I'm sure that if you're telling the truth, we can clear this up there."

Hayley gives me a look that's either asking me if I'm hungry or if I want her to incapacitate or kill the two station cops. I shake my head minutely for her benefit. Though I am hungry . . .

"Sure, Officer," I tell the steadier of the two cops. "We'll come along willingly. If"—I hold up one finger—"you stop pointing those guns at us. My friend here gets really anxious around weapons or violence of any kind. She's a monk. Vow of peace and all that."

The older woman frowns at Hayley. "Doesn't look like any monk I've ever seen. Did she take a vow of silence as well?"

Hayley's response includes vulgarities in three different languages and makes it clear that she hasn't taken any such vow.

Predictably, the older cop shakes her head. "Look, standard protocol. Until we know who you are and what you're really doing here, we have to keep you covered."

My headache is getting even worse. "Fine, but you do know we flew in on that destroyer docked halfway around the station, right?"

She frowns again. She definitely sees where I'm going with this.

"And that my ship has enough firepower to destroy this

entire station, and enough Marines on board to take it over, right?" That last part is a stretch. Gunny Boyd has exactly four other shooters to command, and they're mostly *ex*-Marines. In fact, the only active-duty Marine on our crew is Corporal Eliza Johnson, who happens to be a *Koratan* Marine. I sense that if I were to share that little fact with the two Promethean cops, it would blow their minds, and the kid would definitely shoot me.

Regardless, my statement effectively conveys my point. Five minutes later, without any guns pointed at our backs, Hayley and I are deposited into a very utilitarian interrogation room in Edmonton Station's security office, taking our seats on two hard metal chairs at a table made of the same material.

"Boss?" Hayley asks simply, and I shake my head again. I'm willing to bet I can talk my way out of this, and the fact that we're not handcuffed is a sign that someone might actually listen.

We wait about ten minutes to find out who that someone might be. It turns out to be the older female cop who arrested us, this time without the boy who doesn't know how to use his gun. Now that I can study her closer up, I notice her badge is different from his.

"Marshal," I say, acknowledging her position as the head of Edmonton Station Security. "Have you run our IDs?"

She takes a seat across from us. "I did." She motions at Hayley. "This one comes up blank, which is suspicious enough. But you're Brad Mendoza."

"Guilty as charged," I say. "No autographs, please."

"Funny thing is," she continues, ignoring my amazing joke, "I have two sets of records on you. One says you're an admiral in the Promethean Navy."

"And the other?"

"That you're an ex-captain currently wanted for treason. In fact, I have a warrant for your arrest from the King himself."

That's not good. I sit up straighter in my seat. "You mean you *did* have a warrant out for my arrest from King Charles. But you should also have record of a full pardon from Queen Anne, so . . ."

She shakes her head. "Wrong King. Not Charles. King *Chance,* former Duke Chance Fuller of Serravo."

Oh, that's *really* not good. I look around to see if *this* room has a pillow I can scream into. Like the previous compartment, it's sorely lacking in that regard. "Am I to take that to mean that Edmonton has thrown in with the Duke of Serravo's occupation government?" I ask carefully.

The wonderful Chance Fuller declared himself the new monarch of the Federation after the Jutzens sacked Prometheus and killed King Charles and half the populace of the capital city. The Nazis were quick to endorse Fuller as the head of their occupation government. However, Edmonton is a long way from Prometheus, and far closer to Kipling, where Queen Anne Worthington, Charles's daughter and rightful heir, has set up her government in exile. So I didn't expect to encounter Fuller acolytes all the way out here.

To my small relief, the marshal winces. It's fleeting, but the expression was definitely there. "We haven't endorsed either . . . candidate for monarch yet," she says carefully. "Edmonton's system government is weighing its options." The fact that she says 'its' instead of 'our' adds to my fledgling hope.

I take a moment to collect my thoughts. I can't exactly play the admiral card too enthusiastically here, or even claim that I'm here at the queen's behest. Truth is, Jess and I took our destroyer and our crew and ran the day after Anne—

Annie to me—promoted us and helped Jess stage a surprise wedding on the fleet carrier *King John*. But our queen was expecting me to take command of the *Johnnie* and part of her fleet, so she's definitely not on board with me gallivanting off across the Federation to chase after a random bunch of slavers.

In only the three days we've been gone, she's sent me half a dozen messages expressing her displeasure at my choices, alternating her tone between worried friend pleading for my help and vengeful monarch ready to lop off my head if I don't submit my will to hers. Annie is complex like that. Given that I saved her life as a kid *and* recently helped her forge an alliance with the Koratans to fight the Jutzens, I'm fairly certain she won't really execute me if I ignore her orders to return, but you never can be sure with power-hungry tyrants.

"My dilemma," the marshal continues when I don't speak, "is that if there really are slavers operating in Edmonton space, I have a moral obligation to stop them. You, *Admiral* Mendoza, may be the best hope of doing that. On the other hand, the system governor has given me a direct order to hold you here under lock and key until his people can come up from the surface and take you into custody."

"Where I'll be used as a bargaining chip to strengthen his position with the so-called King Chance and the Jutzens, who want me dead, or with Queen Anne, who would probably like one of her favorite admirals back with his head and limbs intact," I finish for her.

She sits back, folds her arms across her chest, and nods once. "So you get my conundrum. Even if I were, say, loyal to the queen, it wouldn't matter in this instance."

There's that hope again. Still, I suddenly find myself missing the days I was a simple farm boy and son of an accountant on Denton III. Back then, no one outside my immediate family, a handful of friends, and a few unfortunate school teachers knew my name. I definitely didn't have to get involved in these types of Fringe-spanning politics.

I put a hand on Hayley's arm to keep her from killing anyone before lunch. Not that she's moved a muscle since the marshal entered, but because Hayley is the type who needs constant assurance that it's not time to use force to get our way. Looking the marshal in the eyes, I say, "Listen, let's say you were loyal to the queen. Letting me out of here would serve two purposes. First, I hate slavers, so I'll happily kill any I come across and rescue their poor victims. Second, you'd be doing the queen a solid, which can't hurt in the grand scheme of things. And on top of all of that, I'd really like to avoid whatever dungeon your governor has waiting for me. I'm allergic to dungeons—too much despair in the air."

For a long time, the marshal says nothing, just studying me. Once more, no laughs at my terrific jokes. Tough crowd.

Hayley fidgets a little. "Boss?"

The marshal raises her eyebrows. "The monk speaks again?"

"Actually, she's not a monk."

She gives me a droll look. "No, really? I would have never figured that out myself. So what is she?"

"You wouldn't believe me if I told you. But I highly suggest you find an excuse to release us quickly so you don't have to find out. I could threaten your station again with my destroyer's firepower if that would help. You can say I promised terrible calamity upon you and your house, and you had no choice but to let me walk out of here."

To my disappointment, she shakes her head slowly, keeping her arms crossed over her chest. "Won't work. Your reputation precedes you, and no one would believe you'd actually carry out that threat."

I scoff. "Really? No one would believe the *Butcher of*

*Bellerophon* would be willing to kill a few civilians for the greater good?" My formerly light tone darkens despite my best efforts.

She shrugs. "Sure, but no one would believe that of the man who saved Hudson from a Jutzen attack, or who stopped a coup in the Koratan Confederacy, or who saved his XO from a rapist at Gerson. So you see, Admiral, your reputation doesn't back up your threat."

I lean forward, putting my elbows on the table and looking her in the eye. When I was little, my grandpa taught me that to look someone in the eye, you literally needed to choose *one* of their eyes to look at, because you couldn't physically focus on both at the same time. It's one of those little pieces of advice that pops up in your head every once in a while and makes you wonder if you've been doing it right for the last decade. I suddenly can't decide which of the marshal's eyes to focus on. I settle by ping-ponging back and forth between the two, which doesn't seem to work, judging by her confused frown.

Shaking my head to clear it of childhood lessons, I take in a deep breath. "I have a proposal, Marshal."

"I can't wait," she replies drolly.

"Purely off the record, of course."

"Then it's a good thing our interrogation room recording devices are on the fritz."

"Good. I need to get off this station so I can kill slavers. You need that to happen in a way that doesn't make you look incompetent. Hypothetically, of course."

"Of course."

I nod once. "Then how about this? My Marines can storm the station with nonlethal rounds and 'rescue' me"—yes, I make air quotes—"and save you the paperwork of throwing me in whatever lovely cell you've prepared in the back?"

She smiles for the first time in the conversation. "Yes, I suppose that would work nicely. Strictly hypothetically, that is. Especially since most of my deputies are on the lower levels, breaking up a conveniently timed series of bar fights."

I nearly slump in relief, but I force myself to keep my eyes on her left eye, then her right eye, then her left eye—I still can't make up my mind. "Listen, while we're here, what do *you* know about the slavers who hit that ship in the outer system. Pick anything up on the planetary sensor grid?"

Her smile disappears. "No, we did not. I've heard rumors of increased slaver activity in some surrounding systems since Prometheus fell, but that's all they are, rumors, and before your visit, I had no idea any of them might be operating in Edmonton. I'm sorry to tell you that the chances of you finding out who hit that ship in our outer system are slim to none. Not only has that freighter already been cleaned of all evidence and sold for scrap, but the governor declared it the work of pirates, and he's not exactly a fan of folks contradicting him. But . . ."

My implant pings, and I open the file she just sent me, scanning the first few lines of text.

"Andre Bollen." I draw the name out, certain I've never heard it before. "You think he hit that ship?"

The marshal sits up straight and shrugs. "Maybe, maybe not. All I know is that two days ago, I got the wanted bulletin you're reading now. It was sent to all the systems in this sector. According to that, this Bollen guy supposedly leads a new slaver crew operating out of the Corpus Christi Cluster. Now, I have no idea if he's the one who hit our system or not, but I figure taking out any group of slavers is a net positive for humanity in this part of the Fringe."

"So you expect me to go all the way into the Corpus Christi Cluster to hunt down a slaver who may or may not be the one I'm actually after? The Cluster is a big place. Your bulletin doesn't happen to say *where* in its two dozen inhabited star systems this Bollen might be located?"

"Keep reading," she says by way of response.

Frowning, I do, letting my eyes go out of focus so I can study the image my implant projects into my mind, skimming down to the bottom of the bulletin's first page. As I read the system name there, my shoulders slump.

"Poe."

She nods. "Supposedly, there was a sighting of Bollen there a few weeks ago. Seems like as good a place to start as any."

Why does it have to be Poe? "What happens if I say no?"

She graces me with a half smile. "Then your Marines might just encounter more resistance than they're counting on when they try to rescue you. If I'm gonna let you walk, I need to know it's for a good cause. I'm a cop, not a saint. So promise me you'll take out a bigger baddie than yourself, and I'll be able to sleep at night. Got it?"

I could call her bluff. By the size of her security office, she's got maybe two or three deputies in addition to the boy who was with her when she arrested us. Hayley alone could take them all out without breaking a sweat. But still . . .

"Got it," I tell her. "With such scant intel, I can't guarantee anything, but I'll go to Poe at least and poke around."

She reaches her hand across the table. I meet it halfway, and we shake on the deal that no one outside the room will ever know about. But I'll keep my end of the bargain, if only because the Corpus Christi Cluster is about as far away from the war as one can get in Federation space. It seems like a great place for me to go hunt slavers and stay out of Fringe politics, even though I really don't want to go to the Poe system in particular.

Fifteen minutes later, Gunny Boyd and his people stun the

marshal and the two deputies unfortunate enough to be in the office when they arrive to rescue us. Five minutes after that, we're back on *Bainbridge* and blasting away from the station and the single impotent system patrol frigate that mounts a half-hearted chase.

## TWO
# A DECISION TO MAKE

### JESSICA LIN MENDOZA

"You going on that station wasn't the smartest move," I say to my new husband as *Bainbridge* rockets across the Edmonton system toward the jump point that will take us in the direction of Poe and the Corpus Christi Cluster.

Brad and I have been married for exactly four days, and I've done a lot of smiling for that entire period. Now is an exception, as I grace him with my best scowl.

"I thought it was safe," he says from the other side of his ready room desk. He tries to keep his voice even, but it cracks a little on the last word, so my scowl must have done its job. "According to Annie's latest intel, Edmonton was still loyal."

I'm still a bit uncomfortable every time I hear him call our queen by her diminutive nickname, like he's talking about a small child or his best friend. "Oh yes, perfectly safe. Which is why you chose not to wake me up before you went through the airlock, because you knew I'd stop you."

He cringes in a way that tells me he was expecting me to be upset but is still disappointed it's happening.

"Listen, Brad," I tell him soberly, "I'm not just your XO now. I'm your wife. From now on, we're practically one person. That means we can't hide things from each other. Or sneak around behind each other's backs."

His expression changes to one of genuine embarrassment. "You're right, Jess. I'm sorry. It won't happen again."

I sigh. "Yes, it will. But at least next time, tell me you're going to do something stupid before you do it so that I don't have to hear about it from Gunny."

Brad smiles. "That I can promise. Now, aren't you at all curious to know what the marshal gave me?"

Reluctantly, I nod. He uses his implant to throw up the digital wanted bulletin on the room's small display screen.

"They don't even have a picture of this Andre Bollen?" I ask dubiously after scanning the front page. "And not much else to go on except the supposed sighting at Poe."

Brad moves around his desk to stand next to me in front of the viewscreen. "I admit, it's not much, but we wanted to hunt slavers—you know, help out the unfortunate displaced by this war and ignored by the bigwigs while they fight over the scraps? And this Bollen guy is supposedly a slaver."

I chew on the inside of my lip as I command my implant to show me the rest of the file. I read it silently for five minutes, having my implant's AI cross-reference a few things. When I'm done, I focus my eyes back on my husband. "It's really sparse intel. But if someone at Poe can give us more, I agree that it's at least worth checking out."

The smile that breaks out on Brad's face is a mixture of happiness and relief, and I momentarily wonder what he might have done if I'd said no. I dismiss the thought quickly, relegating it to the back of my mind, where it sits with the other things I don't choose to dwell on except in the late hours of the night.

I step closer to Brad and give him a light kiss on the lips.

"What was that for?" he asks.

"Just being you," I tell him honestly. "And for coming back to me. You got lucky with that friendly marshal."

"You kidding?" he says with a lopsided grin. "Hayley was just itching to bust me out of there. It was all I could do to protect the marshal and the other cops from *her*."

I chuckle, but my heart isn't in it. Someday, we might be able to go a week without someone trying to capture or kill us. But apparently, this is not that week. I open my mouth to say more, but I'm interrupted by the chime at the hatch leading from the ready room into the bridge.

Brad uses his implant to command it to open, and Commander Francis Illian steps into the ready room. Or rather, he feels his way into the room with one hand while the other covers his eyes.

"Are you two decent?"

"Of course we are," I snap at him, a little too harshly. "Seriously, does everyone think that the two of us are constantly . . . you know, now that we're married?"

He removes his hand from his eyes, looking sheepish. "Well, not everyone. Okay, so maybe yes, everyone. You do realize I share a bulkhead with your quarters, right?"

The blood rushes to my face, and my ears burn.

"What do you need, Guns?" Brad asks, trying far too hard to hold back a laugh at the man's embarrassment, or maybe at mine.

"Message from the Edmonton System Patrol," he reports. "They've demanded that we heave to and prepare to be boarded, by order of the system governor and someone named Earl Wainscot."

"How close are they?" I ask, grateful for the change in subject. "Any chance they'll catch us?"

Francis smiles. "Maybe if we cut thrust now and fire the retros. That little patrol frigate is pretty sad."

"Hey," Brad says with a fake scowl. "Jessica and I met on a little patrol frigate like that one."

"Even so," Francis replies, "they're not catching us unless we want them to, sir. What should I tell them?"

My husband's expression transforms into a wicked grin. "Nothing. Put Jetta on the comm and have her ask them about their ship's specs. That oughta keep them busy."

I groan. Jetta, who joined our crew after she and I fought off and killed Kayla Carter on Wake, is one of my best friends ever. She's the one who got me through my exile on Lightman Station, after the events at Hothan and Yolandra that were very much my version of Brad's tragedy at Bellerophon.

Despite my love for Jetta, however, I have to admit that even I have a hard time talking to her for more than a few minutes at a time. I've never met anyone who can jabber like her, and her fast speech and frequent changes of topic are hard to follow.

"Aye, Admiral," Francis says with a smile of his own, and then he's gone.

"That was mean," I tell my husband. "Siccing Jetta on that poor system patrol commander."

He smiles at me again. "What? Just being friendly."

## THREE
# NIGHTMARES

### BRAD MENDOZA

"Sir, the children!"

I whirl at the shout from the nearby Marine, losing my purchase on the bulkhead and floating away from it in the zero-g wreckage of the *Cumberland*, the refugee freighter I destroyed at Bellerophon. I immediately see what the terrified Marine is talking about. All around us, the corpses are waking up—but only the children.

"You killed us," one small boy says, pointing at me, and I'm shocked that I can hear his voice in the vacuum.

Then a little girl sneers and lunges toward me, small hands outstretched in claws that—

I jolt awake, gasping for breath, arms held up, crossed in front of me like I'm trying to ward off some kind of wild animal. For a moment, I don't know where I am, and I sit there, panting, desperately looking around for some clue to my location.

A light senses my movement and illuminates, casting a dim glow just bright enough for me to confirm that I'm in my cabin on *Bainbridge,* no longer in the shattered cargo hold of the *Cumberland.* I gulp a great lungful of air in relief.

The nightmares seem to be coming more and more often of late. Tonight, I've had three that I can remember, all from Bellerophon, all as grisly and jarring as the last one.

"Brad?"

The voice catches me off guard. I look down and to one side to see Jess, lying next to me and squinting up like she can't make me out in the scarce light.

"Brad? You okay?"

I nod, then realize she might not be able to see the gesture. "I-I'm fine, Jess. Go back to sleep."

She doesn't argue, just rolls over and promptly falls back into the slow rhythm of breathing that signals she's already drifted off again. If I weren't reeling from my nightmare, I'd smile. Jess is a surprisingly deep sleeper. It's shocking, really, as most spacers, especially those in the Navy, learn early on how to go from sleep to wakefulness in an instant, a required trait in case of emergency. Waking her up before her alarm is usually a violent proposition, verbally at least. This time didn't result in her yelling at me, and I feel a sense of overwhelming relief.

Still, it's a good thing my dear wife has never been on a ship that lost atmo. She'd sleep right through her asphyxiation.

I study her, her back to me now. Jess's hair, longer than when we met but still only just past her shoulders, lies to one side, revealing the back of one ear and the soft skin of her neck where it meets the spine. Underneath the blanket, I admire the curves of her body and sigh.

As horrible as my nightmare was, there are far worse things to wake up to.

If only I could simply lie down next to her and go back to sleep as quickly as she did. But doing so would just invite more of the terrible dreams that have plagued me for the last year since Bellerophon, and even more in the weeks since learning of the fall of Prometheus and Annie's insistence that I rejoin her Navy as a vice admiral.

That line of thinking starts to take me to a very dark place, so I gingerly pull back the covers from my legs and get out of the bed, careful not to wake my wife again. It's a surprisingly hard thing to do, despite how deeply she slumbers. The narrow bunks on Navy ships, even in a captain's cabin, aren't exactly built for two people. It's against Navy regs for a married couple to serve on the same ship. But Jess and I have managed to make it work thus far, even if she did almost murder me when I got out of bed too quickly for a bridge shift yesterday, shaking the mattress enough to wake her up.

Have you ever seen a beautiful woman turn into a fire-breathing monster from the depths of Hades' realm in an instant? I can now confidently say I have.

Still moving slowly so as not to wake her, I slip into a pair of loose pants and a tunic that I conveniently left on the floor, then pad in bare feet out to our cabin's living space. There, I find my shoes and slip them on. A minute later, I'm out of the cabin.

I have no destination in mind as I wander my destroyer's corridors. It's the middle of the night shift, and Lieutenant Laia Gammon has the bridge watch with Chief Cortes, one of our Koratan transplants. I head in the opposite direction, mostly because I have no real reason to go to the command center and don't want my subordinates thinking I'm there because I don't trust them. Eventually, I find myself in the small area that passes for Marine country on an Apollo-class destroyer.

Like most spaces where Marines bunk and gather, it has a gym. I decide that's as good a place as any to spend some time until I'm tired enough to go back to bed. As I turn the corner and head into the compartment, however, I realize someone else is already there.

"Captain—sorry, Admiral?" Heddy Rodriguez, Gunny Boyd's second-in-command, looks up from the weight bench, where she's barely straining under the load of more plates than I can ever recall having bench-pressed.

"Oh, sorry, Heddy, I'll go," I stammer as I start to back out of the compartment.

"You can stay, sir," she says, lifting the bar one more time and replacing it on the stand. "It's your ship."

Unsure of what else to do, I walk with an uncertain gait over to a rack of dumbbells, studying them like they're disease-ridden armadillos that might give me leprosy. Why did I come here again?

"Couldn't sleep, sir?"

I look back over at Heddy. She's sitting up on the bench now, studying me with raised eyebrows.

"Uh, no. Not really."

"Nightmares?"

I squint at her. "Yeah. How'd you guess?"

She smiles wanly. "No offense, sir, but you look a little sweaty, and you haven't even started lifting weights yet. Plus, we're sort of on a perfectly temperature-controlled starship." Her smile shifts. "Of course, there are other things you could have been doing."

Despite myself, I snort an uncomfortable laugh. "Seriously, is that all people think Jess and I do all day?"

She has the good grace not to reply, so I turn back to study the leprous dumbbells again. Finally deciding on a pair that looks only slightly less offensive than the others, I pick them up, grunting a little. I look at myself in the mirror that runs the length of the bulkhead, and I catch Heddy still studying me from behind.

"No offense, Corporal," I say, if for no other reason than to fill the awkward silence, "but isn't it dangerous to bench-press without a spotter?"

Heddy shrugs, the muscles of her shoulders pronounced with the motion. "That?" She gestures back at the weight-laden bar. "It's nothing. Light enough not to get me into trouble, even if the emergency grav plates don't engage like they're supposed to."

I look at the heavily-laden bar skeptically.

"Want to talk about it, sir?"

Her question takes me by surprise. "About the weights?"

She gives me the same look my mom used to when I'd pretend to fall asleep while my dad talked about his boring day as an accountant. "No, sir, the nightmares."

Frowning, I shake my head, which she obviously takes as an invitation to talk anyway.

"I get them, too, sir. All the time. Had one tonight—it's why I'm down here."

My curiosity gets the better of me. "What about?"

Her mouth compresses to a thin line, and I'm about to retract the question, but she answers first. "I never did tell you why I left the Republic Marines, did I, Admiral?"

"No. I suppose you haven't." My voice cracks a little as I start to idly lift the dumbbells, straining my biceps. Heddy has the tact not to laugh at my laboring.

"Republic's a lot like any other government, sir," she says, lying back down on the bench and hefting the bar again. As she talks, she pumps it up and down with considerably less effort than it takes me to keep raising the stupid dumbbells. Am I that out of shape?

Yes. Yes, I am.

"Some of the orders they gave us," she continues, "were easy to follow. Stop these terrorists here; put down this insurrection there; protect a VIP on a fact-finding tour of the outer systems. All simple enough when the good guys and bad guys were straightforward. But sometimes . . ." She pauses, still rhythmically lifting and lowering the bar and the heavy weights at each end.

I'm smart enough not to press her. I give her the time to decide on her next words.

"One day, there came a set of orders that weren't so easy to follow. At Benton. Ever heard of that system, sir?"

I shake my head, still watching her in the mirror as my biceps start to really burn. Belatedly, I realize she isn't watching me, but she doesn't wait for me to acknowledge the question verbally.

"Little system on the border between the Republic and the Jutzen Collective. One inhabited planet and a few asteroid mining stations. Otherwise, a pretty unremarkable system, except for its strategic position. Republic politicians were worried that the Jutzens might declare it one of their protectorates and use it as a jumping-off point to invade us."

"Seems reasonable enough," I say, setting the dumbbells back on their rack as the burning in my biceps gets to be a little too much. "All things considered."

"Maybe," she admits. "But reasonable or not, our Congress felt it would be a good idea for *us* to annex them before the Jutzens did. Sold it to the rank and file as a glorious mission to bring to the people of Benton the wealth, prosperity, and protection the Leeward Republic had to offer."

That's not just idle talk. The Leeward Republic has the highest per-capita income and standard of living of any major Fringe star nation. Sometimes I think I wouldn't mind them annexing *me*. But . . .

"I take it the Bentonians . . . Bentonites . . . Bentons didn't agree?"

Heddy sets the bar back on the rack and sits up again, studying me. "Got it in one, sir. See, someone forgot to ask the Bentonites what they thought about the Republic's offer. Turns out they didn't want us or the Jutzens taking them over, so they fought back. You ever shoot a farmer whose only weapon is a bolt-action rifle and whose only sin was to want a bunch of intruders off his land?"

"Sort of," I admit, flashing back to Belleropon and the *Cumberland*. "Though I did it with a missile."

She winces. Besides Gunny, whose cousin was on the *Cumberland*, I've rarely talked about the details of Bellerophon with any member of my crew. Even Jess knows not to bring it up with me.

"Sorry, sir. I guess you know what I'm talking about. Still, I followed my orders like a good soldier . . . until I couldn't follow them anymore."

"What did you do?" If I were sitting down, I'd be on the edge of my seat by now.

"I decided I was done doing what the Republic Marines told me. I called it conscientious objection. They called it desertion and dereliction of duty. Either way, it landed me in the brig for the journey home."

"Court-martial?"

Heddy nods, a faraway look in her eyes.

"Been there," I grunt.

"Twenty years," she says, still not looking at anything here in the gym with us. "They gave me twenty years in the stockade."

That seems excessive. "How'd you get out?"

Her eyes fix back on me, and she smiles again. "Gunnery Sergeant Quinn Boyd had something to do with that. It's why he and I have to be super careful stepping foot in Republic systems using our real identities."

"Wait, so you're not really Heddy Rodriguez?"

She smiles wider now. "Not saying I am; not saying I ain't. Besides, sir, you should be used to your crew not having the names we were born with. Uvalde rarely uses the same name she gave us last week."

I grunt in agreement. "Is that why you follow Gunny?"

Heddy chuckles, a rich sound that I don't recall having heard all that many times. "Well, let's just say it's not only because he has nice lats, sir."

I can't help but laugh in return.

We say little more as I finish my 'workout' and she finishes hers. For a while, her story makes me feel a tad less alone. But when I leave the gym and head back to my quarters, the weight of my nightmares feels heavier with every step. By the time I finally reach my cabin's hatch, most of the catharsis of my brief exercise and my chat with Heddy have faded.

I enter as quietly as I can, removing my shoes as soon as I'm inside and tiptoeing across the carpeted deck and into the bedroom. There, I stop in my tracks.

A year ago, when Carla finally divorced me after the Bellerophon disaster, I was convinced that I'd never find love again. In fact, I convinced myself I never *deserved* to find love again. Even in my first month and a half with Jess, when I felt myself falling more and more for her, I just knew she'd never love me back. And when I thought she'd died in that explosion in Carter's System, I was convinced it was the universe reminding me that I could never be happy again.

Now, I know the universe was wrong in that regard. Jess is turned back over, facing toward me in the small bed, her face a serene mask that betrays none of the stress we've been under since the day we met. A lock of hair has fallen over it, and I have the overpowering urge to walk over and move it out from in front of her closed eyes.

It's an urge I resist—remember what I said about Visalian crocodiles?

But I do make my way back over and lower myself carefully into bed, facing my wife. I don't know how long I simply watch her sleep, but it stills the demons in my head, at least enough for me to drift off.

# FOUR
# ACROBATICS

## JESSICA LIN MENDOZA

It's cute that Brad thinks he can get in and out of the bed without waking me up. Considering the bed is the size of a postage stamp, that would be quite the feat. So when he comes back to bed after wherever he's wandered off to for the last forty-five minutes, I pretend to stay asleep.

It's really hard given how long he just lies there *watching* me fake sleep before he finally falls asleep himself.

Just as I'm finally drifting off again myself, my implant pings. "Captain Mendoza?"

Ugh, why is someone calling Brad in *my* implant? Then the voice repeats the name again, and I belatedly realize that it's talking to *me*. Having a new last name is taking a lot of getting used to. It's also driving confusion on the bridge when both Brad and I respond to 'Captain Mendoza.' What makes it worse is that I can tell he's still getting used to his new rank, and that he's not exactly happy about the promotion, so he tends to prefer the crew to call him 'Captain' instead of 'Admiral'.

"I'm up," I reply in my implant as I open my eyes. "What's up, Laia?"

"You asked us to wake you when we were about to enter the Poe system," our sensor officer replies. "We'll be emerging from jump space in twenty minutes, ma'am."

I check my implant's clock and see that it's 0320 ship time, far too early for any reasonable person to be up and about. But regulations say a senior officer must be on the bridge every time the ship emerges into a new system, even a supposedly friendly one. Besides, after three days in transit from Edmonton, I'm bored.

"Thanks, Laia. I'll be up before we emerge."

I cut the connection and peer at Brad sleeping next to me. He lies on his side, his face relaxed, looking younger than he normally does. We've been married for just a week, and sleeping together in his—no, *our*—cabin for less than that. But I've already marveled several times at just how different my new husband looks when he's asleep.

Brad has a lot of nightmares, probably about Bellerophon is my guess. He thinks I don't know about those. I haven't figured out yet how to bring the topic up with him, especially since the first time he woke me up in the middle of the night with his mumbling and crying out, I wasn't exactly gracious about it.

However, at times like this, when he isn't having one of those terrible dreams, he looks almost as innocent and serene as a child. It makes me realize how much of a ragged edge he carries with him when he's awake, even when he's happy or joking around. Ironically, I never noticed it before I saw him this way.

Time to get up. I need to be on the bridge in about fifteen minutes. It's regulations.

I stop myself at the recurrence of that thought. When Brad and I first left the Navy, more than nine months ago, I had a very hard time letting go of the order, consistency, and rigid nature of military life. For a while, I missed even the regulations and procedures that were somehow comforting in their relentless conformity.

But now? In the last several months, I've learned to relax and let life come at its own pace. Maybe I'm not as good at that as my new husband, but it's been literally forced upon me as we've learned together that our new lives require a different way of thinking.

Brad and I have technically been back in the Navy for a week, and beyond our formal reinstatements and promotions, nothing has really changed. We're still on *Bainbridge* and still with our crew that feels more like a family. In fact, Brad, Kelly O'Malley, and I are still the only members of the Promethean Navy on board our ship—we actually have more active-duty *Koratan* spacers than we do Prometheans, having kept a good chunk of the crew who joined us to rescue President Fournier in Koratan space, lent to us by the president on a sort of detached duty—a weird sort of interstellar foreign exchange program, if you will.

But despite all that's changed, and for reasons I can't put into words even in my own mind, I've started falling back into the familiar and well-worn patterns of military life. In fact, I feel an almost irresistible compulsion to go back to the old way of doing things. The mere thought of *not* being on the bridge when we exit jump space fills me with unexpected anxiety.

I snort a breathy laugh as I look at Brad. Sleeping with my superior officer is *definitely* against regulations, but the sight of him there in our darkened quarters quells a part of my anxiety. It reminds me that things are, in fact, different now.

Regardless, I need to get out of bed. And therein lies my next major challenge.

Navy bunks aren't built for two people. It's a wonder Brad and I can even fit into this thing together. Worse, like almost every other bunk on the ship, ours is up against a bulkhead, with another bulkhead at its head—the room's corner—and yet another at its foot, the wall of our small private head. That leaves only one long edge open for me, and my new husband is sleeping peacefully between me and that side of the mattress.

Unfortunately, Brad is a light sleeper, so there's almost no way I can do this without waking him. However, since he's had such a hard time sleeping lately and was already awake for a while tonight, I am absolutely resolved to find one.

Briefly, I consider calling Kelly and having him cut the artificial gravity for a moment so I can float out of bed. That, however, would result in a lot of angry crew members when things designed not to float would suddenly do so, no doubt with disastrous results. You've never hated zero-g as much as you imagine you could until it hits without warning, right when you're taking a sip of hot coffee.

As carefully as I can, I sit up and scoot toward the foot of the bed. There, I draw my knees to my chest and use my hands to lever myself up until I'm standing on the mattress near Brad's feet, ducking down to keep my head from hitting the low ceiling. Then I very lightly—in attempt, if not in fact—step over his legs and down onto the deck on the other side.

My movement turns on a dim cabin light to help me see where I'm going. I move across the bedroom as silently as I can in bare feet to the room's sole dresser, in which Brad insisted I take three of the four drawers. I reach inside, going by feel rather than sight, searching for the worn cloth of my typical shipsuit. I'm about to grab it and take it out when the back of one hand brushes a silky garment. Almost without conscious thought, I take that one from the drawer instead and, after only a moment's consideration, put it on in the dim light.

When I'm dressed in it, I move over in front of the room's floor-to-ceiling mirror, where another dim light illuminates so I can make out my reflection.

I pause there, studying myself. For the last several months, I've worn a large variety of shipsuits, skinsuits, dresses, and even my so-called warrior princess outfits: Aurellian leather tunics Harris made special for me to hide my now-healed scars from the explosion in Carter's System. But it's been quite some time since I've worn anything resembling the skinsuit now on my frame.

It's a relatively simple one—blue with white and gold trim, the palette of the Promethean Navy. I used to practically live in uniform skinsuits like this one, until I lost the right to wear it after Brad and I 'died' at Gerson.

Donning it again sends a little rush of mingled excitement and pride through me. Then my right hand moves to my left shoulder, tracing the barely raised fabric of the four gold bars there, and I smile at my reflection. Before, I only had three bars in that spot, one of them thinner than the other two, indicating to all that I was a mere lieutenant commander. After Hothan and Yolandra, I'd assumed that any promotions above that rank would be forever out of my reach. After Gerson, it no longer seemed to matter.

I thought I'd made my peace with all that, but I was wrong, because seeing myself back in the familiar uniform with the unfamiliar four broad captain's stripes fills me with a sense of euphoria.

I slip on a pair of ship shoes and tiptoe back across the

small bedroom, where I lean down and place a light kiss on Brad's temple. He stirs and smiles in his sleep, muttering something too muffled for me to make out. It's a miracle I haven't woken him up by now.

I leave the room, wincing as the opening door sends a shaft of light across the bed and my still-sleeping husband. I close it lightly behind me, looking around the living room and office that make up the rest of our shared cabin. Space is at a premium on a ship the size of *Bainbridge*, but compared to the junior officer quarters in which I spent most of my adult life, the captain's cabin is downright palatial, even for two people.

I'm about to make my way over to the external hatch to leave when a blinking red light under the room's viewscreen catches my eye. For an instant, my heart stops as I remember the last time I was alone and saw a message light like that—back on Jewel, when my ex-fiancé, Jethro Jensen, forced me to run, leaving Brad and our friends behind.

But that was months ago, and there's no way I'm going anywhere now. I walk over to the viewscreen and command my implant to query the ship's AI for the message source and sender. I'm surprised when I see that it was received when we passed the courier ship at the Corsine-Poe jump point, before we entered jump space. It's marked for my eyes only, which is strange. The ship's computer should have notified me immediately upon receipt. A quick scan of the metadata reveals that the AI attempted to do so, but Brad and I were already asleep, and we'd asked not to be disturbed for any nonemergencies.

Frowning, I command my implant to play the message on the room's viewscreen at low volume. The face that appears and stares out at me shocks me almost as much as Jethro's did months ago.

"Captain Lin . . . or should I call you Captain Mendoza,

now?" says Queen Anne Worthington. We've only been gone for a week, but she already looks to have aged years. There are dark circles under her eyes, and her normally lustrous hair is a little limp.

"I've tried to reach Brad several times," she says, "but either he's ignoring me or hasn't gotten the messages." By the way she says that last part, she believes it about as much as I do. He's *definitely* ignoring her. "I need you both back here, Captain Lin—Jessica. I know you're rightfully upset at the way I strong-armed you into taking the mission to Koratan space, but the Federation is bigger than our own personal squabbles. And the Federation needs two of its best officers back on the front lines."

She pauses, blinking rapidly before going on. "Listen, Jessica, you and I both know that Brad isn't running because of what I did to the two of you. He's running because of what happened at Bellerophon."

What is she talking about? Brad hasn't mentioned Bellerophon in over a month now, and I can't even remember the last time I heard him call himself a mass murderer. I'm sure he's not *over* it yet—the nightmares are plenty testament to that—but why would she think that's the reason he and I aren't back with her and the fleet right now?

"He's afraid," the recording continues. "But afraid or not, we need him. *I* need him. I'm honestly not sure how long I can hold what remains of my kingdom together. I need every loyal senior officer I can get, and Brad is one of the best. As are you," she hastens to add. "Please talk to him."

Frowning again, she nods once as if to confirm to herself that she's said what she needed to say, and the recording cuts off.

I stand there for a long time, staring at the darkened viewscreen, running her words through my mind several times. I keep asking myself what she meant by Brad being afraid; it makes no sense. I've never seen Brad truly fearful of anything. And despite what happened at Bellerophon, he's been through so much since then, cheated death so many times, that surely the queen is wrong about that having anything to do with our—

"Hey."

I turn with a startled gasp to see my husband standing in the bedroom doorway, smiling at me.

"What are you doing up this early?" he asks, wiping sleep out of his eyes and yawning. Then his smile disappears. "And why are you wearing that?"

I try to collect myself. "We're about to exit jump space into Poe, and I wanted to be able to use my Navy rank if the system patrol challenges us," I lie, though I'm not entirely sure why.

He squints at me. "Okay. Everything else good?"

Blast. I thought I sounded casual enough, but he's picked up on something in my posture or tone, the lingering shock of the queen's message, no doubt.

"Everything's fine," I lie again, as smoothly as I can. "Sorry I woke you. Go back to bed. I'll make sure we get into the system all right and set course for the planet. You can join me on the bridge when it's time for your shift."

He eyes me with a slight frown but nods his agreement. Then he smiles again. "Uniform still looks great on you."

I return his smile. "Maybe I'll have to wear it more often then."

Despite the playfulness of my tone, my statement makes his smile falter for an instant. But he yawns again and turns back to disappear through the darkened doorway, leaving me alone with the churning thoughts in my head. I leave the cabin and head to the command center to see what awaits us in the Poe system.

# FIVE
# RISK ASSESSMENT

## BRAD MENDOZA

"Admiral, nothing on scanners. A single freighter in orbit of the inhabited planet, but no indications of hostile intent or movement. The threat-board is clear."

I grunt to acknowledge Lieutenant Laia Gammon's report, if not her annoying use of my new rank. We've been out of jump space for close to eight hours now, and *Bainbridge* has already burned most of the way toward Poe's sole, barely inhabited planet.

Jess shoots a questioning glance my way from her XO's chair next to me. I pretend not to notice. She's picked up on a little of my reticence to visit Poe now that we're here. I swear, if the intel on Bollen hadn't mentioned the little star system directly, I would have steered us well around it on our way into the Corpus Christi Cluster.

Of course, in Jess's mind, I should be ecstatic to be back here. My first visit to Poe, after all, was a triumphant one, and I consider my actions here to have been the height of my naval career. In that, unfortunately, lies the problem, but I can't think of a single way to convey to Jess the complex emotions that coming back here causes to roil up in my stomach.

It takes us six more hours to arrive at the planet, allowing Jess and me to take quick naps and to rotate the bridge crew to do the same. When we close enough distance to see the planet up close through the external cameras, it's just like I remembered it: a small, rocky sphere almost too small to hold an atmosphere, and supporting fewer than a million inhabitants.

"Captain, the system governor is hailing us and asking our intentions," Harris says from the comm station. "Do you want to send a response?"

I jump in before Jess can reply—given how forgetful and ignorant of naval ranks Harris is, he's probably talking to me anyway, bless that man. "Mr. Harris, share with them that we're here on behalf of the Navy and that we're looking for information on a possible slaver ring operating in this part of space."

"Okay," he replies, in a true lack of military decorum. I could kiss him.

"Wait," I say, a thought suddenly occurring to me. "Don't sign the message with my blockchain ID. Use Captain Mendoza's—I mean, Captain Lin's." Best to clarify that; Harris is so clueless sometimes, he might not even remember that we're married and that Jess took my last name.

Speaking of my wife, she looks at me funny, and I give her a glance that hopefully conveys that I'll explain later. Whether or not it's successful, she doesn't challenge me there on the bridge in front of the crew. Maybe there's some silver lining to having her behave like a Navy officer again.

An hour later, we successfully insert *Bainbridge* into orbit, and it's time for me to face the music.

Poe is such a small colony that it doesn't have an orbital station. For the first hundred years or so of its existence, it used its old colony ship as one, maintaining it in high orbit as a waystation for the few visitors to the system. But when that giant ship finally got too old to repair and had to be broken down into scrap metal, the citizens of Poe learned to do without.

Which is also probably why, as we pass the lone freighter in orbit, I notice that it's the kind of model with several large cargo shuttles attached to the hull like parasites, so it can load and offload cargo directly from the surface.

It also means we have to take *Bainbridge*'s own small shuttle down to the planet.

"You look good," my wife says, moving up to stand next to me in front of our cabin's narrow mirror before we board the shuttle.

"You're a good liar," I try to say back in a pithy tone, but my voice cracks a little as I study the blue, white, and gold uniform with the admiral's stars on each shoulder. As I intended, I fought Jess on wearing my uniform down to the planet, and as anticipated, I lost that battle. There simply was no good reason I could give her for why I didn't want to don the hated garment.

"Do you know Governor Warren?" she asks, choosing to ignore my comment.

I shake my head, still frowning over the uniform. "He wasn't the governor when I last came through here. Way I heard it, he's only been in office a few months."

"Is that a good or bad thing for us?"

I shrug, mostly because I have no idea, and because my definition of good might differ from hers. I'd actually prefer a governor who wasn't here when I saved that mining base in Poe's outer system over two years ago. It made for one heck of a story—my favorite one to tell, in fact—but coming back to where it happened has me on edge.

Jess leads the way out of our cabin and down to the shuttle dock. A small ship like *Bainbridge* doesn't have a shuttle bay like a battleship or battlecruiser. Instead, it carries a single shuttle tucked up against the belly of the ship like one of those weird suicidal fish that are always hanging around really mean sharks on nature shows. Very similar to how that freighter carries its cargo shuttles.

Our shuttle is smaller than those and can fit eight passengers in a pinch, plus the pilot and copilot. Given the size of our crew and the fact that we expect Poe to be a friendly planet, we travel light. Malina Martinez, one of our Koratans, takes the pilot's seat with me acting as her copilot. If having a Promethean vice admiral looking over her shoulder makes her nervous, then she betrays no sign of it. In the shuttle's passenger compartment behind us are Jess, Gunny Boyd, Hayley, and Darren Beck.

The ride to the surface is uneventful, not that we'd expect anyone to try anything with an Apollo-class destroyer providing support from orbit. *Bainbridge* isn't exactly built for ground bombardment like a Zeus-class battleship with phase torpedoes, but with the small and lightly armed settlements on Poe's surface, she's more than enough to dissuade any would-be attackers. And that orbiting bulk freighter certainly isn't any threat to us.

It pains me that I have to think of things like attackers and threats on a friendly planet, but it's the galaxy we now live in. Regardless, Poe is probably one of the safest places in the galaxy for me in particular. At least, I hope that's still the case these days.

Malina brings the shuttle in for one of the smoothest landings I've ever experienced, on a shuttle pad two kilometers outside of Poe's one major city. When we're settled and unstrapped, Gunny lowers the rear boarding ramp. The instant the seal breaks, a warm and gritty wind whips inside and worries our faces, carrying the dust of the plains around us on the abnormally flat planet's surface, with no mountains or even large trees to serve as windbreaks.

"Is it always like this?" Jess asks, squinting against the onslaught.

"Only on the nice days," I answer absently as Gunny pushes me behind him before I can disembark, insisting I wait until he can give the all clear.

What a sight he must be to the two shuttle port employees who stand outside their half-cylindrical metal shed of an office—I believe it's called a Quonset hut—and watch a giant with a gun larger than most men could hold tromp his way down the ramp and sweep his eyes and the barrel of that monster weapon across the barren landscape. The two men duck back inside their hut in a hurry.

Gunny finally gives the all clear when it becomes obvious there are no hostile tumbleweeds in the vicinity, and Jess and I disembark next, Hayley bringing up the rear. Darren will stay back to guard the shuttle with Malina.

As my feet touch the dusty concrete pad, the door to the distant quonset hut opens again, and a new figure comes out. She's tall and blonde, and that's all I can tell from this distance, but as she jogs toward us, I see she's also built like an athlete. When she reaches us, I'm taken aback by the icy color of her blue eyes. Not that I have an eye for anyone but Jess these days, but because they're a kind of light blue, almost gray, that you seldom see. It's a little startling.

"Captain Lin?" she shouts at Jess, then looks over at me, where I'm standing half-hidden behind Gunny's bulk. "Admiral? Sorry, Captain, but your message didn't say anything about an admiral."

"And you are?" Jess asks, trying to draw the blonde's attention back to her as I attempt to scoot over to better hide myself behind my giant of a crew member.

"The governor's aide," the woman says over the wind, finally tearing her eyes from me and putting them back on Jess. "He sent me to see why you're here."

"That would be a topic best discussed in a secure location," Jess says, a little coldly. Something about this woman has immediately rubbed her the wrong way, though I can't imagine what it might be.

"I understand, but—" the blonde starts to say, raising her voice over a particularly loud gust. She cuts off at a squeal of metal on metal, and we all look to see a gate rolling open a hundred meters away, admitting a large black SUV. "I suppose you'll get the chance after all," she finishes almost absently.

The SUV, an ancient, wheeled model, pulls up in front of the metal hut, and the two front doors open. A short man with thinning hair gets out of the driver's seat, and a medium-height older woman with streaks of gray emerges from the passenger side.

"I'm going to go make some calls to ensure the governor is ready for your arrival," the blonde says. She turns and scurries back to the Quonset hut, nodding to the two newcomers as she passes them. They pay her little mind and continue onward toward us.

"Captain Lin?" the short man asks in a booming voice easily heard even over the wind. "Welcome to Poe. Your message mentioned wanting to discuss something of great importance with the system government. I'm Lars Sorkin, the governor's chief of staff. What is it you'd like to talk about?"

Again, Jess shakes her head. "Like we told your associate, it's a subject better discussed in private, and only with the governor himself."

The man frowns and looks like he's going to argue, but then I hear a loud gasp and the sound of something clattering to the pavement. Gunny reacts instantly, sweeping his gun around, and Hayley shoves me over by Jess so that she and Gunny can defend us more easily. But it turns out to have been only the data pad the older woman was carrying, and when my eyes meet hers, I instantly realize the reason she dropped it.

My heart sinks as she ignores her dropped pad and steps over to the shorter man, leaning down to whisper something in his ear, looking at me the entire time.

Unfortunately, if I had any doubts about what the woman was whispering to Sorkin, they flee when his gaze finally shifts off Jess to focus on me for the first time. The chief of staff frowns, and his eyes go out of focus for a moment as he interfaces with his implant, probably communicating with his boss back in the government offices.

When he focuses back on me, ignoring an increasingly confused Jess, he nods once. "Of course the governor will see you. His office is sending a car now."

"But there's only four of us, and the car you have there—" Jess starts to say, pointing toward the SUV, but Sorkin cuts her off with an almost violent shake of his head.

"Sorry, Captain, but the governor insists. The car will be here shortly."

It takes only five minutes for the governor's car to arrive —Poe's capital city isn't all that big—and I feel a sense of dread when I see it. It's long, black, and a convertible. Not a good sign. At first, Gunny tries to argue that a convertible is too much of a security risk, but Sorkin holds firm, insisting again that the governor demands it.

I end the argument by telling Gunny it's okay. Unlike him, I know exactly what is about to happen. And while it has nothing to do with anyone shooting me from a grassy knoll, I also know that I'm definitely not going to like it.

# SIX
# THE HERO OF POE

## JESSICA LIN MENDOZA

Brad is acting incredibly strange. First, he refused to talk to the governor's people from orbit or let us even share his name. Second, he was reluctant to put on his Navy uniform, though he relented easily enough when I tried to get him to explain why he didn't want to wear it. Third, he practically tried to hide behind Quinn at the port like a little child meeting strangers. Fourth and final, he's now sitting as low as he can in the back of the convertible, looking around furtively.

I want to ask him what's going on, but I daren't do so out loud in case it's not something we want our hosts to hear. Unfortunately, he's ignoring my attempts to establish an implant comm connection. I find my anger building with each kilometer as we ride into town, steaming over what could possibly have my husband so nervous that he won't even talk to me.

I find out when the car arrives at the outskirts of what passes for a city on Poe. There's no grand entrance, just a place where the dirt and scrub brush give way to small, utilitarian houses with equally small but well-kept yards. But what really takes me by surprise are all the people.

Either any visitor to this backwater planet is the social event of the year, or something very odd is going on. As we move into the suburban area, the convertible's driver slows the car to a crawl without explanation. Entire families are standing in their front yards, just watching us go by. Some stare at us in awe, like they've never seen off-worlders before. Others are more brazen, pointing at us and talking excitedly among each other. A few even cheer.

Finally, unable to contain my curiosity any longer, I lean over to Brad. "What's going on?" I demand in a low voice, even though there's no hope of the driver not hearing us.

"Don't ask," my husband answers, doing his best to sink deeper into the upholstered seat.

I frown at him but figure that arguing in front of the governor's employees might hurt our cause, so I compress my lips to a frown that tells Brad he *will* be explaining this later, and in detail. He shrinks down even more in response.

If the families in their front yards weren't bewildering enough, as we leave the residential areas and enter what looks to be more commercial—with two-to-three-story buildings built out of local stone—more people fill the streets. It's as if every shop owner, customer, office worker, and loiterer in the entire city has turned out to watch us go by.

Soon they all start cheering. I know the Navy doesn't make it to Poe much, but this all seems a little extreme. Four more blocks pass, with the crowd getting progressively thicker and louder, and I have no idea what to think at this point. Then, I hear trumpets.

Looking ahead, past the driver, I see an honest-to-goodness marching band, festooned in red uniforms and those big, silly hats bands often wear, blocking the road ahead of us. As we near them, the trumpets and trombones resolve into something approaching a boisterous tune only partially snatched away by the wind, and the band parts in front of the car, then takes up position marching behind us as we pass, still playing for all they're worth.

"Brad," I growl, no longer caring if our hosts hear us argue. "Explain."

"Captain Lin," the driver says, looking over his shoulder back at me. "Welcome to Mendoza Square, dedicated to the Hero of Poe."

Flabbergasted, I look ahead of us and see a large open city square at the street's end. In its middle is a gigantic marble pediment surrounded by a fountain. And on top of the marble is a bronze statue that . . . I don't believe it. Rising high above us is a statue of Brad, complete with his old captain's uniform, depicting him looking off into the distance and standing with his chest jutted out, his hands forming fists at his side.

I look back at him, and he cringes. "Uh . . . yeah. They sort of like me here."

That's the understatement of the year. Of course, I expected the people of Poe to feel benevolent toward Brad, after he saved one of their asteroid mining operations from pirates just over two years ago. But a parade, a band, and a statue? And the city's main square named after him? It's ridiculous.

Before I can voice my feelings or ask for more details, the car comes to a stop in front of a modest three-story building of white stone, with broad steps leading from the street to the second floor's grand entrance. Standing at the base of those steps is a grinning man in a suit that practically screams his identity as Poe's system governor. He's surrounded on both sides by at least a dozen smiling men and women.

We're ushered out of the convertible, and the governor grabs Brad by the hand before he can protest, shaking it so vigorously that I'm worried he might rip my husband's arm off—or worse, that Gunny might try to hurt the governor to get him to stop. Luckily, the handshake ends without incident, and we're led up the steps to find that at the top, someone has hastily set up a wooden podium with a microphone.

The governor steps up to the microphone and stares out over the rapidly growing crowd. "Welcome back to Poe . . ." he starts, then checks Brad's shoulder and smiles even more. "*Admiral* Mendoza!"

At the sound of Brad's rank and name, the entire square, now entirely full of people, breaks into wild cheering. Men, women, and children of all ages clap and yell uproariously. A few voices start a chant that the rest of the crowd quickly picks up.

"Men-do-za! Men-do-za! Men-do-za!" They thrust their fists into the air on each syllable, bouncing up and down like cadets at an Academy football game.

"Would you like to say a few words?" the governor asks Brad, who is blushing redder than I've ever seen him.

"Of course, chico," Hayley answers before my husband can say anything. She shoves him and the governor aside to reach the podium. Before anyone can stop her, she adjusts the microphone height, clears her throat, and smiles at the assembled crowd. "Hola, people of Poe. We come in peace. Take us to your tacos."

Breaking out of my stunned state for a second, I reach over and yank Hayley back by the arm. "The governor meant Brad, Lieutenant," I chide, but she just smiles innocently.

"Come on, boss," she says without a hint of sarcasm, "when have you ever known the admiral *not* to want tacos?"

While Hayley and I argue off to one side, the governor practically pushes my husband to the podium. For a moment —a rather long one—Brad says nothing, just staring in red-faced embarrassment out at the now perfectly silent crowd. Finally, he clears his throat much as Hayley did, but this time the PA system squelches with feedback so loud that we all put our hands to our ears, even cutting Hayley off in the middle of a diatribe about carnitas tacos.

Brad cringes visibly and looks down at the podium, taking a deep breath. He's still blushing when he looks back up at the gathered citizens. "Uh . . . It's good to visit Poe again," he says haltingly. "How have you all been?"

For a second, no one speaks or moves. Then, starting at one side of the square and quickly spreading to the rest of it, the crowd lets out a roaring cheer far louder than ever before. Once again, they start chanting my husband's name, and several teenagers even climb up onto the base of the statue of Brad and hold fists aloft in the air as they cling to his bronze legs with their other hands.

Before I have much more time to process the scene, the governor and his people usher us away from the podium and into the relative peace of the government building itself. As soon as the doors close behind us, and heedless of the governor and the rest of our smaller audience, I whirl on my husband.

"Start talking," I snap at him.

He blushes again. "I guess I forgot to mention just how famous I really am here. The statue is new, though; I didn't know about that."

"Famous doesn't even begin to describe it," the governor says, and I notice right away that he's not smiling anymore.

The small crowd around us quickly disperses, and the man frowns at Brad and the rest of us.

"Governor," I start, "we're here looking for information on—"

"It doesn't matter why you're here, Captain Lin. But I really wish you'd stayed away. Best to speak in my office."

He turns heel and walks away, and we almost have to jog to keep up.

# SEVEN
# OF GOVERNORS AND MONARCHS

## BRAD MENDOZA

Why did they have to build a statue? Seriously, a statue? I mean, it's a good likeness, and I cut a pretty dashing figure in my old captain's uniform. They also made me broader in the shoulders and squarer in the jaw, which I'm not going to fault them for. But still, a statue?

Though, given the way Jess was gaping at it, maybe I should ask them if we can take it with us when we leave.

"We know nothing of any slavers in this system," Governor Warren says for the third or fourth time from behind his desk, ignoring my silent wonderment over the status. "But you being here presents us with a major problem."

Jess looks like she's about to ask what he means, but he keeps talking right over her, and I watch as her face starts to turn red with anger once again.

"The Corpus Christi Cluster is not a safe place for servants of the queen," Warren says, leaning forward across the desk and clasping his hands in front of him. "We're walking a tightrope here. Half the systems in the Cluster have sworn allegiance to King Chance and the Jutzens, and those of us who haven't are trying our best to stay neutral. Having a Navy ship in orbit, and worse a wanted man, Hero of Poe or not, on my planet, is going to make that a *lot* harder."

You can probably guess where the conversation goes from there. Ever been lectured by a third-rate governor from a fourth-rate planet, who's trying to skirt a fine line between a Nazi occupation government and the needs of his own people? Well, if you have, then you know how Jess and I feel. She tries to interrupt the man several times to get to the real reason why we're here, but he just keeps right on talking over her.

I could have told him how that would work out for him, so I'm far less surprised than he is when Jess shoots to her feet and slams a flat hand onto the desk's wooden surface, shocking Governor Warren speechless and making him jump several centimeters off his chair.

"Governor, shut up and listen for a moment," Jess growls. By the look on Warren's face, no one has dared talk to him this way since he was elected. That doesn't seem to dissuade her at all. "We're not here to make your life harder. We're here looking for a slaver by the name of Andre Bollen, and we have intel that says he was sighted passing through this system recently. We need you to tell us everything you know about him, his operation, and where they might have been heading after leaving Poe."

For several moments, Warren just sits where, jaw working up and down like his brain has forgotten to tell his mouth he stopped talking. Then he cocks a head to one side and grimaces. "Slavers? Here in Poe?" He shakes his head. "We've seen no slavers here. And what did you say the man's name was?"

My heart sinks once more, because I'm nearly sure the man is telling us the truth. He's never even heard of Andre Bollen. He confirms it a second later after Jess repeats the name.

"I'm sorry, Captain Lin, but I haven't the foggiest. And if this Bollen fellow did pass through Poe, we'd likely never know it. We don't have a system patrol, and our planetary sensor grid is woefully inadequate to the task of scanning even the area around the planet itself. You say you saw Poe mentioned in a wanted bulletin on this man?"

We both nod.

Warren sits back in his seat, still looking confused. "I'll ask my people. But I don't think we're going to be of much help to you. And, no offense, but the sooner we get you off planet and out of this system, the better. The Cluster has always had close economic ties to Serravo. In fact, King Chance's Serravo Defense Force is rumored to be massing its strength at Linford Commons. If they decide to pass through Poe on one of their patrols, I'd really rather you not be here."

That's enough to make me sit up straight and focus on the conversation again. "Did you say the SDF is here in force?"

"I did, but that's nothing new. We may not be part of the Duchy of Serravo, but the duke had a lot of business interests here. He's always treated it like an extension of his holdings."

"But why now?" I ask, scooting forward a bit on my chair. "I would have thought Chance would keep the SDF close so that . . ." I trail off as I realize the answer to my own question.

Jess reaches the same realization an instant later. "He's trying to flank Kipling and the queen," she breathes.

I nod. Ever since we learned about the conquest of Prometheus, I had in my head that Chance Fuller was an opportunist—that he simply took advantage of the Nazi invasion and his cousin's death to declare himself King and appease the Jutzens while gathering his own power. But if he really is trying to turn the Cluster to the Jutzens so that they can outflank Anne's forces, then it means King Chance isn't just a collaborator, he's a full-on traitor. He isn't just passively accepting Nazi rule—he's actively helping them gain *more* territory.

Warren nods. "For what it's worth, that's my take on it as well." His voice is even more somber now. "The queen, God watch over her always, cannot win." The pronouncement forces its way out of his lips like it physically pains him to say. To me, it sounds like the death verdict in a trial I didn't even know I was part of.

"Who's in charge of Chance's forces in the Cluster?" I demand. "Are the Jutzens here as well?"

The governor chews the inside of his lip for a moment before responding. "Mind you, Poe is a backwater world even by Corpus Christi standards, so I might be the last to know, but I haven't heard anything about the Jutzens actually being here in the Cluster." He shrugs and sits back, looking suddenly exhausted. "But again, I hear rumors, and there's some kind of new leader at Linford Commons—someone indeed backed by King Chance in this sector. No name, just whispers that he or she exists, even one rumor that they may be a member of the former royal family. Take from that what you will."

He lets out a long sigh, turning his chair halfway around and looking out one of the third-story windows that shows a view of Mendoza Square and my ridiculous statue. I can sense that the conversation is over.

"Thank you, Governor Warren," Jess says solemnly, standing up. I follow her lead. "We'll head back to our shuttle now and—"

He shakes his head and waves a hand in my direction

without turning to face us again, still studying the square where knots of people are gathered, left over from our welcome there. "No, no. That won't do at all. I'd have riots outside in the streets if there were the barest hint that I was sending the Hero of Poe away. Besides, I've already ordered a banquet prepared in your honor. Stay the night, please. By morning, I'll have gathered anything my people know on this Bollen, and I'll send it with you before you leave." By his tone, he's not expecting that to be much.

"And anything you have on the political situation in the rest of the Corpus Christi Cluster? Like this mysterious commander at Linford Commons?" Jess prods.

He nods reluctantly, still staring out the window. "Of course. You are the Navy, after all."

# EIGHT
# THE STORM

## BRAD MENDOZA

When Carla and I were married, and even before, I hated fancy dinner parties, balls, and galas. I always felt out of place at such events, especially given my modest upbringing on Denton III, a farming world. Unfortunately, being married to a fleet admiral's daughter meant I was always getting invited to the stupid things, where I'd stand around awkwardly and try to feign interest in conversations about stock markets, Fringe politics, and pork bellies—I never could figure out why there was so much talk of bacon when the fancy buffets never served it.

So, needless to say, I'm dreading another such banquet here on Poe. In fact, 'dreading' is a gross understatement, because this particular party is in my honor, which means I can't stand in the corner nursing a drink until I can think of a polite excuse to leave early.

But when the celebration finally starts, it defies all my

expectations. There's no expensive-looking ballroom with deadly-looking chandeliers. Nor are there petite finger foods carried about by waiters dressed nicer than some of the guests. Instead, Jess and I are led outside into the square that bears my name, where the governor's staff has been hard at work setting up long tables and chairs.

What follows reminds me less of the shindigs on Prometheus and far more of the community get-togethers and county fairs on Denton III. Shortly after we sit down in the middle of one of the central tables, the crowds start to gather and take their seats as men and women wearing aprons, but no fancy tuxedos, bring huge platters laden with a wide variety of foods.

We're definitely not talking finger foods. One of the first platters set down in front of me is heavily laden with a mountain of fried chicken. The next carries an even taller mountain of mashed potatoes, and the gravy boat looks like a bathtub.

There's no standing on ceremony, and the people around us set to eating as soon as each dish arrives, family style. Jess stares at the happening wide-eyed, but I dig in. Before I know it, my plate his buried under copious amounts of chicken, potatoes, green beans, and gravy, and every bite is heaven! As we eat, there's a general hum of chatter around us, interspersed with the welcome sounds of hearty laughs. I get slapped on the back by so many passing folks that I get gravy all over the front of my skinsuit more than once.

Even Jess quickly gets into the spirit of things. Before I know it, she's deep into a conversation with a rancher across from us and a local university professor to her left, while I'm fielding questions from a miner to my right and the rancher's wife.

What's more, after about twenty minutes, those folks closest to us excuse themselves, opening up their seats for others to join us in conversation. Unlike the stilted and forced reception lines at formal events on Prometheus, however, this rotation feels organic and easy.

Halfway through dinner, conversation ebbs, and a small choir of schoolchildren climbs onto my statue's pedestal and treats us to a performance of local folksongs and a few Federation favorites. The crowd cheers and claps for the children, and my wife is entirely enthralled watching them perform, while I remain completely captivated by another helping of fried chicken.

Dinner ends, however, and then my worst nightmare begins. Before I can ask what's going on, the aproned men and women arrive to push all the tables to the square's outer edge, while music starts to play and couples dash into the middle and start dancing. Jess unsuccessfully tries to get me out onto the improvised dance floor with her, but I staunchly refuse to move and expose my new spouse to my two left feet. When a good-looking young man with a thick mop of brown hair asks her to dance, though, it's too much for me. I cut in after the second song and spend the rest of the evening attempting to dance with my wife.

The festivities go long into the night, and I even start to enjoy the music and dancing, until a peal of thunder sounds in the distance and a spattering of rain starts to fall on our heads. Screaming in delight, people start dashing for the overhangs and awnings of the square's surrounding shopfronts, and Jess and I run laughing to the small hotel in one corner, where the governor has put us up for the night.

After checking in with Gunny and Hayley, who spent most of the night seated at a table near ours or walking the perimeter of the dance floor, Jess and I enter our room, and all I want to do is crash. Unfortunately, she has other ideas.

I remember my father once telling me, in a rare moment when he and I weren't fighting, that most women in our family, including my mother, had the rare talent of detecting just when their husbands were getting comfortable, and then asking them to do one of any myriad of tasks in that very moment. It sounds laughable, but it turned out to be universal in my experience. Carla used to get all settled into bed, and the instant I got under the covers to join her, she would ask me to grab her a glass of water or if I'd checked the locks on the front and back doors of our modest home.

Apparently, Jess shares this talent. Because the second I kick my shoes off and shimmy out of my rain-soaked skin-suit, she decides to start a serious conversation.

"Brad, we need to talk." No five words have struck me with the same trepidation as these in at least a month.

When I don't immediately respond, she continues, standing by the door with her hands on her hips and a small frown on her lips. "We can't go on from here. We have no real intel on Andre Bollen, and the queen needs to know about Chance's plans for the Cluster. If Corpus Christi becomes a Jutzen stronghold, they'll be able to harass her on two fronts. She needs to know, and she needs to know now."

I slump down to sit on the edge of the bed and regard her. "So let's send a message to her then. We can warn her, and we can keep looking for Bollen and any other slavers we come across."

My bride flares her nostrils and gives me a look that tells me the thundering storm outside may be the least of my worries. "And where do we go next, sweetheart?" she asks without raising her voice. "Poe is a dead end for us; they've never even heard of Andre Bollen here. So where can we go? Deeper into the Cluster, where the SDF is apparently throwing its weight around? They might just be a system defense fleet, Brad, but you and I both know the major duchy defense fleets are small navies in their own right. They could have dozens of warships, and all we have is our one destroyer, with a skeleton crew to boot."

Everything she's saying makes perfect sense, and up until this point, I might have to agree with her, but then she shows her entire hand. "Listen, Brad. Being out here playing hunt-the-slaver has been fun and all, but it's time to go back to the queen. She needs us, especially if she's about to find herself fighting a two-front war."

This is the moment when my mouth gets ahead of my brain. "I'm not going back, Jess," I snap, with far more vehemence than I mean to. "I'm not going back, *ever*. I'm not going to fight Annie's war. I'm done dying for Prometheus. I'm done."

And there it is, out in the open, the decision that's been forming in the pit of my stomach ever since we learned of Prometheus's fall. By the way Jess's eyes go wide, she's as surprised to hear me say it out loud as I am, but I don't retract or try to walk back the statement. I just return her stare.

"And what if I want to go back?" she asks softly.

It's her tone that breaks me. If she'd responded with the same brash tone I used, it would have put me even more on the defensive than I already am. But no, she has to go and be all gentle and reasonable about it.

I fall the rest of the way back onto the bed, staring up at the ceiling, where I can hear the rain pounding on the rooftop of our top-floor room. It's a sound I've seldom heard since my childhood on Denton III. There's no rain in space, and the storms on Prometheus are far milder what with the planet's advanced weather controls. But here, on this ball of forgotten dust that is Poe, the storm rages unabated. Lightning flashes outside, making the room momentarily brighter, and thunder follows soon behind, so close that it shakes the building around us.

"I just can't," I repeat, almost in a whisper. "I can't go back."

The bed creaks as Jess crawls onto it and settles herself

next to me, lying on her side, using the crook of my right arm as a pillow. Her hair is wet and feels absurdly good against my suddenly hot cheek, as does her hand on my chest.

"Why not?" she asks in the same soft tone. "I can't force you to go back," she hastens to add, "and I would never try. But help me understand why."

I lie there for a long time, thinking hard, studying a water stain on the ceiling that looks like an elephant riding a unicycle. I examine it for a long time, hoping that somewhere in its depths, I might find the way to explain to the person I love most why I'm running away from something so important to me.

Despite her words, I know that supporting me in my decision to stay away from Annie's war would be hard for Jess. I've known it from the beginning, but especially since the other night, when I found her donning her new captain's uniform. Jess has always had a strong sense of duty, far stronger than my own. And while she was initially enthusiastic about leaving the fleet behind so we could help the weaker people of the galaxy, I always knew, deep down, that she'd circle back to her responsibilities as a queen's officer.

I'm still struggling to find the right words when her breathing grows even and her body melts against mine in a deep sleep. But I stay up another hour, at least, studying the unicycle-riding pachyderm on the ceiling and wondering what I'll say to her when we wake up.

Unfortunately, sleep brings the dreams again.

This time, it's not the dead children on the *Cumberland* who wake up to accuse me, rightfully so, of killing them. It's a grown woman. I remember her face distinctly as that of the first corpse I saw when I boarded the destroyed freighter after my Marines declared it free of threats. But in the dream, we're not on board the *Cumberland*; we're in Navy Headquarters on Prometheus, sitting in the courtroom at my court-martial. Still looking like the frozen corpse I first saw, the woman is sitting at the bench with the members of the court, those who will judge me.

"You did this," she says hoarsely, reaching up to point a cold, dead finger at me from across the bench. "This is your fault. You killed us all!" Then she stands and leaps over the table like something out of a horror movie, hands extended and reaching to grasp my neck and—

# NINE
# UNEXPECTED VISITORS

## BRAD MENDOZA

"Admiral?" A voice in my head wakes me from my nightmare.

My eyes fly open. It's still night, and it's still storming outside. I'm still on top of the covers, bathed in a cold sweat, while Jess, slumbering away, has rolled off me and is huddled under a quilt at one edge of the bed, her back to me.

My implant tells me it's the early morning here on Poe, far too early for my crew to wake me with anything routine.

"What is it, Gunny?" I reply quietly in my implant.

"Malina and Daren missed their last check-in, sir. Daren is supposed to be on watch, and I've never known him to fall asleep when he shouldn't be."

Outside, another peal of thunder splits the heavens as if to emphasize his point.

"Maybe interference from the storm?" I ask hopefully.

Hayley breaks into the channel. "I don't think so, chico. I

was talking to Illy on the ship and lost him a minute ago. Just cut off midsentence."

I spring upright on the bed, my heart thudding in my chest. There's a little cry from Jess as my sudden movement awakens her, and she looks over at me with wide eyes in the dim light from the streetlamps outside. "What is it?"

"Hopefully nothing," I answer. "We've lost comms with the ship and the shuttle. We need to—"

"Contact!" Gunny yells into the shared channel. "Hayley, take cover." His shouted orders dissolve into a fit of static just as we hear the boom of a shotgun from somewhere downstairs, somehow far louder than even the raging storm outside. It's followed by another boom and then the rat-tat-tat sound of the big railgun assault rifle Gunny brought to the planet with him.

Needless to say, Jess and I are now fully alert, and we scramble out of the bed and throw our uniforms back on. I'm just putting on my shoes when the door to our room crashes inward and two large figures rush inside. They're dressed in head-to-toe body armor, including black reflective helmets with the face masks down, and each is carrying an ugly-looking short-barreled shotgun with a pistol grip.

"Brad, get down!" Jess yells as she leaps over the bed, rolling across it and then falling into the small space between it and the back wall.

One of the shotguns booms at close range, and part of the mattress erupts into a spray of feathers. With my shoe halfway on my foot, I push room's small table down and crouch behind it just as another gun booms, peppering me with splintered wood fragments that cut into my cheek but thankfully miss my eyes.

Knowing that the thin table is no real defense against the powerful shotguns, I grab the chair I was sitting in, made of a local wood, and stand up again, using every bit of my strength to lift and fling it at the closest attacker. It flies at his chest just as he pulls the trigger again, and the momentary distraction causes his shot to go wild. He tries to duck, but the chair hits his shoulder with a glancing blow. If he grunts or makes any other sign of it hurting him, it's not apparent to me, and he's already straightening back up to take another shot at me.

Not knowing what else to do, I charge him, lowering my shoulder and covering the three meters between us faster than I think I've ever sprinted before. My shoulder slams into his chest and makes him momentarily drop the shotgun, which hangs and bounces on its sling between us. We start to wrestle for control of the weapon.

In the tunnel vision of my fight with the first attacker, I've lost sight of the second, and I don't know if Jess is still cornered behind the bed. Neither of us brought sidearms to the planet—we had Gunny and Hayley armed, and besides, Poe is supposed to be a friendly world. But now, I'm losing the fight for the first man's shotgun while the second may already be rounding the side of the bed to kill my wife.

Suddenly, there's another person in the room, and I catch the brief flash of blonde hair as someone leaps onto the back of my attacker with a scream. It takes the man by as much surprise as it does me, and I almost miss my chance to rip the shotgun from his grasp. Luckily, I keep my grip on it and yank hard while he's momentarily distracted. The sling still around his neck pulls him forward as the newcomer beats on his head with her fists. Then something in the sling gives, and the gun comes loose in my hands.

"Watch out!" I call to the blonde woman, and she pushes off the guy's back and dives to one side just as I unload the shotgun right into his face. If I'd hit him in his armored chest, he might have survived. But humanity has never quite solved the problem of making transparent materials as strong as opaque ones, and enough of the blast breaks through his helmet's face mask that I have little doubt he's dead as he slumps to the floor.

I'm already spinning to point the gun toward where Jess and the second attacker must be, but I stop myself from pulling the trigger when I see them engaged in hand-to-hand combat, though it's clear his armor and greater size are rapidly winning the day.

"Get down!" I shout at my wife, and she doesn't hesitate, letting her legs collapse beneath her as I unload the gun once more. At this farther range, across the room, the second attacker doesn't immediately go down, but the blast is enough to make him stumble and prevents him from regaining the grip on his own shotgun before I hit him with a second shot.

It takes a third shot to finally put him down, and the room is full of the smell of burnt powder and rain outside shattered windows.

"Jess, you good?" I call out, and my wife thankfully pops up, unharmed, from where she'd taken refuge again behind the bed. We both turn our gazes to our rescuer.

It's the governor's aide from the landing pad, the one who first greeted us on Warren's behalf before his chief of staff arrived to take over. She's standing in the center of the room, panting from the exertion of the fight, her shirt ripped in a few places, and blood leaking from a cut on her upper arm.

She looks at me and speaks. "Glad I got here in time. They're jamming comms. Governor Warren sent me . . . he found . . ." She runs out of breath and holds up a hand while she gasps for more air. "He found something on . . . Andre Bollen. Sent me to bring it to you. I—"

Another large figure bursts through the room's open doorway, his massive gun tracking across the room, searching for targets.

"Stand down, Gunny," Jess shouts before I can. "She's a friendly."

The big man nods, relief etched all over his face. "More of them downstairs. Got the drop on us. Sorry."

Jess picks up the shotgun of the second attacker while I continue to cradle the first. With the blonde in tow, we follow Gunny out of the room and down the stairs to the first floor, where it's like a scene out of a B-grade action movie.

There are bodies everywhere, all of them wearing the same black head-to-toe armor as our two attackers, save for an unfortunate hotel clerk who lies slumped over his desk, caught in the crossfire. Standing in the middle of it all, stripping the ammo clips from one of the downed armored bodies, is Hayley, a look on her face as grim as any I've seen since her Confederate Guard friends betrayed us on Serenidad.

"Any word from Illian or Malina?" I ask as I step over a dead gunman.

"No, sir," Gunny rumbles in his deep baritone. "There's some sort of localized jamming in place. We couldn't even warn you about the two who got past us. Sorry."

"It turned out okay, Gunny. Do we think there are more of them?"

The sound of a distant explosion, obvious even compared to the crashing thunder, answers that question for us, as does the accompanying sound of screams.

"Lots more, I think, chico," Hayley says grimly. "So we gotta go."

Motioning for Gunny to lead the way, we charge outside into the dark, rain-soaked streets of Poe.

# TEN
# INVASION

## JESSICA LIN MENDOZA

When we emerge from the hotel, we find Mendoza Square completely deserted. Not surprising, perhaps, at this unholy hour of the morning, but I would feel a lot better if the square was full of cops or our crew come to get us. Even with the rain stopping now, the entire area is already eerily still and silent.

"Which way?" Brad asks.

"Back to the shuttle," Gunny says, always the pragmatist. "We can commandeer a car along the way."

Another explosion splits the night air and draws all of our eyes to the west, across the square toward the governor's offices. The government building itself is dark and intact, but there's an orange glow lighting up the sky behind it.

"The university!" the as-of-yet-unnamed blonde woman shrieks, just as I hear the whine of engines and see two familiar-looking cargo shuttles streak by overhead, bearing in that same direction.

"Follow me!" Brad shouts before any of us can argue, taking off across the square toward a side street, toward the sounds of destruction and fighting, not away from it.

I hear Gunny swear loudly as he starts sprinting to catch up to my husband. The blonde woman and I hasten to follow, with Hayley taking the rear. All of us but the governor's aide are armed, which gives me a measure of comfort. She may have saved us in the hotel room with her timely arrival, but it was almost too timely. I'll feel a lot better at least knowing her name before I trust her with a gun at our backs.

We run like that for three blocks until I see Brad and Gunny stutter to a stop at a T-junction, both their eyes fixed to the right. When I reach them, I see what they're staring at.

One of the cargo shuttles we saw fly overhead, no doubt from the freighter in orbit, has landed in the middle of a wide boulevard, about a hundred meters from our current position. Surrounding it are men and women wearing the same black body armor that we saw on the attackers at the hotel. They're all holding weapons of various types and pointing them at a scared group of people in civilian clothes, maybe a few dozen. There's a fire somewhere out of sight around a corner, but it casts enough ghastly light into the area that I get the impression that most of the civilians are on the young side, as they're herded into the open shuttle.

"They're taking the students," the governor's aide says loudly, drawing the attention of the closest armored troops.

Worse, it seems to embolden some of the young civilians, and a few push past the invaders and try to make a run for it straight at us. Shots ring out and they fall, one by one, to the wet pavement below. My screams join those of the blonde and Brad's shout of anger, even as Gunny holds his rail gun to his shoulder and picks off two of the black-clad troops who start toward us.

"Admiral, Captain, that way, now," he shouts, motioning behind him with a jerk of his head as he continues throwing shots toward the advancing enemy, careful not to hit the students still being rounded up and forced into the shuttle.

I may be enraged at what I'm witnessing; I may even be resolved that I need to stop it. But years of military training taught me to take orders, and when it comes to ground engagements, Gunny is in charge of our crew. That includes me and Brad. So we take off in the indicated direction while he covers us, Hayley and the governor's aide hot on our heels.

We enter the mouth of a side street and sprint down it for all we're worth, until we come to another stuttering stop.

"Dead end!" Brad shouts from up ahead.

"I got this," Hayley shouts back, streaking by me and him and throwing her slight weight at the closed door of a darkened storefront. She must somehow hit it in exactly the right place, because it crashes inward.

We follow her through into the gloom beyond and find ourselves in what looks like a candy shop of all things. The smell of chocolate is sweet in the air, almost overpowering, and in the dim light cast from the street lamps outside, I can just make out glass display counters full of who-knows-what confectioneries.

"They're still jamming us," Brad reports, and a quick check of my implant shows the same.

We can't raise the ship or the shuttle, assuming either is still there. None of us is willing to say it out loud, but the very fact that there's an invasion in process down here on the surface suggests that *Bainbridge* must be dead or disabled above us. That Illian didn't even call down a warning of those shuttles descending suggests the more dire of the options.

"Bollen."

We all turn to stare at the blonde woman, who just uttered the name like a curse.

"You think this is his doing?" I ask, taking a step closer to her.

She nods, though I can only just make it out in the darkness. "It has to be. No one else would be so brazen."

I resist the urge to point out that, until she came along, no one on this planet seemed to have even heard of Andre Bollen, because just then, Gunny comes running into the shop.

"They're on my six," he says in a low voice. "Is there another door?"

It only takes us a moment to locate one, and we come out of it to find ourselves on what looks like a part of the university campus. There are broad, tree-lined walkways going off in every direction across an expansive lawn surrounded by buildings, and there are students like the ones we saw earlier running every which way and screaming. It's pure bedlam, and for a second I freeze, watching with horror as what should be a scene of domestic serenity proves to be anything but.

"Four-o'clock high," calls Hayley, and we crane our heads to see another cargo shuttle hovering above on thrusters. It starts to lower itself to the middle of the quad.

"We have to stop them," Brad growls, and takes a step toward where the shuttle is landing. Before he can do more than that, Gunny grabs him roughly by the arm and shoves him in a perpendicular direction, along the face of the building we just exited and toward the nearest corner of the quad, where I can make out a gap between buildings in the night.

To his credit, Brad doesn't argue. And as much as I hate to admit it, Gunny is right. We're five people, only four of us armed and only one with a ranged weapon, and if the other shuttle was any indication, this new one contains at least a dozen heavily armed troops.

We run, faces hot with the shame of fleeing and leaving behind those we should be helping. As we go, we try to call out to groups of students here and there, urging them to run in roughly the same direction. Some do, while others either don't hear us or stand dumbly, too frozen in shock to understand or care what we're trying to tell them.

Another massive explosion splits the night air, and the ground beneath us rumbles. With the sound echoing off the buildings, it's difficult to get an exact fix on it, but a part of my brain insists it's back in the direction from which we came, at Mendoza Square. If so, there's nothing we can do about it now.

Shots ring out, and a bullet slaps into the pavement near my feet. Gunny turns and fires back toward the newly landed shuttle, and we sprint past him and into a narrow alleyway bisected by a tall wrought iron fence that blocks any escape. Behind us, I can hear shouts and more gunshots, the higher-pitched whine of enemy bullets offset by the deeper bark of Gunny's return fire. There's far too much of the former and far too little of the latter, and I suddenly worry that he might soon run out of rounds. We didn't exactly come down to this planet expecting to fight a war.

"Jess, here," Brad says, and I look back toward the fence blocking our path to see him fling open a nondescript door set into the side of one of the buildings forming the small alley, hidden in shadows where I didn't see it earlier. Without more urging, I shove the governor's aide in that direction and follow her, this time leaving Hayley behind with Gunny to cover our retreat.

I'm surprised to find that we're inside what looks like some sort of chemistry lab. Long white counters run parallel away from us toward the room's far end, a variety of containers and other scientific-looking devices decorating their surfaces. It's been a long time since I've taken a science class, but the warning labels on many of the containers look vaguely familiar.

The door behind us, which I allowed to shut when I came through, slams open again, making me jump and whirl, lifting the shotgun. I quickly lower it when Gunny and Hayley enter.

"I think we lost them for a second," the big man says, surveying the room. "Either that or whoever's in charge called them back to that shuttle to help round up more of the students." Without another word, he starts walking along one of the long counters, examining the various containers on it.

"Why do you think these are Bollen's people?" Brad demands of the aide.

Breathing hard, she holds up a hand to ask for a moment.

"What's your name?" I ask before she can answer Brad's question. I'm sick of thinking of her as the blonde or the governor's aide.

"Terry," she gasps out. "Terry Galpin. And I . . . think it's Bollen . . . because I used to . . . live on . . . his ship."

Involuntarily, the barrel of my gun rises in her direction. "You're a slaver?"

She shakes her head and lifts the sleeve of her right arm and indicates something on the wrist with a nod of her head. I take a step closer, squinting in the scant light, and then gasp.

"Is that a . . ." I can't force out the rest of the question.

She nods. "Slave brand. Bollen's. I escaped six months ago. Came here"—she takes another deep breath—"to Poe. Got a job with the governor. And now . . ." She shrugs and looks around as if to encompass all the terrible things happening outside.

"We're still being jammed," Hayley reports, ignoring Terry. "I don't like this, boss. Illy should be answering."

Surprised by the pain in her tone, though I shouldn't be, I turn to look at her. "I'm sure Illian and the ship are fine, Hayley," I lie.

"It won't matter if we die down here," Brad says, a little more harshly, but his voice carries the ring of command that he's so good at. "So pull yourself together, Lieutenant. Illian and the others may need our help."

Hayley straightens a bit. "Okay, boss. Orders?"

"The mission remains the same," Brad replies. "We've investigated the fighting, and there's little we can do to stop it. So we get to the shuttle, find *Bainbridge,* and intercept and disable whatever ship these shuttles are coming from."

"The freighter," I say for lack of anything better to add.

Brad meets my eyes and nods. "It's the only thing that makes sense. No way Illian or Laia would have let another ship approach without challenging it and at least notifying us. That freighter in orbit was already here, waiting for this."

He stops, but I can read the rest in his eyes: they were waiting for *us,* as well. It throws this entire mess into an entirely new light, and suddenly, everything we thought we knew about this Andre Bollen and the situation here in the Corpus Christi Cluster is suspect. Unless this was the greatest coincidence in the history of humanity, Bollen knew we were coming here. Which means it was a trap.

I just hope our friends in orbit aren't already dead.

# ELEVEN
# AIR SUPPORT

## BRAD MENDOZA

I keep my gaze on Jess, drawing strength from her. She's on the edge of panic right now, though only those who know her well would see it. I'm not quite there yet, but in some way, seeing her being so close to the edge and still holding it together strengthens my own resolve.

"We're four kilometers from the shuttle port," I tell the others. "It's a long way on foot, so let's try and find some transportation."

Jess and Hayley nod. Terry Galpin shrinks a little but doesn't argue. And Gunny . . .

"Uh, Gunny, what are you doing?" I ask, noticing for the first time that the giant ex-Marine is hunched over one of the long, narrow tables a few meters away, pouring the contents of one container into another.

"Just putting together a surprise for anyone who tries to follow us," he says cryptically. "When I say run, run."

I'm about to demand an explanation when he sets the container down hard on the table and shouts, "Run!"

For a big man, he moves incredibly fast toward the exit at the far end of the room, around the corner, and down from the one we came through. Seeing that one of the containers he left behind is now releasing some sort of gas, the rest of us hurry after him.

We burst through the door into a wider street beyond, the one that we were blocked from by that fence in the alley. Once again, in a pattern that seems intent to repeat itself many times tonight, we nearly stumble to a stop.

"Gunny, what's that gas back there?" I ask with a shaky voice.

"Something that'll knock out anyone who tries to follow us," he says in a similar tone.

"Even us if we try and go back in there?"

"Even us," he confirms.

Which is really too bad, because waiting for us in a loose semicircle outside the lab are a dozen armored troops with expressionless shields over their faces and guns pointed right at our chests. But that alone probably wouldn't make Gunny's voice tremble the way it did. It's the light attack shuttle lowering itself on nearly silent thrusters above, and the deadly gatling gun slung under its nose, that are making me and even my giant shooter friend almost wet our pants.

Terry lets loose a cry of despair, while the rest of us drop our weapons and raise our hands high in the air.

"We have them," one of the black-clad invaders says triumphantly. "Tell Mr. Bollen that his prize is intact."

Well, that gets rid of any doubt as to who's behind all this, as does the little squeak of terror from Terry.

"Um, we're just students," I say, my mind racing.

"Students wearing Navy uniforms," the same invader says with a snort.

"Cosplay?" I reply lamely.

Whatever response he might give me is lost in the whirring sound of the gatling gun warming up. I squeeze my eyes shut tightly, waiting for death, wondering if I could somehow leap aside and push Jess to safety in time even though she's several meters away and—

My thoughts are cut off by the deafening sound of the gun engaging, as rounds leap from its whirring cannon and fly toward us. But I don't feel them—maybe they're hitting me too fast for that, ripping holes through my body so quickly they outpace my pain response. Except when I pry one eye open to see what's happening, I'm still in one piece, but the armored slavers in front of me are running for cover.

Opening both eyes wide now, I look up at the hovering shuttle, wondering why it's firing on its own people, just in time to see tracers from the heavens rip it in half. I leap toward Jess, reaching her a second later and pushing her to the ground as fire rains from above and the shuttle slams to the street less than twenty meters away. Lying on top of my wife to protect her, I can feel the heat of the shuttle's flaming fuel tanks on my back. I brace myself for the massive explosion that will surely follow.

Someone grabs my arm and yanks me to my feet, almost wrenching it from the socket. I cry out in alarm, but then I see that Gunny is pulling Jess up next. Soon we're running toward a blessedly familiar sight. Settling to the ground fifty meters down the street is *Bainbridge*'s landing shuttle, its own chin-mounted gatling gun still slowing its rotation after taking out the enemy shuttle.

Behind us, I can hear gunfire, but I keep running, my hand on the small of Jess's back, urging her forward, Gunny's heavy steps putting him somewhere behind and to my left. A bullet pings off the skin of *Bainbridge*'s shuttle just as I reach it, and I watch as Darn Beck jumps down the ramp and starts firing at something behind us, the whine of his gun joining the deep crack of Gunny's as he also turns to cover our retreat. I usher Jess up the lowered boarding ramp and into the relative safety of the shuttle's interior, turning back in time to see Hayley do the same with a frantic Terry.

"Malina, go!" I shout in the direction of the cockpit.

The shuttle starts to slowly lift just as Gunny and Daren step onto the end of the ramp. They brace themselves on its support struts, firing at the regrouping enemy outside as Malina lifts the shuttle up above the buildings and then engages its forward thrusters, rocketing us across the rooftops and almost making Daren lose his hold on the strut.

Moments later, we're all fully inside, and the ramp is rising to shut behind us.

I make my way quickly into the cockpit after a quick check to make sure that no one is injured. Besides a furrow on Gunny's arm from a bullet that grazed him, we all miraculously seem to be in one piece. I settle into the copilot's seat as our Koratan pilot yanks back on the control yoke and sends the shuttle into a dizzying spiral climb, almost making me fall out of the seat before I can finally fasten my restraints.

"Sir," she greets me. "Mind checking the sensors?"

I comply and feel the blood rush from my face as they show another small assault shuttle rising from the city behind us. Apparently, Bollen and his people sent at least two of the deadly craft down to provide air cover for the landing cargo shuttles. One lies in pieces where Malina's shooting left it, but the other seems intent on avenging that one's fate.

"Sir, please man the gun and the countermeasures," she says without taking her eyes off her own display.

"On it," I tell her, ignoring rank and seniority, not wanting to distract her from piloting the ship.

I pull up the targeting sensors on my own display and wince to see the enemy shuttle hot on our six. A red warning pops up, alerting me that they're about to fire at us, but Malina jams the control yoke to the left and takes us in a hairpin turn to avoid the gatling gun rounds that fill the air we just vacated.

"Spacer, come about to oh-two-thirty and dive on my mark," I order, calculating the vectors too quickly to even ask my implant to validate my work.

"No, sir," Malina says firmly. "Just be ready; I'll tell you when."

I look over at the Koratan, incredulous. Did she just refuse an order?

Ignoring me, she turns the yoke hard to starboard and pulls back on it, sending us into another upward spiral that has my stomach doing somersaults. Then, without warning, she reaches out with her right hand and pulls the throttles all the way back.

The roar of the shuttle's thrusters fades to nothing, and my stomach stops its acrobatics to instead rise into my throat as the craft, with us inside, falls powerless backward toward the planet's surface below. I'm about to ask what in the name of Hades she's doing, but she shouts, "Now!"

I look back at my console to see that the enemy craft, its own thrusters still blazing, has overshot us, taken by surprise at Malina's sudden power cut. There it is, in all its glory, streaking by right in front of us.

Without waiting for further instructions, I jam my thumbs down on the fire control buttons affixed to my copilot's yoke, using it at the same time to aim the gatling gun in its limited range of motion. A line of tracers so thick they may as well be a laser beam lance out from our ship's gun, straight at the engine exhaust of the enemy assault shuttle.

I cry out in triumph as our bullets stitch their way across

the enemy's stern, then again as their thrusters snuff out just as ours did seconds ago, but for an entirely different reason.

Malina joins my battle cry and shoves the throttles forward once more, twisting the yoke as the damaged enemy craft starts to fall backward straight at us. It feels like we avoid it by mere centimeters, though the sensors report a full fifteen-meter margin of error. I sit back in the copilot's seat, gasping in relief, and turn to stare at the pilot. "That was . . ." I start, unsure of exactly how to put it.

She winces. "I know, Admiral. I'm sorry for disobeying orders."

I laugh, the near constant adrenaline rush I've been feeling since those soldiers first burst into our hotel room fading and leaving me with only two options in its wake: laugh or cry. I choose the former. "Malina," I tell her when I regain my breath again. "That was amazing. Disobey orders like that again, and we may have to give you the Promethean Cross of Valor."

She blushes, her eyes still on the console in front of her. "I don't know about that, sir. Not sure I'd ever be able to wear a Promethean medal into a Koratan Navy bar."

I laugh again, but I sober up quickly as our continued reality sets in, turning my attention back to the sensor display. Now that we've gained some height, I can see a half dozen cargo shuttles rising from the planet's surface behind us, no doubt all packed with new slaves for Andre Bollen's profit. I feel a cold rage form in my chest, and it's all I can do not to order Malina to go after those shuttles and disable them—doing so would harm the innocent civilians on board just as much as the slaver scum piloting those shuttles.

Instead of dwelling on that, I redirect the sensors to scan ahead of us, desperately looking for *Bainbridge* in orbit. I can see the bulk freighter that was already in orbit when we arrived, its large cargo bay doors open and ready to receive the shuttles, confirming its role in the attack. But I can't see our destroyer.

Then I let out a little cry of relief as our angle of approach changes and I can see *Bainbridge* behind the freighter's bulk. I chart a new course and send it to Malina's console, taking us wide enough around the orbiting freighter that it hopefully can't hit our small moving target with whatever weapons it's clearly packing.

I keep my eyes riveted on my destroyer, searching for any signs of life.

"A Q-ship?" Jess's voice asks near my ear, and I look up to see her leaning on the backs of my seat and Malina's, looking between us at the freighter, now visible to the naked eye out of the forward viewport.

"Has to be," I agree. "Took out *Bainbridge,* maybe with a scrambler or two, then launched the assault on the surface."

"Why now?"

The answer to me is obvious. This was meant for us to see. It was probably meant for us to die, and if that assault on our hotel had gone to plan, we *would* be dead by now. But thanks to Gunny, Hayley, and even our new friend Terry, we're alive.

"Brad," Jess says, pointing to a blinking red light on the console in front of me.

I reach over and press the switch underneath it, and an unfamiliar and heavily distorted voice fills the cockpit.

"Mendoza," it says, somehow managing to make my own name sound ominous to me.

"Sorry, I'm not in the business of giving out my name to strangers," I shoot back. "Who is this?"

"I think you know by now," the voice says, a snide tone coming through even with the heavy distortion.

"What do you want, Bollen?" I demand.

"What every man wants. To see his enemies suffer. Are you ready to suffer for me, Mendoza?"

"Why—"

He cuts me off. "No matter. You'll suffer. You and that tramp wife of yours."

The connection ends before I can say or ask anything in reply.

# TWELVE
# FUTILITY

## JESSICA LIN MENDOZA

"Eight hours, Admiral."

Brad turns red in the face at Kelly O'Malley's dour pronouncement of how long it will take *Bainbridge* to get underway and chase after the slavers.

"Why so long, Cheng?"

Our chief engineer looks almost ashamed. "They hit us with four scramblers at once, sir. Even one would have disabled us for a while, but four at once scrambled the reactor and blew near every power coupling on the ship. We've got the spares in our stores, but I've only got seven engineers, including myself. Even with others on the crew helping, it's going to take time to repair everything. And if we try to bring it all back online at once, we're just as likely to blow it all again. These things take time, sir." He looks away from Brad's gaze and studies the deck at his feet.

Brad reaches out a hand and squeezes Kelly's shoulder. "It's okay, Cheng," he says, using the traditional nickname for chief engineer on Navy ships. "Do what you can. Enlist anyone on the crew to help you, including me and Captain Lin. But only use us where we won't get in the way. You're giving the orders from now until we can get our power back, understood?"

"Aye, sir," Kelly says, looking up again. "We'll get her back up and running for you as fast as humanly possible."

"I know you will."

Kelly whirls and marches off, shouting at his engineers to get back to work, even though none of them stopped while he paused to give us his gloomy status update. Our next stop is the bridge, where the news is even worse.

"We got a few sensors running on backup power," Laia tells us. "That freighter is already done loading and is leaving orbit now. They've got extra drives, sir. The exhaust ports were hidden under false hull plating. They've shed it now, and they're burning hard toward the Gregor jump point."

"How long until they reach it?" I ask, moving to look over her shoulder at her sensor console, the only console on the bridge with any power at the moment.

"AI is down," she admits sheepishly. "So I had to do the calculations in my implant. It says they'll hit the jump point in sixteen hours."

I hear Brad grunt beside me. That means Bollen's freighter will leave the system well before we can catch up to them. *Bainbridge* may be fast, but with drive power a dozen hours away, there's no way we can cover that much space in the four hours remaining to us. And once on the other side of the jump point, with that kind of head start, Bollen can change course and make his engines cold. We might still find them in the Gregor system, but it won't be easy.

"There's a bigger problem, though, sir," Laia says, and I can see her shoulders bunch up a little as if expecting either Brad or me to get upset.

"What is it, Lieutenant?" Brad asks in a surprisingly gentle tone.

"The Poe-Gregor jump point is at mutual conjunction with the Gregor-Hemingway jump point, sir."

We're all silent for a moment.

"How close?" Brad asks softly.

"At the speed I expect that freighter to hit the Gregor jump point, another four hours," she replies.

Brad swears under his breath, and I almost join him. Usually, it takes the better part of a day to transit a star system from one jump point to another. But right now, the jump point that freighter is taking is going to dump it out in the Gregor system a mere four-hour flight from one of the system's other jump points: the one to Hemingway. Pulling up the star charts in my implant, from Hemingway the freighter has a choice of three other jump points, including one to Cillian Heights and another to Linford Commons, where the SDF is supposedly massing their forces.

"So we're not going to catch them," I say, barely above a whisper.

"We have to try," Brad replies at a similar volume. "They did this in front of us, Jess. And you heard Bollen's message—I think he did this because of me, though I can't figure out why. Either way, we can't just let him take all these people."

"I wasn't saying we were going to," I almost snap back, but I catch myself and soften my tone. "But we need to figure out our options."

"No comms yet with the surface?" Brad asks Laia.

She shakes her head. "Harris says if the engineers will listen to him, we can have comms back in two hours. But . . ." She shrugs. There are a lot of other equally vital systems. Harris may have to wait."

"Laia, turn the operating cameras down onto the planet

for a moment. Focus in on the capital city," Brad orders, and she complies.

I gasp as I see the picture of destruction Bollen's people left behind. I gasp again when Brad reaches around Laia and zooms in on a familiar-looking spot of the city. The governor's office building is just . . . gone. That final large explosion we heard when we were fleeing across the university campus —we now know what it was.

"Jess, have Doc Bean load up the shuttle with everyone not working on restoring power. There will be people down there that need our help."

# THIRTEEN
# THREE DAYS LOST

## BRAD MENDOZA

"We appreciate all you've done, sir, ma'am," the planetary police commissioner of Poe says, holding his hat in his hand and surveying the rubble of what was once the planet's seat of government. "But we understand y'all gotta go now, and get our people back."

I nod solemnly, my eyes also on the wreckage. Next to me, Jess is silent. It's been three *days* since Bollen's attack, and we've spent the better part of that time down on the surface helping rescue crews search the rubble of the governor's offices and the other destroyed buildings in the city. Unfortunately, we've found few survivors. Near as *Bainbridge*'s now fully restored sensors and AI can figure out, the governor's office was flattened by a missile fired from Bollen's freighter in orbit. Unfortunately, it happened after the governor and most of his staff had rallied to the building to coordinate what they could of fighting off the attack.

"I lost some of my best people in the raid," the police commissioner goes on, retreading an oft-discussed topic. But both Jess and I seem to sense that he needs to talk things through, convince himself that he and his people did all they could, which they certainly did in the face of overwhelming odds and tactical superiority.

"Some of my best," he repeats, "dead or captured along with those poor students."

The latest estimates suggest Bollen's people captured and took with them nearly three hundred citizens of Poe, most of them students from the University of Poe, the planet's only institution of higher learning.

Slavers. If a vengeful deity offered me the chance to kill every slaver in the galaxy with the snap of my fingers, on the condition that doing so would consign my own soul to endless torment in Hades' realm, I would snap my fingers in an instant.

"We'll get your people back," I promise him. It's not even a question, though Jess and I have debated it endlessly with the other senior officers on our crew. No matter how many times we debate it, the answer is always the same: Bollen clearly did this to get to me, which means that it's our responsibility to rescue those he took.

I just wish I knew who Andre Bollen is and why he seems to hate me so much. It's clear now that the wanted bulletin at Edmonton was planted to lure us to Poe after intel on Bollen. The fact that he was waiting here for us, but Governor Warren had never heard of him, is enough to tell us both that the bulletin was bogus and that coming to Poe was a trap carefully laid for reasons we don't understand.

A lot of people in this galaxy want me dead—often too

many for me to even keep track of—but I just wish I knew why Bollen seems to want me to suffer as well.

"Well, you best be at it then," the police commissioner says, putting his hat back on his head and turning to the fourth member of our solemn little group. "Miss Galpin, it's a shame we never got to know each other under better circumstances."

Terry blushes, the red in her cheeks standing out starkly against her pale, almost Nordic features. "I'm sorry too, Commissioner. I only joined Governor Warren's staff a short time ago."

"And you'll be going with these folks to chase after our people?"

She nods. "I know Andre Bollen. I had no idea he'd come to operate in this part of space. I came to the Corpus Christi Cluster to get away from him."

The commissioner nods slowly, turning back to study the rubble that crushed nearly the entire leadership of this small planet, effectively leaving him in charge, as near as we can tell. "Best of luck to all of you," he says. "May God go with you."

# FOURTEEN
# MAD PURSUIT

## JESSICA LIN MENDOZA

"I don't like it one bit," Brad grouses from the head of the wardroom table after Terry Galpin finishes her proposal as we burn through the Gregor system.

"I second that," Gunny Boyd says from his customary place leaning against the hatchway. "You sure this contact on Gregor's surface is as skittish as you make her out to be?"

Terry Galpin nods, her blonde ponytail bouncing in a way that always made me jealous of the other girls with better hair in high school. Funny to have that thought now, but I blame the lack of sleep. "My contact on Gregor is another former slave of Bollen's," she explains for the third time. "She's . . . traumatized by the things that happened to her, especially at the hands of the men on Bollen's crew. She sees me coming with a man in tow, she's going to think Bollen's people captured me again, and she'll run. Plain and simple, I either go alone or with only female members of your crew."

"Heddy is the obvious choice," Brad says slowly. "And Hayley. That should be plenty if there's trouble. I suppose you could take Eliza Johnson as well," he says, referencing our only other female shooter, a Koratan Marine.

I speak up. "I'm going, too."

My husband gives me an annoyed look, but before he can argue, I keep going.

"You'll need an officer on the ground to command the mission. If something goes awry, I can handle myself, and I can make the command decisions necessary." I meet Brad's gaze in a way that I hope clearly conveys he is *not* going to talk me out of this.

"That's too many people," Terry complains. "She'll get spooked."

"We can leave behind Corporal Johnson," I say, again before Brad can protest. "But Lieutenant Uvalde, Corporal Rodriguez, and I are nonnegotiable."

Terry frowns but has the good grace to recognize she won't gain any more ground in this battle.

We entered the Gregor system several hours ago, after a long slog across Poe to the jump point and then an excruciating six hours in jump space. To no one's surprise, we found no signs of Bollen's ship in Gregor, meaning they've either gone dark or, more likely, headed on to Hemingway and from there to parts unknown.

We were going to chase her anyway, but Terry brought us an alternative while we were in jump space: a friend of hers, another former slave, hiding on the planet Gregor's surface. She has no comm number for this supposed friend, but she insisted she can find her *and* that the woman is likely to have information on where Bollen's base in this sector would be. After a lot of argument, Brad and I both agreed that we were already so far behind Bollen that another day or two lost in transit to Gregor's inhabited planet wouldn't make all that much difference, and could be a huge boon if Terry turns out to be right.

That doesn't mean either of us likes the plan, though, especially with all the conditions Terry keeps putting on it. Something about her continues to rub me the wrong way.

"It's settled then," Brad says reluctantly. "But we still haven't resolved how we're going to get to the planet without being seen. Bollen has to suspect we might stop here for information; he'll have people watching for us."

"I've got a solution to that problem, chico," Hayley chimes in for the first time. "But you ain't gonna like it."

# FIFTEEN
# GIRLS' NIGHT

## JESSICA LIN MENDOZA

"I haven't been on a girls' night in years," Heddy Rodriguez says, practically right in my ear.

"Huh?" I look at her as she slides into the shuttle's copilot's seat next to me while I navigate the small craft toward the massive freighter in front of us.

"I said I haven't been on a girls' night in years," she repeats.

I nod dumbly. My mind is a bit occupied, running in circles. Brad is right about this being a risky plan. But the more he pushed on us not to do it, the more I somehow *wanted* to. Now, however, away from our destroyer and him, I'm having second thoughts.

"You okay?" Heddy asks, pitching her voice lower.

I nod, making a small adjustment to our shuttle's course as a large freighter's airlock comes into view. "Sure. Just try and remember this is a mission, and the girls' night thing is a cover."

She smiles. "You don't have to tell me twice, Captain. I'm an ex-Marine, remember? Even real girls' nights for me have always been about the mission." She waggles her eyebrows in a very suggestive way, and I can't help but bark a small laugh.

"I've *never* been on a girls' night," Hayley says from behind, leaning down to peer between us at the approaching freighter's side. "Unless you count the voices in my head. Then every night's a girls' night."

I have no idea how to respond to that, so I don't even try.

"Is this really the right way to do this?" a fourth voice intrudes. I turn slightly in my seat to peer back at Terry, standing behind Hayley.

"See that freighter up ahead," I say, pointing to the ship growing steadily larger in the forward viewport. It looks a little like the one Bollen used to invade Poe, but it's a different make and model, and just happens to be going to Gregor. "If anyone from Bollen's crew is watching the planet, they'll be watching for *Bainbridge*. So if we arrive on a different ship, like that freighter, we might slip right past them."

Harris's disguises might help a little with that as well. He didn't completely change our appearances—there wasn't time for that. But he added subtle prosthetics, dyed our hair, and made other small changes that should help us not immediately trigger the alarm bells of anyone Bollen gave our description to in Gregor. At least, that's the idea. Even Terry is in disguise, though hers consists only of removable prosthetics, so her contact on Gregor's surface can recognize her when the time comes.

I carefully bring our shuttle in to dock with the freighter's port airlock, waiting until the AI tells me that we've achieved a hard seal. Only then do I unstrap myself from the pilot's seat and make my way back into the passenger compartment with the others. A few moments later, we cycle through the airlock and find the MV *Friendship*'s captain waiting there for us, his eyebrows raised.

"You know," he says skeptically, "when you said the Navy needed to use my freighter, this wasn't what I was expecting."

I nod. The four of us are dressed like single women heading out for a night on the town. Harris even made me wear high heels, which I've always hated. But the man can be quite insistent, and I lost that battle. At least it's not as bad as the time he dressed Brad up like a woman at Carter's World. Either way, we're certainly not dressed like naval officers.

"Undercover mission, Captain," I reply in my best Navy voice. "The Queen's Navy appreciates you helping us out . . . and your discretion."

He shrugs. "Not like you gave me much choice. Anyway, we'll be docking with Gregor Station in about seven hours. I figured you wouldn't want the rest of my crew to see you, so I've arranged for you to wait in my quarters."

I nod, and he leads us through noticeably deserted corridors until we arrive at a nondescript hatch. After ushering us inside, he excuses himself to go back to the freighter's bridge.

Even I was initially very skeptical of Hayley's plan to use the *Friendship* to sneak past anyone Bollen has posted to watch for us on Gregor. Instead of arriving on *Bainbridge,* which is taking its sweet time transiting from the outer system to the inhabited planet, we jumped into our destroyer's shuttle and used it to board *Friendship*. So when the freighter arrives, we'll board the station like we're simply four members of its crew looking to blow off steam while the big ship refuels and offloads cargo.

Brad and I both eventually saw the wisdom in the plan, even if my husband still wasn't exactly thrilled with the idea of me going to the surface without him. He's grown a somewhat troubling protective streak the closer our relationship has gotten, but he and I are going to have to have a real serious talk soon about boundaries. I'm his XO; he can't protect me from everything. In fact, as his second-in-command, a large part of my responsibilities includes going into danger so he doesn't have to.

"So what's it like being a slave, chica?"

The sudden question surprises all of us, no one more than Terry, who stares in shock at Hayley. The Latina has already plopped down on the captain's bunk like she owns the place, and looks back at Terry innocently, like she's asking about the weather.

"It's . . . terrible," Terry replies slowly.

"How so?" Hayley asks, pulling out a package of strawberry licorice from somewhere, tearing it open, and sticking a piece in her mouth to munch happily.

"Is she serious?" Terry asks, looking my way.

"Rarely," I say. "But it might help if you tell us more about your time with Andre Bollen. Give us an idea of what we're dealing with."

Terry shudders visibly but starts talking. "He kept me and a few other women on his ship. I don't think I have to tell you what we were there for." She glares for a moment at Hayley as if daring her to challenge the statement.

Hayley just plops another piece of licorice into her mouth.

"I was there for six months, give or take," Terry continues. "Then I escaped."

"How?" Heddy asks, clearly enthralled.

Terry frowns. "There was a new member of the crew. He liked to look at me and my friend . . . a lot. So we both convinced him we liked him, too. He snuck down to the holding area late one night, and my friend suggested the three of us go to one of the escape pods to be alone. Once we were inside, I—" She pauses, studying the deck for a while. "I strangled him to death while she held him down. Then we launched the pod."

"And they didn't pick you up?" Heddy asks.

She shakes her head. "The ship was in orbit of an inhabited planet, and the pod made it to the surface before Bollen could get his people down to track us."

"That must have been scary," Heddy says. "I'm so sorry you had to go through all that."

For a second, Terry looks like she might snap at her for the seemingly empty platitude, but she seems to sense Heddy is sincere and shrugs. "We got away. The other girls weren't so lucky." She looks down at the deck again, clearly done talking for the moment.

The compartment falls silent. Even Hayley stops chewing the licorice and has the decency to look upset.

I give Terry another ten minutes before I decide it's time for her to tell us more. "And this woman you escaped with, she's the one we're meeting down on the surface of Gregor?"

She nods.

"And is there anything else you can tell us about Bollen himself?"

She looks up, and I can see moisture in her eyes. "He's a sadist." She spits out the words with vehemence, and Heddy naturally takes a step to put herself between me and Terry, who doesn't seem to notice the protective move. "He didn't just use us for . . . well, for you know what. He tortured us, sometimes because we failed to please him, and sometimes just because he was bored." She swears loudly, and I have to agree with her assessment of the man.

"What part of space was he operating in when you were with him?" I ask as gently as I can.

"Mostly the independent systems," she says, maybe a little too quickly, and it suddenly strikes me that Brad and most of our crew spent quite a lot of time in the independent systems just a few months ago, tracking down and capturing the crime lord Baron Dexter Hornsby. Tracking one criminal across that region, it's surprising they wouldn't have at least heard of a slave boss with the obvious power we saw Bollen display at Poe.

There's a lot about this entire situation that isn't adding up, and I continue to feel that Terry herself is one of those things. I look back at her. For the barest instant, I think I see something . . . cold in those icy blue eyes, but then they soften, and I have to question if it was ever really there.

"Be alert for a trap," I tell Hayley and Heddy over our implant comms, purposefully not adding Terry to the channel. "Something isn't right here." I almost go on to explain more, but I stop myself. Right now, all I have are vague suspicions and a fleeting expression I *thought* I saw in the woman's eyes. It's hardly enough to go on, but having both Hayley and Heddy alert for a trap generally is a good idea, so I leave it at that.

They both acknowledge with a quick ping, and then we settle into mostly silence for the remaining trip to the planet on the slow and ponderous MV *Friendship*.

Just over the promised seven hours later, *Friendship*'s captain comes back to his cabin to inform us that his ship has docked with Gregor Station and he's allowed most of his crew to disembark for some R&R. It's now safe for us to come out.

As I pass through the hatch he holds open for us, he stops me with a raised hand. "My payment?"

I smile, having almost forgotten. Reaching into the small clutch purse that Harris insisted I carry, I pull out a small glass cylinder with a plastic top. The captain reaches for it eagerly, twisting off the top and holding the open end to his nose, inhaling deeply. His facial expression turns to one of euphoria, and he takes another deep whiff before replacing the cap and nodding to me. "That's the stuff."

I smirk. Technically, we didn't need to offer the man anything. We could have commandeered his entire ship if we'd wanted, but I knew that we needed his silence as much as his cooperation. However, I was surprised when, instead of credits, he asked for something from our galley as payment.

"Do you know how hard it is to find genuine Tancredi rosemary in this sector?" he asks when he notices my confused look. "Worth its weight in gold and Kaelen diamonds." Then he gets more serious. "My docking schedule has us here for only forty-eight hours to load and offload some cargo. If you're not back by then, we'll have to cut your shuttle loose, and you'll be on your own."

I nod. "Understood. Mind leading us to the other airlock?"

He does so, and the corridors of the freighter are again blessedly empty of other people. It takes about five minutes for us to arrive at the starboard airlock, opposite the one where our shuttle is still docked. Moments later, we're through it and on board Gregor Station at last.

# SIXTEEN
# BARSTOOLS

## JESSICA LIN MENDOZA

If any of Bollen's people are watching for us on the station, they're discreet enough that not even Hayley can pick them out. At one point, I catch a man studying us a little too closely and point him out, but she just smiles.

"He's no slaver, boss. He's just checking out four fine chicas."

I hope she's right, but there's no sense in arguing the point further. Out of the corner of my eye, I see the man I pointed out surreptitiously studying us as we pass, and I can practically feel his eyes on my butt. The skirt Harris made me wear isn't helping things, or as my mother might put it, maybe it's helping things a little *too* much.

We make a beeline across the station's concourse to the opposite side, where we quickly purchase tickets at a kiosk and board the public shuttle that will take us down to the planet's surface. Here as well, we spot no one who seems to take undue interest in us or who looks like a slaver or pirate, though I suspect Bollen's people don't go around wearing the stereotypical metal-studded leather that most pirates seem to fancy.

Regardless, the ten minutes we have to wait on board the shuttle as it takes on more passengers feels like an eternity. Every time someone new enters the small passenger compartment, I have to force myself not to study them too obviously, searching for signs that they may be the scum of the galaxy out to get us. My stress only diminishes slightly when the airlock is finally sealed, and the pilot announces over the intercom that we're ready to undock and start our orbital entry.

Twenty minutes later, we step out of the shuttle and into the late afternoon sunshine of Gregor. Unfortunately, calling it 'sunshine' is a bit generous. I've never liked visiting planets that orbit red stars. The bloodlike rays they cast have never sat well with me. I once had a high school science teacher say that humans evolved with the yellow light of Sol, Earth's sun, and that no other star would ever feel quite as natural to us. I'm not sure I believe that—humans, in my experience, can get used to pretty much anything—but every time I visit a red-bathed planet like Gregor, I become a little more convinced that my teacher knew what he was talking about.

After we clear the perfunctory customs and immigration check, we make our way with the rest of the small crowd of newcomers to the port's one and only exit. There, we secure a robotaxi—a luxury on a planet such as this—to take us into the city, aptly called Landing.

Nearly every human settlement has a city called Landing, usually the first place settlers arrived. They almost always call it that with the full intention of changing it to something more unique later, but most don't ever get around to it. I once had a system administrator tell me it simply wasn't worth the cost of changing the stationery.

So into Landing we go, with Terry giving the robotaxi instructions to take us deep into town, well past the normal spacer bars, clubs, and other establishments set up near the port to service crews on a short leave. That part of town is a little aged and seedy-looking, but beyond it, the place Terry takes us is downright terrifying.

In this part of the city, the streets are oppressively narrow, and not even the dim red light of the star overhead can penetrate their depths, creating a sort of perpetual twilight. Gone are the bright signs and colorful awnings of the spacer's row, and in their place are fading monotone storefront names and a few half-blown bits of neon. One of the latter is outside a bar and is missing half its letters so that it reads 'Sp c r's Gap'.

Hayley stops and studies it. "Spooker's Gap?"

Terry looks like she might correct her, but then thinks better of it. She has no idea who Hayley really is—which is precisely how we want it. But she does know from the frantic flight on Poe that Hayley is a capable operator, so she decides not to potentially insult the obviously insane girl who knows how to fight. She leads us inside, where I have more reason to curse Harris silently.

I argued until I was blue in the face that we'd be best served wearing simply brown or gray shipsuits like the crew of a freighter, like *Friendship,* would normally wear. Harris argued just as vociferously that even freighter crews dress up for a night on the town. I lost the argument.

Unfortunately, my skirt, blouse, and heels don't exactly fit in with the crowd in this dimly lit bar. So, it's no surprise that every eye of the mostly male, working-class crowd rivets on me and the other three women immediately in a way that makes my skin crawl.

Still, I try not to let my discomfort show as Terry leads us to the bar itself, where four burly guys wearing greasy coveralls move aside far enough to let us in, but not far enough that we fit without having to be practically pressed against them on the ends. Hayley looks up at one of them and winks mischievously, and he grins back at her.

I can see we're blending in rather nicely.

"Is Coors here?" Terry asks the rough-looking woman who comes to see if we want a drink of whatever swill they serve in this place.

"Only got Bud on tap," the bartender replies, already turning away.

Terry reaches a hand across the bar and grabs the woman by the arm to keep her from leaving. The bartender looks back at her like she's about to lose that hand, but Terry doesn't flinch. "Tell Coors that Stella is here."

Licking her lips and frowning, the bartender shakes off Terry's hand and quickly disappears through a swinging door behind the bar.

"You ladies looking for a good time?" a gruff voice asks, and I look up to see one of the large men who made way for us leering down at me.

I fight the urge not to shudder at the way his eyes roam over the front of my blouse.

"Depends," Heddy says, saving me from having to converse with the man and inserting herself bodily between us. "What passes for a good time on this rock?"

"All sorts o' things, baby. Depends on what you're in the mood for."

A wave of foul breath washes over me from the side, and I turn to see another man pressing in close next to me. "What's your story, gorgeous?"

Really? Baby? Gorgeous? Do these guys really think that sort of thing works on women? I mean, I suppose Brad has called me both, somewhat awkwardly, but he's *earned* that right. These guys would be far better served by buying a toothbrush and some deodorant, or by occasionally shaving.

"Just here to have a drink," I reply, already turning away, wishing the bartender would return so I could actually order something and look less out of place standing here empty-handed.

Unfortunately, the man with the foul breath doesn't take the hint. He shoves his way closer to me, pushing aside another man to take up position right next to me at the bar, so close that far too much of him is touching far too much of me. "What're you drinking, honey buns? I'm buying."

"I can buy my own drink," I tell him, trying not to sound as annoyed as I feel. Calling me 'honey buns' just might have been a step too far.

"Sure, you can, but no woman looks like you should ever have to," he insists. "'Sides, you look like you came looking for something more than just a stiff drink."

I *really* want to punch this guy, but I refrain. The goal is to blend in—mission failed, but I don't need to muck it up any worse than it already is.

"Come on, little lady," he says, leaning in closer. "I bet it gets all kinds of lonely out there in space. How about you let me show you a good time?"

It's all I can do now not to knee him in the groin, especially since he's so close I can feel his hot, fetid breath on my cheek again. Then, to my horror, he leans even closer, practically pressing his lips to my ear.

"Captain Lin. Don't react. We're being watched."

Hearing my name and old rank from his mouth makes me freeze for an instant, and I almost don't react as he instructed. Then my hand is moving toward the gun at the small of my back. His beefy mitt intercepts mine and keeps me from getting to it.

"Hit me," he whispers harshly in my ear. "And make it look good. Then get out of here as fast as you can. Go west."

My brain struggles to reconcile what's going on.

"Do it, now. Trust me," he hurries to add. Then his voice changes from that of a rough citizen of Gregor to a slick Promethean accent. "For the queen, Captain Lin."

Well, I suppose I wanted to punch him anyway. My foot stomps down on his, not doing much through his thick work boot, but allowing me a moment to wrench my wrist from his grip and use that arm to wind up and sock him right in the cheek.

He grunts and steps back. Shaking his head to clear it, he bellows in anger, and I brace myself for his return blow. Instead, he just picks up a nearby glass of beer and throws it at the mirror behind the bar, shattering both and taking me by complete surprise.

"Tease!" he yells. Then he flips a credit chip onto the bar, stalks away, and leaves the building.

The entire place is silent as every single pair of eyes is fixed on me.

"We've got to leave, now," I tell everyone through our shared implant comms.

Terry starts to protest, but Heddy grabs her by the arm and drags her behind me and Hayley as we rush to exit the bar.

Remembering the man's instructions to go west, I turn and usher my companions east. I'm not in the mood to willingly meet strange men from bars in the quickly darkening evening, Promethean accent or not. Last I checked, Prometheus—what's left of it—is under Jutzen control.

"We're being followed, boss," Hayley says after a few moments, moving up beside me. "That guy from the bar is on our six."

"I figured," I tell her. "He knew me, and I think he wants

to meet. Keep tracking him, but let's not make any moves to lose him." So much for giving the guy the slip, though now that I know a meeting with him is inevitable, I feel a burning curiosity to find out who he is and what he wants.

"Somebody want to tell me what's going on?" Terry asks. "My friend is back there somewhere, and we still haven't found her."

We ignore her, lacking the time to stop and explain, and she falls into a sullen silence that's alright with me. Continuing on for another two blocks, Hayley spots a side street devoid of foot traffic and, with a nod, directs us down it. In the middle of the block, we stop and wait. It's dark out now, with night falling even quicker here in the narrow streets. Only one flickering street lamp lights this particular block, and its on-and-off glow does nothing to still my pounding heart and the adrenaline in my veins.

Luckily, we only have to wait about two minutes before the large man from the bar arrives, shuffling his feet and swaying like a drunk as he moves toward us, fooling no one. Pushing Terry behind me, ignoring her indignant yelp, I take center position while Heddy and Hayley fan out to either side, our hands on our various hidden weapons.

"That's far enough," I tell the man when he's three meters away, pulling out my pistol to emphasize the point.

He stops as ordered, turning around and slowly lifting his work coat above his waist to show he has no hidden weapons there. When he turns back to face us, his eyes fixate on me.

"Who are you?" I demand.

"My sister is a barista," he says nonsensically. "But she can only draw hearts in the foam."

The words trigger a memory, and I find myself almost involuntarily lowering the pistol, though Heddy and Hayley keep theirs trained on the man's chest. "And my brother is a fishmonger, but he only deals in squid," I reply, drawing strange looks from my three companions.

"We need to talk, but not here," he says. "I have a safe-house nearby."

I shake my head. "Not a chance. We do this here, or somewhere else that's more public."

He visibly sighs. "Fine."

"What's ProSec doing on Gregor of all places?" I ask.

Terry swears at hearing the abbreviated name for the Promethean Security Service, the most generally hated intelligence agency in the Federation, and second in skill and ruthlessness only to the Order of the King's Cross.

"I'm here under orders," the man says, offering no more. "What are you doing on Gregor?"

I shake my head. "That's for us to know. Isn't ProSec supposed to help the Navy when you encounter us out in the wild?"

He scoffs. "What do you think I was doing in the bar? There were six guys in there who wanted to do you harm. Three followed you outside, but they're not following you anymore."

I have no way of verifying his story, so I just stay silent.

Finally, he realizes I'm not going to be the first to talk. "ProSec sent me out here to investigate rumors that Duke Fuller was plotting against the king and was making a move to use the Cluster in some way in his plans."

"I think you're a little late on that one, chico," Hayley says with a chuckle.

"No, really?" he asks, laying the sarcasm on thick. "ProSec sent me out here three months ago, *before* Prometheus was sacked and Fuller showed his true colors. Now my accounts are frozen and I'm stuck here. I'm not even sure there's a ProSec anymore for me to go back to. Do you know how hard it is to find odd jobs to raise enough money to get off a dusty rock like this one?"

He looks past me at Terry. "Your friend Coors, the one you were asking about at the bar, I have no idea who he or she is, but your question set off a firestorm. That bartender went to the back room to make a few calls, and those six guys I mentioned were already reaching for their knives when she gave them the signal."

I turn back to see a flash of annoyance on Terry's face, no doubt at missing her contact, but it passes quickly. She's a cool one, possibly a result of living as a slave for so long. Either way, she doesn't reply, just stares at the ProSec agent with a thin-lipped frown.

"How did you recognize us?" I demand.

He smirks. "Seriously? No offense, Captain Lin, but you're hard to miss, even with that so-called disguise you're wearing. Not to mention there's already hubbub about a Promethean destroyer on its way in from the outer system. I heard someone at the bar mention Brad Mendoza, and I put two and two together."

That's not good. It means our supposedly stealthy manner of entering orbit on the MV *Friendship* didn't fool anyone.

"We're looking for a slave ship that passed through this system several days ago," I tell him. "Crew run by a guy named Andre Bollen. Heard of him?"

He shakes his head. "Never. I didn't even know there were slavers operating in the Cluster." It's always hard to tell with ProSec, but he looks sincere to my eyes.

"What about rumors of the SDF massing at Linford Commons? Some sort of plan to open a second front against the queen?"

He thinks about that for longer before responding. "Yeah, I've heard about the SDF. Not a whole lot, mind you. Gregor isn't exactly the center of commerce and trade in this sector.

But I've heard enough to substantiate that rumor for you. In fact . . ." He looks around surreptitiously and takes a step forward. Heddy motions with her gun for him not to come any closer, but he keeps his eyes firmly on me. "There's another rumor going around that Duke Fuller—King Chance, whatever you want to call him these days—sent someone to the Corpus Christi Cluster to run things here. Supposedly, put them in charge of the SDF forces in the region and gave them carte blanche to win the Cluster for the Nazis."

"Any idea who it is?" I ask, excited to hear independent evidence for what Governor Warren told us about a new enemy leader in this sector.

The ProSec agent disappoints me by shaking his head. "No. Rumors say it's some minor member of the nobility, maybe even a distant relative of King Charles who switched sides. Either way, it's just that, rumors. But if you get me off this rock, I still have contacts in Cillian Heights and Linford Commons, and I can find out more."

"What's your name, chico?" Hayley asks before I can respond.

"Volkov. Leo Volkov, at your service."

"Well, Agent Volkov," I tell him. "If you don't have any intel on Andre Bollen, I'm not sure you coming with us will be all that big of a help. So . . ."

"Please take me with you," he says, suddenly pleading. "You have no idea what it's like to be cut off and abandoned on a dustball like this one. I don't even know if the rest of ProSec is still active, and it's driving me insane." He studies me, perhaps seeing that his words aren't convincing me yet. "Look, bring me along, and maybe my contacts can help you find this Bollen guy. It can't hurt, right?"

I wait a beat to see if he's desperate enough to offer more or give anything else away. Then, slowly, I nod. "Fine, let's go to the shuttle station and—"

"No!"

We all turn in surprise to stare at Terry, who speaks up for the first time in the conversation. "We can't leave. Not yet. If Coors isn't here"—her voice breaks—"then she would have left something behind for me. There's a dead drop on the other side of town. We need to go there first."

I study her, frowning. After the scene in the bar, I would very much like to get off this blasted planet. But if Terry is telling the truth, then I can't afford *not* to go see what her contact might have left. It could be the key we need to finding Bollen.

Besides, I've got Heddy and Hayley along, and unlike Poe, here we're actively looking for any signs of trouble. What's the worst that could happen?

"Fine," I say to Terry, who looks supremely relieved.

Volkov shakes his head and shuffles his feet. "I can't go with you to the dead drop. I've got a few loose ends to tie up here on the surface before I leave. I'll meet you in a few hours on the station."

"It's all good, chico," Hayley assures him cheerfully. "You go sulk off into the shadows like a good little spy. We'll be just fine. Entiendes?"

With a last dubious look, he turns and walks away, disappearing around the same corner he emerged from.

# SEVENTEEN
# THE LAUNDROMAT

## JESSICA LIN MENDOZA

Terry's dead drop turns out to be, of all things, a laundromat on the other side of town. I can't remember the last time I saw a real laundromat. Clothing refreshers are generally so cheap that every household on Prometheus has one, even in the poorer areas. However, Gregor is apparently so economically stunted that having your own unit is a luxury. Hence, laundromats.

Even stranger, it has the ancient type of washing machines—the ones that spin clothes around violently for no apparent reason and don't have integrated dryers. Those are separate.

The city isn't all that large, but we took our time moving across it, avoiding the scant public transportation and taking multiple robotaxis in seemingly random directions to throw off any pursuit. All in all, it took us about an hour to arrive at the laundromat, and we stop now to study it from across the darkened street.

"Coors told me, if anything ever happened to her, to check behind the third washing machine from the left in the second row," Terry explains, but as she takes a step to cross the street, I reach out and hold her back.

"What are you doing?" she asks, looking at me in confusion. "It's right there. I can go get it and be back in two minutes."

Frowning, I shake my head. "No, I'll do it. Hayley, stay here and cover me. Heddy, go watch from that doorway. If anything happens to me, call the ship and give them our position."

My two crew members nod their acknowledgments. Terry looks ready to argue with me again, but she clams up when I give her a look.

I set off across the street, entering the laundromat a moment later. As we saw from outside, there are three people inside, and they all look at me with no attempt to conceal their curiosity. Like at the bar, I'm dressed far too nicely, and the clack of my heels on the chipped laminate floor is almost deafeningly loud. I suddenly realize that I'm going to look rather odd walking over and reaching behind a random washing machine for the materials Terry insists her contact would have left there for her.

It's not as if I expect the two housewives and the stoner here washing their clothes to try to stop me—I'm confident I could handle any of them if it came to that—but I am worried about acting in a way so strange that one of them thinks to call whatever passes for law enforcement—or, more likely, whatever gang controls this neighborhood and could possibly be in league with Bollen's people.

I think through my options and decide that I might as well use my outlandish clothing to my benefit. "Excuse me," I say loudly enough for them all to hear, even over the racket of one of the washing machine's spin cycles. "Do any of you know who owns this laundromat?"

They all stare at me blankly.

"I represent a company that's looking to invest in this part of town," I continue. "I'd love to speak with the owner about possibly purchasing this . . . uh . . . establishment."

The two housewives shake their heads and go back to their own wash. Only the stoner is still looking at me, but mostly in a confused and semicurious way. I'm probably the most unusual thing he's seen even while high this week.

"Well," I say, still loud enough for all of them, "I suppose I'll just inspect the equipment to make sure it's worth an investment. Then I can find the owner some other way to discuss terms."

By the way they all don't react, I can already tell I've gone into way more detail than they care to hear. In a neighborhood like this, I just made myself stand out even more than I would have by simply walking in, grabbing whatever Terry's contact left from behind the third machine from the left in the second row, and then walking out.

But there's nothing to be done about it now, so I walk over to that machine and reach over it to feel around in the top left corner, where Terry said to look.

Nothing.

Wondering if maybe her contact meant directionally when looking at the machine from the back, I feel the other corner. Still nothing.

Then I wonder if maybe she meant another machine. The washing machines are in three rows, all back-to-back, with the dryers situated around the outside against the three walls. 'Second row' could mean the first row of backward-facing washers. But checking there yields nothing. Nor does checking the third machine from the right on that row or the original one.

I know I should give up at this point, but I'm starting to get frustrated, like this is a challenge I have to figure out. Soon, I'm running my hands along the back of every washing machine, but all I manage to do is slice open my finger on the jagged edge of an open maintenance panel. My curse draws curious looks from the three others in the laundromat, and by now, they've seen enough of me to give my description to anyone who might care.

I'm about to leave when I pass one of the machines just as it starts its spin cycle. It starts to shake and jump in place, banging up against the machines to either side, and I pause, staring at it, my mind telling me that it's somehow important.

Understanding dawns, and I rush back over to the original machine: third from the left in the second row, as seen looking in from outside. Though it's awkward in the skirt, I lift myself up onto it, drawing funny looks from the housewives and the stoner. Turning my torso, I peer down behind it. In the dim light, I almost can't see to the bottom of the gap between it and the back of the machine behind it, and . . . there's nothing there.

"Captain," Heddy's voice says in my implant. "*Bainbridge* just docked at the station and Admir—" The rest of her voice dissolves in a fit of static.

I try to call her back, but I get nothing. Same with Hayley. Just like on Poe.

Panicking, I practically sprint out of the laundromat, running across the street toward Hayley and Terry, a cry of warning on my lips.

At that moment, a car skids around the corner, its headlights bright and spearing me in the darkness. I involuntarily freeze as I hear it rush forward, its electric motor almost whisper-quiet, but the sound of its tires on the pavement gives away its increasing acceleration as it sprints directly toward me.

# EIGHTEEN
# BUREAUCRATIC FIRESTORM

## BRAD MENDOZA

"No."

By the look on the station administrator's face, few have ever dared to say that word out loud to him before.

"B-but," he stammers, "surely you must realize that we have laws here. The Federation has laws, and those laws state that you must allow us to inspect your ship when it's docked at our station."

We're standing outside *Bainbridge's* airlock, and we're not alone. Four station security officers stare nervously at me and the administrator and beyond us to where Gunny Boyd and Drake Forbes stand, feet apart and hands behind their backs, at military parade rest. The station guards can't know, but they can surely guess, that both of them are armed and their hidden hands hold guns.

"I know the law," I tell the sputtering station administrator. "But I'm guessing the law has nothing to do with you wanting to inspect my ship." I could just reject his claim on the shaky reasoning that *Bainbridge* is a Navy ship. She's not really, of course, but my status as an admiral pretty much means any ship I'm on is Navy . . . sort of. However, I'm not wearing my uniform, and I've introduced myself as Captain Ben Lopez of the MV—not HMS—*Illiad,* one of the fake transponders Harris worked up for us a while back.

Something tells me that making my real identity and that of my ship openly known in this system would not be wise.

"I'm sure I have no idea what you mean," he protests. "I am simply doing my job, and your ship has been chosen for a random inspection. Now move aside, or I will be forced to arrest you."

I smile at him, which seems to confuse the guy. "Nope. Sorry, not gonna happen. I suggest you make another *random* selection and move on. Trying to arrest us would be unwise."

My grandpa was always fond of saying that Hell hath no fury like a bureaucrat scorned, and this station administrator is proving that to be very, very true. His face turns red, and he practically stomps his feet like a toddler throwing a tantrum. "Officers, arrest these three."

Needless to say, the attempt goes very poorly for the four security guards. Their hands go to their weapons, but those weapons are still in their holsters. Gunny and Drake have them all down with stun rounds before a single guard is able to draw his pistol.

Next thing you know, my two shooters have grabbed the furious station administrator each by an arm and are holding him a few centimeters off the ground while his legs kick comedically in the air. He's short, so even in his aloft position, I'm still looking down at him.

"Tell me why you want so badly to inspect my ship," I order him.

He shakes his head, then cries out as Gunny and Drake tighten their grips painfully.

"Last chance," I tell him. "Or I let him start breaking every bone in your body. That sound fun?"

"Sure does, boss," Gunny says with a wicked grin.

"I didn't do anything," the man whines. "Your ship was chosen randomlyyyyy!" His voice goes up an octave on the last syllable as my two shooters tighten their grips once again.

"Fine. Fine. Fine," he gasps. "Someone asked us to inspect your ship."

"Who?" I demand, stepping closer to him. He could try to kick me at this range, but I don't believe he's currently capable of rational thought in that regard.

"I don't know, I swear! We got a call from the surface, but my boss took it. All he told me was to come, inspect your ship, and arrest the captain. I swear, that's all I know!"

I nod thoughtfully, looking him in his frantic eyes until I'm convinced he's telling the truth. I motion to Gunny and Drake, and they set him down almost gently. Reaching up with a smile, I brush imaginary dirt off the man's shoulder and then tug on the front of his tunic to straighten it. After that, I nod to Drake, and he shoots the administrator point-blank with a stun round. The man goes down in a heap, landing across two of the erstwhile security men.

"Want us to go find this guy's boss and figure out who called him?" Gunny asks.

I shake my head. "I don't want to stay here any longer than we have to. But we need to call Jessica and the ground team and get them back here."

Just then, my implant pings. "Admiral, this is Harris," my comms officer and makeup artist says a little strangely. "I was talking to Heddy, but I lost her. I think someone's jamming them."

I swear out loud, drawing looks from Gunny and Drake. I explain to them what's going on.

"Gunny," I order. "Take your shooters, all of them. Go with Malina and get our shuttle undocked from that freighter and on its way down to the surface to our team's last known position. On the double!"

They don't pause to argue, just race back into the ship to gather Malina and the other shooters. I follow them on board and head straight to the bridge.

I don't know what's happening down on the surface of Gregor, or why someone wants so badly for us not to leave this system, but I'm going to make sure everyone in this Crown-forsaken system learns it's a terrible idea to piss off a mass murderer with access to a Navy destroyer. That thinking at least keeps my mind off what might be happening to my wife right at this moment.

# NINETEEN
# CAR TROUBLE

## JESSICA LIN MENDOZA

"Boss, watch out!"

Hayley's cry of alarm snaps me out of my frozen indecisiveness as the car barrels toward me outside the laundromat. I kick off my heels and run barefoot across the pavement, but out of the corner of my eye, I can see the vehicle adjust course to continue charging me.

Gunfire pierces the night air, and I'm not sure if it's from the occupants of the car or my own crew. It really doesn't matter, because I know I'm not going to reach the relative safety of the sidewalk in time. The car is still coming straight at me, and it'll be on me in an instant. I'm no longer looking ahead of myself; my eyes are riveted on my oncoming death. So I don't see Hayley leap off the sidewalk and sprint toward me.

She hits me an instant before the car reaches me, knocking me back toward the center of the street and landing on top of me. I feel the wind of the passing car against the soles of my feet as its driver fails to react in time to my sudden change of direction, speeding through the point where I was before Hayley's daring tackle.

There's a crash and the shriek of metal on metal, accompanied by the brittle crack and tinkling of broken glass. I look up and around Hayley, who is still on top of me, to see that the car's driver, distracted by missing me, slammed the vehicle into a parked car ten meters down the road.

Unfortunately, the parked car took far more damage than the one that tried to run me down, and I watch helplessly as all four of its doors open, disgorging three men and one woman, all carrying assault rifles.

Hayley pushes off of me and leaps a few paces to the right, firing her pistol as she moves, forcing two of the attackers to take cover behind the open car doors. One of the other gunmen goes down, probably from Heddy's gun.

Still on the ground, I roll over, reaching into the holster at the small of my back for my own pistol but finding it empty. At some point, it must have fallen out, either during my run across the street or when Hayley knocked me down.

I spring to my feet, ignoring a twinge in my knee and the bloody scrapes on my feet, and sprint toward the nearest of the two attackers—a man. So intent is he on firing at Hayley that he doesn't notice me approaching until it's too late, and I lash out with a bare foot to take him in his knee. It forces him to stagger back and drop onto the other knee, which allows me to follow it up with a kick to the side of his head that knocks him down and stuns him long enough for me to crouch down and grab for his assault rifle.

He fights me for control of the weapon, but he's dazed, and it's like he's moving in slow motion. After only a momentary struggle, I wrench it away from him and straighten up again, swinging the gun to point it at one of the other attackers, the sole woman of the group.

I start to pull the trigger, but the assault rifle fires prematurely, kicking back hard into my chest.

"Boss!" I vaguely hear Hayley scream as I look down in confusion to see a red spot forming on my white blouse, just above my right breast. Confused, I blink rapidly to clear my vision as it blurs for no apparent reason. Was the gun's kick hard enough to break the skin?

I feel woozy on my feet, and my knees give out. As I slump to the pavement, I hear another shot and a second kick, this time to my left shoulder. That confuses me even more. I didn't even fire my gun. I look in bewilderment at the attacker in front of me, in time to see someone shoot her in the head. Strange. I guess both my shots must have missed her, but they sure hurt me. Maybe the assault rifle was defective and…

# TWENTY
# HOSTILE DEPARTURE

## BRAD MENDOZA

"Sir, station control is refusing to unlock the docking clamps," Manny Cortes reports from the helm. "They're saying we're impounded."

I swear under my breath. "Harris, open a channel."

"Sure, Admiral."

"Captain Mendoza," an imperious woman's voice growls before I can speak, and it confirms for me that my little Ben Lopez and merchant ship ruse fooled no one. "You are hereby ordered to—"

"Shut up and listen if you want to live through until tomorrow," I snap, cutting her off. "In exactly three minutes, I'm going to fire my ship's main drive. Not only will doing so incinerate half this level of your precious station, but it's sure to move your orbit to a far less stable one. However, if you release those docking clamps in the next"—I check my console—"forty-one seconds, I'll be able to get far enough away on thruster power that I won't do much more than char your paint job. You copy?"

The seconds tick away. "You wouldn't dare," the voice replies, sounding far less sure than her words imply. "The damage to your ship would be—"

"Light compared to the damage to your station. And before you even consider that I'm bluffing, you've obviously read my file. Is there anything in there that makes you think I'm *not* crazy enough to do exactly what I just promised?"

Another long pause. I watch the countdown timer in my implant. I'm trying to project outward assurance to my crew and the woman on the other end of the comm, but inside, I'm on the edge of panic. It's been nearly five minutes since we lost comms with Jess's team, and every minute that passes sends me more and more into a near panic at the thought of what might be happening to them.

At exactly thirty-nine seconds since I issued my threat, I feel a satisfying clunk through the deck plates as the station's docking clamps release their hold on my ship, and I heave a sigh of relief.

"Helm, take us out, 20 percent thruster power. Let's leave a mark."

"Aye, sir!"

*Bainbridge* bolts away from the station, her overpowered thrusters not melting the hull metal but leaving several long black scorch marks and pitting on its exterior.

"Guns, any news on our shuttle?" I shout at Illian.

"Coming around the station now, Admiral," he replies. "Gunny reports no problems and is requesting instructions."

I clench my jaw and blow out a frustrated breath from my nose. "Tell him to get down to the planet to Jess's last known coordinates. Weapons hot. We'll cover them from orbit."

I wait as he relays the message, bypassing Harris, who doesn't seem to mind.

"Course, sir?" Chief Manny Cortes asks from the helm.

"Cut thrusters and hold us here for a moment," I reply. "Guns, let's defang this station. Target their defensive systems, lasers only."

"Aye, Admiral. Awaiting your command."

"Fire."

With expert precision, Illian uses our starboard lasers to take out the station's single missile launcher on the top of its spire. Then, lower-powered lances of light reach out from our destroyer and burn off the few defensive laser clusters on our side of the orbital.

After that, all we can do is watch as our shuttle dives toward the planet's surface, its passage through the upper atmosphere making it take on the appearance of a meteor burning downward, hopefully to rescue those we love.

# TWENTY-ONE
# BURIED ALIVE

## JESSICA LIN MENDOZA

It's really loud.

That's my first thought as I wake up. Brad must be doing some kind of construction in our cabin. I open my eyes to find him and tell him to take a break, but something is off. I'm on my back, looking up at a nondescript black ceiling that's far too close.

I start to panic. Did I die? Is this my coffin? What's going on? Have I been buried alive? I—

The coffin shakes and jerks to one side.

"She's awake!" a familiar voice shouts. "Captain, can you hear me?"

Blinking rapidly, I crane my neck to see Heddy's face staring down at me from one side.

I want to ask what's going on, but my voice isn't responding to my commands to speak. I try to suck in a breath, but a sharp pain in my chest stops me.

The coffin jerks again, and I hear a squealing sound. With great effort, I turn my head to look around and see a gap in one of the coffin's side walls. Through that gap, I spy Hayley, gripping something circular.

Wait, is this a car? I'm lying across the backseat of a car. I lift my head to see more, but my neck is weak, and it falls back to the cushioned rear seat.

"No, no, no, go *that* way," another voice calls from the front seat. It sounds like Terry. "Where did you learn how to drive?"

"Who says I ever learned, chica?" Hayley says back with none of her usual cheerfulness. She whips the wheel around, and my entire world spins for a moment before going dark once again…

When my eyes flutter open a few seconds, minutes, or maybe days later, I'm still in the back of the car, and Hayley is still at the wheel, driving like the madwoman she is.

"Why are the cops after us?" Terry asks frantically.

"Because they think we killed four people back there and stole a car," Heddy practically shouts back. I look down to find her still looming over me and notice that her hands are pressing down hard on my chest for some reason. She's hurting me.

I try to find the air to tell her that, but . . . but . . .

Pain!

I wake up again to an entire world that is nothing more than pain. It hurts so bad.

It's also deafeningly loud again. There are pops all around us. Pops like gunfire? Then a whirring noise as a larger, more powerful gun joins the fray. My mind flashes back to the shuttle that tried to kill us on Poe, and I open my mouth to scream a warning, but the sound catches in my throat.

"Almost there, Captain," Heddy tries to soothe me. "Just hang in there. The shuttle is driving those cops back."

I try to nod, to say anything to respond, but my eyelids feel so heavy and I just can't…

# TWENTY-TWO
# RECOVERY

## BRAD MENDOZA

"How far out is the shuttle?" I demand, shouting across the bridge, not caring for decorum at the moment.

"Eight minutes, sir," Illian replies. Then he shouts in surprise. "Contact! System patrol frigate, coming over the horizon. They must have approached on the other side of the planet, sir."

"Harris, hail them."

"They're not answering, Admiral," comes the reply.

"Tell them that if they don't heave to and cease approach, we'll be forced to fire on them."

"They're charging weapons!" Illian warns.

"Harris!" I shout. "Tell them we're the Navy!"

"Still not responding, sir!"

I watch for the barest instant on the battle plot as the little frigate races over the horizon. I imagine I can see light reflected from open missile launchers and feel the energy radiating off charged laser capacitors. Forcing my clenched jaw open, I finally give the order I know I have no other choice but to give.

"Commander Illian, track that frigate and fire the starboard broadside."

I expect him to hesitate—after all, that frigate hasn't fired yet. But military doctrine is clear on this. The enemy ship hasn't responded to hails and has its weapons armed and in range. Waiting for them to shoot first would be to invite damage that we can't afford to repair right now.

Fortunately for us, and unfortunately for the crew of the frigate, Illian either trusts me enough not to argue or understands why I'm giving the order. He fires immediately, and seconds later, the little frigate is nothing more than an expanding ball of gas. With so little warning, we didn't even have time to load a scrambler.

The bridge goes silent as the camera feed shows the other ship practically disappear from the plot and the external camera feeds. Rarely do we see such a sight this close up, and it seems to suck the oxygen from the bridge.

I stand up. "Commander Illian, you have the conn."

"Aye, sir," he says, sounding almost robotic, but I'm already sprinting off the bridge.

I arrive at the port airlock less than two minutes before Malina docks our shuttle. This is the second time she's had to rescue part of our crew from a hot zone, and my anger with Andre Bollen and everyone who supports him is at an all-time high. It's only overpowered and overshadowed by one emotion: dread. Because Heddy's message from the shuttle after pickup was that Jess has been shot multiple times, and she's hanging on to life by a thread.

The airlock opens after far too long a wait, and I rush through, ahead of Doc Bean and two enlisted Koratan spacers who arrived with a stretcher. I stop in my tracks when I enter the shuttle's passenger compartment, a cry escaping my lips.

My wife is covered in blood. There's a makeshift bandage across her chest, and Heddy is kneeling next to her on the deck, applying pressure to her shoulder. She looks up to see me standing there, tears in her eyes.

"Is she . . ." I can't even finish the question.

To my extraordinary relief, Heddy shakes her head. "She's alive. Barely." The last word robs me of my momentary elation.

"Admiral, get out of the way!" Doc Bean shoves past me and falls to his knees next to Jess, examining her from head to toe, including moving aside the various bandages and Heddy's hands to check the wounds underneath.

"We need to get her to the med bay, stat," he says, and I allow myself to be not-so-gently removed from the shuttle by Gunny and Drake.

We wait out in the corridor as the doctor and his two orderlies take Jess off the shuttle and toward the med bay. I follow them, unable to speak, ignoring the other members of my crew who try to get my attention on the way, just as I ignore Illian's calls from the bridge requesting additional orders.

He'll figure it out.

When we arrive at the med bay, I go to follow the stretcher in, but strong hands hold me back. I spin with a growl to see Gunny, tears streaking his dark face, looking down at me with something approaching pity, and it enrages me even more.

"Admiral, you've gotta let the doc work," he pleads.

I struggle in his iron grasp, yelling invectives and threats, until I feel a sting in the back of my neck. Suddenly, my mouth won't form words anymore, and my legs turn to jelly.

"That'll knock him out for a couple of hours so I can save her life," I vaguely hear Doc Bean say as I feel Gunny's hands keep me from falling before everything goes dark.

# TWENTY-THREE
# LIFE AND DEATH

## BRAD MENDOZA

The wardroom is silent, and half the assembled men and women won't even look each other in the eye. I may be the commanding officer on this ship, but if ever there was proof that Jess is *Bainbridge*'s soul, it's in the distraught and wary faces all around me.

"Any word from that ProSec agent you met on the surface?" I ask Hayley, my voice flat and emotionless.

"No, boss. He said he'd meet us on the station."

"Comm chatter says station security had a shootout with someone on the orbital just after we left," Laia Gammon adds. "Sounds like your man. I'm sorry; he died resisting arrest."

I swear, a bit more loudly than I intended. "So we have no idea what intel he had for us?"

No one replies. It wasn't truly a question anyway.

"And nothing from the dead drop?" I ask next.

"Not unless la capitana dropped it in the firefight," Hayley says, looking about how I feel at the revelation.

"So we came all the way to Gregor, damaged their station, blew up one of their patrol boats, and . . ." I can't bring myself to say what happened to my wife. "It was all for nothing?" I lament instead.

Again, no one responds. They don't need to.

"Do we set course to Kipling?"

I look at Illian, who meets my eyes for the first time since I called this meeting after waking up from whatever Doc Bean injected into me. "What do you mean?" I ask.

He looks confused. "I just assumed, with what happened to Captain Lin, that we'd—"

"Run? With our tail between our legs?" I say, far too harshly again. "Go back and throw ourselves on the queen's mercy? Is that what you think, Commander?"

He flinches, and the sight of it breaks something inside me. Tears come to my eyes, and I hastily wipe them away, but more come to take their place. No one else speaks, and it only takes me a minute or so to regain my composure, but in that brief time, all the anger has gone out of me, and left me only with a crippling fear and a burning shame.

"I'm sorry, Francis," I tell him. "I had no right to speak to you like that."

He meets my eyes and nods once to acknowledge my apology.

"We can't go to Kipling," I say, sitting up a little straighter. "It's too far. Doc says that Jessica needs a level one trauma center. He's got her in a med pod in a medically induced coma." I stumble over the words, almost choking on them. "We need to get her to a surgeon as soon as possible."

"So where to then, Admiral?" Gunny asks. He's standing behind me.

"Well," I say, my shoulders slumping, "the last three

planets we visited either tried to arrest us, kill us, or both. So, unfortunately, the only level one trauma center in this sector I think we might be able to trust is at Huff."

A few of them look at me in confusion.

"Huff Naval Base," Kelly O'Malley helpfully explains. "It orbits a moon in the outer system at Cillian Heights. It's where the Navy maintains its command for the Corpus Christi Cluster."

A few of them nod.

"And it's only one jump away," I add, finding my voice once more. "Assuming the forces there are still loyal to the queen, we should be able to get the help we need."

"And if they're not?" Laia Gammon asks morosely.

I meet her gaze and then look at every one of my command officers in turn. "Then," I say carefully, "we'll throw ourselves on their mercy and hope they help us anyway."

If any of them want to argue against giving ourselves over to potentially hostile forces to save Jess's life, they make no indication of it. All I see around the table are solemn nods and determined faces, and I suddenly find myself loving this crew more than I thought possible, even after all we've been through together.

Of course, they might feel differently if they knew what I do—that the Navy commander at Huff is almost certainly going to arrest me the second I enter his sphere of influence. There's a reason Jess and I haven't even discussed the possibility of going to Cillian Heights and the Navy at Huff to ask for help finding the slaves taken from Poe: because we both know who the admiral in charge there is, and he's definitely not a friend.

"How are we doing on fuel?" I ask Kelly, more to get my mind off my impending doom than anything else.

My chief engineer perks up, probably also grateful for the

change in subject. "We have plenty, Skipper. And a little to spare. I refueled us at Gregor Station."

"How?" Illian asks. "They wouldn't even let me connect to their systems to update our star charts. They weren't exactly friendly."

Kelly gives the man a wan smile, though his heart isn't in it. "Been around as long as I have, Francis, and you learn how to get fuel wherever you need it, even under less-than-ideal conditions. Let's just say that the light freighter docked next to us is going to have a little dispute with station command over their bill."

"Kelly, I could kiss you," I say, trying and failing to lighten the mood. "Okay, folks. We sprint full out from here to Huff. I want us at that Navy station in less than twenty-four hours. Anyone gets in our way, we warn first, but shoot if they make any move to stop us. Any issues with those rules of engagement?" I look specifically at Illian, who will have to be the one to carry out that order, just as he did in orbit of Gregor.

He looks like he just bit into a lemon, but he shakes his head. "No issues, sir. Seems like everyone in this sector is a hostile."

I bite back my reply, wanting to break out in a curse-filled tirade about that very topic. No one in this blasted region of space had ever even heard of Andre Bollen a week ago, and most still haven't. Yet the slaver seems to have system commands, patrols, and even police working for him.

I should have *never* let Jess and the others go down to that stupid planet. Which surfaces a sudden thought. "Where's Terry?"

Gunn looks over at me. "In her quarters, sir. Eliza is guarding the door."

"Put her in the brig," I say. "Let her sweat there for a few hours. Miss Galpin and I need to have a very unpleasant conversation."

# PART TWO
# SURRENDER

# TWENTY-FOUR
# QUEENS AND PAWNS

## BRAD MENDOZA

"Brad, since you've ignored my last six messages, I can only assume you're not coming back. I wish you'd reconsider. Hecate has fallen. We tried to hold it, but the Jutzens sent two of those dreadnoughts of theirs through a C-class jump point in the outer system. So long as they have those special jump drives, we can't defend all the jump points in a system without spreading ourselves too thin."

Annie stops talking and looks at something off camera. Then her eyes return to peer through the screen at me, seeming to search my soul, despite this being a recorded message. "I can't get any messages to Fleet Admiral Oliphant at Gerson. Everyone we've sent either can't get through or never returns. Without him and his fleets . . ."

She doesn't need to finish the rest of the thought. I know as well as she does that without the bulk of the surviving

Promethean Navy at Gerson, her small forces have no chance to retake any territory, nor can they likely hold the territory she has for much longer, especially if the Nazis manage to take the Corpus Christi Cluster and open a second front.

Eventually, even Kipling will fall.

I pull up the latest reports she attached to her message. Even now, she's managed to hold on to a few systems only because the Koratans have sent a few task forces to support her. But with the troubles Nanette Fournier's government is facing back in the Confederacy, I doubt more help will be forthcoming from that quarter.

Annie stares into the camera pickup silently for several seconds, possibly debating her next words. "Brad, I need to talk to you as your friend, not as your queen. I'm scared. We're going to lose. I can't say that out loud to anyone. I shouldn't even be saying it to you. Something needs to be done about Admiral Oliphant. You know him better than anyone else; I need you here advising me. I need you *and* Captain Lin. Wherever you are, whatever you're doing, come quickly. Please."

With that, the message ends, leaving me to stare into the blank screen and my dim reflection in it. For a fleeting moment, in my mind's eye, I see Annie as she was when I first met her: a mere child whose life I somehow managed to save after her father used her as bait for assassins. The mental image breaks my heart, and part of me wants nothing more than to turn my ship around and make all speed to Kipling, join her fleet, and fight for her and the Federation.

But even if I didn't have myriad reasons for not surrendering to that desire, my only concern right now can be Jess. We're ten hours out from Huff Naval Base, and Doc Bean won't give me a straight answer when I demand to know if she'll last long enough for us to get there.

Still, Annie needs to know about what King Chance has

going on here in the Corpus Christi Cluster, so I record a quick response, warning her of the rumors of the massing SDF fleet and the potential second front. I encrypt it using the highest-level codes, then transmit it toward the courier ship waiting across the system at the jump point back toward Poe and onward to Kipling.

My warning to her will have to be enough for now, though it may be all I can ever give her.

Angry, I leave my ready room and head down to the brig. Arriving, I stare through the transparent door of the first cell at Terry Galpin, asleep on the cell's hard bench. She must sense me watching her, or she's faking sleep, because her eyes almost immediately flutter open and she sits up to regard me.

"Admiral, what is this all about?" she asks, her tone carrying a challenge. "Why am I in here?"

"Tell me how long you've been working for Bollen," I demand, a ragged edge in my own voice.

She shakes her head. "I've already told you about my time with Bollen and how I escaped and—"

"Shut up," I cut her off. "Tell me about *now*, Terry, if that's even your real name. You're still working for Bollen, and I need to know what he has planned for us and why he wants me and Captain Lin dead so badly."

She sighs. "Look, I know you don't trust me, but I promise you I'm not working for Bollen. After all he did to me, the only thing I want from Andre Bollen is to see him dead!" She screams the last part, making me take an involuntary step backward.

Unsure of how to reply, but knowing I'm in no mental state to handle interrogating her further right now, I turn and walk out of the brig, back to the bridge.

# TWENTY-FIVE
# THIS IS MY FAULT

## BRAD MENDOZA

When I close my eyes that night and dream, I'm back in Gerson, on HMS *Persephone,* fighting the heavy g-forces in the wardroom as Lieutenant Commander Jessica Lin, Junior Lieutenant Petra Yesayan, and I try to figure out a way to escape the Koratan Scimitar-class destroyer following us.

"What about a Chitoran Slide?" I suggest, remembering that I've had this conversation before. It's a terrible idea, but it's important to keep the flow of ideas going, even if a real option seems out of reach. At least, that was my reasoning back then.

Jess shakes her head. "*Persephone* doesn't have cold reaction thrusters." I knew that, of course, but I remember hoping that maybe someone had installed them without updating my briefing packet or that maybe it was in the part of the packet I still hadn't read. No such luck.

"Sir, do you mind if I go back to my station? Sometimes I think best when I can view the vectors in a familiar setting," Yesayan asks.

I nod to her. "Of course, Lieutenant. Commander Lin and I will join you shortly."

Jess throws me a look but doesn't argue, and we wait in silence while Yesayan exits and closes the hatch behind her.

I know what I want to talk to Jess about, though why I feel the need to do so in the middle of a combat situation I can't explain even to myself. But I just can't figure out how to start.

Finally, she gets sick of waiting and speaks first. "Sir, can I ask you a question? And will you give me an honest answer?"

Uh oh. "Depends," I hedge.

"Why are you here?"

It's not the question I was expecting, though it is related.

"What do you mean?" I ask, playing for time, much as we're doing with the Koratan destroyer.

"I think you know, sir. You were exonerated of all wrong-doing by the court. And you were on a fast track to flag rank, by all the stories I've heard. But obviously . . ."

She leaves the rest unsaid, but it's clear. Obviously, I'm a drunken has-been with no hope for further advancement and no shred of remaining dignity or self-respect. She's right on that, even if she didn't say it out loud. She's wrong about the exoneration.

"Commander," I start. "There's too much to explain. And now really isn't the time."

I see her frown and hope she'll drop it. She doesn't. "Sir, with all due respect, now may be the only time. And I need to understand. You didn't do anything wrong. The military court said so. So why are you here?"

I grunt in frustration. When I speak, my voice is sharp and angry, almost a shout, which surprises me now just as it did then. "Blast the court! They got it wrong, Commander. All wrong. They swept it under the rug because my father-in-law called in some favors, not so that I could walk free but so that he wouldn't be tarnished by association with me. Is that what you want to hear? It was a cover-up, all of it. I'm a murderer, plain and simple. Happy?"

"No. You're not." She speaks the words with such conviction that they surprise me all over again and stop my tirade in its tracks. "I had a friend on *Lancer*. If you hadn't fired when you did, the station could have been destroyed."

"It was a *refugee* ship, Commander. Over five hundred innocents dead. It doesn't matter why I fired, only that I did, and there are families who are gone because of it."

"Sir." Jess just isn't going to let this go. "They wouldn't respond to your hails, wouldn't even use their lights to signal you with flash code. You had no way of knowing it was a refugee vessel, and their captain had put them on a suicide vector with Bellerophon Station. How were you supposed to . . ."

"A captain is supposed to know!" I cut her off in exasperation. "There were signs I missed that should have told me what I was dealing with. A ship matching her description fled Langosta space a few weeks before, loaded with Rotingan refugees. If I'd been current on my briefings, I would have known that. They had a sputter in their starboard engine that no self-respecting pirate or smuggler would have allowed for. And they certainly weren't a warship!"

I stop, breathing hard, both from the topic and the long hours in heavy gravity. I meant to use this time to interrogate Jess about her treatment at the hands of Jessup and Jacobs, but she's somehow turned this around on me to discuss the one topic I most didn't want to discuss with *anyone*.

I've lived this once before, so I know what she's going to say next. She'll try to argue with me, but I'll open my big, stupid mouth and blurt out what I've been wanting to ask her, about the vids I saw of her with Jacobs and Jessup.

But when I turn to look at her, it's not the Jess I remember, staring at me with wide-eyed hope or a desire to understand. She's scowling, and her eyes are hooded under stern eyebrows. "You're right."

"What?" I ask, not sure where things got off the rails.

"You're right, Captain—Brad. Bellerophon *was* all your fault. You're a murderer, and I wish you'd never come aboard this cursed ship."

"Jess, I—"

"We'd all be better off without you, Mendoza," she sneers. "No one needs the Butcher of Bellerophon."

I watch in horror as half her face seems to melt in front of me, taking on the burn scars that once marred her beautiful features after the explosion at Carter's System. Then her face morphs again, the scars disappearing but her skin turning ashen, so pale it's almost translucent.

"I'm dead now, Brad, and it's all your fault," she says in a soft voice. "I wish I'd never met you. We'd all be better off if we'd never met you."

My jaw is stuck open in shock, but I still jump when the hatch flings open. I look up to see Senior Lieutenant Richard Ingbar, not as I last saw him before he knocked me out and took my place, sacrificing himself to save *Persephone*'s crew, but as I imagine he might have looked after the explosion that took his life, his skin covered in burns.

"This is your fault," he says, staggering into the room, raising a charred arm to point right at me.

"This is your fault," Jess repeats, raising her own arm to point at me as well.

"This is your fault," a chorus of 504 voices chimes in, and I—

I scream, jolting upright in my bunk, cold sweat covering my entire body.

"Boss?" a voice yells, and the door to my bedroom flies open.

I look up and yell in fright, expecting to see the burned body of Lieutenant Ingbar standing there, accusing me. Instead, I see the shorter, thinner stature of Hayley Uvalde.

"Boss, you okay?" she asks. How long has she been in my cabin, watching over me? How did she even get in? Stupid question with Hayley, I suppose.

"I'm . . . I'm fine, Lieutenant," I say stiffly. "Just a dream. I'm okay now. I'm going to go back to sleep. You should get some rest, too."

She looks at me skeptically, but apparently none of the personalities in her head are therapists, because after studying me for a few seconds, she nods and shuts the hatch. However, I don't hear the outer hatch to my quarters open, so my guess is that she's curled up on my couch, standing guard against threats that she can't see, and that she can't defend me against.

No one can. No one can save me when the enemy is me.

# TWENTY-SIX
# BLOCKADE

## BRAD MENDOZA

There was a time in my life when, despite everything I'd seen and heard, I truly believed the Promethean Navy represented the good guys.

I don't know when I stopped believing that. The easy answer would have been at Gerson, when my own Navy betrayed me. Except I think it was before that. There were too many orders that didn't make sense, too many times we were called upon to do what was best for the nobles and the royals, and not the people we were supposedly sworn to serve. Just like the story Heddy told me of her time in the Republic Marines, there were times that we just didn't feel like we were doing the right thing.

Thinking back now, it's hard to remember a time when I was so naïve that I thought it was as simple as the good guys versus the bad guys. But regardless of when I lost that innocence, I know now that going to the naval base at Cillian

Heights is likely to be the last thing I do. Because I don't believe that they're the good guys in this—not at all. I'm only hoping that maybe, just maybe, they're slightly less evil than Andre Bollen.

Jess's life depends on it.

I know the base well. I was stationed at Cillian Heights for several months back when I commanded *Lancer*. Huff Naval Base is named for the gas giant it orbits, Huff, the fifth planet in the system. When I was here, it was home to a full task force—fifteen ships strong, anchored by two monster Zeus-class battleships that rarely left orbit, there more to intimidate and discourage any Koratans who might see the Cluster as easy pickings.

According to the latest intelligence reports, however, those days are over. Huff has only an understrength task group of six ships, with just one battleship, the aptly-named HMS *Liberator*. It's a force not nearly enough to patrol an area as large as the Cluster, which is perhaps why the current base commander doesn't even seem to be attempting to do so. From what little we've heard from the locals in transit, the Navy has barely left the Cillian Heights system in months.

Some of that may be due to their commander. He's the last person I would ever go to for help, and if our circumstances weren't so dire, I wouldn't consider it now. Unfortunately, I have no choice, though trusting him to save my wife is far from a sure thing.

He may say no just out of principle.

"Sir, something's wrong," Illian reports from his station as I stride onto the bridge.

"What is it, Guns?" My voice is flat and devoid of emotion. I'm running off adrenaline and caffeine—I haven't slept, spending every moment of the last twenty hours when not on the bridge holding vigil next to Jess's med pod.

"I can see the Navy fleet in orbit of Huff, sir, but they're not alone."

"Show me."

He puts the tactical plot onto the main forward viewscreen, and I study it for only a moment before I see what he's talking about.

"Who's that second fleet?" I ask no one in particular.

"I might know, sir," Laia Gammon says from the sensor station. Like everyone else on the bridge, she looks ragged, with dark circles under her eyes. I would take her aside and ask her what's troubling her, but I know. We all know—having Jess so close to death is killing us. "Based on comm chatter, I think that second fleet belongs to the Serravo Defense Force," she finishes.

I swear under my breath. The rumors from Poe and Gregor suggested the SDF was massing at Linford Commons, three jumps away from here, so I was hoping to find the Navy still in control of this system. It seems I was overly optimistic.

Or worse, maybe the Navy forces here are in league with the SDF and King Chance. Except . . .

"Guns, take a careful look at the placement of those two fleets. What does this look like to you?"

"Hold on." He takes a few seconds to have a second look. "Sir, I think it's a standoff."

"I think you're right, Commander Illian."

The Navy fleet is in close orbit of the gas giant, huddled around their station there. But the SDF fleet is arrayed farther out from the planet, in a classic siege formation, blocking any attempt by the Navy to venture out from their base.

It fills me with a small measure of hope to confirm that the Navy and SDF aren't working together, but only a small measure.

"Harris, hail the Navy station and fleet," I call out.

A few minutes pass before he replies, allowing for

message transit time. "They're not replying, sir. I think those other ships are jamming the area."

A murmur of concern ripples across the bridge, and I suddenly feel that I'm on the edge of losing my entire crew. Inside, I'm dying. My soul hurts. But outwardly, if I don't start projecting some calm and confidence now, my friends are going to break.

"Very well," I say a little louder for all to hear, forcing as much strength into my tone as I can, even though I haven't felt as flat as this since my first days on HMS *Persephone* at Gerson. "Apollo-class destroyers were originally built as blockade runners. There's no reason we can't get through that siege formation and into the Navy base's defensive umbrella. So let's talk, people. I need options."

We start brainstorming, throwing out ideas. All the while, I'm dying a little more inside with each passing minute as I think of Jess back in that med pod. My last check-in with Doc Bean was twenty minutes ago, and there's been no change in her status, but each time I speak with him, he impresses on me again how important it is to get her to a trauma center as soon as humanly possible.

As if I needed any reminder.

The problem we need to solve is fairly simple on the surface. The SDF and Navy fleets are evenly matched, more or less. Actually, I'd give the Navy the edge—their Zeus-class battleship is both larger and more heavily armed than the SDF's older generation Kronos-class battleship. Which means that the SDF commander might hesitate to move any of his ships out of position to block *Bainbridge*'s approach directly. Doing so would open a gap in their formation that the Navy might be able to exploit.

I wish I knew how long this siege has been going on, as well as who the SDF commander could be. Either piece of intel would help me determine how the enemy might react to the introduction of a new element: my destroyer. On one hand, they might aggressively try to stop me from getting to Huff Naval Base, even if it does weaken their lines, in the interest of not letting me add a seventh ship to the Navy's arsenal. On the other hand, a single additional destroyer won't tip the scales of power in this standoff, and the SDF commander might be all in favor of letting me inside the blockade so he can bottle my ship up along with the rest.

Either way, I need to hope for the best and plan for the worst, against an enemy who's already seen me coming. With that in mind, I settle on a plan of attack. Slow nods start across the bridge as I explain it, along with the risks, and we quickly reach consensus.

"Execute phase one," I order Illian, and he relays the order. *Bainbridge* starts to change course toward the edge of the gas giant, skirting well clear of both fleets.

I turn over the conn and stride off the bridge once we're on course, and head straight to the med bay, ignoring the rumbling in my stomach; it's well past lunchtime. When I arrive, I go immediately to the med pod containing my wife.

When I was a little kid, my mom showed me this really ancient Earth movie about a princess who eats an apple and falls into a deep sleep. She stays like that, under a dome of glass, until one day a prince comes along and kisses her, waking her up from her slumber. Naturally, they live happily ever after.

Looking at Jess now through the transparent med pod cover, she looks twice as serene and five times as beautiful as that fictional princess. She almost looks like a wax statue, devoid of life, and I have to check the pod's readouts to assure myself she's still with us. I suddenly have the totally irrational urge to lift the cover and kiss her, even though I know it will do nothing for her. In fact, it would do a lot more harm than good.

Feeling a presence at my side, I look over at Doc Bean. He looks as haggard as the rest of us, but his mad scientist hair and thick anachronistic glasses enhance the effect, making him look even worse.

"No changes," he tells me, voice more solemn than usual. "I'm afraid it's all in Captain Lin's hands now."

I look at him in confusion, so he elaborates.

"I've seen it a hundred times, Admiral. Two different people with the same injuries and the same treatment—one dies and the other lives. No medical explanation for it, though I have colleagues who have certainly tried to come up with one." He shrugs. "I just always figured it was either God or the will of the injured person."

"Which one is it, Doc?" I find myself asking, looking back at my sleeping wife.

"Honestly, probably both."

I tear my eyes from Jess to look at him again. "What happened to you, Doc? You're obviously a skilled doctor. Why did we find you living hand-to-mouth on a random station in the Fringe?" I've always wondered it, but never found occasion to ask. When we first picked him up, he claimed to be from Earth, though I'm not sure I believe it at all.

He takes a long time to respond, and I start to think he never will. When he does speak, his voice is so low I have to strain to hear.

"I killed a man."

When I don't respond, he looks at me sharply. "Didn't you hear me, Admiral? I said I killed someone."

I snort. "So what? I've killed a lot of people, Doc. This week, even. So if you're expecting me to react with shock and awe, you're going to have to give me more than that."

He looks at me in a way that I can only classify as disappointment. I suppose I ruined his big, dramatic reveal. "You kill people in battle or in the course of your duties, Admiral Mendoza. I killed a man whose life I was supposed to *save*."

When I still don't react, he rolls his eyes, and I hold up both hands in surrender.

"Sorry, Doc. I'm shocked. I'm aghast. I'm horrified. I'm . . . out of synonyms."

He growls in annoyance and shakes his head, the tufts of white hair on the sides of his scalp bobbing and weaving to keep up with his rapidly rotating cranium. "You are an extremely annoying man, Admiral."

"Right back at ya, Doc. So who was this guy you killed?"

"A dictator of an Inner Rim star nation, a monster who killed millions of his own people. He got a rare form of cancer and came to Earth for a cutting-edge treatment. I was one of his doctors. But I couldn't bring myself to save him, so I did the opposite. If they could have proven what I did, I'd be in prison, but I covered my tracks well. It was still enough to get my medical license revoked permanently."

I sense this is where he's expecting me to look genuinely surprised, but I'm not in the mood, so I give him a little frown and nothing more.,

"Do you regret hiring me now, Admiral?" he asks. "Do you regret that a killer without a medical license is treating your wife?"

I put my hand on his shoulder. "Doc, the way I see it, you're the only reason Jessica is still alive. Just keep doing what you're doing, and I'll get us to that trauma center."

Taking one last look at her sleeping under the glass, I sigh. "I'm going to go get lunch, Doc. Listen, do you regret killing that guy on Earth?"

He looks me in the eye. "Not for one moment."

I give him an unenthusiastic smile. "Then it sounds to me like you did the right thing."

He stares after me as I leave the med bay to head toward

the galley. Lifting the glass and kissing Jess isn't going to save her. And if I'm going to get to that Navy base, I need a sandwich.

It's likely to be the last decent meal I'll have for quite some time. Especially given the part of our plan I haven't shared with the rest of my crew. Earlier, I felt guilty keeping such critical information from them about my rocky relationship with Huff Naval Base's commander, but my visit to Jess strengthened my resolve. I'll do whatever needs to be done to save her, and then I'll do what I have to in order to save my crew.

It will probably be the last heroic act of my life.

# TWENTY-SEVEN
# BLOCKADE RUNNERS

## BRAD MENDOZA

We rocket toward Huff's atmosphere, entering orbit far from the naval base's location and the two opposing fleets. As we pass, the SDF launches a few missiles our way, but the speed differential is too great, and they have no real hope of catching us.

As soon as we're over the gas giant's horizon and out of sight of either fleet, I order *Bainbridge* to turn over and start burning hard to kill our velocity. This is the riskiest part of the plan. The SDF could send a ship around the planet from the other side, and with our main drive's exhaust pointed in that direction and the interference from the planet's upper atmosphere, we'd have a hard time detecting them until they put a missile up our tail pipes.

Luckily, no such enemy ship or missile appears, and as we near the two-thirds point of our orbit, we cut the drive and turn back over in our direction of travel, firing the engines again to slow down.

"Sir," Laia calls across the bridge, "we're picking up comm signals bouncing off one of Huff's moonlets. An SDF ship is coming around the planet to cut us off."

They're a little late, but they're still dangerous.

"Take us deeper into the atmosphere," I order the helm, and we pitch down and move into a lower orbit where the high winds and gases of the giant planet buffet our little ship mercilessly. Manny tenses up at the helm station, his knuckles turning white as he grips the control yoke, even though the ship's systems help keep us on course. For a brief moment, I remember Saki Hashimoto sitting in that chair, and it makes me feel somewhat empty, but I quickly shake off the thought and focus on the matters at hand.

"Enemy ship coming into visual range now," Laia reports. "Light cruiser class, on a direct intercept course."

"Steady as she goes," I order, studying the specs on the SDF light cruiser on the sensor plot. It's almost twice as large as our destroyer, with thicker hull plates and more weapons. Normally, our speed would be our key advantage in the engagement, but our head-on course with the enemy ship negates any help from that quarter.

"Guns, are my weapons ready?"

"Aye, sir," Illian replies. "Fifty-fifty loadout as ordered."

I nod, studying the plot and counting down in my head. At the right moment, I call out a series of orders: "Helm, yaw port. Tactical, fire the starboard broadside. Comms, continuously signal the Navy fleet until we can get through the jamming."

Underneath me, the ship rotates hard, then the deck shudders as we spit out six kill shots, half our starboard loadout. The light cruiser, perhaps taken by surprise that we chose to be the ones to start the engagement, or maybe having a hard time seeing us through the atmospheric gases, reacts slowly, hesitating a beat before cutting its drive and turning to present its own broadside.

Missiles from the SDF ship join ours on the plot, flying directly at us. Illian launches the six antimissile interceptors from our remaining starboard tubes, and then Manny yaws the ship back to a head-on aspect to our direction of travel, presenting the enemy missiles with a smaller target cross-section.

I watch the plot, calculating the vectors, travel times, and a thousand different things, both by gut and utilizing the AIs from both my implant and my ship. Again, as my internal countdown winds to zero, I shout a new series of orders.

"Helm, new course, up 20 degrees, two-thirds thrust. Tactical, ready on the bow tubes."

A chorus of acknowledgments answers me as my ship pitches upward and burns on a course that will take us out of the atmosphere and up and over the enemy light cruiser. I watch the plot eagerly, fingers crossed on my command chair. It's going to be close.

The two dozen missiles the SDF ship launched at us revector their thrust to account for our course change. For a moment, maybe two, it looks like they might adjust in time to catch us, slamming into *Bainbridge*'s belly and breaking our spine. But gravity is a cruel mistress, and the massive pull of Huff combined with the enemy missiles' forward momentum is enough to prevent them from rising to meet our new course in time. We rocket by them, and then I order another course change.

Two things should be happening on that light cruiser as its captain sees me changing to a direct collision course with his ship. First, he's got to be thinking I'm insane. He's right on that count. Second, he's starting to worry that his missiles, still looping around to pursue me from behind, might miss

*Bainbridge* and hit his own ship. And as much as I'm sure the SDF trains their commanders, he's not Navy. Up until today, it's quite likely the most exciting engagement he's ever commanded was against a smuggler or pirate scow.

So he does what any human without enough training would do in this situation. Rather than rolling his ship to present his other broadside and blow me out of the sky, he hits his main drive hard to move out of my way at a perpendicular angle to my approach. Then he sends the command to disarm the missiles chasing my stern.

"Guns, fire!" I order Illian, and our destroyer's bow tubes unleash a trio of scramblers.

The light cruiser's defensive fire has already taken out all six of the kill shots we first launched at him, but the three scramblers that streak from *Bainbridge*'s bow tubes take him by surprise, so intent is he on moving out of my way. And just as the enemy ship barely clears my approach vector, but before its captain can overcome his panic and target us with offensive lasers, one of our trio of scramblers gets through.

The SDF ship's drive sputters and dies out as the scrambler blows its internal systems, tripping breakers all over the ship and forcing the reactor into an emergency scramble. It's not nearly as devastating as the blow Bollen's freighter gave *Bainbridge* at Poe—the SDF commander will need only an hour or two to reset his systems and get everything back online—but it's enough for us to streak by him and over the horizon, in sight now of both fleets.

I'm about to declare mental victory when Laia's voice freezes my blood. "Admiral, one of the SDF battlecruisers is breaking formation to intercept. Five minutes out!"

"Harris! Any response from the Navy?"

"No. Nothing. I think we're past the jamming, but they're just not answering."

"Illian, take the conn," I shout at the man. "Go to full military power and get us to that base. I'll be back in two minutes."

I spring out of my chair before he can protest and almost sprint off the bridge and through the hatch into my ready room. I run straight to my desk and the console there, and start recording a message for the Navy commander at Huff.

"This is Vice Admiral Brad Mendoza recording a personal message to Rear Admiral Christoph Turly," I say as formally as I can. The name of the hated man who tried to arrest me and Jess at Hudson after we saved the system from the Jutzens more than five months ago tastes like ash on my tongue. But I have to keep going, or Jess won't be the only one to die today.

"Listen, Admiral Turly . . . Christoph. I know you're not my biggest fan; the feeling is, as you no doubt know, mutual. But by now you've seen the blockchain codes attached to my messages." Despite the urgency of the situation, I pause and almost reconsider, but I've come too far now. "You know that my promotion is real, Admiral Turly, but I'm going to set that aside. My XO is dying in a med pod, and I need to get her to your trauma center. In exchange for letting us approach and saving us from that SDF battlecruiser, I will formally surrender myself into your custody." My voice falters, and it takes a monumental effort to finish the message.

"You've wanted to arrest me for a while now, Turly. Well, here's your chance. Just save my XO—my wife. Please."

I press the transmit command before I can overthink it, then run right back out onto the bridge.

"Any movement from the Navy ships?" I ask as I take my seat again.

"No, sir," Illian reports. "And the SDF battlecruiser is entering weapons range in two minutes."

I swear under my breath, eyes glued to the plot, willing the Navy ships to move—to do anything.

At first, I think I must be imagining it, or conjuring it out of pure hope, but slowly, one of the Navy battlecruisers seems to twitch in the SDF fleet's direction. Then a heavy cruiser joins it in charging the enemy. With breath held and heart pounding, I almost explode in relief when the enemy battlecruiser sees the movement and turns over to burn back to its lines and away from us.

"Sir, enemy ship is disengaging!" Illian shouts an instant after my own eyes confirm the same. "It worked."

That it did, but at a high cost. I look around my destroyer's bridge with moisture forming in my eyes. Around me, my crew is celebrating in muted fashion. We're still in a combat situation, and Jess is still dying in a med pod, but I take it all in, knowing it might be my final moments with them. We'll dock with Huff Naval Base on an hour, and after that, I'll likely never see this bridge or most of these people again.

"Admiral, I'm getting a message from the Navy," Harris calls out, quieting the whisper of celebration around me. "It says . . . Sir? Admiral Turly says, 'Terms of surrender accepted.'"

You could hear a pin drop on my destroyer's bridge as everyone turns and gapes at me.

## TWENTY-EIGHT
# UNDER ARREST

### BRAD MENDOZA

"I don't like this, Admiral," Gunny growls from next to me as we hear the clang of *Bainbridge*'s airlock mating to the docking port of Huff Naval Base.

"Noted," I say dryly. I'm not sure who's angrier at my surrender to Turly: Gunny, Hayley, or Illian. Heck, my entire crew is pretty pissed at me right now. The only one who seems to get why I did what I did is Doc Bean, who gave me little more than a grim nod when I explained the situation to him and asked him to get Jess's pod ready for transfer to the station and the Navy's trauma center.

The pod is already waiting here, my wife deathly still inside. Doc Bean hovers next to it and gives a sharp glare to the two Koratan spacers who are helping him move it when one of them jostles it slightly. Next to me at the airlock door are Gunny and Hayley. Gunny wanted all his shooters here and armed, but I forced him to settle for himself (unarmed) and Hayley (supposedly unarmed, but likely hiding a few weapons on her person).

None of us is happy about this, but we're not dead or in the brig yet. And where there's life, there's hope. Or something cheesy like that—I don't expect to survive this little ordeal. Christoph Turly *hates* me, and he's got the human decency of blue cheese past its expiration date. But at least Jess will live. She has to.

The airlock finally swings open, and we find ourselves facing two ranks of a dozen Marines flanking two medics and a sour-faced commander. He looks at me with thinly veiled contempt as he steps forward and speaks first.

"Brad Mendoza?"

I huff a laugh and shake my head. Who else does he think is waiting here?

Gunny answers for me. "It's *Vice Admiral* Mendoza," he growls.

Despite himself, the commander falters a little and keeps his eyes on me while studiously ignoring the muscular, hulking, and very pissed-off giant next to me. "Sir," he at least adds, "I've been ordered to take you into custody and escort you to Rear Admiral Turly's office."

"Not before you take Captain Lin's pod to the trauma center," I tell him, trying to keep my voice even and dispassionate.

To the commander's credit, he doesn't argue. "Of course." He motions to the two medics, who quickly come through the airlock and, under the judgmental eye of Doc Bean, take the pod containing my half-dead wife into the station, our doctor following them and jabbering all the while with so much medical terminology I'm worried their heads might explode. Only when they're out of sight around a bend in the corridor do I nod to the man in charge. "Let's go, Commander."

He motions again, and two of the Marines step forward,

one of them holding out a pair of cuffs. Before I can say anything, Gunny shoves me behind him and glowers at them with murder in his eyes.

"It's okay, Quinn," I say gently, stepping around him and offering my hands to the man with cuffs. "Stay with the ship. I'll comm with orders as soon as I can."

"Uh, sir," the commander practically stutters. "We've been ordered to escort your crew to a holding area and put a prize crew on your stolen—"

"No." My one-word response cuts him off. "I surrendered myself, but *Her* Majesty's Ship *Bainbridge* is an active destroyer in the Queen's Navy. Command reverts to my XO, who is in a medically induced coma right now. In which case, Commander Francis Illian will take command until such a time as Admiral Turly and I negotiate terms." I take another step toward him, shrugging off the Marines now that they have me in cuffs. "Trust me, it's better for everyone this way." They may not realize it, but Hayley alone could kill the commander and likely half of his Marines before they even figured out she's a threat.

He frowns but, to my relief, gives in. "This way, then . . . uh, Admiral."

Ordering Gunny and Hayley to stay behind on the ship, I follow the commander as six of the twelve Marines fall into step around me in a prisoner escort formation, taking me to my doom.

# TWENTY-NINE
# ARMCHAIR ADMIRAL

## BRAD MENDOZA

Christoph Turly and I have always loathed each other. We served together for six months when we were both stationed on the Harper Line. Back then, Turly was a self-important blowhard, the arrogant captain of the battleship HMS *Stalwart*, while I was the newly promoted captain of the heavy cruiser *Queen's Pride*.

The source of our antagonistic relationship goes back to one of our first meetings, when we attended Vice Admiral Krishna's staff meeting for our task force at Harper. I was the youngest and newest captain in the room. But for some reason, Turly, who was the most senior captain in the meeting, decided to single me out. When Admiral Krishna asked for recommendations on deployment patterns for our patrol, I spoke up and offered my two cents. Turly immediately jumped on me, berating me in front of the others for the 'obviously flawed plan' I was proposing.

Now, I'll admit, my plan wasn't great. But his response was way out of line, and Admiral Krishna, usually a self-important blowhard himself, wasted no time in rebuking Turly for his overreaction. From that moment onward, Christoph Turly and I hated each other's guts.

Of course, the events at Hudson over five months ago, when Turly looked like an idiot by ignoring our warning of the Jutzen invasion, didn't exactly build any new bridges with the guy.

So when my escort finally leads me through the broad hatch into his command office on the Navy station, I'm not expecting a warm reception. What I get is downright frigid.

The rear admiral makes no move to get up from his chair when I enter, even though I do technically outrank him. Turly sits behind his desk, hands steepled in front of him like some kind of B-movie villain, his thinning red hair and pasty complexion doing nothing to tone down the fire of the evil, triumphant grin he shoots me.

"Ah, Brad," he says, voice thick with condescension and arrogance. "I always knew I'd catch up to you eventually."

Normally, this would be the time that I would very enthusiastically and aggressively poke the bear by saying something snide and rude, like reminding him that he didn't, in fact, 'catch up' to me, but that I brought myself to him. However, the image of Jess in her pod flashes in my mind again, and I bite my tongue—literally, hard enough to draw blood.

"I hope you know that your fake, trumped-up rank doled out by an embattled queen on a contested throne won't do you any good here," he continues with a sneer, and now, at least, I know which side of said contest he comes down on.

Except, if he were on King Chance's side, why would the

SDF, Chance's attack dogs, be blockading Turly's force here at Huff? Something isn't adding up.

He watches me under his flaming eyebrows, and I realize he's waiting for me to talk now. I bite my tongue hard again, the pain reminding me of the stakes. "Admiral Turly," I say, purposefully and painfully omitting the diminutive 'Rear' from his title. "As noted in my earlier message, I surrender myself to your custody. And I . . . thank you for rendering aid to my XO."

"Don't worry, Brad. We'll save your wife's life. She'll need to be healthy to stand trial with you for your crimes."

My heart sinks. None of this is a surprise, but if I held out any hope that Turly might be reasonable, it flies out the airlock. I can expect no help from this man beyond what I've already gotten. Little does he know, however, that even the relatively small act of allowing my wife to be treated by his medical center has put me forever in his debt. It will have to be enough.

"Should I take this to mean that you've given your allegiance to King Chance?" I ask, keeping my voice as calm as I can. As long as I'm here, I might as well find out what cards everyone is holding.

I hear the commander and at least two of the Marines behind me suck in sharp breaths, but I keep my eye squarely on Turly.

He snorts a laugh. "Nice try, Mendoza. My loyalty is to the Navy, which has yet to officially endorse either *candidate* for our next monarch. I'm awaiting orders from Naval Command at Gerson."

My heart sinks a little more. This idiot is waiting for my even bigger idiot of an ex-father-in-law, Fleet Admiral Terrence Oliphant, to decide who the new king or queen will be. Not a promising sign. I'm frankly surprised Terrible Terrence hasn't tried to crown *himself* yet.

I open my mouth to say something snide, despite my self-injunction, when I happen to study Turly a little closer. To my consternation, I see beads of sweat forming on his forehead. What does *he* have to be nervous about in this conversation?

"I see," I say, swallowing my original rude rejoinder. "Either way, Admiral, my surrender stands. Do with me what you will."

He nods resolutely, the sweat on his brow the only sign that something might be amiss. "Commander Lukas," he orders the officer who brought me here, "take *Mister* Mendoza to the brig. I understand from your report that his ship has not fully surrendered. Let's not press the issue quite yet, but keep our station weaponry trained on it in case his crew decides to try an escape. That will be all."

I stare at Turly in what I hope looks like defiance as the Marines wrestle me out of his office. Just before we go through the hatch, I catch something else in the other man's eyes. It's only a brief flash, so quick I might be imagining it, but I swear he looks relieved.

# THIRTY
# JAIL IS NOT FUN

## BRAD MENDOZA

Brigs suck. I mean, they *really* suck. Imagine being put in a little box, with a transparent bulkhead and hatch so that there's not even the semblance of privacy. Now, make sure there is nothing in that little box except a hard bench that's barely large enough to lie down on, and a head with an integrated sink. Next, put a general-purpose jamming field over it so that you can't use your implant to connect to anything outside the cell.

What you end up with is a very boring brig cell where the unfortunate detainee can't even play a stupid game on his stupid implant because, like an idiot, he forgot to download an update before losing his stupid connection!

Several hours pass. I have no idea what's going on back at my ship, or even what Jess's status is. My constant questions to my Marine guards go unanswered. There are two of them, and I've nicknamed them Hulk (he's the big one) and Conehead (trust me, if you could see the shape of his head, you'd get it).

They don't like their nicknames. In fact, their hatred of them is about the only reaction I've been able to get from either of them.

But never let it be said that Brad Mendoza can't be annoying even in the worst of situations. I listened to a lot of music as a kid. I've had less time to do so as an adult, but I remember enough of it to be able to sing an entire playlist, though I've forgotten *a lot* of the lyrics. That's not a problem —I just make up my own.

I run out of songs after the first few hours. There are only so many verses, even to the aptly titled "The Song That Never Ends." So, I change to popular commercial jingles. Again, I've forgotten a lot of the words.

"The best part of waking up, is reactor fuel in your cup!

"Like a good neighbor, Strike Force is there! For all your world conquest needs.

"Double the destruction, double the fun. NSX Arms!"

There are more than that, but you get the picture. At this point, I'm even starting to annoy myself, and my next move is to begin a word-for-word recitation of the last four episodes of *The Adventures of Firebrand's Marauders*. Luckily for all of us, I'm interrupted shortly when a senior lieutenant I've never seen before comes to my cell's hatch.

"Mr. Mendoza?" she asks, and I sit up and smile.

"That's *Admiral* Mendoza, but what can I do for you? I'd invite you in and offer you scones, but I wasn't aware I'd be entertaining this evening."

"Admiral Turly has asked me to bring you to his office so he can interrogate you on events outside the Cluster."

That intrigues me. Why is Turly himself asking to interrogate me? He should have people for that. Maybe he just wants to gloat some more in person. But my mind flashes back to the sweat on his brow and the momentary look of relief when I surrendered without a fight earlier.

"Uh, okay. Sure." I say as meekly as I can.

She turns to Hulk and Conehead. "Open the cell hatch, Marines. I can take it from here. I'm sure *Admiral* Mendoza plans to behave." She turns back to me and raises an eyebrow.

Maybe it's because I want to see what this is all about, or maybe it's because I recognize in her one of the small portion of humanity who, like me, has the supreme skill of being able to raise just *one* eyebrow at a time. Either way, I nod. "Of course, Lieutenant."

Moments later, I'm being led, again in cuffs but without a hulking or pointy-headed Marine escort, back to Turly's office.

"What—" I start to ask the lieutenant, but she shushes me. It takes me by such surprise that I'm speechless until we reach our destination. Then she ushers me inside and closes the hatch behind me, *without* following me inside. Nor do I see any Marines waiting for us.

Stranger and stranger.

Turly himself is alone in his office. I'm about to ask him what's going on, but I catch his appearance. It's like Rear Admiral Turly is an entirely different person from the one I met with just a few hours ago. Gone is the sneer and arrogance. In its place is a man who looks haggard and exhausted. There are bags under his eyes, and his face shines with a sheen of sweat.

I finally find my voice. "Turly, what's going on?"

He motions to a seat in front of his desk, a luxury he didn't grant me on my first visit, and then I'm doubly shocked when he sends a command with his implant, and the cuffs around my wrists unlatch and fall to the deck with a clatter.

"I don't . . ." I start to say, but I'm so flabbergasted, I have no idea how to go on.

"Sit down, Brad." He reaches under his desk and pulls out a bottle of what looks like scotch along with two glasses. He pours one and offers it to me, but I decline with a wave of the hand. He shrugs and downs it himself in one large gulp, then refills it.

"What's going on, Turly?" I repeat after several moments.

He looks up from the second glass and frowns at me. "How is the queen?"

The question surprises me. This doesn't feel like the lieutenant's promised interrogation. Regardless, I answer cautiously. "She's healthy and holding the line against the Jutzens, I suppose. What do you want to know?"

He slumps further in his seat, a smile on his lips, as if my words took all the tension out of him. "I met her once, you know," he says, almost dreamily.

I decide now is not the time to point out my own long-standing, close relationship with our new pain-in-the-butt monarch. "Really, when?"

If there's one thing men like Christoph Turly love, it's talking about themselves. "The King sent her to Harper a few months before you arrived, for an inspection tour. She reviewed the fleet's captains and even spoke to us for a few minutes on behalf of her father. She was just a teenager back then, but still one heckuva leader. I felt a real connection when I shook her hand."

I nod in agreement, but mostly because I can't figure out what to say.

He smiles wanly. "She inspired all of us to do our duty to the Crown. I . . . I used to know what that meant. These days . . ."

I give him a few moments, but when it's clear he's waiting for me to say something else, I decide to prod just a little. "It still is clear, to my way of thinking. The Jutzens sacked Prometheus and killed our king, then installed Duke Fuller as their puppet. But Charles's daughter is the true heir."

"You and I know that," he says, closely examining the amber liquid in his glass under the overhead lights. "But others aren't so sure."

Is this for real, or is he playing with me? I imagine a kill squad of Marines outside the door, just waiting for his signal that I've said something incriminating. But I've always been good at poker, mostly because I'm aggressive and know how to play the bluff. So I decide to trust my instincts.

"You mean others like that commander who brought me to your office the first time?" I ask carefully.

Turly looks up at me sharply. "You caught that, eh? Commander Lukas, that rat." His voice is like acid. "He's thrown in with that pretender, Chance, with reckless abandon. I'd love to throw *him* in the brig."

I still wonder if Turly is playing me, but if he is, then he's a much better actor than I ever would have expected. "And you, Chris?" I ask, still a little cautious. "You're still loyal to the Crown of Prometheus?"

He nods and removes any last worry that this is for show. "With all my heart. You and I have never seen eye to eye on much, Brad. But you were always loyal to the king, as was I. It was the only thing we ever had in common. Even after you deserted at Gerson, you still served Prometheus in your own twisted way."

Ignoring the implied insult and deciding to go for broke, I lean forward. "You mean our loyalty to the Crown is the only thing we *still* have in common, don't you? Our loyalty to Charles's daughter?"

He smiles again, not in triumph, almost wistful. "Indeed. So imagine my surprise when she went and made you a vice admiral." He says it like it's a big cosmic joke and not an indictment.

I lean back and smirk just a little. "Trust me, it wasn't on my bingo card either." Then my voice cracks. "How is she?"

He leans forward, not having to ask who I mean. "Captain Lin is stable and recovering, the doctors tell me. You got her here just in time. A few more hours, another day, and . . ." He shrugs. No more words are needed as I sag in relief.

"Thank you," I tell him sincerely.

"What are you doing here in the Cluster, Brad?" he asks, voice a little sharper. "And don't lie and tell me the queen sent you to collect me and my little force. We're not worth the fuel."

Darn, that's *exactly* what I was planning to tell him. But I sense that maybe honesty is actually a better path right now. "Actually, the queen didn't want me to come here at all. She wants me commanding on the front lines. But I—" I stop because I'm still not even sure why I chose not to stay. Then, in a startling moment of clarity, I speak the actual truth that's been hovering at the edges of my mind since Annie had to go and make me an admiral. "I'm not ready, Chris. I'm not flag officer material. Bellerophon showed that, if nothing else."

Turly frowns at me. "You really are an idiot, aren't you, Brad?"

"So I've been told many, many times."

He shakes his head. "You misunderstand me. I've had a lot of time to think since my exile from Hudson to this lovely assignment." He waves a hand to vaguely encompass the base and perhaps the entire Corpus Christi Cluster. "And truth is, maybe one of the reasons I hated you so much for so long is that I always knew you were simply a better commander than I was."

The startling and unexpected admission forces me to swallow whatever I was going to say next.

"So if the queen didn't send you here, what are you really doing in Cillian Heights?" He watches me closely, waiting for my response.

Honesty is like a battleship. Once you start moving in one direction, it's incredibly hard to stop or change course with that much mass and inertia. Before I even realize what I'm doing, I'm relating to Turly *everything,* from the derelict freighter we found at Edmonton months ago, to the events at Poe and Gregor. When I mention Andre Bollen, he frowns and shakes his head.

"Never heard of the man. Chance has supposedly installed some new leader at Linford Commons, but I would hardly believe even he would choose a slaver to conquer this sector for him. Besides, what little intel I have suggests that Chance's chosen commander for the Cluster is a member of the royal family who's defected to join the other side and collaborate with the Nazis."

That matches up with our intel thus far, and I tell him so.

"Good to get some independent confirmation," he says. "My fleet has been bottled up here in Cillian Heights since word of Prometheus's fall reached us and the SDF showed up to hem us in. So any intel I have about what's happening at Linford Commons or really any other system in the Corpus Christi Cluster is spotty at best."

He pauses, downing another sip of scotch. "You realize, Brad, that this whole legend of Andre Bollen seems to be tailor-made to lure you into a trap."

Jess and I have been thinking much the same thing, but to hear Turly reach the same conclusion so quickly is surprising. "How so?"

He sets his glass down on his desk and looks at me with surprising soberness. "First, you run from the queen's fleet with the stated goal of hunting slavers, starting in the Edmonton system. Those slavers are long gone without a trace, but the station's marshal just happened to have received a bulletin on this Bollen fellow days before your arrival, a bulletin that leads you to Poe.

"Then no one at Poe has heard of Bollen either, but the man again just happens to be waiting there in a disguised freighter and kidnaps three hundred students right in front of you. I mean, Brad, he's perfectly playing to your hero complex."

"I . . ." Do I have a hero complex?

He keeps talking right over me. "But the biggest proof of all is that he only disabled your ship at Poe, when he could have just as easily destroyed it. He was hedging his bets. If you didn't die when he sent those men after you on Poe—assuming he really expected them to kill you, rather than just piss you off—he wanted to make sure you'd be able to follow him on a Quixotic quest to rescue those slaves. And when you stopped at Gregor, he saw another opportunity to urge you along by nearly killing Captain Lin. Whoever this Bollen is, he doesn't only want you dead, Brad, he wants you to suffer greatly. Any thoughts as to who in the galaxy might hate you that badly?"

"Unfortunately it's a pretty long list," I admit.

Turly barks a laugh. "I'm sure it is. So what are you going to do about it? Furthermore, what am *I* going to do about it?"

His second question shocks me so that I cock my head to one side and stare at him in silence.

"Don't act so surprised, Brad. You may be an annoying little punk, but I'm still the senior queen's officer in this sector. Present company excluded, of course."

"Of course," I reply dryly.

"So the safety of those three hundred people taken from Poe rests on my shoulders just as much as yours. And frankly, I'm getting sick of just sitting here in this base while the rest of the galaxy burns around us."

"So, what do you have in mind?" I ask cautiously.

Any brief levity disappears from his features. "I'm hoping you can help me with that. See, we have a bigger problem. I estimate about a third of the officers and spacers under my command are still loyal to the queen. Another third, including the ever-so-annoying Commander Lucas, is solidly in Chance's camp. Lots of Serravans transferred to this base over the last several months, no doubt in preparation for what the duke already knew was coming."

"And the other third?"

He shrugs. "No telling. I think most of them are waiting to see who comes out on top. Having the SDF blockading us here at Huff may actually help in that regard. I think a lot of my people who might have fallen in line with Chance's occupation government are just pissed enough at the SDF to keep them from doing so.

"I'm afraid you may have saved your wife's life by getting her here, but now you're both stuck here unless we can do something about the SDF. My task group could take them in an even fight, but I'm worried at least half my ships will side with them if it comes down to it."

He absently picks up his glass of scotch again to study its depths. "The SDF has us all hemmed in. So far, they've been content just to keep us from venturing out from the base, but their admiral has made it clear that he expects me to eventually declare my loyalty to King Chance. The deadline is approaching. After that?" He shrugs and knocks back the scotch, slamming the empty tumbler down on his desk and looking angry for the first time in this very surreal conversation. "I'm stuck between a rock and a hard place, Brad. But maybe you showing up when you did is the card my hand needs."

Am I dreaming? All my dreams have been nightmares lately; maybe the universe is screwing with me by sending a good dream to get my hopes up. I suddenly expect I'm going to wake up in the brig, somehow in my underwear, while my entire grade school class points and laughs through the transparent bulkheads.

Because, if I'm not mistaken, Christoph Turly just sort of said he's *glad* to see me.

"What do you mean, exactly?" I ask him very carefully, searching the room for some sign that this is, indeed, all a dream, like a purple leopard wearing a tutu and balancing a chainsaw on its nose. There are no chainsaw-juggling leopards, though, just me and Turly and a shadow on the back wall that could pass for a cat if you hold your head sideways and squint just right.

"Let's face it, Brad," he says, pouring himself yet another scotch. Maybe that has something to do with his radical honesty. "I'm not exactly the type of leader who inspires the troops. I was hoping to maintain the peace here by refusing to publicly take a side in the conflict between Queen Anne and Chance Fuller. But I'm afraid all I've managed to do is alienate both sides—not even the loyalists are likely to trust me. You, however, are very clearly a queen's man.

"On top of all that, I'm a by-the-book type of commander. You, on the other hand, have the infuriating habit of doing the impossible while somehow even getting sworn enemies like the Koratans to follow you into battle. Oh yes, I know all about your little side quest to save President Fournier; some of the queen's messages have gotten through the SDF blockade.

"So I'm going to make a deal with you. I saved your wife's life. In return, I need you to save my fleet, *Admiral* Mendoza."

It's like all the oxygen just got sucked from the room. I just finished telling Turly that I'm not fit for command, and now he's trying to hand me his fleet? Now I'm certain this is a dream, and not the happy kind. It just turned into a nightmare almost as bad as my recurring nighttime visits to Bellerophon.

"Vice Admiral Mendoza," he says before I can stop him, burping halfway through the title after all the alcohol he's imbibed. "I am formally transferring command of Huff Naval Base to you, effective immediately."

My mind races, and for several moments that stretch the definition of the word, I'm stunned—and frankly terrified—speechless. When I finally find my voice, it's hoarse. "Chris, I . . ."

He must sense what I'm about to say, drunk or not, because he shakes his head emphatically. "Sorry, Brad. This whole thing is your problem now. Orders, Admiral?"

I sigh, realizing that I really have no choice. When that SDF fleet decides to finally press the issue of Turly swearing allegiance to King Chance . . . Well, coming all this way to save Jess's life will end up meaning nothing if we both find ourselves in front of Chance's firing squad.

"Fine," I say, forcing out the word like the curse it is for me at the moment. "But I request that you defer transferring command to me to a later date."

He scrunches up his face in confusion, overemphasizing the motion as the drunk tend to do. "And why would I do that?"

"Because," I say, leaning forward to meet his red-rimmed eyes. "You just told me that not even the loyalists are apt to trust you. So, if this is going to work, I can't actually have you transfer command to me. I have to *take* it from you."

I go on to explain my hastily formed plan, and it's a good thing Turly is as drunk as he is, or he would never agree to it. Even with his inebriation, it takes me the better part of an hour to talk him into it.

# THIRTY-ONE
# ANOTHER LIFE

## JESSICA LIN MENDOZA

"Captain Lin, can you hear me?"

My eyes flutter open to see the fuzzy outline of a man's face peering down at me. I blink rapidly to try to clear my vision, confused by a sort of numbness that seems to pervade my entire body. When I can finally see more clearly, I find myself in an unfamiliar med bay, looking up at the face of a Navy doctor I've never seen before.

"Where?" I ask, the words barely coming out through a dry and sore throat.

"Sorry," the doctor says, and hands me a cup of ice chips. "We just took out the breathing tube; talking is probably going to be painful for a while. You died once on the operating table, you know."

I consider that for a moment. Then I mentally shrug, recalling the doctors on Carter's World telling me much the same thing after Kayla's bomb almost killed me there. Not the first time. Probably not the last. It's amazing the things you can get used to. "Where am I?" I repeat my original question, the words coming out hoarse and scratchy.

"Huff Naval Base. Your ship got you here just in time. I can't believe they made it through the blockade."

Sounds like I missed a few things. "Admiral Mendoza?"

He looks suddenly chagrined. "Sorry, ma'am. He's in the brig. He's been arrested pending trial by the station commander."

"Turly?" I'm suddenly out of breath.

The doctor nods and answers in an overly neutral tone. "Aye, ma'am. Rear Admiral Christoph Turly."

I try to swear, but it turns into a coughing fit. Really? What was Brad thinking, coming to Turly for help? If he had to pick the worst person in the galaxy to ask for help, the man would be at least in the top five.

The Navy doctor pretends not to notice my reaction. "Captain, I regret to inform you that, as soon as you're well enough, I have orders to send you to the brig as well." He frowns a thin line. "Fortunately for you, I don't think that will be possible for at least several days—maybe as long as a week. As I said, you came to us with a lot of damage."

My heart goes out to this man, who is obviously stuck between his sworn loyalty to his command structure and his duty as a doctor to his patient. I admire his resolve; there's no way Christoph Turly will let me stay in his care a moment longer than absolutely necessary.

The snake. I have only a vague idea how we must have ended up in his custody, but I swear I'll help Brad find a way to—

My thoughts are interrupted by the wail of a klaxon as all the lights in the med bay dim and start flashing red. The doctor startles, staring up at the lights. "Now what? SDF attack?"

He disappears before I can ask what he means by that. In his place, a short nurse wearing a surgical mask walks in and starts checking my IV bags.

"What's happening?" I demand of her, but she just ignores me, whistling softly through the mask as she works, seemingly oblivious to the loud klaxons and shouts of confusion from outside my field of vision. "I asked you a question, Nurse," I say, trying to mimic Brad's command tone but failing miserably, as I can still barely force out any words.

"Nothing to worry about, princess," the nurse says, turning to look at me. Despite the mask covering the lower half of her face, I have the distinct impression she's grinning at me. Then a small lock of her hair, peeking out from under her cap, momentarily but unmistakably turns bright green before quickly fading back to brown.

"Hay—" I start to gasp, but she puts a hand on my mouth to stop me.

"Keep quiet, boss," Hayley says with a wink. "Admiral's got a plan."

"But Brad is in the brig," I protest as she moves her hand off my mouth.

She shrugs. "You know the admiral, boss. He ain't gonna let anything happen to you or the rest of us."

Before I can ask for more information, she's gone, pulling shut a curtain behind her so I can't see what's going on around me in the med bay. But I can still hear all the continued shouts and alarms, and I start to look around at the various lines and leads attached to me to see if I can free myself and make my escape.

However, my eyes start to feel heavy, and my last conscious thought is to swear at Hayley, who surely slipped some sort of drug into my IV bag specifically to *keep* me from trying to get out of bed.

# THIRTY-TWO
# JAILBREAK

## BRAD MENDOZA

My second stint in the brig is only slightly less boring than the first. Once the initial shock and excitement of the bizarre conversation with Christoph Turly fades, I'm left with nothing to think about but the questionable plan I presented to him in his office.

Back in my cell, I've already run that plan through my head a few dozen times, until I finally have nothing left to think about. And the longer I have to think about it, the more I start to second guess myself.

So it's with immense relief that the klaxons start to sound, and I watch in silence as Conehead chokes out Hulk just beyond my cell door. Seconds after the giant Marine is slumbering peacefully on the metal deck, Conehead has the hatch to my cell open and is ushering me outside.

"He's with them?" I ask, motioning to the prone and snoring Hulk.

Conehead nods. "He's from Serravo, sir. Can you handle a gun?" He hands me a pistol without waiting for my reply. "Stay close behind me, Admiral. If we encounter resistance, don't try to talk your way out of it." Apparently, he's heard of me. "Just shoot first and ask questions later." He takes the gun out of my hand, flips the selector switch to stun rounds, and hands it back to me.

"Sure, Marine. You got a name?" I'm guessing that continuing to call my rescuer Conehead would not be conducive to a productive working relationship.

"Matthews, sir. From Hecate. Is everything they say about you true, sir?"

"Only the bad parts."

He barks a single laugh, and we're off, moving quickly down the corridor outside the brig. Just as we've moved about five meters, a second Marine appears out of nowhere, a woman, and I start to raise my pistol.

Luckily, Matthews holds out a hand to stop me. Without any exchange of words, the female Marine falls in with us, her weapon at the ready.

We round a bend up ahead and encounter the first resistance. It's my old friend Commander Lukas, accompanied by two Marines of his own, clearly on his way to the brig to secure the prisoner.

We have the element of surprise, but we're still evenly matched. My stun round takes Lukas in the chest before I realize he's not the right target to prioritize. By then, one of his Marines is down, but the other gets a shot off before he falls.

Unlike our guns, the rebel Marine's is *not* set to stun, and I cry out as Matthews falls dead to the deck, a bullet in his forehead, before the female Marine with me takes out his killer.

I stare down at Matthews almost uncomprehendingly. I've been around a lot of death, even a lot of close-quarters death, over the last year, and well before that also. But to see my first protector on this station dead so quickly is nearly too much to bear.

"We need to keep moving, Admiral," the female Marine says, and I nod dumbly before following her down the corridor, doing my best to kick the unconscious Commander Lukas hard in the ribs as we step over him and his two sleeping, traitorous Marines.

Luckily, we encounter no more hostile Marines, but we do collect friendly ones as we make our way deeper into the station. By the time we arrive at the command center, we're a dozen strong, all armed, and all seriously pissed off.

We enter the command center, which is quite a bit larger than *Bainbridge*'s bridge, to find several officers standing with hands raised, covered by the guns of a half dozen other armed officers and an equal number of Marines. Right in the center of the room, standing next to his command chair, hands raised and a panicked expression on his face, is Rear Admiral Christoph Turly.

"Mendoza!" he barks. "What in Hades are you doing? You'll hang for this, you dirty—"

Whatever foul word he's going to call me is cut off when my fist connects soundly with his jaw. He goes down like a sack of potatoes, not knocked out but stunned. He stares up at me in shock from the deck as I turn to the other Navy officers —the ones holding their peers at gunpoint.

"Who's the next senior officer here?" I demand.

"That would be me, Admiral!" a middle-aged woman with commander's stripes says as she steps forward, lowering her gun from the head of a man wearing the insignia of a lieutenant commander as a Marine moves to replace her. "Commander Chelly Lund, sir!"

"Which ships in the fleet can we count on?"

"Sir," she replies crisply, "we can count on *Gunslinger* and *Charger*." Those are both of the battlecruisers in Turly's little fleet, which is a relief. I *love* battlecruisers.

"Unfortunately," she continues, "the heavy cruiser *Jack's Gambit* and light cruiser *Cambridge* are both sympathetic to the SDF and King Chance. We can probably count on Lieutenant Commander Rickers on the destroyer *Vancouver*, but her sister ship *York* could go either way."

Not that bad, so far. About what my conversation with Turly led me to expect. "And *Liberator*?" I ask, naming the sole battleship that is the center and anchor of Turly's small fleet. *Liberator* alone has more firepower than the other ships combined, and armor thick enough that even the two battlecruisers working together would be hard-pressed to breach it before she killed them both.

Commander Lund frowns. "Not good news, sir. Captain Borisev is from Serravo, so his loyalties are not with us. Same for his XO, Commander Chatterly. But the rest of the crew?" She shrugs. "Like *York*, they could go either way. They're not exactly big fans of their CO, but that doesn't mean they'll side with us."

"What about the Marines?"

She stops and considers that for a moment. "Major Early is the Marine commander on *Liberator*, and she's from Kipling. But about a quarter of her people are from Serravo."

I nod thoughtfully and then look down at Turly, still on the floor, glaring daggers at me and Lund in turns. "What do you think, Admiral?" I ask. "Does Captain Borisev hate you enough to want you in his own brig rather than here on the station?"

Predictably, Turly spits on the deck at my feet and refuses to answer. He's not a bad actor after all.

"I'm willing to bet he does," I say with a smile. "Comms?"

"Here, sir," an older enlisted salt says from across the room.

"Call *Liberator*. Tell them that Vice Admiral Brad Mendoza has taken command of the fleet here at Huff and that I will be bringing myself and the prisoner, Rear Admiral Turly, to *Liberator* to discuss our strategic options." I pause and look back down at the red-faced admiral at my feet. "And so that I can get Admiral Turly into the battleship's brig, where he'll be more secure in the event of an SDF attack."

Now, all I have to do is hope that Captain Borisev on that massive, indomitable battleship will be just curious enough to hear what I have to say—and just greedy enough to take both me *and* Turly captive—that he won't blow our shuttle out of space en route.

# THIRTY-THREE
# HOME IS WHERE THE BIGGEST GUNS ARE

## JESSICA LIN MENDOZA

"Ahhh!"

My scream as I jolt awake brings Doc Bean bustling over to my bed back in *Bainbridge*'s med bay, looking supremely annoyed that I interrupted whatever he was doing.

I sit there, eyes wide, breathing hard as he checks the readouts on all the various machines attached to me, clucking to himself as he goes as if he's deciding whether or not he approves of the work the station's doctors did on me.

"How am I back here?" I ask when I catch my breath.

Bean shrugs. "A few Marines showed up at the airlock with you on a stretcher, and here you are?"

"Marines?" That makes no sense.

He scowls like he's put out by having me question him.

"Where are those Marines now?" I ask.

"I don't know," he says curtly, like it's a stupid question.

"Probably still at the airlock measuring bicep circumference with Boyd and Rodriguez to see who the new alpha is going to be. Now hush up so I can get a better read on your oxygen levels. Those hacks on the station did passable work, but if I'd known they were going to return you in such a state, I would have . . ."

I tune him out as my mind races. Using my implant, I try pinging Brad, but there's no response. So, I ping Gunny and Illian for a status check. Boyd replies first, letting me know that the Marines who returned me to our destroyer claimed to have been acting under Brad's authority. That's good news, I suppose, but I'm still out of the loop. I need someone to fill me in on just what in Hades is going on.

Illian chimes in a moment later, letting me know that we've separated from the Naval station and are standing off a few thousand kilometers in case they decide to open fire. Again, with no real context, I can't tell if that's a good or bad thing.

I try pinging Brad again. Still no response. Same for Hayley.

I'm about to order Illian to fill me in on everything when my implant connection suddenly cuts out, and I look up to see Doc Bean glaring down at me.

"Captain Lin," he says sternly. "I didn't put you back together so that you can overexert yourself now. No more using your comms until I say you're ready."

I look up at him and then down at the tubes and needles in my left arm. Reaching over with my right hand, I grab them in a bundle and rip them out, only gasping a little at the flash of pain. Then I stand up, shoving him out of the way when he tries to stop me.

Swaying on my feet for a moment, I reach out to grab the bed for support and glare at Bean. "Doctor, you will cease jamming my implant now, or I will throw you in the brig. I'm going to the bridge to take command. Assuming we survive the next few hours, depending on whatever stupid, asinine plan my husband has concocted, then you can strap me to a medical bed and force me to rest. But not a second before. Got it?"

Frowning like an angry gym coach I once had, he nods regardless.

"Good, now out of my way."

Grunting in frustration, he stands aside, and I walk unsteadily past him. Just as I'm nearing the hatch, he clears his throat loudly. I look back over my shoulder to see him blushing and looking anywhere but at me.

"Uh . . . Captain," he says. "There's one thing you might—"

"What is it, Doctor?" I demand harshly. "Spit it out!"

He blushes an even deeper shade and points toward my back, but a little farther down. I crane my neck to look over my shoulder and feel my own face turn red and my ears go hot as I see that the hospital gown I'm wearing is open in the back, exposing my rear end for all to see. I'm suddenly conscious that we're not alone in the med bay either, and there are two enlisted Koratans there, both studiously pretending I don't exist as they blush just as furiously as the good doctor.

"Well," I huff as I reach behind myself and use one hand to hold the gown partially shut. "I suppose I'll need to go to my quarters first, then, won't I?"

No one answers, and I catch one of the Koratans, a man, sneaking a peek. "Spacer?" I ask, and he immediately averts his eyes.

"Yes, Captain?"

"Take a picture. It'll last longer."

I turn to go again, but my next step in my bare feet somehow goes wrong, and I have to reach out and brace myself against the open hatch with both hands, feeling the gown flap open again behind me.

"Oh for Hades' sake!" I hear Doc Bean behind me. "Miss Encarnacion, get that hoverchair over there and help our stubborn mule of a captain back to her quarters and then to the bridge. If she tries to walk on her own, shoot her."

# THIRTY-FOUR
# INTO THE LIBERATOR'S DEN

## BRAD MENDOZA

"*Liberator,* this is Shuttle T-17 on approach to your starboard docking bay. Request that you open the outer doors now."

The forty-minute ride from the station to the enormous Promethean Navy battleship has been one of the tensest of my life. Captain Borisev's reply to my 'request' to come to his ship was terse and not all that encouraging. I've half expected him to open fire on our shuttle at any moment during the journey.

But if he were going to do so, he surely would have done it by now, and I breathe a sigh of relief when the massive ship's docking bay doors start to open at my shuttle pilot's request. I turn to face the rear of the cockpit so that I can see through the hatch and into the passenger compartment. With us is a squad of Marines, ostensibly an honor guard for our prisoner, Admiral Turly. Commander Chelly Lund is also on board, along with three junior officers.

I turn back to stare out the shuttle's viewport as the battleship's starboard flank fills our entire field of vision. I'm telling you, you never quite grasp the size of a Zeus-class battleship until you're right up close to one like this. They are *huge*. Of course, *Liberator* isn't nearly as big as the Jutzen dreadnought we destroyed at XB-411, but those monsters are in an entirely different class and don't really count. In this sector of space, *Liberator* is unequaled. Even the SDF battleship, one of the older-generation Kronos-class bruisers, is 20 percent smaller than its Navy cousin.

As long as eight football fields and as wide as two, *Liberator* has a crew of nearly two thousand officers and spacers plus an entire company of Marines. And it's quite possible that every single one of them is going to be hostile toward us.

Unfortunately, it's a chance we have no choice but to take, and I absently rub at the admiral's stars on one of my shoulders as I contemplate the lion's den we're walking into.

Our shuttle finally slips through the docking bay's outer door, where our pilot stops and hovers in place in the large airlock's zero-g. Behind us, the outer doors close, and we wait the long minutes for the airlock to pressurize. The inner doors finally open, and the pilot handles the transition to the gravity inside the bay with a deft touch, setting us down gently on the deck.

The shuttle's rear boarding ramp drops, and a young female ensign moves to my side to help me hobble down it, crippled by injuries I supposedly sustained in taking the station from Admiral Turly. I'm also accompanied down the ramp by my prisoner and his honor guard of Marines, plus the other Navy officers. Together, we round the shuttle to walk toward the front of the bay and find a corpulent man in a Navy captain's uniform—Borisev himself—and a dozen armed men and women waiting for us.

The first thing I notice is that none of those with Borisev are Marines, and that gives me a glimmer of hope. The fact that he handed small arms to a bunch of spacers and junior officers tells me that he can't trust the Marines on board to stay loyal to *him* instead of to a ranking officer.

However, that momentary good feeling is quickly replaced by a cold certainty that the lack of Marines also means Borisev does *not* intend to recognize my command authority. Too bad; why can't things ever go the easy way?

"Captain Borisev," I say, as the ensign helps me limp up to him. "I am Vice Admiral Mendoza. As of 0525 this morning, I have assumed command of Huff Naval Base and Task Group 34.2. I'm here for a report on your ship's readiness to engage the SDF forces arrayed against us and to transfer our prisoner, Rear Admiral Christoph Turly, to your brig for safekeeping. I was injured in the fighting on the station, and request the use of your med bay before we discuss—"

In front of me, Borisev yawns theatrically. When he's done, he gives me a cruel smile. "Sorry, *Admiral* Mendoza, was it? I regret to inform you that the rightful monarch of Prometheus, King Chance, has issued an order for your arrest. But I do thank you for removing this idiot"—he motions toward Turly—"from power and bringing both of you to my ship. Saves me the trouble."

"You traitor!" I hear Turly growl behind me, but we both ignore him.

"Captain, you want to think very carefully," I start, but he cuts me off again with a chop of his hand.

"Shut up, Mendoza. Just because the pretender queen gave you a battlefield promotion doesn't make you fit for leadership. I will assume operational command of the fleet here at Cillian Heights, and I have already negotiated a cease-fire and alliance with the loyal SDF forces in the system. And don't think your queensmen on board our battlecruisers are going to come to your rescue. I've got them positioned in a crossfire with the SDF, so they're not going anywhere."

Blah blah blah. It's an eternal rule that bad guys always want to monologue and tell you how smart they are. Borisev looks so proud of himself that I'm shocked he's not drooling.

"You won't get away with this, you dastardly traitor," I say, *really* trying to sound indignant but just so bored with his jabbering that I come across as reading from a really terrible script.

He goes on, of course, for another few minutes, telling me all about how he's backed me into a corner. He insults Turly a few more times for good measure, calls me the Butcher of Bellerophon once or twice, questions both our parentage, implies something about the size of his manhood versus ours, and generally pats himself on the back. Only after subjecting us to that cruel and foul torture does he *finally* command his armed spacers to disarm my Marines.

Amateur. He's just lucky my Marines have strict orders not to fight. That's not why we're here, at least not yet.

When Borisev is finally done preening in front of us, I follow his instruction to precede him out of the bay so he can gloat at my back as he marches me to wherever he plans to take me. Fortunately for me, he allows my helper, the young ensign, to keep assisting me with my injured knee.

Borisev's people take my Marines and most of the Navy officers down one corridor toward the brig, while he and a smaller group lead me, Turly, and my helpful ensign forward toward the crew portions near the bridge. He mumbles something about setting aside quarters for our 'arrest'. It's good to see at least *some* respect for our rank afforded to us, though I'm pretty sure he's only treating us so kindly so as not to piss off the loyal elements of his own crew or the onboard

Marines, none of whom we encounter on our forced journey through the long ship's corridors.

Finally, we arrive at the quarters set aside to hold me and Turly. One of our escorts opens the hatch and ushers us through, but I turn around as the young ensign helps me over the threshold and glare at the battleship commander. "You won't get away with this, Captain," I tell Borisev soberly. "I'll give you one last chance to do the right thing. Will you take it?"

He scoffs. "Shut up, Mendoza. There's no way I would ever take orders from the Butcher of Bellerophon, even if you were a real admiral. Not get inside and be glad you're not in the brig with those other fools, you—"

The young woman in the ensign's uniform moves like a flash. One moment, she's still supporting part of my weight with my arm across her shoulders. The next, I have to reach out and steady myself on the hatchway as she leaps at Borisev.

His first warning that something is amiss comes as her blade slashes his jugular. Before he can finish his final gurgling gasp of surprise, the four armed spacers with him meet similar fates. The first loses his gun to the diminutive ensign, who then spins him around and uses him as a human shield while she calmly shoots his three companions dead. He's the last to fall, joining Borisev and his companions on the cold metal deck.

"Hayley," I hiss when she's done, "I didn't want you to *kill* them all. I wanted to question Borisev at least."

My favorite assassin smiles brightly at me as she tucks the stolen gun in her waistband. Next to me, Turly gapes at her, despite my telling him what to expect.

"Sorry, boss," Hayley says, not sounding sorry in the least. "But you told that hombre it was his last chance, so I figured that meant . . . well, you know, that it was his last chance."

I shake my head, exasperated. "Well, next time, try to take him alive."

She looks at me funny. "You mean next time I have to rescue you from him? He's dead, boss; there won't be a next time. Or do you mean next time I help you board and take over a hostile battleship that's supposed to be on our side?"

Reaching up to rub my temples against the encroaching headache, I sigh. "Never mind. Turly, I've never served on a Zeus-class. You know the quickest way to Marine country?"

The short rear admiral steps up to my side, glaring at me. "Of course I do." He reaches up to rub his jaw. "Did you have to hit me so hard back on the station?"

I shrug. "Had to really sell it. Not even the loyalists would have bought you and me working together. And Borisev would have never let us both on board if he thought we were on the same side." I grin at him. "Besides, I still don't really like you all that much."

He grunts. "The feeling is mutual, trust me. Now let's get going before someone else happens along and sees all these dead bodies your psychotic whatever-she-is left bleeding in the corridor."

Hayley grins at him and licks her lips, and I have the pleasure of seeing Christoph Turly turn from red-faced to white as a ghost.

## THIRTY-FIVE
# CHICKEN NOODLE SOUP

## JESSICA LIN MENDOZA

"Any word from Brad?" I ask for perhaps the fifteenth time in the two hours since awakening back on board *Bainbridge*.

"Nothing yet, Jessica," Harris reports from the comm station. He seems to always forget I'm his commanding officer. How come he never does that with Brad?

"Well, let me know the instant you hear anything," I say grumpily, not because my comm officer is far too familiar with me—the man has held me when I cried, after all—but because I'm seriously pissed off at my husband for doing something so stupid as traveling to a hostile battleship, even if he did at least have the two braincells to take Hayley along.

"What about those SDF ships?" I ask no one in particular.

"They came in closer but stopped just outside missile range." Illian confirms what the battle plot already tells me.

"They must be waiting for *Liberator*'s captain to confirm that Admirals Mendoza and Turly have been neutralized."

I open my mouth to also tell *him* to notify me the second something changes, but I close it quickly. I'm on edge, but the entire crew already has their orders, and I can count on them to follow them to the letter and then some.

I hear the bridge hatch open behind me and the sound of heavy footsteps, and I fight a sigh as Karen O'Malley comes into view with a thermos and frowns down at me.

"Yes?" I ask when she just glares at me for several moments.

"You should be in bed, lass," our cook and ship's surrogate mother chides. Has *everyone* forgotten I'm in command?

"After this is over, I'll sleep for a week," I tell her dryly. "First, I have to make sure we live that long."

She frowns again, but at least doesn't argue with me. Instead, she twists off the top of the thermos, and I wrinkle my nose as a savory smell fills the air.

"Is that chicken noodle soup?" I ask sourly.

"Aye, it is," she says in her light Irish brogue.

"I don't really like chicken noodle soup," I tell her honestly, if not a little too sharply.

She snorts. "I don't care if you like it or not, *Captain*." At least she remembered my rank this time. "You're gonna drink every last drop and eat each and every noodle, or so help me, I'll wrestle you into bed myself. Clear?"

I clench my jaw but do the only thing a captain can do in a situation like this: nod meekly and accept the thermos. And when it's clear she won't leave until she sees me start drinking the foul stuff, I take a hearty sip and try not to wince too much.

Satisfied, Karen throws a look behind me at Illian. "Francis, see that she drinks it all, you hear me, lad? Or you'll be eating emergency rations for a week."

"Yes, ma'am," my tactical officer and acting XO says as if he's talking to an admiral.

The tyrant leaves the bridge, so I set the thermos down. Illian clears his throat behind me. Grimacing, I surrender once again and take another sip. Blast it all, I've always hated chicken noodle soup, but somehow Karen managed to make even this swill taste not half bad.

# THIRTY-SIX
# I LOVE MARINES

## BRAD MENDOZA

When we reach Marine country, we find the hatchway that separates it from the rest of the ship being surreptitiously guarded by four spacers with holstered pistols. It's ridiculous, of course, as any single Marine worth their salt could easily subdue them all before they even got their guns drawn. But something tells me they're more of a symbolic guard than anything else.

It also confirms that while the ship's Marine commander wasn't going to participate in my illegal arrest, she also wasn't going to commit mutiny against her captain. I can work with that.

Hayley makes short work of the four wannabe guards, using *stun* rounds this time.

"Where did you find her?" Turly whispers next to me as she takes out the last of the armed men.

"Believe it or not, she found me," I answer honestly.

Hayley hears and smiles, then opens the hatch, and we step through and into what always seems to be the smelliest part of any ship I've served on.

There's a healthy rivalry between Marines and the Navy. They think we're a bunch of dandies who sip tea and pat ourselves on the back—somewhat true—and we think they're a bunch of knuckle draggers who always smell like sour sweat—*always* true. But I've typically had good relationships with my Marines, even if they do stink. It's not really their fault; they just can't help but work out *all* the time. I swear they have to go lift weights and work up a good sweat just as soon as they step out of the shower.

We don't have to go far to find the Marines. As soon as we step through the door, a muscular woman wearing major's bars on her collar greets us with a full squad of riflemen, guns out and pointed right at our center mass.

"Major Early?" I ask the obvious. "I'm—"

"We know who you are, sir," the woman says, not sounding impressed. "Where is Captain Borisev?"

With angry Marines, I find honesty is typically the best policy. "The captain and I had a little disagreement over the chain of command. I'm afraid he didn't survive the argument."

That does seem to surprise her. "He's dead?"

I nod. "Not my ideal outcome, I assure you. But he committed treason, so I was well within my rights under the Military Uniform Code of Justice, section four, paragraph—"

"No need to read the book to me, Admiral," Early says, holding up a hand. "Borisev was a pig. Have you taken command of the ship yet?"

I regard her carefully, despite her glowing assessment of her former ship's CO. "That depends, Major."

"On what, sir?"

"On whether or not you and your Marines are still loyal to the Crown."

She smiles, showing far too many teeth in the process. "Depends on which Crown you mean, sir. If you're talking about the pretender who sent those SDF goons to hem us in, then we're going to have a problem, you and I."

"Well, then it's a good thing I can't stand the Fullers or the SDF. You ready to help score a victory for Queen Anne and the Federation?"

Her smile turns even more predatory. "Sir, you have no idea."

"I heard a quarter of your Marines are Serravan, Major."

She shrugs. "They were. The rest of us convinced them of the error of their ways." She motions to a nearby corporal. "Davis, you used to be Serravan, didn't you?"

The boy steps forward and salutes sharply. "Aye, ma'am. But I'm just Promethean now. I converted."

Needless to say, the ship falls under my command very quickly after that. Even the traitorous XO's attempt to seal off the bridge fails when the ship's AI recognizes Turly's flag rank blockchain ID and allows him to override the security systems. What an odd couple he and I have turned out to be. I still hate the guy—mostly—but he's not a total jerk.

Unfortunately, a company of 145 angry Marines still isn't enough to truly take command of a queen's battleship. For this to work, I need virtually the entire two-thousand-strong crew to have my back, lest one of them find an opportunity to put a knife in it during battles or in between.

My thoughts go back to the first day I took command of HMS *Persephone* in the Gerson system, when Jess tried to get me to give a speech to the crew as we left the station for our doomed patrol. I recall how disappointed she was when I did little more than announce myself and our patrol and didn't even try to be inspiring.

Why did she marry me, again?

Well, now I have no choice. I'm about to give another speech, and this one needs to be the most inspiring one I've ever given. No pressure, right?

The bosun's whistle sounds throughout the ship as I stand next to the command chair on the truly enormous bridge of the battleship. At a nod from the chief of the boat, I clear my throat and begin.

"Crew of Her Majesty's Ship *Liberator*, this is Vice Admiral Brad Mendoza of the Promethean Royal Navy, here under assignment from Queen Anne, long may she reign." I figure the white lie is worth it at this juncture.

"I have taken command of *Liberator* following the unfortunate death of Captain Borisev, who attempted to illegally imprison me and Rear Admiral Turly when we boarded the ship under legitimate authority." The only thing in the universe that travels faster than a ship in jump space is Navy scuttlebutt, so everyone by now already knows of Borisev's death. I have to address it head-on.

"I truly regret your former captain's passing," I tell them honestly. "Unfortunately, he was a traitor to the Crown and was conspiring with the Serravo Defense Force fleet to surrender control of this fleet and the Huff Naval Base to their forces. Therefore, his death was justified, if not the outcome any of us desired."

Now to the most critical part. "Ladies and gentlemen, most of you don't know me. Or if you do, you've probably not heard great things." I try to ignore one of the bridge officers choking on a gasp. "But despite my many flaws, I am the senior Navy officer in this sector, and as such have a responsibility to Queen and Federation to ensure the security of the citizens of the Corpus Christi Cluster.

"I arrived in the Cluster on board my destroyer, HMS *Bainbridge*, to hunt down and stop the activities of a group of slavers I know to be operating in this sector. However, my mission has changed, and at Admiral Turly's request, I am now faced with the task of liberating Huff Navy Base from the SDF forces blockading us."

Several of the bridge officers are smiling now, so maybe I'm not doing so terribly at this.

"Ladies and gentlemen," I continue. "None of us wants to fight against our former comrades. However, the SDF has proven its treason by challenging the legitimate authority of this fleet and the queen. That cannot stand. After the conquest of Prometheus at the hands of the Jutzens, I hate that we must fight amongst ourselves when we should be focused on our true enemy.

"So I'm going to make you all a deal. I'm fully aware that some of you are loyal to Duke Chance Fuller. I can even respect your position in many ways." That's a lie, but it's a necessary one. "If you feel you cannot accept my command, I will understand. I invite you to leave this ship under a flag of truce and take up residence on the station. I won't force you to fight against your allies in the SDF.

"But for those of you who wish to stay and pledge your loyalty to the rightful queen of the Federated Systems of Prometheus, I offer you this: First, full clemency for anything you may have done up until this point in the service of Chance Fuller. Second, and more importantly, my trust that you will do what needs to be done now to retake the Cluster and join me and the Navy in fighting off the Nazis and their collaborators."

I pause, swallowing. "But know this. If you choose to stay under a false allegiance, I will give no quarter and no mercy. As with Captain Borisev, treason will be punishable by death. We are at war, ladies and gentlemen, and can do no less, as much as it may pain me to carry out such sentences."

I don't think I'm being nearly inspirational enough. I take a deep breath and collect myself.

"Listen, folks, I'm not really good at this admiral stuff. Queen Anne made me a flag officer about fifteen minutes before I left to come to the Corpus Christi Cluster. So I'm going to level with you. I know Anne personally; I actually met her first when she was just a kid, but that's a long story. And while I wasn't the biggest fan of her dad, especially in his later years, he didn't deserve to go out the way he did, in a cowardly Jutzen bombardment that killed millions of civilians along with him.

"Anne isn't perfect. No monarch is—no *person* is. I'm certainly not either, though my wife comes pretty close." Uh oh, I'm rambling now. Pull it together, Brad! "But the queen is our best hope to fight off the Nazis and retake our star nation. She deserves our loyalty. Back at Kipling, her temporary seat of government, even the Koratans have pledged to work with her. Can you believe that? The Jutzens are so terrible that even the Hades' cursed Kories have set aside three centuries of cold war and vowed to help Anne fight them off. Crazy, right?" Wow, I definitely don't sound like an admiral now.

"Listen, stay with me on this, and we'll play a vital role in helping to win this war. For all of us, it starts here, today, by standing up to the SDF bullies, and by extension, to the Nazis. Please, help us do that. That is all."

I take another deep breath, looking around at the bridge crew. It may be my imagination, but I think they're all sitting up a little straighter, so maybe something I said worked.

"Crew of the *Liberator*," a new voice intones, and I look over, shocked at Christoph Turly, who is standing next to the comm officer. What is he doing? "This is Rear Admiral Turly. Many of you know, and the rest of you no doubt suspect, that I've never been a big fan of Brad Mendoza. In fact, I've now tried to arrest him *twice*. But I find myself realizing that the best thing I can do for Queen and Federation is to follow his orders. He's actually good at this sort of thing. Join me in helping him liberate Cillian Heights and the Cluster, and may God watch over us all."

I swallow a sudden lump in my throat and nod at Turly, just as my eyes start to water. Stupid Navy—why can't they ever keep the blasted air ducts free of the dust that always makes my allergies flare up at the absolute worst of times?

## THIRTY-SEVEN
# A VERY PUBLIC PRIVATE CONVERSATION

## JESSICA LIN MENDOZA

"Captain!"

I look over at Harris eagerly. "What is it?"

"Admiral Brad is on the line. He says—"

"Just put him on the bridge speakers, Harris," I say, practically leaping out of my command chair before groaning and settling back into it when both my healing gunshot wounds protest loudly.

"Hiya, Jess," a far-too-cheerful voice says for all to hear.

"Admiral," I reply in a warning tone to tell him this isn't a private channel, not that it will make any difference to him.

"Glad to hear your voice, pookie," he says a little more somberly. "You had me scared there for a bit."

Pookie? Really? He's going to pay for that one. "Brad, honey," I say, unable to keep up the pretense of professionalism. "Did you really take over an entire Navy base and fleet just to get me to a hospital?"

"Well, sort of. But now I'm going to use them to spank those SDF ships. Wanna help?"

"Just try to stop me." I blush ahead of my next words, almost reconsidering them, but I figure that almost dying earns me a little leeway with my crew. "Listen, Brad, whatever you do, don't die doing it. At least not until I've had a chance to properly . . . thank you for saving my life again."

I can practically hear him grinning like an idiot over the voice-only comm channel. "Um, maybe you want to hop on a shuttle and come on over? *Liberator* needs a new captain."

Despite the absurdity of the conversation, I laugh. "Sorry, Brad. *Bainbridge* is going to need a captain as well for the battle. But I can send Illian if you'd like." I ignore the sound of my tactical officer choking behind me.

"No, that's okay. I'm sure I can rustle up an officer senior enough over here to repeat my orders."

Suddenly, in the background, I hear harsh whispers that I can't make out. But I can understand Brad's voice whispering back. "Open channel? Really? The entire fleet can hear?" Then, he speaks up again. "Uh, listen, Jess—uh, Captain Lin—I gotta go. Battle to fight and all that. I'd ask you to keep our little undermanned destroyer behind the main line, but . . ."

"But I'd ignore that order, no matter your rank," I say with a smile of my own.

"Yep. Listen, take care of yourself and our crew. Talk to you soon. Love you!"

The line cuts before I can tell him how madly I love him back. I look around to see the entire bridge crew grinning at me.

"What are you all looking at?" I ask, pretending to be cross. "Didn't you hear the admiral? We have a battle to prepare for."

# THIRTY-EIGHT
# ONWARD TO BATTLE

## BRAD MENDOZA

"I can't believe I'm under your command now," Christoph Turly says dryly from the chair next to me on *Liberator*'s bridge.

I look over at him and smirk. "Trust me, I wasn't ever planning on going into battle with you either. But as much as you annoy me, Chris, I seem to remember you being a halfway decent battleship commander. Mind taking the conn of this one while I direct the overall battle?"

He looks surprised for a moment, either by my offer or my continued use of his first name, and nods. "I suppose I can do that. But one thing, Admiral."

"What's that?"

"When this is over—at some point when you least expect it—I'm going to return the favor from the station and punch you so hard it'll knock you into jump space."

I can't help but laugh out loud, drawing a few confused

glances from the officers around us. Something tells me Borisev wasn't quite so casual on the bridge.

"Any issues with the rest of the fleet?" I ask when I compose myself again.

Turly frowns. "The Marines on *Jack's Gambit* had to arrest Commander Pierce. She's on a shuttle back to the station with most of her command crew. That leaves them pretty short-staffed, and the senior remaining officer is a lieutenant. Not ideal for a heavy cruiser. Luckily, Commander Ravenfeather on *Cambridge* said he'll support you and follow orders. He's technically Serravan, but he's from Wayside."

I nod knowingly. Wayside is one of the vassal worlds in the Duchy of Serravo. But of the five worlds in the Duchy, it's the most tumultuous, with a population that often seems to want to be on its own rather than be part of Serravo or even Prometheus.

Still, Ravenfeather's willingness to go against King Chance was far from a given, so it's a relief.

"What about *York*?" I ask, referencing the final questionable ship, a destroyer.

Chris, as I'm truly starting to think of him more often now, grimaces. "That one was a surprise, and not in a good way. I thought Lieutenant Commander Young would side with us at the end of the day, but apparently, he felt strongly enough about things to sprint over to the SDF side."

I look at him sharply. "Why wasn't I informed immediately?"

He bristles but, to his credit, doesn't snap back at me. "Sorry. Lots going on. Sensor officer just told me two minutes ago, while you were on the comm with your wife. Didn't want to interrupt while the entire fleet heard you making plans for your reunion later."

I bite back the retort already forming on my lips. "Okay. Anything we can do about them?"

He shakes his head. "*York* was already the farthest out on the starboard flank. We could send *Cambridge* after them, but I wouldn't advise it."

I nod. No sense in testing Commander Ravenfeather's fledgling loyalty by having him shoot at his former consort. That might have him switching sides far too quickly. The loss of the destroyer *York* is a hard blow, but at least the majority of the fleet stayed loyal.

As for *Liberator* herself, only about 10 percent of the crew took me up on the offer to leave and go to the station to sit out the battle. I'm sure some of those who remained are still loyal to King Chance, but I've had Major Early post her Marines around all the ship's most sensitive areas just in case. I also asked her to tell them to act as discreetly as they can—no need to rub it in that I don't trust my new crew—but they're Marines, so their discretion will no doubt involve glaring and barking at everyone who passes within sight.

"Very well, Admiral," I say to Chris, turning my voice more formal. "Is my flagship ready for battle?"

"Aye, sir. *Liberator* stands ready in all respects, awaiting your orders."

I bite my lower lip for a second, studying the battle plot in front of me on the extremely large viewscreen—it makes *Bainbridge*'s look like an entertainment screen—searching the positions of our ships and the SDF's to see if I've missed anything. Nothing jumps out, so I nod. "The order is given, Admiral. Comms, message to the fleet: execute Plan Delta."

# THIRTY-NINE
# TIME TO GO

## JESSICA LIN MENDOZA

"Orders from the flag, Captain," Harris says with unusual gravitas. Illian must have coached him on proper protocols prior to the battle. "Attack Plan Delta."

"Very well. Helm, come about to oh-one-four mark two and go to flank speed. Tactical, get me firing solutions on that SDF destroyer, designate Tango Six. Sensors, full active scans. If that light cruiser so much as twitches in our direction, I want to know about it."

I pause, listening as my bridge crew calmly relays my orders, repeating them to each other and then to themselves to make sure there are no mistakes and no misunderstandings.

It's the first time we've entered battle as part of a larger force, and it's a new experience for most of my crew. Frankly, it's a new experience for me outside of war games. And despite the scrapes Brad and I have gotten into over the last nine months, a formation-driven battle like this is nothing like the single-unit tactics we're all used to.

I take a deep breath, trying to think of what Brad would say—probably something short, pithy, and hard-hitting. I'm not Brad—I'm not nearly as pithy as him—but I can do short. I key open the ship-wide comm.

"Ladies and gentlemen. Let's go hunting."

# FORTY
# TANGO ONE

## BRAD MENDOZA

"Tango One is moving to intercept *Gunslinger* and *Jack's Gambit*."

"Tango Two is coming about and presenting port broadside."

"*Vancouver* reports engaging the enemy on the port flank."

"Admiral, *Charger* reports a firing solution on Tango One and is requesting permission to disengage from Tango Three."

I listen to the flurry of shouted voices on the expansive bridge. Tango One is the enemy battleship, while Two and Three are their battlecruisers, and so on. The red enemy ship icons move across the forward viewscreen's battle plot toward the green friendly ones, all of them dancing, jinking, and driving forward to meet each other like the galaxy's most chaotic football game.

My mind flashes back to the last time I commanded a fleet action like this—nearly seven years ago at Jalisco, as a very junior commander, thrust into the thick of things when Duchess Charlotte's forces ambushed my task force and left me as the seniormost surviving officer.

Back then, I didn't know how far over my head I really was. Now, staring at the plot, I feel it in my bones. I'm not ready for this.

"Sir, orders?" a voice asks from one side.

My breath quickens, and I feel sweat breaking out on my brow. Unbidden, my eyes dart to one of the green friendly ship icons on the plot—*Bainbridge*, with everyone I love on board—driving hard toward two red dots that suddenly seem much larger. I lick suddenly dry lips, and my mind goes completely blank.

I can't do this. I thought I could, but now I'm sure I can't. I never should have even tried. I—

"Admiral, orders?" the same voice asks, more urgently now.

I look over with wide eyes at Chris, who is frowning at me from his command chair, taking a short break from the battle to check up on me. "You okay, Admiral?" he asks carefully.

I want to shake my head, to tell him he has to take command, but the words won't come. It's like my brain can no longer even form language.

"Brad," a new voice says in my private implant comm, relayed by the ship's AI. "What are you doing? We need support on the left flank. You've got this, sweetheart."

The sound of Jess's voice, calling over our private comm channel, snaps me out of my fugue state. My brain suddenly fills with vectors and figures as it falls into old patterns of training in choreographing the movement of ships and missiles.

"Tell *Charger* to stay on Three," I call out, my voice cracking a little. I clear my throat before continuing. "And tell *Cambridge* to tighten up in formation. I need her covering

*Gunslinger's* starboard flank. Get Captain Quarrie to take out that cruiser sneaking up on *Bainbridge*! Admiral Turly, move *Liberator* up the middle to engage Tango One."

The bridge had started to fall silent when I was frozen with doubt, but now it fills with the shouts of orders repeated and other orders given. Some of it relates to the fleet as a whole, while Turly relays other orders directed at *Liberator* herself. Which is good; I may not like the man, but I need to trust him to fight the flagship so I can stay focused on the battle in its entirety.

Beneath me, I feel *Liberator* shudder, and I check the main battle plot in time to see the icons of nearly *fifty* missiles lance out from our starboard broadside. Among those are half a dozen of the larger icons denoting ship-killer nuclear missiles, all aimed at Tango One, the SDF battleship.

Unfortunately, the plot also shows a similar number of missiles and ship-killers coming straight at us from the enemy. I do my best to ignore those as *Liberator* rolls on her long axis and uses her port broadside to spit out dozens of antimissile interceptors. What I wouldn't give for a carrier full of fighters right now to stop those incoming missiles and pound on Tango One at the same time.

Then I spot something else on the plot as one of the enemy ships halts its forward advance and begins to turn. "Comms, message Captain Walsh. Tell him I've changed my mind and he should launch a broadside at Tango One's flank. Have him coordinate with *Jack's Gambit* to keep Tango Three off him for a few minutes."

"Aye, Admiral!"

Taking a deep breath and driving away the last of my demons—there will be ample time for them later—I close my eyes and connect my implant to *Liberator*'s fleet operations tactical system. In my mind's eye, I'm no longer looking at a two-dimensional plot. Instead, it's as if I'm standing in the middle of space, except that I'm roughly the size of a planet. Even the staggering distances between the battling ships appear as nothing more than a few meters here or there around me. I watch as ships bolt ahead, spin and turn, disgorging wave after wave of missiles. Again, almost involuntarily, I seek out one of the friendly ships, outlined in green.

*Bainbridge* is right in the thick of things. She used her defensive weaponry to stop a wave of missiles fired at the battlecruiser *Gunslinger*, then somehow managed to get a couple of missiles past an SDF destroyer's defenses. The small enemy ship is now dead in space and venting atmosphere, on a ballistic course that will take it straight into Huff's atmosphere and crush depth if the engineers can't restore power in the next few hours.

Now my wife and our crew are charging an SDF light cruiser, trying to get within laser range and depending on her own defensive lasers and gatling guns to intercept missiles lobbed their way. When we sustained damage saving President Fournier, the Koratan engineers upped *Bainbridge*'s top acceleration by 5 percent, but Jess doesn't seem to be using that extra speed. I briefly wonder why but am forced to reluctantly tear my eyes away from my loved ones to take in the battle as a whole again.

My orders to *Charger* pay dividends. Her last-second broadside at the SDF battleship is enough to make Tango One split her defenses. As a result, half a dozen of *Liberator*'s medium and heavy ship-to-ship missiles get through and slam into the enemy's hull. Most of them don't breach it, but they do weaken it, and in one case, they open a deck or two to space.

Then, my implant simulates a brilliant flash of light as a ship-killer missile slips through and detonates its nuclear fire right against Tango One's port bow. When the momentarily flash clears, I grin in satisfaction. A large chunk of the enemy battleship's bow is just gone. It's not enough to slow her down all that much—battleships are built to take a beating, even from nuclear warheads—but it's a solid start. If we can get another ship killer into that breach and detonate it *inside* the enemy ship, it'll explode into a billion pieces like that Jutzen dreadnought back at XB-411.

The SDF battleship's captain knows that just as well as we do, and rotates his ship to show us his relatively undamaged starboard flank.

"Order *Charger* to disengage from Tango One and reengage Three," I say aloud, then watch as only a few seconds later the battlecruiser does as I command.

A flashing red light from my left grabs my attention, and I turn in time to see a dozen missiles impact the light cruiser *Cambridge*. In an instant, the recently repentant Everett Ravenfeather, a man I would have very much liked to have met in person, meets his end along with 250 other souls as one of the SDF battlecruisers snuffs their lives out.

Resisting the urge to order a revenge run, I instead command *Gunslinger*, my other battlecruiser, to do a mirror image of *Charger*'s earlier attack on Tango One, but this time from the SDF battleship's newly damaged port flank. I time it just right and watch a few minutes later in satisfaction as two of *Gunslinger*'s missiles make it through to damage the enemy battleship, while the distraction once again clears the way for *Liberator*'s broadside. Another ship-killer missile takes the SDF ship in the starboard stern this time. Unfortunately, that's the area of heaviest shielding around the reactor and engineering compartments, but the nuclear blast is still enough to open a few surrounding decks to space. Secondary explosions cascade along the starboard flank and take out several missile tubes and laser clusters, and just like that, Tango One has lost a third of its offensive punch since the battle started.

Space seems to jolt around me a second later as three missiles bash against *Liberator.* I turn my attention to my implant's 3D rendering of my own command ship, relived to see that none of the three missiles were ship-killers. But one deck is open to space, and we lost a few missile tubes and laser projectors of our own.

I resist the urge to yell at Chris and whirl to find *Bainbridge* again. There she is, still charging at the enemy light cruiser, but not using her max speed advantage yet. The two ships disgorge missiles at each other and knock them out of space with defensive fire. I watch in horror as my little destroyer enters the larger ship's laser range and beams of potent energy streak out toward them.

## FORTY-ONE
# KNIFE FIGHT

### JESSICA LIN MENDOZA

"Light damage to the enemy's starboard hull. No breaches!"

"Decks three and four on our port flank are open to space, Captain. Damage control crews responding!"

I know that said damage control crews consist only of Gunny Boyd and his shooters, but I resolve to let them do their jobs as I fight my ship.

"Helm, come about thirty degrees port, up two. Tactical, fire our last two scramblers. Ready the starboard laser barrage for another pass."

The deck rocks beneath me as a medium ship-to-ship missile gets through our defensive fire and, for a moment, I worry that the blast may have somehow broken through to explode inside the ship. But when the crazy earthquake stops, I'm relieved to see only light damage to our ventral hull—a near miss, not a contact detonation.

"Laia, work out a vector to drive that light cruiser toward *Gunslinger*," I order. "Signal Captain Quarrie to be ready."

"Aye, ma'am."

"Illian, ready on those lasers?"

"At your command."

"Fire!"

Invisible beams of destruction reach across the vacuum between *Bainbridge* and the enemy light cruiser. Our little ship rocks again as the enemy fires back at us almost simultaneously with its own, more powerful laser banks. But as strong as that light cruiser is compared to our destroyer, its captain failed to account for the speed of the Apollo-class. Chief Cortes at the helm jinks our ship faster than seems possible so that the enemy lasers don't find purchase for more than the barest instant. They still burn through our hull in a few places, but none of them reach sensitive areas.

"Kelly, get ready to give me a surge of power!" I call down to Engineering. It's time to use what the Koratans gave us, when the enemy will least expect it.

"On your mark, Captain," he calls back.

I silently count down the time in my head. "Now!"

*Bainbridge* bucks so hard that it jams me painfully into the back of my seat, the temporary surge of 5 extra percentage points in our acceleration too much for the inertial compensators to handle. My mind flashes back to a similar time on *Persephone*, when Kelly found a way to get more acceleration out of our ion drive and we all felt like pancakes for hours under the heavy g-forces.

This time isn't quite as bad, but my barely healed wounds scream in protest until I hear an actual scream issue from my own lips.

Forcing my head down to survey my console, I see that our sudden burst of speed threw off the enemy light cruiser's aim, and its latest laser volley speared the space behind us as we surged forward.

"Fire!" I shout again at Illian, and our own lasers do better, hitting the light cruiser in the flank and ripping into its hull. Two of those lasers concentrate on the ship's stern, just ahead of its drive nozzles, and I stifle a cheer as something there explodes and the enemy ship's acceleration cuts in half.

# FORTY-TWO
# A HIGH-COST VICTORY

## BRAD MENDOZA

I somehow resist the urge to check in on Jess for a full five minutes. When I finally look again, I'm almost shocked to see the light cruiser she engaged venting atmosphere and accelerating at a snail's pace. Finding my little destroyer, I see it's damaged as well, though it's certainly given more than it's gotten in what should have been a one-sided battle in the other direction.

I watch in satisfaction as the battlecruiser *Gunslinger* swoops in from the light cruiser's other side and the larger ship's much more powerful lasers practically cut the enemy in half, taking it out of the fight entirely.

"Sir, *Charger*," a voice intrudes from outside my virtual bubble, and I turn in time to watch in horror as one of my mighty battlecruisers takes fire from both sides by what remains of Tango One, the SDF battleship, and a nearly undamaged SDF battlecruiser that, until now, was hanging back and mostly playing defense.

*Charger* doesn't even have a chance to cut its reactor and surrender before it's hit from both sides by concentrated laser power aimed almost entirely at its stern quarters. One or more of the enemy lasers burns through to the reactor itself. I cry out in rage as *Charger* and its eight hundred souls follow the light cruiser *Cambridge* into whatever afterlife awaits spacers and Marines.

It's too little too late when, mere moments later, one of *Liberator*'s ship killers finally makes it inside Tango One's open port bow. The nuclear-tipped missile burrows its way deep into the enemy battleship's decks before exploding, and I watch with teeth bared as the massive warship breaks apart at the seams. It's a satisfying sight, though it does nothing for the brave men and women who died on *Charger*.

The battle finishes quickly after that. Only two enemy ships manage to escape—the battlecruiser that helped destroy *Charger* and, ironically, the traitorous Navy destroyer *York*.

The day is won, but at a high cost. Of the seven ships I started with, all are damaged. *Liberator* is in the best shape, with only a few hull breaches and no critical losses. Surprisingly and by some miracle—a miracle named Jessica Lin Mendoza, thank you very much—*Bainbridge* is only moderately damaged. Likewise, the battlecruiser *Gunslinger* is still battleworthy. Unfortunately, the two final ships are capable only of limping back to the station: the heavy cruiser *Jack's Gambit* is missing a chunk of its bow, and the destroyer *Vancouver* has a damaged engine and has to be towed in after its sputtering drive gives out halfway to the station.

Still, all told, it's better than we could have hoped for, though not as good as we prayed for.

"Good work, people," I say when the last two enemy ships are well out of range. I meet the eyes of every man and woman on the bridge, including Turly's. They look back with a mix of pride, exhaustion, and horror. For most of them, this was almost certainly their first real battle, and as the adrenaline wanes, they'll feel the full force of what just happened.

As do I.

"Admiral Turly," I say as calmly as I can, standing up from my chair. "Permission to use your day cabin to check in with the rest of the fleet?"

"Of course, Admiral Mendoza."

I walk stiffly across the bridge to the day cabin's hatch, and I barely get it shut behind me before my knees give way and I have to brace myself against the bulkhead to keep from collapsing.

My entire body shakes and trembles. My mind rebels and starts racing through every moment of the battle—every order I gave, every order I failed to give, and everything I might have done differently.

Over a thousand dead on our side and thousands more of the enemy, and I can't help but think a better commander would have found another way. A better commander wouldn't have hesitated. A better commander would have found a means to save more.

My implant pings with a call from Jess, but I ignore it, stumbling over to the day cabin's couch and throwing myself down onto it before my legs give way yet again.

# FORTY-THREE
# HOMECOMING

## JESSICA LIN MENDOZA

I bounce on my toes inside Huff Naval Base, ignoring the wheelchair one of our Koratan enlisted women has waiting behind me, too intent on watching the airlock cycle between the station and HMS *Liberator*. The battleship has just docked with surprising delicacy and grace for such a giant ship, after towing in the disabled destroyer *Vancouver*. Finally, I hear the environmental systems equalizing the pressure between the ship and station, and then the hatch on my side swings ponderously open.

I rush through before it's even halfway there, throwing myself at Brad, though the action fiercely hurts the wounds in my chest and shoulder. I simply don't care.

"Miss me?" he asks in a subdued voice as I squeeze him hard.

"What can I say? Almost dying twice in one week makes

me sentimental honeybuns." Where did I come up with *that*? Brad and I really need to figure out our pet names for each other.

Someone clears their throat, and I disengage from my husband and frown at the short, red-haired man next to him.

"Admiral Turly," I say, failing to keep the coldness from my tone.

Turly squirms under my gaze, but Brad waves me off. "Relax, Jess. Chris and I have arrived at an understanding."

I look at him in surprise. Did he just call this man 'Chris'?

"Captain Lin," Turly says, taking a small step forward. "I want to apologize for my actions at Hudson, and I need to thank you for risking your life and your ship to defend this base and the fleet."

Wow. "Um . . . thank you, Admiral. And I suppose I should be thanking you for the use of your trauma center."

He smiles.

Looking back at my husband, conscious that we're holding up an increasingly large crowd of spacers, officers, and Marines seeking to board the station, I lead him by the arm out of the airlock, waving off the wheelchair and its minder. Turly trails wordlessly behind us.

"How are things on the station?" Brad asks in a low voice as we go. "I would have liked to have gotten here a lot sooner."

"Delicate," I answer. "The Chance loyalists are being held on the residential levels. Turly's people have Marines posted at every stairwell and access point to keep them away from any sensitive areas, but there are just so many of them."

Brad frowns grimly but stays silent as we reach the main concourse, which, on a dedicated Navy station, is free of the typical shops and restaurants, though there is a bar and grill where the spacers can blow off steam, next to the guarded entrance to the Officers' Club. We head to the latter now, the

Marines flanking the door coming to rigid attention as the two admirals pass through.

Once inside, Turly leads us to a secluded booth in the back, and we take our seats. "Safer to talk here than in my office," he says after a server takes our drink orders and leaves. "I have the office swept three times a day for bugs, but I'm sure some of Chance's people planted more while we were away fighting."

He pauses when the server returns with our drinks, and we send her away without ordering any food. Leaning conspiratorially across the small table, Turly speaks in a low voice.

"What comes next?"

Brad frowns. "We originally came here to find and stop slavers. There's a freighter somewhere in the next line of systems with three hundred innocents from Poe. We owe it to them to do whatever we can to bring them back."

To my complete lack of surprise, Turly shakes his head. "We have bigger problems, Admiral." He must see my stormy expression, because he at least has the decency to look embarrassed for a moment. "Listen, I'd love to go rescue those slaves—you have no idea how much. But the SDF force we just took on was only a fraction of what they have here in the Cluster. I haven't been able to do any recon of Linford Commons, but rumors suggest as much as an overstrength task force could be waiting there to take the Cluster for King Chance. If they take over Cillian Heights and this base, we're in real trouble."

"If they do that, they can meet the Jutzens in the middle and cut off Anne from all the western territories *and* open a new front in the war," Brad says with a frown. "I've thought a lot about that. But we think Bollen's freighter went in that same direction, toward Linford Commons. What if they're all working together?"

Turly sits back, frowning. "Seriously? You think the SDF and your slavers—this Bollen—are in league with each other?"

My husband nods. "I can't prove it, but I don't like coincidences, and there are far too many of them at play here. A guy like Bollen doesn't just kidnap hundreds of people from a Federation world unless he's sure he can get away with it, and what better way to get away with it than to do it with the support of the largest fleet of warships in the sector?"

The other admiral chews on that for a few moments, as do I.

"Brad," I say to break the tense silence. "I want to find those people from Poe as much as you do, but maybe Admiral Turly is right." I can't believe I just said that. "Our first responsibility has to be to the Federation. We need to figure out a way to stop that SDF fleet at Linford Commons, at least until the queen can send reinforcements."

"Reinforcements aren't coming," my husband says curly, throwing me a look. "The latest reports from the front are . . . Well, let's just say we're not winning. Anne can't afford to send any more forces to the Corpus Christi Cluster right now."

"Did she actually tell you that, or did—" I start to argue, but he cuts me off.

"It's obvious. Hecate has fallen," he says somberly. That statement is like a punch in the gut. Hecate is one of the largest systems in the Federation, and a source of much of our industry. The naval shipyards there are among the largest in the Kingdom as well.

"The Navy lost two task forces trying to hold the system," Brad continues. "Anne has only two fleet carriers left, and no ships to spare. If we're going to stop the Jutzens and King Chance from taking over the Cluster, we're going to have to do it ourselves."

I want to argue with him, but there's an iron in his voice that tells me he's beyond hearing. On the surface, his words make sense, but I've rarely seen Brad as tense as he is right now, so much so that I can feel his muscles clenching next to me in the booth.

"Besides," Brad says, "if I'm right about Bollen and the SDF working together, then either way, our next stop is Linford Commons."

"Okay," Turly says carefully. He may not know Brad as well as I do, but he's clearly picking up on his new boss's intensity. "But with all due respect, sir, we're weeks away from repairing all the damage to our ships. Even then, we'll certainly be outnumbered by whatever the SDF has waiting for us at the Commons. I recommend we fortify our position here and send to the queen for help anyway. Maybe she can spare a single task force, or even a few battleships to—"

"No." Brad's blunt, one-word response makes Turly go red in the face, but he's wise enough not to press the issue. Maybe he's smarter than I've always given him credit for. "We'll find a way, Admiral Turly," Brad continues. "We have to."

A sudden thought comes to my mind. "The Cillian Heights shipyards!" I exclaim, and they both turn squarely to me.

Turly cocks his head to one side. "What about them? I've already ordered a tow ship from there to come and take *Jack's Gambit* and *Vancouver* in for repairs."

I shake my head vigorously, sitting up straighter in the booth's padded seat. "No, I'm talking about the shipyard's mothball fleet."

He looks at me like I'm crazy. Every sector has a mothball fleet, used to store decommissioned ships in a decentralized fashion across the Federation. The original idea was that it would allow for quick refurbishment and reconditioning should the Koratans ever attack—sort of like ready-made fleets in whatever territory the enemy might choose to invade. But after three hundred years of cold war with no large-scale battles, most mothball fleets aren't even maintained anymore, becoming little more than warship graveyards.

"There might be fewer than a dozen usable ships there," Turly argues, "and even those would be horribly out of date. Not to mention we don't have the crews to man them."

"But they *are* working ships," Brad says, catching on to my nascent plan and leaning forward eagerly in his seat. "If we drained this station of resources, we could get some of them up and running with skeleton crews, right?"

The red-haired admiral doesn't look convinced, but he at least pretends to consider things.

"Listen," I say, leaning closer across the table toward Turly as I put a hand on Brad's knee under the table and squeeze. "Sometimes it's less about actual power and more about the appearance of it. Like what Brad did at Poe the first time he went there. If we arrive in the Linford Commons system with a legitimate show of force, even an understaffed and out-of-date one, it might be enough to make the SDF think twice about engaging us. We could drive them out of the system without firing a shot."

Turly still isn't convinced, but Brad takes up the narrative. "It just might work, especially if we can get some intel first on the disposition and placement of forces at the Commons. I could take *Gunslinger*," he says, referencing the surviving Navy battlecruiser, "and we could do a fast recon of the system. Then we'll know what we're up against. We might even be able to find that slave ship's trail while we're at it."

Turly starts to nod slowly. "It's risky, but then so was our little trip to *Liberator*. It could work, I suppose."

"And while I'm gone," Brad continues, "the two of you

can head over to the Cillian Heights shipyards, have them start on the worst of the damage to *Liberator, Bainbridge,* and the other ships, and poke around the mothball fleet to see what we can do with it."

I'm opening my mouth to tell him that I will absolutely *not* be staying here to do anything of the sort while he goes gallivanting off to Linford Commons in a battlecruiser, but he gives my knee a return squeeze under the table in a way that tells me he's pleading for me to hold my arguments for now. Reluctantly, I do.

"Sounds like a plan," Turly says, just as reluctantly.

"Good." Brad sounds more cheerful again. "Then let's get that server back over here and order some food. Battles always make me hungry."

Despite his attempt at humor and his excitement for our new plan, there's an edge to my husband's voice. Something is eating at him, and it must have to do with the thing none of us have mentioned: the way he froze at the beginning of the battle, those few crucial moments that might have doomed us if luck hadn't been on our side.

# FORTY-FOUR
# LOVER'S SPAT

## JESSICA LIN MENDOZA

"Do you want to tell me what that was all about?"

"You're not going with me, Jess. You almost died less than twenty-four hours ago. You're staying here and resting. Doctor's—and admiral's—orders."

I glare at him across the small space of our cabin back on *Bainbridge*, where we finally retired after finalizing plans with Admiral Turly.

Brad doesn't flinch as I give him my best angry look, the one that usually has him preemptively apologizing for half a dozen things he might have done. This time, however, he's not going to back down. Maybe because I realize he's actually right, I slump in surrender. "I don't like the idea of you going to Linford Commons with only one ship."

He steps over to me and wraps me in his arms, and I collapse into him as the fatigue and trauma of the last few days catch up to me all in an instant. My husband gently half carries me over to the couch, lowering me carefully before taking the seat beside me.

"I know, sweetheart," he says softly. "But you and I both know that that *one ship* is a Hermes-class battlecruiser. *Gunslinger* may be damaged, but she's almost as fast as *Bainbridge* and packs an offensive punch only second to *Liberator*. I'm going to be fine."

I want to argue with him more, I really do, but I just sit there, burying my head in his shoulder and doing my best not to cry. This is all so much, and the thought of him leaving fills me with a dread I can't put into words. Why does the galaxy seem so intent on constantly separating us?

Worse, I know there's something majorly wrong with Brad, even if he tries to hide it from me. If I'm not there to help him work through it, whatever it is, then the next time he freezes in battle could be his last.

Despite all of that, he's right. I'm in no condition to go with him, and if he's going to do this, then taking *Gunslinger* gives him his best chance at survival. And, as much as he and I are married, in matters of the Navy, he is still my superior officer.

He puts his arms around me and pats me lightly on the back, careful not to hold me too tightly given my injuries. "I'll come back," he whispers. "That's a promise."

It's not a promise he can make, but the words lighten the weight on my soul regardless. "Just don't do anything stupid," I mumble, my head still buried in his chest.

"That eliminates pretty much every strategy in my playbook," he says, "but okay. For you, I'll be smart about it."

He gently disengages us and holds me at arm's length on the couch so he can look me in the eye. "I need you here, Jess, not just to heal, but to get those mothballed ships up and running. Turly and I may be on better terms now, but he's too naturally cautious. He doesn't have the kind of experience you and I have of making the impossible work. I'm going to leave him with orders putting you in charge of the efforts to get those ships back in service as quickly as possible. Can you do that?"

I nod, because I know this isn't some sort of consolation for leaving me behind. This is Brad putting his trust in me. He needs me to do this for him. "I'll do it. You can count on me."

He smiles. "I never doubt that. Take Kelly with you; if anyone can figure out how to restore a broken-down old ship, it's him. He can leave Lieutenant Vargas in charge of repairs to *Bainbridge* with the yard monkeys."

I nod. "Aye, aye, sir." Then, maybe because of the fatigue or stress of the last several days, I bring up the topic I've been avoiding in the least thoughtful way possible. "What happened during the battle? Why did you freeze, Brad?"

My question catches him off guard, and he looks at me in confusion. Then he swallows and seems to deflate, shrinking in size. "I don't know what you're talking about," he says lamely.

"Don't do that, Brad," I say, trying to pull him toward me, to close the distance between us. "Don't shut me out. Talk to me."

He gets up abruptly, moving around the coffee table to stand on the other side of the small room, his back to me. "I was just double-checking the formations."

"Brad, please don't do this. Talk to me," I repeat. "I'm your wife right now, not your XO or another officer. Your *wife*. Please tell me what's going on with you." Tears spring to my eyes.

He doesn't answer, still refusing to even *look* at me. The tears are running down my cheeks now.

"I'm fine," he says after far too long a pause. "It was nothing."

His dismissal turns my despair into anger faster than a

reactor going critical. I practically leap to my feet, my legs receiving sudden strength, and I glare at him so hard he seems to sense it as he turns to face me.

"Brad, stop being like this. I know you've been having nightmares about Bellerophon. I know you think you're not up to this, but you are. You just need to stop lying to yourself and to me. I can *help* you. Let me help you."

The last I say in a pleading voice, but his face turns to stone as he turns and glares right back at me. "You're wrong, Jess. This has *nothing* to do with Bellerophon. Don't you ever bring that place up again!"

I flinch back at the vehemence in his tone. His eyes bore into mine, and I can see that we've both crossed a line. But I'm too upset to moderate my own words and tone. "How dare you lie to me!" I snap. "I'm your wife, Brad. And your XO. Did you ever lie to your XO on *Lancer*? Would you ever have even considered it? So why do you insist on lying to me?"

My words aren't sinking in, and Brad's face turns red. I have the fleeting thought that what I'm seeing might be shame instead of anger, but it's a quiet thought, and it doesn't gain purchase. I'm pissed, and not just because I think he froze at the beginning of the battle or because he's refusing to talk to me.

No, I'm pissed mostly because I know I'm not helping the situation. But in the exhaustion and heat of the moment, my mouth is moving faster than my brain. Which is why I don't stop myself from saying the next words to come out of it, even though I instantly know they're wrong.

"Brad, it's time for you to be an admiral. Stop running away from responsibility. The queen needs us. And you need to stop being a coward."

I desperately wish I could take back the words. But before I can, my husband's face turns completely impassive, and he whirls, flinging the hatch open and leaving our quarters. I try to go after him, but the sudden movement to get up from the couch did something to the wounds in my chest and shoulder, and I'm suddenly having a hard time breathing. Unwillingly, I slump back to the couch, using my implant to call Doc Bean to the cabin, my vision blurred with tears.

# FORTY-FIVE
# PHANTOMS

## BRAD MENDOZA

Suddenly, *Bainbridge*, my home for the last five and a half months, feels oppressively small. Before I know it, I'm through the airlock and back on Huff Naval Base, walking quickly through the station's corridors, my mind spinning in circles.

Jess is right. I *am* a coward. Maybe I've always been one. Maybe it was my cowardice that made me fire on that refugee ship at Bellerophon in the first place, hiding behind standard operating procedures when the *Cumberland* failed to respond to my hails or deviate from its collision course with Bellerophon Station. Perhaps if I'd been just a little more willing to take a risk, I could have saved those 504 refugees rather than inflicted death upon them.

My wife may not know it, but she just drove home why I can never go back to Annie's fleet. Because at some crucial moment, when we can least afford it, I'll screw up, just like I did then, and just like I did in the battle this morning with the SDF. Next time it happens, rather than hundreds or even thousands, it may be millions who pay the price of my cowardice.

As my thoughts spin out of control, I'm not paying attention to where I'm going, so I'm surprised when I find myself on the station's command level. Returning the salute of two Marines guarding the entryway to the command center, I step through.

Commander Chelly Lund looks up from where she's studying a console over the shoulder of a senior enlisted man. "Admiral on deck," she calls out, snapping to attention as the others do the same.

I wave them down. "As you were."

"How may I assist you, Admiral?" she asks as she relaxes marginally. "I was unaware you'd be on board the station this evening."

The meaning behind her words is clear. My presence here, in the middle of the station's night shift, especially without any warning, is both unexpected and frankly disruptive. You might think that an admiral could go anywhere he pleases at any time and without anyone's permission. He can, but that doesn't mean he should.

"Map room?" I ask.

She nods toward a hatch off to one side of the command center. "Do you need any assistance, sir?"

I shake my head, making my way across the deck toward the indicated door. "No, thank you, Commander. I can handle things."

A moment later, I'm alone in the map room, the hatch shut behind me. The compartment is shaped like a cylinder. On the curved walls are flexible viewscreens that create a mostly uninterrupted image of the space surrounding the station. In the middle of the compartment is a flat table with an interactive surface.

Connecting my implant to the room's AI controller, I have it call up a map of the Corpus Christi Cluster. I look hard at the location of Cillian Heights, and three jumps away, Linford Commons, where the SDF is marshalling its forces and where I'm increasingly convinced that Andre Bollen may have taken those three hundred slaves from Poe. I study the map for way too long, as if staring at the systems and stars involved might somehow make them yield their secrets.

My implant pings, and I see it's Jess trying to reach me. I reject the call and instruct my implant to ignore further comms from her until I tell it differently.

Ironically, this is our first major fight since being together as a couple. Sure, we've disagreed on things since professing our love for one another, but we've never had a fight where either of us *purposefully* tried to wound the other.

It brings with it flashbacks to my final months with Carla, when I was trying my best to drink myself into an early grave and she was trying to make sense of why I was shutting her out. Those arguments culminated in first me finding her in bed with Horace Clarrington, and then in our bitter divorce, expedited through the courts because her father, the fleet admiral, was gleefully applying pressure to the judge to make it so.

I have the sudden mental image of the judge's chambers, where my marriage to Carla ended in a shouting match. But instead of Carla, I see Jess there, telling the judge all about how I've let her down—and not just her, but our crew, the Navy, and the queen.

Almost unbidden, my mind sends the command to the map room to zoom out to show the entirety of the Promethean Federation, overlayed with the latest maps from Naval Intelligence. Three distinct territories trisect the map, each shaded in a different color: red for the Jutzen-occupied systems, green for those held by Queen Anne, and blue for those with either uncertain or unestablished allegiances. Another command, and roughly half those blue areas turn orange, indicating that Naval Intelligence feels they're on the verge of going over to the puppet government of King Chance.

The Corpus Christi Cluster, of course, is bright orange, updated as such by Turly's intel people.

My eyes wander over the map, pointedly avoiding a spot in the southeast quadrant of the Federation, until they can no longer do so. When they alight on that portion of space, another orange system makes me stop and focus in.

Bellerophon. Where my old life ended. Where I learned that I was not, in fact, the good commander, officer, and man I'd always thought myself to be. Where I learned that Terrence 'Terrible' Oliphant had been right: I was just a kid masquerading as a ship's captain, and 504 innocent lives had to be lost for me to finally realize what everyone else had seen all along: I was—*am*—a fraud.

Annie doesn't need me. My queen needs me as far away from her command structure as possible. *Maybe* I could have rejoined her fleet as a ship's captain, my old rank. Maybe I could have been trusted with a single ship again; after all, I've learned and grown since Bellerophon. But as an *admiral*? No way.

I lied to Jess. *Gunslinger* doesn't need me aboard to do recon in Linford Commons. Captain Quarrie could do the mission just as easily without me. But I need to get away—I need some space away from my wife, my crew, and my responsibilities over the fleet. And I *need* to find those slaves. That Poe got hit was my fault as much as Bellerophon was. Whoever Andre Bollen is, he's obviously decided he wants to lure me into his web. I just wish so many innocents didn't need to suffer for him to do it.

In this moment, I make myself a solemn promise: I will find Andre Bollen, I will kill him, whoever he is, and I will rescue those he's abducted from Poe and anywhere else along the way. Then I'll surrender my rank and command and go back to doing what I do best, which is operating as a mercenary with one ship and a small crew.

I shove aside the thoughts that eat at the edges of my consciousness, that my wife might not follow me back into that life.

I turn and stride out of the map room. "Commander Lund," I say as I emerge back in the command center.

"Aye, Admiral?"

"Is my aide already on board *Gunslinger*?"

Her eyes go out of focus as she checks the logs. "Aye, sir. She transferred your prisoner to the battlecruiser three hours ago and is awaiting your arrival there."

I nod. "Good. Contact Captain Quarrie. Tell her I'll be arriving shortly. And instruct her that I'm pulling the mission timeline earlier. *Gunslinger* should be ready to set sail by 0500."

"On it, sir. Anything else?"

I stop and nod at her. "There is. Please send a runner to *Bainbridge* for my footlocker. I won't be returning to my ship prior to the mission."

It took six years of marriage for Carla to finally realize that I'm a fraud. I'm terrified that Jess may learn it much sooner than that.

# PART THREE
# RECONNAISANCE

## FORTY-SIX
# MOTHBALLS

### JESSICA LIN MENDOZA

"What do you think?"

Kelly O'Malley shakes his head inside his bubble helmet as he withdraws himself from a floor-level panel, crawling on all fours. "She's a no-go, Captain," he says sullenly through our vacsuit comms.

"We're alone, Kelly. You can call me Jessica."

He snorts. "Sure. Anyway, half the control lines are just missing. My guess is some yard monkey salvaged them for parts. Without those lines, this battleship is basically a floating slamball. There's no way she's getting underway anytime soon."

"We can't just replace the lines?" I ask hopefully.

He snorts again as I help him up to his feet. "Sure. But in a Kronos-class, those lines are over a kilometer long. Finding that much unused line that can handle a battleship's reactor loads is one thing; installing it takes a dedicated crew weeks of yard time. If you want, mark this one up as a very distant maybe, but we haven't even checked engineering yet. For all we know, the reactor housing could be cracked, or worse."

I try my level best not to let his words drag me down even more. The fight with Brad is still fresh in my mind, as is the fact that he moved up the timetable for *Gunslinger*'s departure without so much as a message to me—no, *ignoring* the many, many calls and messages I sent to him.

For the first few hours, I was pissed at him for walking out on me and then refusing to take my calls. After that, I was mostly upset at myself. I cannot believe I called my husband a coward. With all we've been through, I *know* that's anything but true. But I had to go open my dumb mouth and say it anyway. I could use the trauma of my injuries or the adrenaline crash after the battle as excuses, but the bottom line is, all of us still have a responsibility to be decent human beings, even in our weakest moments.

My last few calls to Brad after that realization were attempts to apologize. I even tried to find him on the station and went so far as to stake out the docking airlock where *Gunslinger* was waiting. But he must have already been on board, because I never saw him before the battlecruiser undocked and went on its way, burning toward the first jump point en route to Linford Commons.

Now, more than twenty-four hours later, I have even more reason to be upset. For the last day, against doctor's advice but fueled by caffeine, shame, anger, and painkillers, I've been crawling through the guts of old ships with no atmo, only to find that the prognosis is *not* good. Along with Turly's engineers, Kelly and I have thus far only identified five mothballed ships that are battleworthy with no repairs or refurbishment required: two battlecruisers, two light cruisers, and a destroyer. We've already sent those off with skeleton crews to Huff Naval Base for resupply and rearming. But the rest . . .

There are seven decommissioned battleships in the mothball fleet, and so far we've checked four of them with no luck. If the state of those is any indication, we're unlikely to find a miracle hidden among the final three.

"There's got to be something we can do," I growl in frustration. "Brad was right; we don't need to have every ship necessarily ready to fight. We just need to look scary enough to send the SDF running away with its tail between its legs."

It physically pains me right now to talk about Brad, but if Kelly notices the tremble in my voice at my husband's name, he at least has the decency to pretend not to.

He sighs and shakes his head again inside his helmet. "I know, Jessica. But we're not talking broken weapons or auxiliary systems. One of the battleships has no functioning life support. Two have no artificial gravity or inertial compensators. This one has no control lines. I wouldn't trust these things to fly us from here to Huff, much less through three jumps to Linford Commons."

I return his sigh. "Well, then we'll have to hope the last three are in better shape." Sure. I believe it as much as he does.

Then an idea hits me. "Kelly, those two battleships with no grav or compensators, can they fly?"

He looks at me oddly. "Sure, I guess, but unless we kept the acceleration under a few g's, they'd kill anyone on board."

"What if there wasn't anyone on board?"

Cocking his head to one side inside his helmet, he studies me like I've gone insane, but I see the moment he realizes what I'm getting at. "Jessica, the AIs can't fight the ship; they can load or launch any weapons. All they can do is fly the ship, and that only with very specific orders and a flag-level override."

"The orders and overrides we can supply," I tell him with a growing smile. "And like I said, we don't need them to fight, just to look scary."

He starts nodding slowly. "And few things look scarier than a battleship."

"Exactly."

# FORTY-SEVEN
# A NEW SHIP AND CREW

## BRAD MENDOZA

"Admiral on the bridge."

I stride onto *Gunslinger*'s bridge, nodding to Captain Risa Quarrie, a trim Black woman in her early forties who runs as efficient a ship as I've ever been on. And it is quite a ship. *Gunslinger* is a Hermes-class battlecruiser, just like my old command, HMS *Lancer*, and the resemblance is uncanny. In fact, I can nearly believe I'm back on my old ship until something subtly different—like the color of the wall in my shower—jars me back to the reality that I'm effectively a visitor on someone else's command.

That's undoubtedly a good thing given what happened the last time I was on *Lancer*.

Already seated on the bridge is Hayley Uvalde, prim and proper in her fake ensign's uniform, playing the role of my aide. Since no one but Chris Turly saw her in action back on *Liberator*—no one who survived, at least—we're able to continue to pass her off as a simple, young Promethean officer, and not a deadly Koratan assassin with multiple eccentric personalities. It's got to be killing her to keep a low profile, with that drab brown hair and gray eyes, rarely speaking lest her accent peek through.

Captain Quarrie waits until I sit in the observer's chair before settling into her command chair next to me. "We're about to exit the jump point into Linford Commons, sir," she tells me. "We're ready for trouble, even if we're not necessarily expecting pickets at the jump point."

I nod my appreciation. Risa Quarrie is my kind of officer, far more focused on doing her job well than playing the political game many senior officers find themselves overly embroiled in. She has attempted to suck up to me exactly zero times in the two and a half days I've been on her battlecruiser as we've transited three jump points and two intermediary systems to get to our destination.

As a result, we've fallen into an easy professional rhythm. Of course, I've had to moderate the more colorful aspects of my personality. Vice admiral or not, I get the feeling Captain Quarrie wouldn't appreciate me cracking jokes on the bridge or in the wardroom. So it's been a little boring, but it's also surprised me how easily I've fallen back into old Navy habits.

It almost worries me. In some ways, it's nearly as if the last sixteen months since Bellerophon never happened. But at least the familiar patterns have helped occupy my mind. Except each night, in my bunk, when I lie awake, Jess's final words to me running on repeat through my mind. And when I finally fall asleep, the nightmares return.

"Helm, be ready to take evasive maneuvers if we detect anyone waiting when we emerge from jump space," Quarrie orders across the bridge, snapping me out of the beginnings of another self-pity spiral. "Weapons, how are we looking?"

"All tubes loaded with a fifty-fifty loadout, ma'am. Defensive and offensive clusters are at full charge."

I smile my approval. It's somewhat of a faux pas to enter a supposedly 'friendly' system loaded for bear, but Quarrie insisted upon it. She argued that we could no longer consider Linford Commons to be all that friendly. If she hadn't, I would have ordered her to do so anyway, but it's nice when you don't have to overtly exert your authority.

"Exiting in thirty seconds," the navigation officer calls out. On smaller ships, like *Bainbridge*, the helm covers nav functions as well. But on a queen's battlecruiser, there's room for a separate station, and the young senior lieutenant who fills the chair is as efficient as her boss.

We watch the countdown on the main forward viewscreen, and when it reaches zero, the gray of the void outside the ship gives way in a flash to the stars of normal space and the Linford Commons system.

Linford Commons is an extremely rare inhabited binary system. While binary systems aren't all that uncommon—a decent number of systems have two stars orbiting each other—what *is* rare is for one to have worlds capable of supporting life. It would make the place a tourist attraction if it weren't in the middle of nowhere in the obscure Corpus Christi Cluster. There's a running joke in the Navy that the only reason Koratas never invaded the Cluster was because no one in their right mind would want it. I've always disagreed—a habitable world is a habitable world, and any place humans can live has some value. Except for that mud planet where we rescued Koratan President Nanette Fournier last month—no one should *ever* want to live there.

"Scanning the system, Captain. No contacts so far."

"Thank you, Lieutenant Commander," Quarrie says to her sensor officer. "Comms, what does traffic look like?"

"Normal, ma'am. No sign of conflict and no overabundance of military-level encryption. I'm getting signals from a few SDF ships patrolling near the fifth planet, but nothing else strong enough to distinguish from here. Though at our current speed, I'm likely missing quite a few signals."

Quarrie nods. When entering a hostile system, it's standard operating procedure to first accelerate to a significant portion of the speed of light. We helped that along by using a gas giant in the previous system for a slingshot maneuver, hitting the jump point at speed so we'd emerge in the Commons at the same velocity.

This way, no one could reasonably hit us with any weapons when we entered the Commons, even had they been waiting for us at the jump point. It's the reason most defense fleets cluster around inhabited planets or patrol near mining stations rather than try to guard the constantly moving jump points. Only systems with large fleets, like Prometheus, try to guard the jump points, because they have plenty of backup if someone tries what we're doing and gets past the first line of defense.

The downside to this approach is that the faster we're moving, the harder it is to pick up on comm signals and get sensor readings. It has something to do with relativity, even though we're moving at a painfully small percentage of lightspeed. Still, we could have conceivably flown right by a few enemy ships at the jump point and not seen them.

"Execute turnover and bleed velocity," Quarrie orders. "Active sensors on full; they're going to see us regardless of what we do. Let's make sure we see them first."

That's how this entire journey has been: calm professionalism, reasonable tactics, and efficient operations. No one has shot at me, tried to stab me, attempted to arrest me, or make me save a head of state yet on this trip. And no one I love has called me a coward.

I'm not mad at Jess. Not exactly. Because, as hurtful as her words were, she was absolutely right. I realized it in the map room back at Huff Naval Base. I *am* a coward, running from duty with Annie's fleet way out here in the Cluster. But I have good reason to be scared: I don't want to be the reason Annie loses the war, and I know I would be, because she would put far too much trust in me. I would inevitably let her and everyone else down.

This is the problem with space travel over such astronomic distances: it gives you far too much time alone with your thoughts.

*Gunslinger* burns off enough of her speed over the next few hours for us to start getting usable sensor readings at long range. We slowly start to get a picture of what's happening here in the system.

Like Chris thought, the SDF has an entire task force here: seventeen ships that we can see, anchored by two massive battleships. Both are the older Kronos-class—King Charles never let system defense fleets have the latest and greatest hardware—but those are enough to single-handedly destroy the entire small sector fleet we have back at Cillian Heights.

The good news, if there is any, is that the SDF ships are spread across the system. A small task group of just four ships is burning hard in our direction and will reach us in a few hours if we don't head back to the jump point soon. But the rest are too far away to make a difference. Several are in orbit around the planet Linford itself, and the others are at various points around the system. Some we only determine are there from comm chatter, as they're too far away for us to see them with our sensors.

"Admiral, time to send your packets?" Quarrie asks from beside me.

"Make it happen," I tell her.

At her command, the comm officer sends the several prerecorded messages I put together en route to the system.

These messages are aimed at completing my secondary mission: finding Andre Bollen and the three hundred slaves from Poe.

Some of the messages are meant for the commander of those SDF forces, both demanding any information they have on the slave trade in the area in general or Andre Bollen in particular, and warning them to stand down to the legitimate authority of Queen Anne over this system—I don't expect positive responses to either, but I have to try. Other messages are meant for the planetary government, the system patrol, the local Navy office—little more than a recruiting center on the planet's surface—and even the Girl Scouts. I want to leave no stone unturned in the short time we have here. All of the messages ask for any information on the freighter we saw fleeing Poe and anyone named Andre Bollen.

It's the equivalent of a hunter throwing stones into a bush to startle a flock of birds, and I'm hoping we bag at least one trophy before we leave this system to return to Cillian Heights. Assuming I'm right about this being the slave freighter's destination, *someone* saw that freighter enter the system—maybe even saw where it went. We just have to hope they're willing to talk to us.

## FORTY-EIGHT
# INGENUITY

### JESSICA LIN MENDOZA

"This should work."

Kelly O'Malley wipes dust off his hands and looks over at me and Admiral Turly with a smile to punctuate his words. Behind us in a loose, floating semicircle are senior engineers from across Turly's fleet. Almost to a person, they were skeptical when we first presented our plan to turn mothballed warships into drones. Kelly and I decided the best way to overcome their doubts was to stage a demonstration.

We're currently on the bridge of one of the mothballed Kronos-class battleships, HMS *Excalibur*, one of the ships with no working gravity or inertial compensators.

"Everyone hold on to something," Kelly admonishes, and we all push off the various stations we've been clinging to and find handholds against the rear bulkhead. My chief engineer then opens a comm channel. "*Vancouver*, we're ready for the test."

For a moment, nothing happens, and I can imagine the command crew of the destroyer *Vancouver*, stuck in a shipyard slip for repairs to its battle damage, nervously checking and rechecking every step of Kelly's improvised process. Then, slowly at first but with growing thrust, *Excalibur* starts to accelerate.

Without the inertial compensators, and even at less than 1 percent drive power, the move presses us all against the rear bulkhead.

"*Vancouver*," Kelly says after a minute, "change course to oh-four-one mark neg two and ramp thrust to 1.2 percent."

This time the change is much faster, and the massive battleship fires its thrusters to turn the nose onto its new course and then increases acceleration, causing one of Turly's engineers to lose his grip on his handhold and tumble across the curved bulkhead before he manages to catch himself on a support joist.

"That's good, *Vancouver*," Kelly finishes. "Fire retros to zero relative to the shipyard."

This time, we all grip our holds more tightly as the battleship's retrothrusters, located in the bow and designed for use at lower speeds, ease *Excalibur* to a stop.

When the thrusters cut out and zero-g returns, I turn my body to face Turly's engineers. Four of the six are smiling broadly, and the other two are wide-eyed in disbelief.

"So, ladies and gentlemen," I say with a grin I can't help, "are we ready to execute Operation Marionette?"

The nearest engineer starts nodding, and the move spreads to the others down the line. Satisfied that we've overcome any skepticism, Kelly and I start laying out the specifics of the operation, giving each of the engineers their assignments and then dismissing them to go work with their people.

Kelly, too, takes his leave, and I'm alone with Admiral Turly.

"What happens if the enemy knows exactly what we're doing?" he asks when Kelly is far enough down the corridor to the docking bay and the shuttle waiting there to not overhear us.

"You think Bollen and the SDF have spies here?" I ask with raised eyebrows.

"Don't you?"

I nod. "Even if we had managed to root out all the Chance loyalists from your fleet, there are enough civilian contractors at the shipyard who are likely sympathetic to the occupation government and the SDF. As far as Bollen goes, he seems to have the uncanny ability to have people waiting for us at every port of call, so I have zero doubt he will know soon what we're doing."

"Then why do it?" he asks. "I thought the point was to trick the SDF into thinking our fleet is bigger than it is."

"Two things," I tell him, speaking slowly, letting the words out only after running them through multiple mental filters. If I do this wrong, Turly could attempt to axe the entire project, and I cannot risk that. "First, even if the SDF and Bollen think they know what we're doing, they'll have to be wondering if we have another trick up our sleeves. And second, Brad Mendoza destroyed a Jutzen dreadnought with a single bomb and an unarmed spy ship. I find that if we give Brad the tools and the options to use them, he'll find a way to do so that surprises all of us."

Turly chews on that for a moment and then, to my relief, nods appraisingly. "He does have the infuriating habit of winning against impossible odds, doesn't he?"

"That he does."

"But by all accounts, so do you," he adds, and I feel myself blushing slightly. "Don't sell yourself short, Captain Lin. You forget that I served with Brad before he met you. He was always resourceful and a force to be reckoned with, but even from our short few days together here, he and you together form the kind of potent combination that could take over the Fringe if you set your minds to it."

Before I can think of a response to that, he turns and pushes himself out of the bridge and into the corridor beyond. Feeling an oddly warm glow in my chest, I follow him.

# FORTY-NINE
# UNLIKELY HELP

## BRAD MENDOZA

Four hours after sending my messages across the system, we have exactly nothing new. No one has replied in any helpful way, beyond the Girl Scouts offering me a deal on Thin Mints. A bulk discount of only eighteen thousand credits for five thousand boxes would be enough to make our entire fleet happy, and I'm severely annoyed that we don't have time to stop by the inhabited planet and pick some up. Being the shrewd negotiators that they are, the Girl Scouts set a one-day expiration date on the offer and assured me that they'll be unlikely to offer as good a deal the next time I come through Linford Commons.

By now, we've used a rocky planet just inside Linford Commons' asteroid belt to turn without bleeding too much velocity, and we're burning back toward the jump point through which we entered the system. The closest SDF task group is accelerating hard to meet us there, but the latest numbers show we'll beat them by four hours.

Unfortunately, that gives us no margin for error. If we don't hear back from anyone about Bollen's freighter by the time we hit the jump point, we're out of luck. It eats away at me, because even if we succeed in returning in a week or two to liberate this system, it will be too late for those poor souls he took from Poe.

More time passes, and as we draw closer to the jump point, I grab a short nap on the ready room couch. Two hours out from our planned exit, I'm back on the bridge with Quarrie, frowning at our imminent failure in what to me was the most important part of our mission.

"Admiral, we've got something."

I perk up and leave my chair to practically jog over to the comm station. "What is it, Lieutenant?"

The young man on duty pulls up what looks like a garbled transmission. "It's a response to one of your data packets, heavily encrypted. Code looks . . . Koratan, sir."

I suppress a little squeak of joy. This was the last and final message I sent, and perhaps the longest shot of them all. Linford Commons isn't a particularly important system, but for some unknowable reason, the Koratans long ago decided to put a small consulate here. Maybe it's because there used to be an earl of some reputation here, before he died of heart trouble, though there's always been some tabloid rumors about him still being alive somewhere.

Either way, using the authorization codes Nanette Fournier shared with me when I saved her life, I sent a Hail Mary message to the Koratan Consulate on the Linford's surface, and the inevitable intelligence agents assigned there, and it looks like they actually replied.

"Sir, I can't decrypt this," the comm officer says,

chagrined. "I don't have the latest Koratan encryption schemas."

I smile and pat him on the shoulder. "Just send it to my implant, Lieutenant."

"Of course, sir. Done." He gives me a questioning look, but I ignore it.

I catch Quarrie's eye and motion toward her ready room, where I shut the hatch behind us.

"Can you decrypt that message, sir?" she asks.

"Sort of," I say, quickly sending it over to Hayley. She pings back the plain text a moment later.

I grin at Quarrie's confused expression, as she's oblivious to the messages between me and my friendly neighborhood Koratan intelligence officer and assassin.

"And what does the message say, pray tell?" the captain asks, clearly intrigued.

"Four words, Captain."

"Only four, sir?"

I can understand her skepticism, especially given the source. I may trust the Koratans these days about as much as I trust the average Promethean—which isn't a whole lot—but she's only known them as the enemy for her entire life.

"Sixth planet, third moon," I tell her.

"I'm not sure I understand, Admiral."

I shake my head and sigh in exasperation. "Come on, Captain. They're telling us where to look for that freighter, or Bollen, or both."

She keeps frowning. "Sir, how can you be sure of that?"

"Easy. Let's scan the third-largest moon of the sixth planet and see what there is to see."

Quarrie shakes her head. "Admiral, the sixth planet is way out in the outer system, beyond the jump points and well out of sensor range. It's a full quarter turn around the system from us right now as well. We'd have to change course, burn right past our exit jump, and spend a day traversing the outer system the long way to even get within range. That gives the SDF fleet all the time in the galaxy to cut off our escape route. There's no way we can make it all work."

"Yes, we can," I argue, grinning at her.

She studies me for a moment, still frowning like my mother used to when I lied that I'd already fed the cat because I didn't want to pause my video game. Quarrie shakes her head slowly. "Why, sir, do I get the impression I'm going to hate whatever plan you've come up with?"

I keep grinning. "Oh, Captain, I think you might actually like it." It's the first mirth I've felt since leaving Jess after our fight three days ago.

# FIFTY
# THE FINAL TALLY

## JESSICA LIN MENDOZA

"Twenty-five ships isn't all that bad," Christoph Turly says with a half smile as we review the latest numbers in the shipyard's command center.

"Even if only thirteen of them can fight?" I ask.

He nods. "I'm trusting Admiral Mendoza, just as you suggested. Besides, having *Adjudicator* alone almost doubles our offensive punch."

That draws a smile out of me. *Adjudicator* was the last of the mothballed battleships we checked, and we were surprised to find it almost entirely spaceworthy and battle-ready. Of course, staffing it with its normal crew of two thousand is a nonstarter—we don't have that many to spare—but by careful movement of crews and Marines across the fleet, it has a large enough skeleton crew to put up a fight. It's amazing how many shipboard functions aren't truly necessary when you don't need to do any maintenance because you only need the ship to last for a week.

In addition to *Adjudicator,* we found three operational battlecruisers and a variety of escorts. Then there are the twelve drone ships we've set up as part of Operation Marionette, each of their flight controls slaved to multiple other ships in our fleet, so even if we lose some of our operational ships, we can keep making those drones fly. Two of them are even battleships, including *Excalibur,* so I'm pretty happy all told.

"Will they be ready in time?" Turly asks the third member of our group.

Kelly nods. "*Adjudicator* needs a lot of work, and only about two-thirds of her weapons are operational. But give me a few days, and I'll have her and the others ready to fight. The drones were the easy part."

"How are the repairs to the Huff fleet coming along?" I ask Turly.

He perks up a bit. "The damage was lighter than we initially thought on *Liberator.* Crews worked through the nights and got most of the hull breaches already sealed. Another forty-eight hours, and she'll be spaceworthy with about 85 percent of her weapons operational. Two weeks and we can fix most of the remaining damage."

Unfortunately, we all know we're unlikely to have two weeks. Whether we go to them or they come to us, I can't imagine the SDF fleet at Linford Commons is going to take the destruction of their task group at Huff sitting down. They'll force the battle sooner than we're ready for it, assuming they're not already on their way.

Regardless of the tight timelines, things are looking up, and we'll be ready to hand Brad quite a toolset when he returns from his recon mission, assuming . . .

I don't let myself go down that line of thought. Brad is resourceful; there's little chance the SDF will ambush him and keep him from coming back to us—to me. But the worry remains, as does the echo of our last conversation.

*Come back to me, Brad,* I keep thinking. *Come back.*

# FIFTY-ONE
# THE MAILMAN

## BRAD MENDOZA

Two hours after the message from the Koratans, we enter the jump point. In a flash of light, *Gunslinger* disappears from the sensors of the pursuing SDF ships.

Or, at least, that's the idea. The moment our battlecruiser hits the otherwise unremarkable stretch of space that is your typical jump point, we do *not* engage our jump drive.

Being an admiral is turning out to be extremely useful in some instances. For example, the moment Annie entered my promotion in the Navy's systems, my implant was updated with a series of new blockchain IDs. These IDs, to my delight, prove to be a sort of backdoor into many Promethean systems and operations across Federation space.

Unfortunately, transmitting those codes to the local system command was the first thing I tried when we arrived in Linford Commons. Not surprisingly, they'd already reprogrammed their system to block them all soundly, sending me API error messages in thinly veiled language that made it clear it was no error at all. But while they may have locked down command, defensive, and even information systems against my codes, they forgot the mail.

The courier ship network is truly one of humanity's biggest boons. Dedicated small ships—little more than a jump drive and a computer core—some manned but most automated, sit at the entrance and exit to nearly every jump point between inhabited human systems. On a fixed schedule, often multiple times a day, they enter the jump point and travel to the next system, taking with them mail, messages, and updates to the Internet. Then they ingest the same via comm signals from across their destination system and head right back home with the new data.

The system, as rudimentary as it may seem, has managed to keep humanity's far-flung colonies on the same relative page in terms of general knowledge for thousands of years. One can know that it's only a matter of time before your local system's Internet contains all the updates from the surrounding systems, and even from the core worlds, like Earth. It's remarkable how well it all works.

It's also what is going to make our recon of Bollen's possible location possible. Because whoever programmed blocks against my command codes in Linford Commons forgot to update the local courier ship's programming. Why would they? It's just a harmless mail carrier.

Except that with my codes, I'm able to take full control of that harmless mail carrier, and the flash that the SDF fleet saw was *not* Gunslinger entering jump space—it was the courier ship, jumping at precisely the same moment that our battlecruiser reached the jump point, cut its engines, and turned over to put the bow and bulk of the ship between our hot drive nozzles and the thermal sensors of that enemy armada.

"Did it work?" Commander Jonathan Smith—Quarrie's XO has the most boring, vanilla name I've ever heard—whispers, as if the SDF might somehow hear us.

"We'll know in fifteen minutes," Quarrie chides. That's the amount of time it will take the light of our fake jump to reach the SDF, and the light of their reaction to it to reach us.

The minutes count down as sweat forms on my brow. If this works, the SDF will think we left the system. If it doesn't, and they see through the ruse, we'll never be able to reverse thrust and reach the safety of the jump point in time to evade them. They'll hunt us through the outer system until we run out of fuel or make it to another jump point, driving us far away from Jess, Chris, and our support back in Cillian Heights.

It's a huge gamble, but the other advantage of being an admiral is that I didn't have to fully convince Quarrie of the wisdom of my plan. I only had to *mostly* convince her, then bridge the gap with a direct order.

"Ensign," I call over to Hayley, who jumps up from an auxiliary weapons station at the bridge's rear and scurries over to me.

"Yes, Admiral," she says, doing a passable job of hiding her Koratan accent.

"Head down to the galley and see if they have any ice cream," I tell her, and she's gone before even acknowledging my order.

Quarrie and Smith look at me in confusion.

I smile. "We're holding on to our waste heat so those SDF ships don't see us on thermals. It's going to get really hot in here. I find that ice cream helps."

"Are you suggesting we eat ice cream on the bridge of a warship in a combat situation, sir?" Quarrie asks, sounding scandalized, her voice rising high enough to draw worried glances from around the bridge.

I raise my voice to address all of them. "Folks, let me tell you about the time I played cat and mouse with a Koratan Scimitar class four jumps away from their capital planet, and came within five thousand kilometers of them without the Kories even knowing I was there, all while having an ice cream *party* on my destroyer's bridge."

It's a terrific story, and by the time I'm done telling it, the temperature in the bridge has risen noticeably, but I can see smiles all around, including—to my surprise—from Quarrie herself.

Just then, Hayley returns, leading several confused cook's mates pushing carts laden with ice cream and toppings. As they start to serve the sweet, frozen treat, there's a cry of triumph from the sensor station.

"Admiral. Captain. They're turning over!"

"Some decorum, please, Lieutenant Commander Behr," Quarrie lightly rebukes the woman, but by the small smile on her own face, I can see she shares the younger officer's relief.

"Well done, Admiral," she says. "I honestly didn't think they'd fall for that."

"No one ever suspects the mailman," I say as Hayley brings me a bowl of chocolate ice cream with rainbow sprinkles. "Now we just have to stay off their sensors until we can see what's happening at that sixth planet and get back to the jump point with our intel. Easy."

Quarrie scoffs and shakes her head, accepting a bowl of ice cream from a cook's mate. She catches me watching. "Yes, Admiral? Can I help you?"

"Rainbow sherbert and strawberry syrup?" I say with awe. "No offense, Captain, but I would have figured you more for vanilla with a side of regulations and procedures."

For the first time since I've met Risa Quarrie, she laughs, startling several of the bridge crew. Then, to my continued shock, she winks at me. "I think you'll find I have hidden depths, Admiral."

Next to her, Commander Smith chokes on his first bite of rocky road and breaks into a fit of hacking coughs. More smiles break out across the bridge.

I grin back at Quarrie. "Captain, I really think I would. Have you ever considered dating an ex-Marine? There's a gunnery sergeant I'd really like to introduce you to when we get back to Cillian Heights."

"Married, sir."

"Well, pardon my saying so, but he's a lucky man."

She nods. "I keep telling him that, sir. And pardon my saying so, but you're a lucky man as well. Captain Lin is quite something. I admire the way she helms that destroyer."

I nod, but then give her a confused look. "Wait, aren't you supposed to say something like she's a lucky woman to have married me? I gave you a compliment, so . . ."

Picking up her bowl of rainbow-colored ice cream, she smirks at me. "I said what I said, Admiral."

# FIFTY-TWO
# FINALLY!

## BRAD MENDOZA

"Sensor picture resolving, sirs. On screen now."

I whistle appraisingly. The Koratans, it seems, were spot-on. There's a station in orbit of the third moon of Linford Commons' sixth planet. The facility is shaped like a large disc, clearly of industrial design rather than military. As we get closer, we see that it's not the only thing orbiting the moon.

"Is that a battleship?" Quarrie asks grimly. "Sensors, can we see the markings on that ship?"

"Aye, Captain. It's not SDF. No markings to speak of. Just plain black. The AI can't identify class either."

Quarrie shakes her head. "Who ever heard of an unmarked battleship?"

"Bollen," I growl. "It has to be him."

"When you said this supposed slaver had a warship of his own, I didn't believe you, Admiral."

I nod. "Ensign," I call to Hayley. "Take some Marines and go get our guest from the brig."

Ten minutes later, Hayley returns with Terry Galpin wearing handcuffs and glaring at me with her icy blue eyes.

"Miss Galpin, does this ship look familiar?" I ask her, ignoring her sullenness and putting the image of the distant battleship on the screen.

Her eyes go wide, and she seems to momentarily forget how mad she is at me for keeping her in various brigs for the last week. "That's it," she breathes.

"Are you sure?" I press, knowing how little she claims to have known about Bollen's ship.

She nods. "It looks like the ship I saw out of the escape pod window. All black and big like that one."

That's not the best confirmation I could have hoped for, but it's something.

"Admiral, Captain, there's another ship coming into view." The woman at the sensor station throws a new image onto the forward viewscreen, and I feel my breath catch.

"Is that the freighter from Poe?" Quarrie asks in a low voice.

I nod. "Almost certainly. Sensors," I call across the bridge, "compare that ship's signature with the one I provided you from *Bainbridge*'s sensor records at Poe."

"Scanning," she says, and a moment later, "It's the same ship, sir. The AI puts it at 87 percent probability of positive match."

I let out a long breath. "We've found them. We've really found them."

"Orders, Admiral?"

I gulp. What I really want to do is command Quarrie and her ship to charge the station and take out that battleship so we can rescue those slaves, assuming they haven't already been offloaded and transshipped elsewhere. But to attempt such would be suicide. Even if that battleship is more luxury cruiser than warship, as Terry suggests, I doubt Bollen removed its teeth.

"Continue as planned, Captain," I order, the words tasting of ash in my mouth. "Now we know where to strike when we return to the Commons."

"Very good," Quarrie says, sounding extremely relieved. "Navigation, maintain course and alert me as we near the next waypoint. Tactical, Sensors, if that battleship so much as twitches in our direction, I want to know immediately. And I'll want firing solutions on it and the station in that event. Good job, people. It's time to make our way home."

I watch with satisfaction as the plot updates to show our vector back to the jump point. By the time we return to Cillian Heights, a full week will have passed since we left, but we'll be returning with the location of Andre Bollen and the slaves he took from Poe.

Something has finally decided to go right for us.

## FIFTY-THREE
# ELEVATOR TROUBLE

### JESSICA LIN MENDOZA

"Captain Lin," a voice calls over my comm.

"Here."

"This is Lieutenant Commander Grayson on the *Guardian*, ma'am."

My mind races and then locks in. *Guardian* is one of the three ready-for-a-fight battlecruisers we found among the mothball fleet. "Can I help you, Commander?"

"Yes, ma'am. We have an issue over here, and we may need your help deciding how to tackle it."

"What kind of issue?" I ask.

"Honestly, ma'am, it's a bit hard to explain. Much easier to show you. It's not an engineering thing, but we need a ship commander's opinion."

"You can go, Jessica," Kelly says from underneath a nearby console in *Adjudicator*'s engineering section. "I can wrangle the crew here to get this lady flying on schedule."

I shrug. I'm not doing much to help anyway. Kelly has adamantly refused to let me crawl into any conduits or service hatches, insisting that being shot twice and dying on the operating table a few days ago disqualifies me from that type of work. I've honestly been getting bored, and being bored has given me far too much time to think of and regret my last words to Brad.

"On my way, Commander," I tell Grayson gratefully. "Give me forty minutes." The docking arm of the shipyards servicing the mothballed battlecruisers is all the way on the other side of the massive facility, and all of the shuttles, carts, and trams are being used to ferry supplies and engineers back and forth. The walk will be good for me, even if I have to take it slow.

"That will be perfect, Captain. We'll wait for you here."

With a last nod toward Kelly, I make my way out of the battleship's engineering section and back toward the airlock to the shipyard beyond.

I'm only ten minutes along when Gunny calls. "Captain, heard you're headed to *Guardian*. Hold there, and I'll come escort you."

"Don't worry about it, Gunny," I reply, grateful that he can't see me roll my eyes. He's been far too overprotective since I was shot on Gregor. I can't blame him, but I'm on a shipyard taken over by the Navy. Besides, he and his people are far away, helping lift heavy supplies into one of the light cruisers we're preparing to get underway.

"I'd really prefer it if you'd wait, ma'am," he argues back, but I keep walking. And by the simple fact that he'll never catch up to me if I don't stop, I win our little argument.

Nearly thirty minutes later, I enter a small lift that will take me four levels up to the specific docking arm I'm looking for. Just as the doors start to close, a woman in a lieutenant's uniform cries out, "Hold the lift!"

I press the button to stop the doors and reopen them as she scurries into the lift car, carrying a small crate full of electronic components. "Thank you, Captain," she says with a smile. "I'd salute, but I don't want to drop this."

I wave her off and return her smile while a sense of comfort and pride fills me. I forgot how much I *loved* being a Navy officer. To be part of something so much bigger than yourself is almost intoxicating. And while I've found a family with Brad and our crew on *Bainbridge*, I didn't realize how much I missed the larger community of Navy officers and spacers before now.

The doors close, and the lieutenant sets her crate down and reaches up to wipe the sweat from her brow, giving me another apologetic smile. I turn away slightly to give her some semblance of privacy to fix herself and her uniform.

I start to turn back as I hear her step toward me, but I never make it. Something jabs hard into my right kidney, and I feel the shock of high voltage electricity before the deck rushes up to meet me.

The pain of my fall racks through my body, aggravating my still raw injuries. Just before I lose full consciousness, I register the lieutenant's voice, now cold and hard: "Don't worry, Captain. Andre Bollen has plans for you."

# FIFTY-FOUR
# ANGER—LOTS OF ANGER

## BRAD MENDOZA

My sense of hope from finding Bollen and the slave ship at Linford Commons dies the moment we enter Cillian Heights and reestablish comms with our forces there.

"What do you mean, she's gone?" I scream into the comm at Chris.

He explains what happened in short, terse sentences, obviously upset about it, but in my own anger, I continue to yell into the comm. Luckily for both of us, he ignores my outbursts.

"Why didn't you go after her?" I demand when he's done.

"What do you think we're doing now?" he shouts back, finally losing some of his composure. "I've got every spaceworthy ship mere hours out from the jump point. But we didn't even know she was gone until twelve hours ago, and getting twenty-five ships ready to fly takes time!"

I want curse him and his over-cautious nature. If I'd been

here, I would have sent *Bainbridge* after the ship that took Jess without waiting for the rest of the fleet to be ready. But I have to bottle that anger up—it's not Chris's fault I wasn't here, it's mine. If I hadn't insisted on going with *Gunslinger* to recon the Linford Commons system, maybe I would have been with Jess and stopped her from—

"You can't blame yourself, Captain," Quarrie says softly at my side, momentarily breaking me out of my doom spiral. "All you can do now is rescue her. Focus on that."

Nodding my thanks, I check the sensor picture on the display in Quarrie's ready room. Sure enough, there are twenty-four ships burning toward us and the jump point we just emerged from. They're close enough that the shouting match Chris and I are having is nearly in real-time.

How did they get twenty-four ships operational in a week?

"How long ago did they leave the system?" I ask Chris, straining to control my tone now.

"Exactly eight hours and seventeen minutes ago," he replies in like manner. "In a fast courier ship, so not even your *Bainbridge* would have had a hope of catching up to them. We would have had trouble even pinpointing the ship that took her, but they . . . advertised it."

The console pings, and I command my implant to open the attachment now displayed there. An audio-only message starts playing, and a familiar but distorted voice plays from the console's speakers.

"Mendoza. If you're hearing this, you survived your little foray to find me at Linford Commons. Which is fine—I *want* you to come there. I want you to watch when I kill your wife in front of you. I want you to hear her beg for her life like the tramp she is, and then I'm going to torture you and her until you'll wish you never crossed me. I'm waiting, Brad. Let's see what the Butcher of Bellerophon can do. See you soon."

The message cuts out, and I scream in rage, picking up a paperweight from Quarrie's desk and launching it across the room to shatter the viewscreen on the opposite bulkhead. To her credit, she doesn't even flinch.

"It's a trap, Brad," Chris tells me unnecessarily.

"Of course it's a trap," I growl. "It's always been a trap. But . . ."

But what? My mind goes blank. I can't think of a single thing that doesn't involve turning around and charging headlong into Bollen's trap. Whether I know the ambush is there or not, he's taken the one thing from me that guarantees I'll have to play his little game. But I don't have to take the rest of the fleet with me.

"Admiral Turly, I'd like you to hold your forces here. I'll transfer to *Bainbridge,* and we'll go after Captain Lin alone. No sense all of us falling into Bollen's trap."

He licks his lips. "I'm sorry, Admiral Mendoza, but your last transmission was garbled. Say again."

I frown at him crossly. He can definitely hear me, but I'm not sure what game he's playing.

Suddenly, the transmission cuts out, and I look at the blank console in near panic.

"Oops," Quarrie says next to me. "I forgot that the comm system needed to reboot. Should only take an hour or so, Admiral. Apologies for the inconvenience."

"This is mutiny, Captain. You know that, right?" I growl.

She shrugs and smiles. "Sorry, Admiral, I'm having a bit of trouble understanding you as well. Maybe you need a nap so you start making more sense. I'll rouse you after we head back through the jump point and are well en route to Linford Commons."

Before I can formulate an angry response, she flees out of the ready room and back onto the bridge, where I hear her shouting orders to turn over and burn back to the jump point so we can match speed and vector with the rest of the fleet in time for them to join us.

I sigh, rubbing my temples. I'm pissed, but I'm also grateful. With only *Bainbridge,* Bollen's plan, whatever it is, would undoubtedly work. With the entire fleet . . . well, we'll see.

# PART FOUR
# IMPOSSIBLE CHOICES

# FIFTY-FIVE
# MORE PAIN

## JESSICA LIN MENDOZA

Pain.

Pounding, piercing, blinding pain.

Nothing else exists but the pain. As I rise from the void to meet it, I want to turn around and retreat far away, where I don't have to feel anything. But it inexorably pulls at me, and I have no choice but to ascend and face it.

For some time longer, it's my entire universe. Then, slowly, in fits and starts, I become aware that other things exist: the hard grate of a metal deck beneath my back, my shoulder blades digging into it with a different kind of pain, the soft hum of a ship underway, and from somewhere, a steady drip of water.

"She's waking up!" an unfamiliar voice cries.

I try to open my eyes to see the speaker, but the lights

above immediately blind me, so I involuntarily shut my eyelids tight again.

"Stay still. You need to drink something," a voice says, a woman, and I feel a hand lift my head up from the deck and another press the rim of a plastic water bottle to my lips.

Gradually, cool liquid starts to flow into my mouth and down my throat. The first few drops ignite a ravenous thirst, and I start to gulp it down greedily, almost crying out as the bottle suddenly departs.

"Nice and easy," the woman's voice chides. "Drink too much too fast and it'll do more harm than good. You had us scared there for a while. We weren't sure you were going to wake up."

I keep my eyes squeezed shut, but when the light filtering through my eyelids seems to dim a little, I start to open them. At first, the brightness is still unbearable, but slowly and surely, my eyes adjust. As my vision clears, I find myself staring up into the smooth, round face of a young woman I've never seen before.

"How's the pain?" she asks.

I try to answer with words, but all I can force through my lips is a whimper.

"That bad, huh?" she asks with a grimace. She turns and addresses someone out of my line of sight. "Tell those brutes outside we need pain relievers."

I hear someone respond, but my head is still pounding so hard, I can't make out the words.

"I know they'll just say no," the woman above me snaps. "But we owe it to this officer to at least ask."

Whatever response or outcome might come from the conversation eludes me. I find myself growing drowsy, and then my eyes squeeze shut again of their own volition as I sink back into the void.

When I awake next, the pain is only somewhat lessened,

but it's enough for me to sit up with the same kindly young woman's help, gratefully taking more of the water she offers. I'm lucid enough now to see that we're far from alone.

We're in what looks to be a cargo hold, but it's impossible to tell for sure. It's packed so tightly with people that I can't see more than a couple of meters to either side of me, and behind me is a plain utilitarian bulkhead. But the ceiling is several meters high, which gives me a clue to the compartment's function.

The people around us are standing shoulder to shoulder, like sardines in a can. I see mostly women, and most of those are young, but there are men of various ages scattered here and there as well. They're all wearing civilian clothes, most appearing homespun and rough.

It reminds me of what I saw the people wearing at Poe.

Gingerly, I raise a hand to press it to my left temple, which seems to be a focal point for the pain that still pulses through me in waves. My fingers find a large bump and what must be dried blood. A sudden memory flashes through me: a lift, a Navy officer, a stun rod, and the deck rising to meet me as I fell. I must have hit my head when that happened.

Oh no! Brad. My crew. Bollen. I try to get to my feet so quickly that I immediately feel woozy, but what stops me is the other woman putting a gentle but firm hand on my shoulder to hold me down.

"You have a head wound," she says in the tone of a patient schoolteacher, "and you've been out of it ever since they brought you here. You shouldn't try to get up."

"Where?" I croak out, my throat and mouth not cooperating enough to speak clearly.

She sighs and shakes her head. "We'll get to that. First, how are you feeling?" She helps me scoot backward so I can prop my back against the bulkhead, then hands me a newly filled water bottle.

Before answering, I chug the water greedily, unabashed at how a good portion escapes my lips and wets my chin and the front of my Navy skinsuit. When I finish, I wipe my mouth with the sleeve of my other arm. "Like I got hit by a battleship," I answer honestly.

"Any dizziness? Double vision? Blurriness?"

"All of the above. Where are we?"

She frowns. "You're not going to like the answer, Captain Lin."

"You know me?"

She shakes her head and points to my chest. "Your nametag and rank insignia. Plus, I remember seeing you from afar at the governor's feast for Admiral Mendoza," she says, confirming my assessment about her clothing and that of the others. These have to be the slaves Bollen took from Poe.

I try to nod but abandon the effort when the simple movement triggers a wave of pain. "Where are we?" I ask a third time. I don't mean to sound so angry and impatient, but it comes out that way regardless.

She sighs again, looking over her shoulder at the assembled crowd as if to seek permission or support from them. All of them stand like statues, eyes riveted on me, and ignore her. "We're on a freighter of some kind. We're all from Poe, picked up there a little over two weeks ago. We think they mean to make us . . . slaves."

She says the last word like she expects it to shock me, but all I can think is that I've finally found them, and now I'm in no position to help them. It feels like I've just been told I won the lottery, but also that I have a terminal disease and won't live to spend any of it.

"Any idea where the ship is right now?" I ask, ignoring her confused look at my lack of surprise about being on board a slave ship.

The woman shrugs. "We were actually hoping you could

tell us, Captain. We've been in this hold long enough to be anywhere in the Federation, or outside of it. Where did they capture you?"

I decide there's no sense keeping it a secret. "Cillian Heights."

There's a murmuring of voices among those in the crowd close enough to hear us. The woman helping me looks semi-relieved. "So we're probably still in the Corpus Christi Cluster, at least. That's good news."

"How so?" I ask.

Her relieved look disappears. "Because if we're still in Promethean space, they probably aren't going to sell us quite yet. Slavery is illegal in the Federation, right? So they'd have to take us somewhere else."

I decide not to dash her hopes. While she's right that slavery has been illegal in the Promethean Federation since its inception, it hasn't stopped some of the seedier elements of society from trading in the suffering of other human beings.

"What's your name?" I ask, realizing she hasn't shared it.

"Mary. Mary Sullivan. I'm a nursing student at the University of Poe. Or I was."

With no small effort, I reach out and put a hand on her shoulder where she crouches next to me. "You still are, and you'll get back in time for midterms."

By the look on her face, she doesn't believe me one bit.

I take a deep breath, and another wave of dizziness hits me, along with a sharp pain in my chest and shoulder. Again, involuntarily, I feel my eyes start to close.

When I open them again, it feels like seconds later, but my implant helpfully informs me that three more hours have passed. Unfortunately, that's all it will tell me. All my attempts to query the ship's AI or other systems return nothing more than an error, like my implant is being jammed, though it can't seem to detect the jamming field either.

At least I feel a bit better this time around, and Mary Sullivan, seeing I'm awake, helps me sit up again.

"You okay, Captain?" she asks, concern etched all over her face.

"Please, call me Jessica."

"Call me Mary. Not that it matters anymore."

I consider that for a while. My first reaction is anger at her defeatist attitude, but I remind myself she's been in this cargo hold for more than two weeks already, and apparently, I just arrived less than half a day ago. So, I imagine there are few here with any hope of rescue left.

"How many guards are there?" I ask, changing the subject to the true matter at hand: escape.

Mary regards me with blatant skepticism, guessing where I'm going with this. "Four, I think. Whatever you're thinking, don't. They almost never come inside the hold except . . ."

"Except for what?" I prod when she doesn't continue.

"Except for when they take out a girl or two for—well, you know."

A upswell of rage fills me as I think of these poor prisoners going through what I did on *Persephone*, but without even the hope of transfer or a new captain to look forward to. I try to tamp it down, but it must show on my face.

"Don't," Mary repeats. "We've already tried just about everything to get out of here. We're separated from the rest of the ship by an airlock. They open it from their side, put our twice-daily meals inside, and then close their side before they open ours. The doors never open at the same time. A few of the stronger men tried to go inside the airlock and wait for them to bring the next meal, but the guards kept our side of the door open and sent in the drones."

"Drones?" I ask, perking up at the unexpected word.

She nods. "Nasty ones. They come out of small vents where the bulkheads and ceiling meet. There are a dozen or so, with guns attached. They shoot some really nasty stun rounds. Those who have gotten hit are out for hours and wake up in a lot of pain." Mary frowns. "They cause a lot more pain than typical stun rounds should, or so one of the men said, like they're engineered that way."

"Fun," I observe, tentatively shifting my weight as I contemplate getting to my feet. "Any good news?"

Her lack of an answer tells me all I need to know.

"Help me up," I tell her. "I need to see more of where we are."

She does so, reluctantly, but a moment later, she has to lower me to the deck when my head starts to swim and I almost fall over.

# FIFTY-SIX
# CAGED RACEHORSE

## BRAD MENDOZA

I may have accepted that it would be foolhardy to transfer over to *Bainbridge* and sprint ahead of the rest of the fleet to find Jess at Linford Commons, but that doesn't mean I like it one bit. At one point, I was pacing the bridge of *Gunslinger,* my chosen flagship, and looking so upset that Captain Quarrie gently but no less forcefully advised me to get some rest.

I went and paced in my temporary cabin instead.

I hate every second it takes us to traverse the three jump points and two intermediary systems to get to Linford Commons. Every second is one that may see Jess getting farther away from me.

So when my cabin door chime sounds, I welcome the interruption.

"Boss, I have a thought," Hayley says, entering and closing the hatch behind her. The instant it's shut, she changes her hair from drab brown to bright green, and her entire posture transforms. She also kicks off her shoes.

"Make yourself at home, Lieutenant," I say dryly from my place on the couch, where I've taken a short break from pacing a trail into the metal deck.

"Thanks, boss," she says, though without the full measure of her usual cheerfulness, sitting down on the floor and leaning back against the bulkhead opposite me, much like she does on our destroyer's bridge.

I raise an eyebrow at her. "You had a thought, Hayley?"

She nods, wrinkling up her nose. "Why does this Bollen hombre hate you so much?"

I scoff. "If I knew that, I might know who he actually is. Or if I knew who he is, I might know why he's doing this. See the dilemma?"

"Sí, chico, but he seems to hate la Capitana Lin, too, no?"

I'm opening my mouth to answer, but I stop. "What do you mean?"

"He called her a tramp, boss. Twice, in his messages to us. Why do that if he only hates you?"

"Maybe just to piss me off?" I offer lamely.

She shakes her head. "No way, boss. Distorted voice or no, he hates both of you. It's obvious. So who do you know who hates you both this badly?"

"A lot of people, I suppose," I answer honestly. "Duchess Charlotte, but she's dead. Same with Hernandez. Lady Jacobs and her son, but I imagine they have enough to worry about with her brother, King Charles, dead. Baron Hornsby supposedly died in his dungeon cell when Prometheus was bombarded from orbit. I'd normally add Chris Turly to the list, but he seems to like me now, plus he's not smart enough to pull off anything this elaborate. Maybe the Jutzens or King Chance himself? No, they may hate me, but they're already winning the war, and this feels much more personal."

"Sí. This Bollen hombre wants you both to suffer a lot, boss," Hayley says, a haunted look in her eyes now. "I think he's not sane."

"A lot of people think the Jutzens aren't exactly right in the head," I point out. "Kind of comes with the territory of the whole evil Nazi thing."

"But like you said, boss. They're already winning. They don't need this kind of sneakiness anymore. They'll just kill you in battle one day."

"Gee, Hayley, thanks for the vote of confidence."

"There's another problem, boss," she adds, ignoring my sarcasm.

"Oh great, because I thought this was going to be simple." I lay it on a little thicker this time.

It doesn't faze her. "There are better ways to lure you and la Capitana Lin into a trap than by pretending to be a slaver."

My mind races, as it often does, trying to follow Hayley's logic. "Explain."

"Capturing those people at Poe was risky, and I've been checking around, boss. It wasn't just on Poe."

I cock my head at her. "But no one else in the Cluster has heard of Bollen or reported any other slave activity."

"I'm not talking about the Corpus Christi Cluster, boss. I checked all the news reports across the Federation and the Confederacy. Tapped into some of my old Guard sources, too. There was that ship we found at Edmonton, and there have been reports of ships just like that one drifting derelict all over the place."

She pings my implant, and it opens a map in share mode, so we both see it superimposed on our vision as if it's floating in the center of the room between us. The map shows a zoomed-out view of this area of space, with the Corpus Christi Cluster at its center. Scattered around the map's edges are systems outlined in red.

"Hayley," I ask in awe, "are you telling me that *all* these red systems have evidence of slaver activity?"

"Sí, boss. And all in the last two months. And not just women taken, but men too. I think two to three thousand slaves."

I swear under my breath. The map tells a clear story. Until the attack at Poe, no system in the Corpus Christi Cluster had seen any evidence of slaver activity. However, the space surrounding the Cluster on all sides is speckled liberally with red. It's as if someone purposefully drew an exclusion zone inside the Cluster and then tried to hit as many systems as possible outside of it, but as close to that exclusionary line as possible.

"I think Bollen isn't a fake slaver, boss," Hayley says soberly. "I think he's real, and he's been gathering people from outside the Cluster and bringing them to his base at Linford Commons. You saw a large orbital station at the sixth planet where he's hiding, no?"

I nod, studying the map in my implant. "An industrial one. You think he's keeping the slaves there?"

"I did some more digging, boss, but that station used to belong to the Adamsons."

I focus back on her. "You mean the family of the late Earl Adamson?"

She nods. "They were shippers, chico. At least for the last fifty years, until they went bankrupt right before the old earl went kaput. But before that, they made weapons, lots of weapons."

The revelation hits me like a physical force to the chest. "Hayley, are you saying that station is an old weapons factory?"

She nods.

"Like the one we found underground with Hernandez?"

"Sí, boss. What if this Bollen hombre is working with the

same people as Hernandez, Duchess Charlotte, and Baron Hornsby? And what if he's using those slaves to make more weapons for the Jutzens, or even for the Koratan rebels?"

I swallow and lick suddenly dry lips. "You think it's all connected? Seems like quite a leap."

She shrugs. "Not really, boss. We know Hernandez and Hornsby had connections to the Jutzens. And you think Bollen is working for King Chance and the Jutzens, right?"

"I do. So you think the Jutzens are behind everything?"

To my surprise, she shakes her head. "I don't think so, boss. I can't explain it, but it feels like maybe someone else is in charge."

I wait for her to continue, but she clams up, clearly not ready to elaborate on that massive supposition. "Wait," I say. "What kind of munitions did that factory specialize in?"

She smiles, as if glad I finally got to the real point of the conversation. "Missiles, boss. Like the others. No phase torpedoes, though. But a long time ago, it used to make mines, también."

My jaw drops. "Hayley, we need to tell the fleet."

She nods. "Of course, boss."

"Hayley, if you're right, we've been going about this all wrong. Bollen isn't some fiction invented to trap me or Jess. But he's someone who hates us enough to make his existence known and break his own exclusionary zone by hitting Poe to lure us into his trap. And he's got access to resources we never even considered. This changes everything about our plan of attack at Linford Commons!"

She smiles and nods again. "Sí, boss."

"Hayley," I say crossly. "How long ago did you figure all of this out?"

Still smiling, she shrugs. "I figured it out this morning. But sometimes you gotta come up with the idea yourself, sabes, or you have a hard time accepting it? Lots of hombres are like that, especially the ones that think they're smart."

I scowl at her. "First of all, I don't think I'm smart . . . You know what, never mind. Next time, just tell me your theory instead of handholding me through it."

She shrugs again in a way that tells me she has already decided to ignore this latest order. "So whatcha gonna do about it, chico? Does this give you any hints about who Bollen is?"

I shake my head. "No, but it virtually proves that he's working with King Chance, the Jutzens, and the SDF. And that we're likely to encounter mines when we get to the system. Which means I need to call Chris and the other captains and start redesigning our plan of attack accordingly."

Hayley squeaks in surprise as I step over and crouch in front of her. I grab her face in both hands, pulling it forward and placing a kiss on her forehead. She doesn't fight it, and when I look back down at her, she's smiling, and suddenly I realize that I've started thinking of her the way I might if I'd ever had a little sister. Our entire crew is my family now, but a few—Hayley, Gunny, Illian, O'Malley, Laia, Harris—have risen to an even higher level than that. Jess, I realize now, is far from the only member of our crew I would die for. Or happily spring a trap set by a psychotic slaver boss for.

"Hayley, you're a genius. Have I told you that lately?"

"I don't think you've *ever* told me that, boss. You've called me loca, which is fair; dangerous, which is also true; but never a genius."

"Well, I'm saying it now." I release her face and beam down at her. "Of all our crew, I often think you're the one we're most lucky to have." The words come naturally, and I mean them.

Hayley stares up at me with unusually wide eyes and starts blinking a lot, turning away and using her uniform sleeves to wipe her eyes. "You'd better think hard about who this Bollen hombre is, boss. I'll leave you alone to do that. But I'll tell Captain Quarrie to call that meeting with the other bosses."

She's out the hatch an instant later, and I check my implant. Our fleet should be entering the final jump to Linford Commons in ten hours. Then we'll have six hours in jump space. That doesn't leave me a lot of time to figure out who Andre Bollen really is. Nor does it leave us a lot of time to completely rethink our plan of attack.

I only hope we're not too late.

# FIFTY-SEVEN
# HOPELESS SITUATION

## JESSICA LIN MENDOZA

When I wake up yet again, many hours later, Mary Sullivan is crouched over me and looking worried. Everything hurts, from my back to my head, and especially the two recently healed bullet wounds from Gregor. I groan as I try to sit up again.

"You still need rest, Jessica," she chides, gently pushing me back down. I'm only a nursing student, but you look like you've been through a meat grinder. All due respect, Captain."

I smile up at her. "You have no idea. But help me up anyway, because it's time for us to find a way out of here."

Her only response is a frown.

"Come on," I urge her. "There's always a way out of any situation."

If living with Brad for the last nine months has taught me anything, it's that there truly is always a way out. Someone could make a movie out of the times we've escaped places and people that we had no right escaping. He's often commented that our lives have turned into the kind of story a sadistic author might write, where he's trying to ramp up the tension more and more with every book, without actually killing us so that his readers don't hunt him down for taking out their favorite main characters.

Brad has some truly bizarre ideas sometimes.

Mary doesn't share my confidence or enthusiasm. "The airlock is the only way in or out of the cargo hold. There are bathrooms, but they're portable latrines set up in one corner. So no plumbing goes in or out. Same with the showers—just disinfectant sprayers, and thank goodness for that much, or this entire place would smell terrible."

I choose not to point out that it doesn't exactly smell like springtime in here.

"A few of the smaller folks talked about getting into the air vents," she continued.

I feel a momentary glimmer of hope, remembering how Tina DeJong saved Brad's life on Serenidad by doing just that.

"But they're all welded shut, and from what they could see into the lowest ones, far too narrow for even a child. Besides, the last person who tried got shot by a drone." Just like that, my fledgling hope evaporates.

"Help me get up and walk," I tell her again.

She looks at me like my mother did when I told her I wanted to quit riding lessons. But when I meet her gaze defiantly, Mary sighs and waves over another nearby young woman, who introduces herself in a small voice as Diedre, an English student. Together this time, the two of them help me to my feet and support me on either side. Moving slowly as the crowd parts for us at a glacial pace, we start to make our way around the edge of the hold, sticking close to the bulkheads.

Between the denseness of the crowd and my needing to stop and rest every few minutes, it feels like it takes us hours to walk the full perimeter of the cargo hold. At first, there's nothing to see. Then, we reach the promised interior airlock. Even though I'm sure it won't work, I try fiddling with the control panel to find that someone has severed the power to it. Nor can my implant connect to it. Despite having no real expectations that it would be that simple, the confirmation kills a little more of my hope.

The next notable attraction on our journey is the set of portable latrines Mary told me about. I smell them before I see them, and it doesn't surprise me that there's a relatively large open space around them as the crowd pushes as far away from the odor as they can. I make a stop there, availing myself of the facilities, and nothing I see encourages me in any way.

Right after the latrines, I find the source of the water Mary has been giving me. It's a small pipe extending from the bulkhead, with a steady and fast drip that falls right to a small drain set in the deck. I try to fit my nails around the edges of the drain to see if I can somehow pull open the deck plates, but they're welded in place, as I'm sure are the others throughout the hold.

At this point, we're joined by a fourth prisoner, a young man named Peter, who takes in my uniform with wide, hopeful eyes that break my heart a little more.

Brad once told me that when he first came on board HMS *Persephone*, back when he was still a drunk loser (his words, not mine), Kelly and I looked at him with the same hopeful expression. He laughed it off at the time, but thoughts of how much he was certain he'd disappoint us contributed to his several bouts of drunkenness while on board that ill-fated frigate. Now, I can understand a measure of what he felt, because I'm suddenly certain that

I'm going to disappoint Peter, Diedre, Mary, and everyone else.

That insight makes me stop in my tracks, drawing confused looks from companions. I say nothing to them, but my mind spins in circles as I finally understand both why Brad froze in the battle at Huff and why he is so against the idea of going back to join Queen Anne and taking the command she desperately wants to give him.

It's not cowardice—not that I ever truly thought it was, despite my poorly thought-out words the last time I saw him. It's fear, sure. But not fear of failing himself or getting himself killed. It's fear of letting others down, like he's always felt he did at Bellerophon.

As we start walking again, Peter takes over supporting my right side from Diedre, who was starting to sweat and strain under my half-dead weight. Mary, on my other side, shows zero signs of fatigue.

We continue our circumnavigation of the cargo hold, stopping more often now to rest. I suppose I could simply choose to slump to the deck anywhere and go back to sleep, and my throbbing head is certainly a motivation to do just that. It's pure stubbornness that has me absolutely resolved to reach the spot we started from, even if it drives me to complete and utter exhaustion.

When we're three-quarters around the hold, almost ready to turn the final corner and head back to our starting point, I feel a small sliver of renewed hope.

"Don't even think about it," Mary says when she catches me studying the *second* airlock in the hold, the one that leads *outside* the ship. "Unless the Navy has somehow developed a way to breathe in a vacuum, that's a one-way trip."

She probably expects me to turn away from the exterior airlock, but I step closer to inspect its control panel. My heart leaps when I see a single, small red light indicating the panel has power. I say as much to her.

My skinsuit is built for decompression and even has an integrated emergency hood in the collar to protect my face and head. What it *doesn't* have is an oxygen supply, so I'd be stuck with only the air trapped inside it, but at least I wouldn't die immediately.

Unfortunately, getting outside the ship presents two major problems. First, if the ship is under acceleration—and I can feel the vibration of its engines through the deck plates—I'll be instantly ripped off the hull and sent tumbling through the void. Second, even if I managed to cling to the moving ship, I'd have nowhere to go without an air supply. Unless the slavers helpfully left another external airlock unlocked and wide open for me, I'd be dead before I could work my way back inside.

Mary gives me a third reason it likely wouldn't work. "There are access codes," she explains. "And we don't have them."

I nod to acknowledge her words but don't fully extinguish the small wellspring of hope in my chest. If I could get my implant to connect to the ship's AI, opening this lock would be easy. Then again, if my implant were able to connect, opening the inner airlock and accessing the rest of the ship would be just as easy.

Still, it's *something,* and now that I know about it, I may alight on an idea for how to use it, even if nothing comes to mind right now.

I let Mary, Diedre, and Peter lead me away and back to our starting point, where I promptly lie down on the deck and pass out from the exertion of our single loop around the relatively small cargo hold.

## FIFTY-EIGHT
# STRATEGY

### BRAD MENDOZA

"You want to enter the system going *that* slow, sir? It's suicide. If the SDF is waiting for us at the jump point, we'll be sitting ducks."

I stare across the wardroom table at the speaker, Commander Jonathan Smith, he with the super boring and generic name. He's not currently serving on *Gunslinger*, but he's taken the role of CO for *Dasher*, one of the battleworthy mothballed battlecruisers.

Around the long conference table on *Liberator*, where I gathered all the fleet's COs to meet in person, there are several nods of agreement. I can see I'm going to have to give them the full story.

So I do, explaining in detail what Hayley and I discovered. By the end, the nods are replaced with mouths agape.

"Mines, sir?" Admiral Turly asks incredulously. "But the

Accords of Centauri outlawed the use of mines at jump points a century ago."

He's absolutely right. It used to be a fairly standard practice for warring star nations to mine their jump points to protect against invasion. But the problem with mines is that they tend to go off whether or not the ship triggering them is a true enemy. So, when a starliner with an Earth registry was destroyed at an Inner Rim system a little over a hundred years ago, the Sol Federation stepped in and put a quick stop to the practice. They dressed it up as a voluntary treaty, of course, but also made it clear that any star nations that didn't sign the Accords would receive heavy economic sanctions. Earth may be prone to largely ignoring its far-flung colonies, but when they do choose to pay attention, no one wants to be the nation that makes them angry.

As a result, only pariah states have dared to mine jump points since. Until now.

"Think about it," I urge Chris, "one of the munitions factories at Linford Commons specialized in manufacturing mines. When the Accords were signed and demand dropped, they stopped manufacturing the things, but records suggest they kept the production lines intact and just shut down that part of the factory. It was apparently cheaper than dismantling them or replacing them with other production lines.

"And so far as the Accords go, if Bollen is really the man in charge of the occupation of his sector, we know he's already stooped to piracy to further his aims, why not mining jump points as well?"

"It's a stretch, sir," he argues, and justifiably so. When Hayley and I figured all this out, even I had to admit it was far from a sure thing. But every time I've thought about ignoring this intel and entering the system at speed, my stomach feels like it's going to fall out of the bottoms of my feet.

"Wouldn't even Andre Bollen be afraid of the Sollies?" Risa Quarrie asks from her place next to Smith.

"Earth has never liked the idea of Nazis continuing to exist in human space," I shoot right back. "The Jutzens have been under Sol Fed sanctions for decades. Hard to imagine them caring if Earth slaps more of those on them, and hard to imagine the Sollies caring enough to send their own Navy way out here to enforce the edict."

There are a few slow nods around the table as the other commanders absorb my counterarguments.

One of the destroyer commanders ventures a question. "What happens if you're wrong, sir?"

I smile at him. Technically, as an admiral, I can simply order the fleet to follow my revised plan—I sort of already did that, as all ships are already turned over and killing their forward momentum—but the best admirals I served under were the ones who took time to listen to the opinions of their subordinates. I may not be fit for this kind of command, but I am resolved to at least do this little piece to be a good admiral before I can convince Annie to demote me back to captain.

"Lieutenant Commander Wright," I say to the man, "that's a terrific question. Let's game it out. If I'm wrong, we'll enter the system at a slow enough crawl that any SDF forces waiting for us at the jump point will have all the time in the world to pound on us before we can get out of range. But we'll have equal time to fight back, and we'll be able to use our drone ships to draw their fire and maybe eke out an advantage before they figure out which of our ships can shoot.

"But if I'm right, and we exit the jump point at speed, none of us are likely to survive. Imagine several hundred heavy missiles waiting for us, floating in space, not lighting up their drives until they're already inside our close defensive envelopes. We might get some of them, but it only takes a few getting through to take down even a battleship. That's what it's like to go into a minefield."

Silence once again dominates the room as everyone digests that. I hear a few breathed swear words, a definite breach of protocol in the presence of two admirals, but neither Chris nor I is keen to punish our officers for simply voicing what we're all thinking.

"There's one more piece," I say after about thirty seconds of quiet. "I'm starting to think I might know who Andre Bollen is."

Every eye in the room rivets on me in shock.

"It's too early to share a name," I tell them honestly. This is more hunch than anything. "But if I'm right, then Bollen is a bully and a coward. Now that he knows that we know exactly where his base is, he won't risk putting the SDF fleet at the jump point, lest we get by them and make it to his location before they can catch up. He'll keep the fleet with him at the sixth planet. I'm sure of it."

I make eye contact with each of them as I speak, and for about half of them, I see the moment they decide to believe me. Which almost makes me recant everything. If I'm wrong about any of this, we're all likely dead, despite my earlier statement to the contrary. My eyes find Francis Illian, sitting at the far end of the table with the other junior commanders, and he gives me an encouraging nod that lends my spine a little more steel than a moment ago.

"Admiral Mendoza, I'm convinced."

Perhaps it shouldn't surprise me anymore that Chris Turly is the first to openly support my plan, but it does. Years of loathing are hard to undo in just a few days, and I give him a silent nod of thanks.

"I'll have my people on *Gunslinger* start working up the math," Risa Quarrie says next. "Assuming that you'll be keeping *Gunslinger* as your flagship, Admiral."

I nod to her as well. "Of course, Captain. I'm a battle-cruiser man. But please coordinate with Admiral Turly's people on *Liberator* to double-check things. We have to get this perfectly right.

One by one, the other COs all voice their support.

# FIFTY-NINE
# BEING WATCHED

## JESSICA LIN MENDOZA

Mary wakes me up at some point to eat a meal. The food is bland, survival rations that taste worse than the slop they used to serve us on Navy training exercises. But at least it's edible, and I feel a small measure of my strength returning. My head has even mostly stopped swimming.

"There's just no way," Mary tells me as I reiterate my desire to escape after dinner—or maybe it's breakfast, I can't tell. "You saw how everything is set up. There's no chance we can get out."

Peter, who was also by my side when I woke up, along with Diedre, frowns at Mary's fatalistic words but doesn't argue. Though he looked at me with some hope earlier, it's clear that in the intervening hours, they've all convinced themselves that my arrival is not a harbinger of freedom.

"There's always a way," I tell them, doing my best to

sound resolute. "If we can gain access to the rest of the ship, there are enough of us to overpower whatever crew they have guarding us. Then we can—"

"People will die," Mary interrupts me. "Say you get us out. Some of us will die trying to overpower the guards and the crew, and there's nothing you can do to prevent that. Better that we just wait until they offload us. At least then we'll be alive."

Peter frowns again and trades a look with Diedre, but neither of them speaks to contradict the other woman.

"Don't you get it?" I argue back. "Whatever is waiting for us on the other side is *worse* than death. At least if we escape, most of us will live and be free." Buried underneath my words is a growing certainty I've had since I first woke up and remembered the traitorous lieutenant's words to me in that lift at the shipyard. Bollen is using me as bait for Brad—I'm sure of it. Which means he doesn't intend *any* of us to survive this.

"How do you know that things will be worse?" Mary demands. "Have you ever been a slave before? Maybe we'll just be indentured servants on a farming world. Or house servants on one of the metropolitan border worlds. How could you possibly know what waits for us?"

I open my mouth to respond, then shut it. How can I explain to them what I've been through? I was never a slave, but I might as well have been one on *Persephone*. It's not a time I like to think about, much less speak of. So I don't.

"Listen," I say instead. "All I want to do is explore our options. I won't do anything rash, but if you help me, I'm confident we can find *something* that we can use to either escape or increase our chances of surviving the voyage and whatever comes at the end."

This hedge seems only to mollify her slightly, but Peter

and Deidre are both nodding encouragingly. Mary sighs. "Fine. Where do we start?"

"We have to assume they're watching us, right?" I ask.

The three trade uncomfortable glances, but they don't claim otherwise.

"So we need to make it look like we're not up to anything. Let's do another lap of the hold. I want to see it with fresh eyes."

This time, I spend less time on our journey examining the hold itself and more time inspecting the people.

Roughly 60 percent are women, but the rest are men, as if the slavers simply didn't care what gender they took. Which doesn't make a whole lot of sense given standard slaver M.O. Unless Mary really is right, and we're all destined for some sort of farming world.

But the ages are consistent: almost all are young, with few over thirty. That fits with standard slave trade practices and also with Bollen's decision to focus on the University of Poe.

Most of the prisoners are rather listless. The few who look up as I pass start at the sight of my Navy uniform, but they quickly go back to studying the deck near their feet, as if they don't want to allow themselves even to think hopeful thoughts.

At least they're not filthy. Mary tells me that by some unspoken consensus, everyone uses the latrines for their intended purpose, and most avail themselves of the waterless disinfectant showers every few days. Those who don't are practically forced to when the smell becomes too bad for the people immediately around them. It's a good sign to see that even if they've abandoned hope, the occupants of the hold haven't abandoned their humanity. It means they might be persuaded to fight back.

There *have* been a few acts of violence between prisoners. Fights over food were common at first, but ended after the guards deployed the drones a few times. The use of stun rounds is encouraging: the slavers at least don't want us dead. Dead slaves aren't worth as much money.

The drones are a problem. As long as they're operational, the guards won't ever have to step foot inside the cargo hold, unless it's to take a new female prisoner for themselves. But even then, with the drones covering the guards, it would be hard to convince any of the listless prisoners to fight back.

When we reach the latrines, I once more go inside to make use of them. There are two sets, each with four toilets, but no dividers between stalls. So the prisoners have naturally self-designated one set for men and the other for women. When I'm done in the women's latrine, I hold my breath and peer down into the waste tank. From what I can see, it's half full. So, there's no hope that someone might come to empty them anytime soon.

After leaving the latrine, I make my way over to the water pipe and examine it more closely. Nothing helpful comes from that. Same with my second inspection of the outer airlock.

By the time we get back to our starting spot, I'm starting to feel as hopeless as my new companions. I do my best to hide it, but from the way Mary frowns at me when Peter and Diedre aren't looking, she's picked up on it.

I square my shoulders and glare back at her, her disappointment being the catalyst I need to decide that there is no way I'm giving up. We will find a way out of here, even if it kills me.

Nothing much happens for the rest of the day. We eat another meal of the same slop as before. I take two more laps of the hold, the first with my three friends and the second alone, but learn nothing new. I even stop and question a few of the other prisoners, but most of them either ignore me or answer in terse, one-word responses that give me little hope of help from that quarter. Beyond Mary, at least some of them recognize me as Brad's companion during the celebration the governor threw for us, which was all over the news on Poe. At least a few of them rightly blame me and Brad for their imprisonment. If not as the direct causes—which we are—then at least for not stopping it.

At the end of the day, or perhaps it's the next morning, I'm exhausted and I have to sleep again. My rest is filled with nightmares of what happened to me on *Persephone,* and of what certainly *will* happen again if I don't find a way to escape.

# SIXTY
# WHY IS THERE AN ASSASSIN ON MY SHIP?

## BRAD MENDOZA

"Admiral, we've entered jump space at our target velocity. We'll reemerge in the Linford Commons system in five hours and thirty-eight minutes."

I nod to Risa Quarrie on *Gunslinger*'s bridge. "And our guests?"

"Came aboard as requested prior to the jump, sir. They're waiting for us in the wardroom."

Five minutes later, with the bridge watch handed over to the jump space detail, Quarrie and I arrive at the battlecruiser's wardroom to find Major Early and Captain Lamar, our fleet's two seniormost Marine officers, waiting there with two other individuals: a prim and proper-looking Hayley Uvalde in her ensign disguise, and Gunny Boyd.

"All due respect, Admiral," Early says the moment introductions are made and I've taken my seat, "but I should be back on *Liberator* prepping my people to storm Bollen's station when we get to Linford Commons."

"I understand, Major," I tell her soberly. "I promise this will be worth your time. Tell me, when's the last time you stormed a hostile station in wartime?"

The muscular woman immediately bristles, though she hides it relatively quickly. "Sir, my people and I have trained for this—"

I hold up a hand to stop her. "I'm not questioning your training or your competency, Major, or that of your people. I'm simply pointing out that it's been a long time since the Federation has truly been at war." I nod toward Gunny. "This is Gunnery Sergeant Quinn Boyd, formerly of the Leeward Republic Marines and now the head of my personal group of shooters on *Bainbridge*. In just the last nine months, he's successfully stormed multiple hostile stations against superior forces. He's also in large part responsible for saving Koratan President Nanette Fournier six weeks ago in Confederacy space."

Major Early bristles even more and doesn't try to hide it this time. "Admiral, if you're suggesting that I yield command of my Marines to a foreign noncom Marine just because he's led boarding actions on a couple of stations, then I'm afraid I must refuse."

"Relax, Major," I say sternly, and she has the good sense to look momentarily cowed. "I'm suggesting nothing of the sort. However, I did ask Gunnery Sergeant Boyd to put together some initial plans to share with you. During the operation, he and his people will operate under your command, along with the full contingent of our fleet's Marines. But given the circumstances, I felt you would benefit from his experience."

She looks slightly less upset but far from convinced. Next to her, Captain Lamar is red in the face as well. I decide to play my trump card.

"There's one more reason I've asked Gunny to help with planning the boarding action," I say slowly. "There's an important asset in our attack that neither you nor Mr. Lamar knows of, with whom Gunny has worked with several times in the past."

"Asset, sir?" Early asks cautiously.

"That'd be me, chica," a cheerful accented voice says from next to me, and I see every pair of eyes in the room go wide except mine and Boyd's.

"Koratan!" Risa Quarrie hisses, and both Early and Lamar jump up from their chairs, hands going to their sidearms.

"Stand down, Marines!" I bark, as Hayley simply sits there and grins at them, slouching in her chair, her hair turned bright pink, all pretense at being a simple Navy ensign and my aide out the airlock.

"Sir, what is the meaning of this?" Quarrie asks angrily.

I sigh. I wanted to ease them all into this, but leave it to Hayley to go for the shock factor. She's enjoying this way too much. "Captain Quarrie, Major Early, Major Lamar"—I give Lamar the unofficial promotion to have only one captain present on the ship—"may I introduce Agent Sparrow of the Koratan Confederate Guard. You can call her Lieutenant Uvalde if you'd like."

The two Marine officers stand there, hands still on their sidearms, but neither makes a move to draw their weapons. Of course, I'm not worried about them hitting Hayley; she's quite good at moving out of the way when people shoot at her, but I don't particularly relish the thought of being caught in the crossfire.

"Agent Sparrow is on special assignment to my crew from President Fournier herself," I say firmly, "with the *full* knowledge of Queen Anne, I might add. In fact, she's been in the presence of the queen on multiple occasions, including at my wedding reception, so if our monarch trusts her, perhaps you can as well."

The two Marines take their hands off their weapons but stay standing and ready for action.

I sigh again and decide to tell them everything, starting with Hayley first helping Jess rescue me from Kayla Carter's clutches, and then about her role in taking down Duchess Charlotte in our first trip to Koratan space, all the way to the details of her role in saving President Fournier. By the end of my lengthy story, Early and Lamar are still pissed, but at least they're sitting down. Quarrie looks only thoughtful, her initial anger gone without a trace.

"In other circumstances," I tell the two Marine officers, "I'd have Hayley beat up a few of your best fighters on the sparring mats to show you just what she can do, but we don't have that kind of time. So I'm going to ask Gunny Boyd and Agent Sparrow to share with you the plan they've put together to storm Bollen's station. Then I'm going to let you all discuss things with the promise not to kill each other until you've hashed out our final plan of attack."

I do just that, sitting patiently as Gunny and Hayley describe their plan, and even hanging around a little while to hear Early and Lamar poke some very real holes in it and 'suggest' several changes. Finally, when I'm confident they won't hurt each other and that they're on their way to an actual, workable plan, I leave them be. They have just under three hours left to finalize things before we surface in the Linford Commons system, where we'll also find out if I was right about the minefield.

# SIXTY-ONE
# CONFRONTATION

## JESSICA LIN MENDOZA

When I awake next, after another nearly twelve hours of sleep, Mary and Diedre are there, but Peter has disappeared. When I ask about him, they evade the question. It's obvious to me what's happened: whatever hope the boy had in me is gone, and he's chosen not to hang around and be disappointed any further.

I'm about to suggest another futile lap of the hold when the crowd around us parts and two large men step through. Both glare down at me where I sit with my back to the bulkhead.

The bigger of the two, a wide-faced man with a buzzcut, levels a finger toward me. He's probably in his late twenties, but his voice is surprisingly deep, and with a pang, it reminds me of Gunny Boyd. "You're Navy?"

I nod.

"It's your fault we're here!" he bellows. "You people were

on Poe when this happened. So what are *you* going to do to get us out of here?"

I look around, eyebrows raised. "What do you mean? The exit's right over there." I point in the general direction of the inner airlock.

I don't know why I said that—it's more like something Brad would say. He likes to poke the proverbial bear; I don't. From the look on the big newcomer's face, he doesn't appreciate my lame attempt at a joke, either. He takes a step forward, and I rise to meet him, stopping him in his tracks, but he's so close to me that I can smell his fetid breath.

"I asked you a serious question," he growls. "I expect a serious answer."

"Or what?"

Again, very much the wrong thing to say—I know that. I'm shocked to even hear it escape my lips. Brad has been a *terrible* influence on me. Big Boy thinks so too, and growls again, the sound low and primal, that of a man at the end of his rope and trying to utilize his last few brain cells.

"Listen, you…" he says, calling me a word that I haven't been called for a long time. "Your job is to protect Federation citizens, right? So you'd better figure out a way to get us free, since you did such a great job at protecting us on Poe."

"Or what?" I ask again, taking a small step forward and bumping him with my chest, glaring up at him with hard eyes and ignoring the surprised look on his buddy's face. "If you touch me in here, then *after* I kick the snot out of both of you, the guards will send in their drones and finish the job. Heck, I'd even take a stun round myself for the pleasure of beating you to a pulp."

Again, completely the wrong thing to say. I blame the head trauma. Or maybe the poor diet. Or maybe the fact that I'm on a slave ship, probably being used as bait for some kind of trap to ensnare and kill my husband and all our friends.

Either way, I'm feeling just as belligerent as this guy and his only slightly smaller friend.

To my surprise, however, Big Boy's face almost immediately lightens up, and he breaks out a big, toothy smile. "You've got fire in you," he says. "I like that. Listen, sorry about what I called you. We're all a little on edge."

The apology takes me by such surprise that the words don't register in my injured brain for a couple of seconds. When they do, I have a hard time coming up with a response.

Perhaps sensing my confusion, he steps back and holds out a hand. "Gunter Upton. Formerly of the Poe Constabulary."

Still stunned, I reach out and take his hand, letting him shake mine. "Jessica Lin. Formerly of . . . well, everywhere lately."

If his smile was friendly before, his entire face lights up now. "No kidding? *The* Jessica Lin?"

"I think so?" I answer, having no idea what he means by that.

"You're a legend!" he practically shouts. Then, to my chagrin, he turns and addresses his buddy. "This is *the* Jessica Lin. The one that shot up those Koratans at Serenidad and took down Dexter Hornsby!"

I decide not to correct him that it was Brad who took down Hornsby while I was busy killing Kayla Carter.

"How—" I try to ask, but now the giant raises his voice and yells to the assembled crowd. He's tall enough and loud enough that I'm entirely certain the entire cargo hold can hear him.

"Everyone! This is Jessica Lin. She's a hero! I would know, I was a cop on Poe. I've heard all about her." He looks back at me and blushes. "Mostly on wanted bulletins, mind you, but everyone in my precinct thought you were a hero and got a bad rap, just like Admiral Mendoza."

I'm stunned. I literally can't think of a thing to say. It seems everywhere we go these days, people have heard of Brad. But me? A hero?

"So," Gunter says, still excited. "What are you thinking for us to get out of here?"

I want to tell them that I have no idea. I want to tell him to shut up and leave me alone before he draws the attention of any slaver who hasn't already wondered why the entire crowd is now staring at me. But the sheer joy and excitement I see in his face, mirrored now on the many faces around me, is both intoxicating and terrifying. Like if I tell them the truth, they'll wither and die of disappointment, but also like I *want* them to have hope in me.

So I hedge. "I'm still working on that. But when I finish figuring it out, I promise you'll be the first to know."

That seems to satisfy him, for now, and he nods. "Great. And don't hesitate to ask for any help you may need. Me and Frank"—he jabs a thumb over his shoulder to point to his only slightly less giant friend—"are all in. We're with you all the way, Captain." He rises to his full height and throws a sloppy salute.

I return his salute, and he turns and pushes his way through the crowd. Frank lingers for a second and gives me his own shy smile before heading off after Gunter.

The crowd watches me as I stand there for a while. When it's clear I'm not about to do anything remotely interesting, they slowly disperse, which, in the crowded hold, basically means they start ignoring me, since there's nowhere else to go.

I'm heartened by Gunter's faith in me. Maybe after his pronouncement, I can get the crowd to help in some sort of escape attempt. At the very least, I have what looks to be two physically powerful new allies.

Unfortunately, I have no idea what to do with them.

Or do I?

I turn to Mary, moving close to her and speaking in a low voice. "How long does it take the drones to deploy after a fight starts?"

She jerks her head back and gives me a confused and disapproving grimace, but I lean closer and put my ear near her mouth so she can whisper her response without being overheard.

"I don't know," she replies. "One, maybe two minutes. I think the guards like to watch the fights before they break them up."

"Perfect."

# SIXTY-TWO
# MOMENT OF TRUTH

## BRAD MENDOZA

"Something tells me we wouldn't have been friends at the academy," Risa Quarrie says dryly as we count down the minutes until *Gunslinger* and the rest of the fleet leave the void to enter the Linford Commons system.

"What makes you say that?" I ask from my seat next to her on the bridge.

"This plan of yours is either the dumbest thing I've ever been a part of, or it's brilliant. I've always been more by the book. I largely stuck with the textbook battle plans in my academy courses. I imagine you were more of the type to throw a lot of spaghetti at the wall and see what stuck."

I look at her oddly. "Why would anyone throw spaghetti at a wall?" All I can think of is the disastrous time Jess cooked me a spaghetti dinner on that yacht in Koratan space. But I don't recall throwing the dish at the wall as being any part of that.

Quarrie gives a short laugh. "That's an excellent question, sir. It's a saying back home on Hecate. Never quite understood it. My sister and I once tried it. We found a box of noodles and threw them at a wall. None of them stuck, and our mom yelled at us when she saw the mess. Never attempted it again after that."

I chuckle. "Maybe we might have gotten along after all, Captain." I'm not really feeling all that humorous, but I can appreciate what she's doing: distracting me from the fact that we're about to exit jump space, potentially straight into an ambush, with my wife's life on the line.

"Captain, ten seconds," the navigation officer calls out, and we clam up, watching the countdown timer on the forward display.

When it reaches zero, the stars are back, and I hold my breath, waiting.

"No contacts," the sensor officer finally reports. "Scanning on X-band and increased PRF."

We continue to wait as the sensors switch to a shorter wavelength and a higher frequency, searching for objects usually too small to show up on the scans.

"Reading multiple contacts at close range," shouts the sensor officer. "Resolving."

I wait, gripping the arms of my chair so hard my knuckles turn white. Then I practically hear the sensor officer's sigh of realization across the bridge. "Mines, sirs. They're mines."

"Are we close enough to trigger their proximity fuses?" Quarrie demands.

There's a momentary pause that seems to stretch into eternity.

"No, ma'am," the tactical officer answers. "They're just

out of range, and at our current closing rate, the fleet has plenty of time to turn and avoid them."

"Message the fleet to come about to one-two-oh mark zero and burn at flank speed," I tell the comm officer.

All around me on the bridge, I see bunched-up shoulders relax. Against all odds, entering a system at a crawl actually paid off. Instead of the SDF waiting here to blow us to bits, we've found the mines, just as Hayley and I predicted.

I can't believe that actually worked.

We're alive and unscathed, having foiled the enemy's first attempt to kill us in this system. Of course, I'm sure Bollen and the SDF have backup plans upon backup plans.

"Boss?"

We all turn to see that Hayley has wandered onto the bridge. Now that she isn't posing as an ensign anymore, she's given up all pretense of military discipline as well. She's shed her uniform and is wearing a pair of shorts, a bright red T-shirt, and a short leather jacket. Her hair is still bright pink and, disconcertingly, her eyes match it. She catches one of the male lieutenants studying her a little too closely and winks at him before turning her attention back to me.

Did I mention she's also barefoot, on the bridge of a functioning warship?

"What is it, Lieutenant?" I ask crossly.

"That Major Early chica says she's ready to command the Marines to transfer to *Bainbridge* whenever you give the order," she says, innocently enough.

"And she couldn't just call up here and tell us that herself?" I chide.

Hayley offers a laconic shrug. "I was bored, boss. Figured I'd take the message for her."

"Understood. Thanks, Hayley. Tell Major Early I'll give the order as soon as we're fully clear of the minefield."

"I'll tell her, boss," Hayley says cheerfully. Then she

throws another suggestive wink at the gaping lieutenant and practically skips off the bridge.

"I'm not going to have a problem with her and my male officers, am I?" Quarrie asks with a hint of real distaste in her tone.

I laugh. "No, you won't, Captain. Believe it or not, she's practically engaged to Commander Illian on *Bainbridge*."

Quarrie's jaw drops open. "Illian? That boring man with the personality of a rock?"

Now I can't help but laugh a little louder. "He's not *that* boring, but yes."

"Really? How? Why?"

I shrug. "No one knows. But even Victoria wouldn't cheat on Illian."

"Who's Victoria?"

"Well, she's Hayley. Sort of. It's hard to explain. Needless to say, she might flirt with your crew because she likes to mess with people and throw them off, but she won't do anything more than that."

"Good, because from what Major Lamar has told me, there's not much we could do to stop that woman from doing just about anything she wanted on my ship."

I look at her wryly. "Try sleeping a few doors down from her every night, knowing her implant can hack Navy locks."

Quarrie visibly shudders and turns to her console, trying very hard to study the vectors projected there and probably not think about a rogue, overly flirtatious Koratan Confederate Guard assassin loose on her ship with the master key to every lock.

Welcome to the club, Captain.

Unfortunately, my good humor evaporates almost instantly. The enemy missed their first chance to take us out. But we still don't have eyes on Bollen's ship, the freighter from Poe, or the courier ship that took Jess. The sixth planet is still too far away, and our sensors won't have a clear view of its environs for the better part of a day yet.

For all I know, Bollen and the SDF have already left the system with Jess as their prisoner, trusting their minefield to take us out. But I take a sort of cold comfort in knowing that Bollen wants me and Jess to see each other die. So I have to believe—*hope*—that he's still here, waiting, watching, and preparing for the fight to come. And that she's still somewhere nearby as well.

# SIXTY-THREE
# FIGHT!

## JESSICA LIN MENDOZA

I wait a few hours for the tumult of Gunter's announcement to die down completely before I whisper instructions to Diedre and send her off to find my two large admirers. She returns with their response, and I give them another two hours to spread the word. Only then do I get up and start my usual lap around the cargo hold. This time, I walk slowly and stop to loiter just short of the inner airlock door.

I wait there for a few minutes until a young man just as large as Gunter and Frank pushes his way through the crowd, his face stormy. His eyes meet mine, and he glares daggers at me. "You! This is all your fault!" he shouts, his voice booming and startling everyone around us. He steps forward and, before I can react, reaches down, seizes my throat in his gigantic, meaty paws, and starts choking the life out of me.

"You! My brother is dead because of you!" he screams,

spittle flying from his mouth and wetting my face as I gasp for breath. He doesn't let me get any air but lifts me off my feet so that they flail helplessly in the air.

I try to kick him, aiming for the groin, but he turns a hip and deflects it, sneering at me.

"I'm gonna choke the life out of you!" he roars. "You were supposed to protect us." Then he calls me a word very similar to what Gunter called me hours ago.

"Let her go!" an angry voice shouts from a speaker somewhere overhead. The guards have finally noticed.

The giant doesn't put me down. He looks up at the ceiling high overhead, searching for the cameras the guards are using to watch us. "Make me!" he yells with laughter in his voice as I vaguely hear the sound of hatches opening high above and the buzz of deploying drones. "Hit me with a stun round and my hands'll spasm. I'll snap her neck!"

For far too long, I think the guards aren't going to do anything. Certainly no one from the crowd seems keen to intervene, and through the tears in my eyes, I can see several drones hovering around us, just out of reach, but not daring to shoot the man either.

Most of the crowd is pushing backward, trying to put as much distance between themselves, my attacker, and the circling drones as they can.

"Last warning!" the guard's voice shouts from the speakers overhead.

The man choking the life out of me responds with another booming laugh.

I hear the guard swear, but his foul word is cut off halfway as he stops transmitting. Nothing happens immediately, but as darkness starts to infringe on the edges of my vision, I finally hear the sound of my salvation over the rushing noise of blood in my ears and the buzzing of the drones.

The airlock cycles and then opens.

Shouts fill the hold as footsteps pound across the short distance toward me and my would-be killer. He roars again and flings me aside. I crumple to the deck, gasping for breath, stars filling my view as I struggle to suck in enough oxygen to get back to my feet. Everything hurts as I watch four guards in riot gear slam shock sticks into my giant attacker.

He goes down like a sack of potatoes, twitching and spasming on the deck. All four guards make the mistake of circling him, taking turns kicking the giant man while he's down, just as I hoped they might.

Their focus on the downed man makes it so much easier for me to get to my feet unseen and leap toward the back of the guard closest to me. Just as I charge into him, forcing him to trip over the body of the large man he's gleefully kicking, Gunter and his friend Frank emerge from the crowd and football tackle two of the other guards.

Shots ring out as the drones fire repeatedly, but I pull the guard I grabbed on top of me. He grunts as multiple rounds hit him. I feel an overwhelming sense of relief when none of them hit me—this was by far the riskiest part of my plan.

Someone yells, and they must throw something, because I hear a collision overhead, and then one of the drones falls to the deck next to me, sparking. The buzzing of the other nearly dozen drones gets farther away as their little AI brains identify the threat and either go after whoever threw the object or move high enough to evade another missile.

Unfortunately, one of the guards is still standing. But so, by some miracle, is Gunter. And as I roll the unconscious guard off me, I watch as the two men trade blows.

The final guard never stands a chance. Gunter's fist takes him on the chin, under his helmet, and he drops to the deck. The drones turn back to us, but several more men materialize from the crowd, leaping on top of both of us and shielding us with their bodies as more stun rounds fly.

This isn't going as well as I'd hoped. Luckily, my implant pings me. It's finally managed to identify the control channel for the drones, the *only* channel seemingly not being jammed in the hold. Their small onboard AIs are no match for my military implant. Less than two seconds after the ping, I cry out in triumph as the remaining drones fall to the deck, completely deactivated.

"Go!" I shout, and Gunter and I push our unconscious human shields off us. I'm surprised he and Frank were able to get so many to help us, and I breathe a silent thanks to those who literally sacrificed their bodies so this plan would work.

We rush to one of the prone guards, and I help Gunter drag him toward the still-open airlock. Just as we reach it, I hear the sound I've been dreading: the drones coming awake.

I knew it was only a matter of time before their onboard AIs rebooted and cycled their frequencies. I throw myself through the open airlock hatch and pull on the guard's deadweight as Gunter shoves him over the threshold from behind. Then I watch in horror as, instead of following me inside the lock, the big man grabs the door and shuts it in my face. I watch through the porthole, the cry of protest dying on my lips as four drones empty their stun rounds into Gunter's back.

I'm alone, in a sealed airlock, with the unconscious guard. This had better work.

I search the guard's pockets until I find what I'm looking for. I drag his body across the airlock to the sealed door that leads into the rest of his ship. Praying that his friends inside haven't been able to reset the security systems yet, I strain to lift him enough to place his palm against the reader on the hatch controls. At the same time, I insert the key fob from his pocket into the small receptacle next to the palm reader.

With a satisfying click, the hatch lock disengages, and I reach down to take the stun rod from the guard's belt before I pull the hatch open and leap inside, weapon at the ready to find . . .

No one.

An empty corridor stretches in both directions, with no sign of other guards, crew, or anyone else for that matter.

# SIXTY-FOUR
# OVERCROWDING

## BRAD MENDOZA

"Sir," Francis Illian reports over the ready room's comm. "Captain Lamar and his Marines docked their shuttles and transferred to *Bainbridge* without incident. Same for Major Early's company. It's a bit crowded over here, sir. And it kind of smells."

I might laugh if I were in a better mood. "Thanks, Guns. Don't worry, you'll have them off your ship soon enough."

"Aye, sir," he says with clear doubt in his voice. This may be partially his girlfriend's plan, but he's not exactly enamored with it.

"How's Hayley?" I ask, if for no other reason than to distract him.

He sighs. "Happy to be home, sir. I had to kick her off the bridge because she kept trying to nibble my ear. I think she and Gunny are sparring with the Marines in the gym right now."

"Remind them not to injure any of Early's or Lamar's people. We're going to need each and every one of those Marines."

"Aye, sir. You okay?"

The direct question surprises me so much that I almost don't even realize he's asked it.

"No," I answer honestly.

"We'll find her, Skipper," he tries to reassure me. "Assuming she doesn't find us first. If there's anyone better than you at pulling off the impossible, it's Captain Lin."

I nod, trying so hard to believe him.

"Admiral, did I ever tell you what I went through when you, Hayley, and Tina went missing on Serenidad—when Hayley's old Guard buddies captured and almost killed you all?"

This question surprises me as much as the first, and I shake my head dumbly over the video call. I really should be signing off, but as the fleet accelerates on a straight line to the sixth planet, there's really not a whole lot for an admiral to do right now.

"I was in a pretty dark place, sir," Illian goes on. "I tried not to show it—Captain Lin needed my help taking out those two Koratan ships that tried to intercept us in orbit. But I thought I'd lost the woman I loved and my captain all in one day. I was a mess. When I wasn't on the bridge, I was back in my quarters, either pacing back and forth or shouting into my pillow."

I've rarely heard Illian raise his voice, so the image of him screaming into a pillow is a bit hard to picture.

"How'd you get through it?" I find myself asking despite the bleakness that still fills me.

"By thinking that if I didn't, and if I wasn't at the top of my game, then it wouldn't matter if you and Hayley and Tina survived, because *Bainbridge* wouldn't be there to pick you up. Not unless I gave Captain Lin and the rest of the crew everything I had to help save them and our ship. It was the same thing, I think, that got Captain Lin through thinking she might have lost you."

I nod slowly. "Thanks, Francis. That helps. It helps a lot, actually."

We end the call, and I stand up and ball my hands into fists. Illian is right. Jess is still alive out there—I refuse to believe Bollen has already sacrificed his primary bait now that he failed to kill me with his minefield—and she's going to need me, *Bainbridge*, and *Gunslinger*, the whole fleet, at the top of our game to rescue her and make sure she has a home to come back to. Taking a deep breath and letting it out slowly, I square my shoulders and march back onto the bridge.

On the forward display, I see an external camera view of the stars ahead of us. It's not like the movies, where the stars move apart and to the sides as we fly through them at breakneck speed. Space is far too large for that. Virtually all of those stars are so far away that no human eye could ever perceive them moving as we fly toward them. The one exception is the bright pinpoint of light that's center screen. It's noticeably bigger than when I was last on the bridge a few hours ago, but it's still too far away to make out any details.

Somewhere around that pinpoint of light, assuming he hasn't run and hid somewhere else, is Andre Bollen. And hopefully there with him is Jess.

"Penny for your thoughts, Admiral," I hear a soft voice at my elbow. I turn to see Risa Quarrie standing beside me, though with my attention fixed on the light of the sixth planet, I didn't even notice her arrive on the bridge. As it is, we're both standing in the rear, and most of the bridge crew hasn't noticed us yet. Those that have go about their jobs; we're in a combat situation, so all the jumping up and saluting when senior officers enter the bridge has taken a necessary and welcome backseat.

"Just wondering where that SDF fleet is," I lie.

Quarrie gives me a knowing smile. "I think you're right, Admiral. They'll be huddled around Bollen's base, just like you said. And don't worry, sir, I'm sure we'll find her there, too."

I suppress a grimace at realizing how easily she's read me and simply nod to acknowledge her words of support. Then I turn my attention back to the sixth planet and silently will it to grow big enough for us to see if I am, indeed, right about what we'll find there.

# SIXTY-FIVE
# NO ONE

## JESSICA LIN MENDOZA

We've searched the entire ship, four times.

Disabling the drones again was the hardest part, but when I did so, the crowd was able to crush their flight surfaces and prevent them from taking off again. After that, I came back through the airlock and organized those still conscious, which was thankfully most of them, into search parties. We searched the entire freighter four times and found exactly no one. It's like the four guards represented the only crew.

That alone might have been a good thing, except for what we *did* find.

"So you're saying that we can't change course or even slow the ship?" a now conscious Gunter asks as we survey the bridge for the fifth time.

I slam a fist down on the broken console in front of me and swear. "No. They haven't just locked everything down;

they've outright destroyed every control, even the direct control consoles in Engineering. The drive is burning happily along on a fixed course with no way to shut it off, power up the thrusters, or do anything to change our course and speed."

"And that course leads to?"

I shrug. "Sensors are gone, too. We literally can't see where we're going. There are a few windows here and there, but all the star positions tell me is that we're probably in Linford Commons, and most likely heading out of the system."

"Probably? Likely? Doesn't inspire much confidence."

I glare at him. "Well, excuse me. The astrogation app on my implant isn't exactly designed for this exact scenario."

Gunter takes a step back, reacting to my acid tone. "At least we're out of the cargo hold," he says, trying to sound upbeat.

I wince. How can I tell him that we left one prison only to find ourselves in another? I've already checked, and every escape pod has been launched. I'm sure this is the armed freighter Bollen used to capture these people at Poe, but all its cargo shuttles are missing as well. With the controls destroyed, we're stuck inside this ship until someone comes to get us out of it. Not that we can even call for help; the comms are dead.

"Do we have any engineers in our group?" I ask, purposefully avoiding calling us prisoners or slaves or anything else that might hurt morale, since there are half a dozen others on the bridge with us pretending not to listen to every word I say.

Gunter blows out a long breath. "Dunno. Let me go ask around."

I nod, and he takes off, while I go back to examining the mess of cut and melted wires under the helm controls for the third time. Maybe if I try to talk to the ship's AI for a seventeenth time, it will answer. I've confirmed now that they weren't actually jamming our implants in the hold—there was simply nothing outside the hold to talk to. Even the various hatch and external airlock controls have been rendered dead or responsive to manual codes only.

Unfortunately, the ship has stayed completely silent despite my many attempts to communicate with it. Which makes me certain that whatever is happening here is by design. Andre Bollen has a plan for us, and we're powerless to fight against it.

# SIXTY-SIX
# THE MESSAGE

## BRAD MENDOZA

"Admiral, we're getting a signal from the sixth planet."

I perk up at the comm officer's words. Next to me on *Gunslinger*'s bridge, Risa Quarrie furrows her eyebrows.

"On bridge speakers," I order after only a moment's hesitation.

A moment later, a familiar distorted voice echoes across *Gunslinger*'s bridge. "Mendoza, nice to see you've continued to be so predictable. So you figured out my little trick with the mines, did you? Well, no matter. As nice as it would have been to show your wife the sensor readings of your death this morning, you won't live to see tomorrow."

"Hello?" I call out in reply, ignoring Quarrie's shocked look. "Andy? Are you transmitting? I can't make out what you're saying."

It takes a few minutes for my response to make it to the sixth planet and for Bollen's next message to arrive. When it does, I can sense an edge of frustration in the distorted voice.

"Don't play games with me, Mendoza! Or poor little Jessica will pay the price. It's bad enough you brought an entire sector fleet to their doom just to try and rescue her; imagine how bad it will be when I torture her and let you hear her screams as she begs for death."

"I'm sorry," I say back, doing my best to sound genuinely puzzled. "But if you're transmitting, it's coming through pretty garbled. How about this, Andy? I'll just come to you. You can tell me what you want to say while I'm killing you. See you soon!"

I signal to the comm officer to cut the connection, then force a smile at a very concerned-looking Risa Quarrie.

"What exactly was that?" she asks in a low voice so the rest of her crew can't hear.

"Villains like to monologue," I tell her with a shrug. "Take that away from them—don't let them tell you all about how smart they are—and they tend to make mistakes. Trust me on this. Sometimes it's fun to hear all about their dastardly plans. But in this case, Bollen can't taunt me into doing what he wants if I can't even hear him."

"But he *knows* you can hear him, right?"

"He *thinks* I can hear him, but he can't know. So he's got to be doubting just a little that I'm going to dance to his tune, because he simply can't be 100 percent sure I'm listening to the music."

"You're a very strange man, Admiral," Quarrie says dryly. "Have you taken many hits to the head lately?"

"Several, why?"

Despite the banter, there's a ball of cold dread in my chest. What if messing with Bollen ends with him killing Jess to retaliate like he's threatening to do? What if he really does torture her until she screams for it all to end? So much could go wrong—likely *will* go wrong—and it will be all my fault.

But I have to stick to the plan. Otherwise, I have *no* hope of seeing my wife alive again.

# SIXTY-SEVEN
# TAUNTS

## JESSICA LIN MENDOZA

It's been exactly twelve hours, forty-two minutes, and eighteen seconds since our daring escape. And in that time, we've made exactly zero progress on gaining control of a single ship's system.

"There are no spare parts or tools anywhere, ma'am," says a tall woman who worked as a mechanic in her father's shuttle repair shop prior to enrolling in the university. Her name is Kimberly, and she's become my de facto chief engineer. She's also the twentieth person to tell me there's nothing on board that we can use to repair the ship.

"Even if there were," adds an older, shorter man next to her, a retired former engineer's mate on a freighter who was visiting his son's dorm the night of the raid, "most of the damage we've found would need a shipyard and months to repair." What a fun-loving group this is.

"How is the drive still operating?"

He scrunches up his face. "Not sure, ma'am. By all rights, it should have automatically shut down when the controls were damaged like that. Something, somewhere, is keeping it going. But without tools, we can't even open up the panels in Engineering to get at the inner workings.

"Are the guards talking?"

"Nothing helpful." This is from Gunter. He cracks his knuckles. "And I've been *real* persuasive. I get the impression that they don't actually know much."

"Why is that?"

"Well, mainly because they claim to have been lured on board in this system with promises of great pay, but never met their employer. They were told the ship was automated and not to worry about it. And frankly,"—he pauses for effect—"they're imbeciles. If they've got a fourth-grade reading level between them, I'd be shocked. My guess is they're low-level scumbags looking to make a quick buck."

"So the real crew must have abandoned ship at some point," I muse, not sure what to take from that.

He nods but has nothing more to add.

"Okay, well, then let's—"

I'm cut off when the bridge speakers overhead squelch loudly. Then a familiar distorted voice booms in our ears.

"Well done, Captain Lin. I'm so glad to see you've escaped and learned the futility of your situation."

"Who are you?" I demand, wondering how this is even happening. A prerecorded message from the crew before they abandoned ship? Or is the comm actually working?

I have to wait for my answer, but the wait itself confirms that this is, indeed, a live comm message. After several minutes, the time it takes my response to get to Bollen and his next words to get to me, I finally hear his terrible voice again.

"I doubt you're smart enough to figure out who I am, Captain Lin. But let's see if you can guess anyway."

"It doesn't matter who you are, only that you've chosen to hide behind the name Andre Bollen," I shoot back, not in the mood to play by the slaver's games.

Another long wait.

He laughs, a cruel sound even through the distortion. "Jessica, Jessica, Jessica," he says, like I'm some small, unruly child. "You've got more fire in you than I remember. Too bad, really. I do miss our time together. Breaking you again would be so much fun."

My breath catches. It can't be. There's no way.

"It's such a shame," he goes on, oblivious to the way my entire body has frozen on the freighter's bridge, or the way my heart is pounding so hard in my chest that I worry I won't be able to hear him over its rapid thumping. "I'll just have to take my pleasure in forcing your idiot husband to watch you die."

The line goes silent, no doubt as he waits for my response. But I can't talk. I can't muster the will or the air to do so. Because distorted voice or not, I now know exactly who Andre Bollen is.

He must guess that my lack of response is a sign that I've finally figured it out, because when his voice next intrudes into the freighter's bridge, the distortion is gone, leaving behind only the oily, conceited, haughty voice that once caused me panic attacks.

"That's right, Jessica. You thought I'd forgotten what you did to me, you . . ." What follows is the worst litany of words I've ever been called, but they have no impact. My entire being is still frozen, my fight-or-flight response short-circuiting as the most hated voice in the galaxy continues to tell me how small, unimportant, and useless I am.

When he's done, he laughs again, the sound like that of an executioner's blade. "Now, Jessica," he says smugly, "witness your husband's downfall. And die knowing he couldn't save you—that *no one* could ever save you from me."

# SIXTY-EIGHT
# HADES

## BRAD MENDOZA

"Well, there's no longer any doubt of the SDF being under Bollen's control."

I nod grimly at Risa Quarrie's assessment. We're close enough now to see the ships waiting for us in orbit around the third moon of the sixth planet. There, as before, is Bollen's station and his battleship. But surrounding it are *twenty-nine* SDF ships, far more than we saw on our recon pass of this system a week ago. And as we get closer, there's something else.

"Admiral, Captain, we're getting a better scan of Andre Bollen's battleship," the tactical officer says from his station behind us. "But we still can't identify the ship class."

"Admiral Mendoza?" a voice from the overhead speakers interrupts us.

"Go ahead, Admiral Turly," I reply.

"Admiral, I've got a match on that enemy battleship."

I sit up straighter in my seat. "We were just discussing that, Chris. How did you get a match? Our AI can't identify it."

"Give the AI your flag rank override codes," he suggests.

I hadn't even thought of that, but I do so, following his instructions. I know the second it works, because the tactical officer gasps.

"Sir, the AI is insisting it's a Hades-class," he says in disbelief.

Beside me, in a very out-of-character move, Risa Quarrie gasps. "But, the Hades-class . . ."

"Is still theoretical?" I finish for her, watching new data pour into my implant from a previously locked portion of *Gunslinger*'s AI memory. "I thought so too, or that it was just a rumor. But it seems our dearly departed king had three of them made."

"Brad," Chris adds over the speakers, his voice subdued, "can we speak in private?"

I quickly make my way into Quarrie's ready room, which I've essentially made my own that this point. The comm officer transfers the call to the console there.

"Go ahead, Chris," I say, looking into his worried face over the camera feed.

"If the specs on the Hades-class are accurate, that's the third one built, *Vigilant Dagger*. And it heavily outguns even *Liberator*."

I mull over that for a few moments. "Any recommendations?" I ask. "Not just for *Vigilant Dagger*, but for that entire fleet? We're more outnumbered than we expected."

I almost expect Chris to suggest we turn around and head back to Cillian Heights, but as usual these days, the man surprises me.

"We won't get another shot at this, Admiral," he says somberly. "We'll need to keep our speed advantage if we want a chance though—control the time and angle of each attack."

I nod. "Multiple passes around the sixth planet then. After the first attack, we enter its orbit. We can use it to keep our velocity and attack the SDF fleet each time we come around to the third moon's location. Hit them at speed, like you said."

"I think that's best," he agrees. "Also gives us the advantage of readjusting our next pass after whatever happens on the previous one."

"But we won't be able to see how Bollen is adjusting his forces when we're on the backside of the gas giant," I argue back, playing devil's advocate to my own plan.

Turly licks his lips. "No plan is perfect, Brad. But this one gives us the most flexibility and advantage over a superior force. Though if we play our angles right, we could lure the SDF away from that station, make room for *Bainbridge* and the Marines to board her."

"That's exactly what we'll do then," I agree. "Bollen is hungry to fight. He wants me dead, and he's probably looking on this as his chance to destroy the entire sector fleet and hand the Cluster over to the Jutzens on a silver platter. He'll be prone to be too aggressive. Let's use that against him and ruin his plans, shall we?"

Two minutes later, I'm back on the bridge, sharing the new plan with Quarrie and her people. There are several gasps when I explain the specs on Bollen's battleship.

According to the intel locked away in the AI's memory, four years ago, King Charles commissioned three prototypes of the ultrasecret and superadvanced Hades-class battleships, so secret because they supposedly incorporate weapons tech illegally secured from the Outer Rim. It's amazing he hid their existence so long—Navy scuttlebutt is often far more effective than official secrets can withstand—but in this instance, he managed to do so, building all three Hades-class ships in closed drydocks at a secret shipyard far out in Prometheus's outer system. Unfortunately, he didn't hide them well enough, because the Jutzens apparently found them. And all three ships, codenamed *Vigilant Sword, Vigilant Shield,* and *Vigilant Dagger,* must now be in the hands of the Nazis and their collaborators.

"How did a Hades-class get out here?" Quarrie asks. "And in the hands of a slaver."

"Because Andre Bollen is no slaver," I answer soberly. "Well, he is, but first and foremost, he's what we've suspected. He's King Chance's new commander for the Corpus Christi Cluster, the man he entrusted to take over this sector and open a second front against Queen Anne. And he's a member of the royal family."

*Gunslinger*'s normally professional bridge is bombarded by curses and chatter from every present crew member. The captain herself has to call for decorum. When it's silent again, she looks at me with haunted eyes. "Admiral, are you telling us you've figured out who Andre Bollen really is?"

"Not exactly," I lie. "Not yet. But I expect to soon enough."

# SIXTY-NINE
# IN VAIN

## JESSICA LIN MENDOZA

"I'm sorry, Captain, but there's nothing at all we can do," the tall ship's mechanic, Kimberly, tells me, her face red with shame. She's young—far too young to be suddenly in charge of fixing an entire starship, and too young to have to deliver bleak news such as this. "They just destroyed too much, and there's literally nothing we can use to even get at the damaged components, much less fix them."

"I know," I say, putting a hand on her shoulder. My entire body is still trembling from my horrible realization of who Andre Bollen is, even though nearly six hours have passed since he revealed himself to me. I finally had to leave the bridge, unable to stand the thought that he could call me there at any time. So I've spent most of that time down here, in the aft engine room and surrounding sections of the ship, helping Kimberly and others try every access panel and search every compartment, cabinet, and locker.

"I know you're doing all you can," I tell her gently. "So are the others. We just all need to keep looking. There *has* to be something we can do to access the ship's systems."

She nods but won't meet my gaze. She's already given up. It's obvious, and with her goes our last chance of improving our situation, because if she's already surrendered, then so have the others.

But surprisingly, to myself especially, I *haven't* given up yet. Even knowing who Andre Bollen really is, I haven't once let myself think our situation is hopeless. I'm not sure why, but there's something in me that won't give up, even when my traumatized psyche keeps screaming at me to curl up in a ball and sob until either Brad or death find me.

I search Kimberly's eyes now, searching them for the same kind of hidden strength. What might Brad say to her in this situation? Probably something mildly inappropriate and wildly motivational. However, I'm not Brad, with his sharp wit and ever-present repertoire of witty comebacks. But maybe I don't have to be.

"Kimberly, what do you want to do with your life?"

She blinks at me in surprise. "I'm not sure I follow, Captain Lin."

"First off, call me Jessica. You've more than earned that right. Second, you're already a highly competent mechanic. What prompted you to go to the university?"

She looks at me as if trying to decide if I'm serious, then shrugs. "My dad never went to college. He wanted me to have that chance, even if all I did afterward was come back and work with his mechanic business again. But I guess I thought I could do something more, something that might get me off Poe one day. I'd love to be the chief engineer for a starship." Her expression, briefly softened, turns downcast again.

"Looks like this might be my only chance, though fat lot of good it did any of us."

Fighting back my own encroaching despair, I smile at her. "Not to worry, Kimberly. Something tells me you'll get your chance. Any ship would be lucky to have you in its engine compartment. You've got people older and more experienced on this freighter taking your lead because you're good at what you do and a natural born leader."

She blushes a little but looks no happier for my words.

"Right now," I tell her gently, "I need you to keep being that leader. Bollen's people may have done a number on this ship, but they're not perfect. They missed *something;* I guarantee it. We just have to figure out what it is so we can exploit it. I need you to rally your people. We've been over the ship seven times—let's do an eighth, ninth, and even tenth pass, however many it takes to find that one sure mistake they made. Because it only takes one mistake on their part for us to crack this thing wide open."

I can tell I haven't actually encouraged her all that much, but she does her best to stand up straight and throws me a relatively sharp salute before she turns to leave. I watch her go in silence.

"Did you mean all that?" a voice intrudes on my somber thoughts.

I turn to see Gunter, with the mostly silent Frank, his ever-present shadow, standing a couple of meters away. I nod. "Every word. There has to be *something* we're missing—something we haven't found yet. This is a big ship, and I refuse to believe Bollen's people did a perfect job of disabling our ability to control her."

"How long until we run out of air?"

I look at him oddly. "Why would we run out of air? We can't control the ship, but it's still operational."

Gunter looks at me oddly and points to a vent on the nearest bulkhead. "It's not blowing," he explains.

I study the vent for a moment, unsure if he's right. To prove it, he walks over and stands on his toes, reaching up to put his beefy hand in front of it. "There's no air flow, Captain. Frank and I have checked all over the ship. No air, anywhere. For at least the last few hours."

I bite back a curse. I don't know why it never occurred to me that our torturer would play by some sort of rule book—he's proven since I first met him that the rules of fair play mean nothing to him, and that he enjoys the suffering of others. Cutting off our life support is just one more obvious step in his sadistic plan, apparently.

"How much air do you think we have left?" Gunter asks, staring at me hopefully.

Sighing, I shake my head. "Hard to tell exactly, but days, certainly. It's a big ship, and even with three hundred of us on board, it'll take a while for the air to go stale. Do me a favor, though, don't tell anyone else. No sense in causing more anxiety than they already have."

Gunter frowns, but both he and Frank nod. Then they're gone, off to help continue the search for something—*anything*—we can use to better our situation.

I watch them go, feeling guilty, because I lied. It took my implant seconds to analyze the CO2 levels already in the air and extrapolate from there. We do have days, as I told them, but not many, a little less than three, in fact. Then, it won't be the lack of oxygen that kills us, but the buildup of $CO_2$. Once there's too much carbon dioxide in the air, we'll become drowsy, listless, and unable to think straight. The first sign will be headaches. After that, it'll be a fast decline until we're all gone.

That will all start to happen in roughly sixty-six hours, if we don't find a way to restore life support or get off the ship by then. After that, my implant is a little less specific on how long it will take until we're all dead—there are too many factors, like preexisting health, levels of physical activity, etc. —but it will be too quick to stop yet likely too long to be merciful.

I bite my lower lip, hard, trying to break myself out of the fast-approaching despair that wants to once more envelope me in a cocoon of hopelessness. Surely Brad would find a way out of this. I so wish he were here.

For lack of anything better to do, and perhaps to face my fears a little more head-on, I make my way back up to the bridge. The moment I walk in, I notice something new. One of the hitherto dead consoles is now lit up brightly.

I approach it with trepidation, entirely certain that this can't be a good thing for us. When I arrive, I study the screen carefully. It shows a navigation plot, complete with vectors, times, and other figures. I analyze it for a while, and with understanding dies any remaining hope.

Assuming this plot is telling the truth, we won't have three days for our air to go bad. In less than a day and a half, this freighter will slam into a small asteroid at high speed. The collision will obliterate us, and all three hundred slaves will join me in becoming a permanent part of the Linford Commons system.

We must find a way to change course or shut down the engine. Either would change our approach timing, and we'd miss the asteroid altogether.

"Jessica?" a voice says in my implant comm.

"Go ahead, Kimberly," I answer, trying to keep my voice steady and not give away that I'm panicking again.

"You know how the exterior airlocks were all sealed shut? Well, their inner doors all just opened. I'm at the one in the cargo hold; you'd better come check it out."

# SEVENTY
# ULTIMATUM

## BRAD MENDOZA

"Admiral, we're receiving another transmission from Andre Bollen's battleship at the sixth planet."

I frown in the direction of *Gunslinger*'s comm officer, then over at Captain Quarrie.

She frowns back. "Best you take it in my ready room, sir. You can always share what it says afterward."

Acknowledging the wisdom of the suggestion, I leave the bridge and am soon settled behind her ready room desk, where I accept the transmission. We're closer to the sixth planet now—close enough that 'Bollen' and I can talk in near real time.

The signal, no surprise, is audio only, but I recognize the arrogance of the disguised voice regardless. "Mendoza, so good of you to come visit me all the way out here."

"Cut the crap, Bollen. What's on your mind?"

He laughs. "Getting worried, are you? I should think so, Brad. You can't beat my SDF fleet. You can't even hope to match them, not with half your ships nothing more than drones."

I grit my teeth. We knew he had to be aware of what we did with the mothballed ships—he's clearly always had spies among us—but I'm still disappointed to confirm that our ruse has failed.

"Brad, if you could go back and do Bellerophon over again, what would you do differently?"

The non-sequitur shocks me back to complete focus on his words. My mind races—it's a question I've asked myself thousands of times, so the answer comes to my lips before I stop myself. "I would have tried to nudge the freighter off course before it hit Bellerophon Station. I would have treated it like the refugee ship it was, not the terrorist ship we wrongly thought it to be. I wouldn't have killed those people."

He laughs. "Oh, you're so predictable. Ever the Boy Scout, even when you were a drunk slob. Tell me, Brad, how much have you had to drink since I kidnapped Jessica?"

"Where are you going with this?" I demand, already sick of his games. "Spit it out, or you and I are done talking."

"Bellerophon forced you to make a choice, Brad," he continues, ignoring my outburst. "Between saving a few or saving many. And you never could live with what you did there. I've studied it, Brad, and I've studied *you*."

The pure arrogance of his statement enrages me, and though I'd intended to keep my theory of his true identity to myself, I blurt it out now in my anger. "You know what. Get to the point! And drop the charade, because I know exactly who you are."

The man called Andre Bollen laughs, and the distortion shuts off halfway through, revealing the posh and snide

Promethean accent of my old nemesis, the man who raped Jessica repeatedly on *Persephone,* and who has tried to kill her and me numerous times since, though never in person. Not until now.

"Jacobs." I hiss the name like the curse it is.

Nedrin Jacobs, King Charles's nephew and now King Chance's lackey, laughs again. "Took you long enough, Mendoza. Imagine Jessica's reaction when she found out."

"Jacobs, I swear if you've touched her, I'll—"

"Do what, Brad?" he shouts, losing all semblance of calm. "You can't do anything now unless I say you can!"

I stop, recognizing a man on the edge. Jacobs may think he's in control of this situation. He may even think he's secure behind his SDF fleet, but deep down, he's scared. And the realization of that fills me with something new that I can't quite describe.

"So what's it going to be, Nedrin?" I growl. "You want me? Take me. You let Jessica go, and I'll surrender myself to you, and you can take me back to King Chance in a box."

"No. You're not getting off that easy. *He* wouldn't be happy if I let you off that easy, Brad." The way he says 'he' makes me almost stop and ask him if we're both talking about the same person: King Chance. I've never met the former Duke of Serravo, so I can't imagine he cares about me beyond removing an annoying piece from the chessboard. But the way Jacobs refers to his master, he makes it sound a lot more personal.

"Then torture me," I urge, filing away my suspicions for later. "Cut off my limbs like the coward you are. Or face me man-to-man and show me how you fare against someone who fights back!"

He roars, and I have the satisfaction of hearing something crash in the background of his message. The sound isn't clear, but I imagine he's just thrown something heavy at something fragile, and it makes me show my teeth in a smile, though he can't see it.

"You're going to suffer plenty, Brad. But I'm going to let you choose how. Come here and face me and my fleet, and watch everyone you love die, including your precious wife. Or save her and betray everyone else who has put their misplaced trust in the Butcher of Bellerophon."

Before I can respond, the console screen comes to life as he transmits a video. I look in horror at what seems to be a live image of people, standing about or lying down, all dirty and disheveled, despair writ large on their features even in the small picture. They seem to be in some massive cargo bay, and the video zooms out to show that there are hundreds—no, *thousands*—of them.

"What you're looking at are the more than two thousand slaves working on my factory station here. Two *thousand* people, Brad, here in my station at the sixth planet. Only you can save them—assuming you can fight your way through my forces."

"Jacobs, I swear, if you're planning to use them as hostages, I'll—"

"You insult me, Brad." He cuts me off. "I can be magnanimous. If you manage to defeat my fleet, all these people will be yours for the saving. But I don't think it's going to matter, because I don't think you're even going to try."

I'm without words, my mind trying desperately to keep up with what he's telling me. As if sensing my shock, he laughs.

"That's right, Brad, you're not even going to try to save these two thousand souls. And do you know why?"

The transmitted video shifts, and instead of four thousand people, I'm looking at one—only one.

"Jess!" I choke out. It's her, standing on what looks like the bridge of a freighter, the consoles and controls around her shattered and damaged. She looks stricken but seems completely unaware that we can see her.

"That's right, Brad," the taunting, arrogant voice of Nedrin Jacobs continues. "Poor little Jessica, your precious wife. The one person you value above all others, though I have no idea why. She's here in this system too, Brad, but she's not with me. Come and face me here at the sixth planet, and you might defeat me—you might save thousands of so-called innocent people—but you'll *never* save her."

The console updates again to show a navigational plot, with the icon of a solitary ship—by the specs, the slave freighter we saw at Poe—on a collision course with what looks like a small asteroid. But the other parts of the plot are stripped away; there's nothing that would give me even a hint of their coordinates. I'd have to search the entire Linford Commons system to find them. Impossible.

"Her time is running out, Brad. Hers and the hundreds of people I took from Poe. Ah, Poe. They practically worship you there, don't they? Imagine their disappointment when not even their hero could stop me from taking their best and brightest. Oh well, at least I'm giving you the chance to save them.

"You see, Brad, I'm going to give you the opportunity to do Bellerophon all over again. This time, the choice is even simpler for you, because you know all the stakes. Come to the sixth planet and face me, with the chance to save two thousand people. Or turn your fleet around in the next ninety minutes, and I'll send you Jessica's coordinates. You'll have just enough time to reach her and save her before she slams into that asteroid."

"That's the game, Brad. Come after me and save a few thousand but sentence your wife to death. Or save the woman you claim to love but betray everything you stand for. No need to tell me your decision now. I'll be watching."

The line cuts before I can say anything back, before I can beg him not to do this, curse him for doing it anyway, or promise to come after him with all the fires of Hades' realm at my back. Instead, I'm left staring at a blank and silent console, my hands clenched into fists so tight I can feel my fingernails cutting into my palms.

With a roar of rage, I stand, flinging the chair back behind me, and punch the console, bruising my hand and not even marring the screen.

# SEVENTY-ONE
# DESPERATION

## JESSICA LIN MENDOZA

I finish listening to the conversation between Brad and Jacobs, transmitted to our ship by the royal nephew-turned-slaver himself. Unfortunately, I'm not the only one who hears it. Mary, Gunter, Frank, and Kimberly are all on the bridge with me when the transmission plays from the overhead speakers. Like me, they all hear the horrible ultimatum the wretched slaver gives my husband.

At the transmission's end, they all stare at me, wide-eyed. I want to freeze again; I want to curl into a ball and sob, not just at hearing my abuser's voice again but also at the horrible thing he's just asked my husband to do.

But whether it's that the shock of learning Bollen's true identity has worn off, or the knowledge that the others on the bridge are looking to me for strength—either way, I don't devolve into a sobbing mess. Instead, I meet the gazes of each of the others, almost defiantly.

"He'll save you, right?" Frank demands, uncharacteristically the first to speak.

I know what he's really asking. Will my husband let me and all the rest of them die, or will he abandon the hunt for Jacobs, those two thousand slaves, and the fate of the whole Corpus Christi Cluster, and come save me instead?

I have no idea which he'll choose. I know which one I want him to choose, as much as it pains me. Two thousand is greater than three hundred. What's more, failing to stop Jacobs means that thousands more will suffer under his hand. Maybe millions. If he manages to open a second front from the Cluster against Queen Anne, the entire Federation may very well fall.

Brad needs to stay the course—he needs to kill Nedrin Jacobs and stop him and his Jutzen masters.

"It's not important," I reply carefully, ignoring the looks of borderline shock and rage on the faces of those around me, and ignoring them all trying to talk over each other at once in protest. "Our job remains the same. We need to fix this ship. Jacobs—Bollen—is getting these messages to us somehow, so let's shift focus to the comm system. I want everyone working on that problem."

I turn to Kimberly. "Tell the rest what we found at the airlocks."

She scowls but accepts my change of subject. "Explosives. Every external airlock door is wired to blow if someone tries to open the outer door, from the inside or outside."

The bridge goes silent, the overlapping conversations coming to an abrupt end.

"Can't you disable them?" Gunter demands.

Kimberly blushes. "Not without tools. And if we had tools, we wouldn't be in this mess."

Unfortunately, we are in this mess. The outer door of every airlock in the ship is rigged with enough C8 explosive to destroy a good portion of this ship and any ship that tries to dock with us. Even if Brad does find us, he'll have one more nasty surprise courtesy of former Petty Officer Nedrin Jacobs. At the very least, I need control of the comms so I can warn him off.

"I need ideas, people," I say sharply as they start to argue again. "How do we get control of the comms?"

"I have an idea."

We all turn to see a young man standing at the bridge hatch, his body outside in the corridor but his head inside, staring sheepishly at us.

"And you are?" I prompt him.

"Jimmy Nevins," he says, blushing. "Sorry, I didn't mean to listen in. But I had an idea and wasn't sure where to—"

"Come inside and tell us then."

He creeps onto the bridge, looking around with wide eyes. When he reaches our little circle, he tries to throw me a salute, but it's clumsy, and his flailing hand basically just slaps his own forehead. I wince on his behalf.

"What's your idea?" I ask softly.

Once he's composed himself, he looks at me sheepishly again. "I was thinking, Captain Lin, that there might be a way to hack into the comms."

"How?" Kimberly demands before I can ask the question. "The comms system is behind locked panels, and we don't have a pry bar or a screwdriver on board to open them. And it's not responding to any of our implants. Even the captain's is locked out. No, scratch that; she's not locked out, as far as we can tell, there isn't even a wireless signal for her to connect to."

The boy shrinks back a little. "Uh . . . that's just it. There *is* a wireless signal."

"Okay, we're listening," I say before my de facto chief engineer can object again. "Tell us what you're thinking."

"The drones."

At those two words, I feel my eyebrows shoot up, an expression quickly mirrored by every other person on the bridge with us. Kimberly gasps. The drones. Why didn't any of us think about that?

"You see," Jimmy says, talking faster now, "I figured the guards were controlling the drones somehow, so that means a wireless comm signal. And if this freighter is like every other ship, then the internal comm system is tied into the external. There's a firewall, but once we're in, couldn't your implant hack through that, Captain?"

By this time, we're all nodding along with him.

"I think it just might work," Kimberly says without a hint of begrudgment. "But the drones are in pieces. We knocked all of them down when we broke out of the hold."

Jimmy smiles for the first time. "We did. But they're made of pretty simple plug-and-play hardware modules. No tools required. All I had to do was cobble together enough parts from the broken drones to rebuild one, *minus* the gun, of course."

"That's amazing!" Kimberly says, now fully enthusiastic. "Say, aren't you in my Systems 204 class?"

The boy blushes again and nods. "I sit behind you a few rows."

"Well, Jimmy," she says with a broad smile that sets the boy's cheeks all rosy again. "Go get this drone of yours, and let's see if this works."

As everyone rushes to take advantage of this new hope, I do my best to keep a smile plastered on my face. Because I alone know what getting comms will mean, and it isn't rescue.

## SEVENTY-TWO
# DEBATE

### BRAD MENDOZA

"Admiral, with all due respect, the math is clear. Nedrin Jacobs and his forces are a clear and present danger to the security of the Federation. Not to mention that he has two thousand slaves that we might rescue if we take on his forces."

I stare hard at Chris Turly through the vid screen in *Gunslinger*'s wardroom. Captain Quarrie is with me for this conference, acting as my flag captain, and Illian is also on the call.

What surprises me the most, I suppose, is not that Chris and Quarrie both support prioritizing taking out the SDF fleet over rescuing Jess—they're right about the math on this one—but rather that they're not advocating turning around altogether given how superior his force is to ours.

Apparently, learning Jacobs's true identity and hearing the

recording of him taunting me has pissed off a lot of people in the fleet.

"I'm sorry about Captain Lin," Turly says, his voice softer now. "But even if we did turn over as Jacobs is asking us to, you have to know he won't give you those coordinates. Not the real ones. He wants you to suffer, and he clearly wants her dead."

"But if there's a chance of saving those people from Poe," I argue, knowing from the start that it's a futile argument at best. Chris is right, even if I can't admit it out loud.

"Admiral, I don't think we need to choose."

I look at the screen in confusion, surprised to hear Francis Illian's voice. He's been quiet up until now, on the call only because I needed a friendly face.

Illian visibly steels himself and continues. "Admiral Turly is right, sir. We owe it to the people of this sector to stop this Jacobs in his tracks. He's obviously afraid of you, sir, or he wouldn't have laid those mines and he wouldn't be trying so hard to get you to turn around. That means he knows we can win, and we have to win, sir. Otherwise . . ." He trails off, giving me a pleading look. I know what he's trying to say, but I can't bring myself to finish his thought for him.

"But Jessica," I say instead.

Illian shakes his head, tears in his eyes mirroring my own. "What would Captain Lin tell you if she were here, sir? She'd tell you to take on Jacobs, save the cluster, and rescue those two thousand slaves, sir, and you know it." The words sting like an ice storm, and me without a jacket. "And how would the captain feel afterward, sir, if you saved her instead of all those people? If she knew that she was alive only because all those people died, or worse?"

I have to blink rapidly to clear my vision enough to see my supposed subordinate. Chris and Quarrie look just as shocked, as the man I counted on the most to back me up in this argument just turned and bit the hand that feeds him.

Illian and I are going to have words later.

"We can send *Bainbridge* out to find Jessica while we . . ." I trail off, immediately seeing the poor logic in my own argument. *Bainbridge* may be our fastest ship, especially with our other Apollo-class, *Vancouver*, still damaged from the engagement at Huff. But sending her alone to search the massive sphere of space that is the Linford Commons system would be an exercise in futility, and it would require us to change our entire plan of attack.

*Bainbridge* already has most of our fleet's Marines on board, crammed into her like sardines, stretching her life support and environmental systems for all their worth. It's her job to dock with that station while we fight Jacobs and the SDF fleet. If they can liberate that station before we defeat the enemy, they'll cut off any attempts by Jacobs to use those two thousand people as hostages to stop our attack.

"Sir," Chris says gently. "I know how difficult this is for you. I'm a big fan of Captain Lin. The way she rallied the troops at the shipyard to salvage the mothball fleet was a masterclass in leadership. But Commander Illian is right, blast it. There's no other way.

Just like that, any last vestiges of hope deflate inside me like a balloon. My shoulders slump forward, and I hang my head, still blinking to clear away the tears. He's right. I don't want to admit it, but Chris is spot-on. They all are.

"Except that Nedrin Jacobs didn't count on one thing," Illian says, his voice as fierce as I've ever heard it. We turn our gazes back to him. "If there's one person in this galaxy who can beat the trap that coward has set up for her, it's Jessica Lin."

I have to hope he's right.

"Admiral, Captain," a new voice calls over the intercom.

"The ninety-minute deadline Bollen—excuse me, Jacobs—gave us is about to lapse. Orders?"

I can't find my voice, but I meet Risa Quarrie's gaze and nod slightly, asking her to speak for me.

"Signal the fleet, Commander," she replies to the voice on the intercom. "We continue with Attack Plan Alpha. All units, prepare for battle with the SDF."

She cuts the connection and looks over at me. "For Queen and Federation, Admiral."

I nod, still not able to find my voice.

"For Queen and Federation," Chris echoes her. Even Illian joins in on the last word, though he's technically not subject to either.

With that simple statement, our fates, along with that of my wife, are sealed.

# SEVENTY-THREE
# COMMS

## JESSICA LIN MENDOZA

I wish I could talk to Brad *now.* Or that I could at least see his fleet on the freighter's nonfunctional sensors. Jacobs's ninety-minute deadline has passed. Has Brad turned his fleet around to come for me as our enemy desired? Or is he even now on his way to the sixth planet to kill the snake and rescue thousands?

I try very hard not to think of what he might be doing, or which of the terrible options I would prefer he choose. Sometimes, logic and the heart go to war.

At least, if all goes right in the next ten minutes, I *will* be able to talk to him soon.

"We're ready to test it, Captain," Jimmy Nevins says from beside me in large open expanse of the cargo hold. With the rest of the ship open to the survivors, none have opted to return to this hated space, so we're alone here with Kimberly, Gunter, Frank, and a young woman named Pauline, who was a computer science major at the University of Poe prior to her capture.

"Okay, making the connection," I reply, commanding my implant's AI to repeat its earlier trick of connecting to the drone's wireless signal and hacking its control systems.

The drone itself is on the ground, seemingly dormant, a blinking red light on its frame the only indication that it has power. It does nothing to betray the moment my implant seizes control of its command interface. Nevertheless, I can practically feel the drone's small AI brain trying to cycle the frequencies as they did earlier when I temporarily hacked the drones to escape. But this time, my full attention is on the task at hand, as is my implant's AI. I lose my connection momentarily as the drone kicks me out, but I'm back in and gaining control again in less than five seconds. This time, the drone takes longer to kick me out. The third time, it fails to do so entirely.

"I have full control," I announce to the others. "Pauline, what am I looking for?"

"There should be a root directory. See if you can find it."

I only have a vague idea what she means, but my implant's AI takes the instruction and runs with it, pinging me a moment later with a mental image of a file folder with no name.

"Okay, I think I've found it," I tell the girl.

"Open it and look for a folder labelled 'Comms'."

I want to gape at her. It can't be that easy. My implant confirms I'm right almost immediately. "Nothing with that name."

"Well, it was worth a shot," she says, not sounding discouraged in the least.

For the next forty minutes, she painstakingly talks me through various attempts to find a way to use the drone to communicate directly with the ship's comm systems. I lose hope after the first twenty minutes, but Pauline is patient and relentless. I almost can't believe it when my implant's AI finally announces success, which I echo in a little shout of triumph and by thrusting my fist into the air so exuberantly that Frank takes a step back in surprise.

"We're in?" Gunter asks, practically bouncing on his toes. "Can we get access to the ship's AI, take control, and change course?"

"No," Pauline says with an apologetic frown at the big constable. "I wish we could, but civilian ships have a hard block between the comm systems and the main AI. It's so that no one can hack your ship remotely without your permission. Think of it like a virtual airgap."

From the look on Gunter's face, he has no idea what she's talking about, but he's still happy. Next to him, Frank is grinning widely at the girl.

"Quiet for a moment, everyone. I need to send the message," I tell them.

Together, we crafted a carefully constructed message that tells Brad and his fleet as much about our situation as we can. It includes the turnaround time for Jacobs's messages—which can give a rough idea of how far we are from the slaver's base—as well as some star sightings we were able to get out of the ship's few windows that *might* help the Navy ships triangulate our position within a few dozen light-minutes.

Everyone watches me eagerly as I select a message and send it. When I nod to say it's done, they all grin widely and high-five each other.

I try not to think of how different their reactions would be if they knew that I did *not,* in fact, send the message we so meticulously crafted together. Instead, I sent another, far shorter one that no one had a part in preparing except for me.

# SEVENTY-FOUR
# MY HEART

## BRAD MENDOZA

"That may be the bravest woman I've ever seen," Risa Quarrie says in a low voice as Jess's message stops playing in *Gunslinger*'s ready room. On the vid screen, Chris and Illian nod their agreement.

Me? I just feel numb as I command the screen to play the message again, as if I might have misheard my wife the first time.

There's no image, only audio, but in my mind's eye I can see the grim set to Jess's jaw as she relays her instructions. "Brad, don't come after me. I have a plan—a way to miss that asteroid. I need *you* to focus on getting Jacobs and freeing all those people. I love you. I always will. Promise me you won't worry about us. This isn't Bellerophon all over again, Brad. There, you were alone. Here, you have me. I need you to trust *me*, sweetheart. I'll be waiting when you're done with the fight."

"See, sir," Illian says when the message is done playing the second time. "I told you Captain Lin would figure out a way to save herself and everyone on that freighter."

I nod mutely, because I know my wife well enough. She doesn't have a plan. But she knows me well, too, and she knows what I need to hear.

"Can we triangulate her position?" I ask, my voice sounding robotic even to my own ears.

In the room with us, *Gunslinger*'s comm officer shakes her head sadly. "No, Admiral. The signal bounced off a comm satellite in orbit around the sixth planet. We tried to run a backtrace, but the SDF figured out what we were doing and blocked us." She ends her dour report with a preemptive wince, maybe expecting an outburst from me.

"Thank you, Lieutenant," I tell her, still monotone. "I'm sure you and your people did your best."

"Do you wish to send a reply, sir?" she asks, almost sounding hopeful.

I shake my head. "Since we don't know where she is, we'd have to go wide band, omnidirectional, right?"

She nods.

It kills me, but I know what I have to do. "Then no. Jacobs no doubt heard her message, too. But that doesn't mean we have to broadcast to him what our plans are. Maintain comm silence outside the fleet."

She leaves, looking almost as dissatisfied as I feel.

"Admiral Turly, is *Liberator* ready for battle?" I ask, voice still dead flat.

"Aye, Admiral Mendoza."

"Commander Illian?"

"*Bainbridge* stands ready to do her part, sir!"

"Captain Quarrie?"

"All ships report readiness, sir. *Gunslinger* is ready in all respects and yours to command."

"Then message the fleet. Execute Attack Plan Alpha."

# SEVENTY-FIVE
# ANGER

## JESSICA LIN MENDOZA

"How could you do this to us?" Gunter bellows at me.

I'm sitting in the captain's chair on the bridge, but I feel less like an actual captain and more like a schoolgirl called to the headmaster's office. Gunter, Frank, and a dozen others have taken turns yelling at me and berating me. I never intended to tell them of the contents of my message to Brad, or that I didn't send the message we agreed upon together. However, Kimberly asked me to transfer control of the rebuilt drone to Jimmy so he could help her use it to examine the explosive charges at each airlock. Apparently, he found a copy of my outgoing message in the device's small memory.

"You've doomed us all!" Gunter shouts, spittle flying from his lips when I don't answer his question.

A few others yell various things at me, and I just sit there and take it. I deserve it. I don't regret telling Brad to stay away—it's the right choice. But it sucks that three hundred people have to die with me. I have a sudden new understanding of what Brad must have felt like when faced with the impossible decision at Bellerophon . . . and what he's feeling now, faced with yet another impossible decision.

I don't shy away. I meet the gazes of each member of the angry group as they shout at me. A few talk in more reasonable tones, but their words sting just as badly. The only one who hasn't said anything is Mary Sullivan. She sits at the ruined helm station, looking at me with something approaching understanding or even pity. Maybe it's because she's studying to be a nurse, where triage is often a required way of thinking. Either way, I get the sense that she alone among all the others realizes why I did what I did.

"I don't believe this. This can't be happening," Gunter says, hands covering the top of his head like he might somehow pull his buzzed hair out by the roots. "You've doomed us all. Your husband could have *saved* us. Don't you get it? He could have saved us!"

"How?" I demand, finally done being silent. "Do you really think Jacobs ever intended to let us live? Those charges at the airlocks tell the story sure enough. The second a ship tried to dock with us, to help us gain control or to evacuate us, those charges would blow, and goodbye to our rescuers. Don't you get it? We were never meant to win this game. Jacobs rigged it that way. You heard him; he loathes my husband and me. Do you really think he won't do whatever it takes to kill us both?"

I glare up at the big man the same way I did when he first braced me in the cargo hold. "I did what needed to be done. There are thousands of people on that station at the sixth planet. We're going to die anyway." The statement hits him like a physical slap, and he flinches backward as I finally say the quiet part out loud. "Do you really want to die with that many people on your conscience? Or how about the Marines and spacers who would die trying to bypass those explosive charges at each airlock? In fact . . ."

I trail off, breaking eye contact and feeling the blood rush to my face in embarrassment as I realize how monumentally stupid I've been. All this time, the solution was there, practically staring me in the face.

"I have a plan," I mutter.

"What?" Gunter demands. "Don't lie to us again, Lin."

I look back up at him and smile. "I have a plan, Gunter. A real one this time. And it just might work. Jimmy, how many more of those drones do you think you can cobble together? And can you put the guns back on them?"

## SEVENTY-SIX
# RELIEVING MYSELF OF COMMAND

### BRAD MENDOZA

"Brad, you wanted to talk before the battle?"

I nod at the image on the ready room console. "Thanks for taking my call, Chris. I know you're busy over there."

He nods but doesn't reply, waiting for me to get to the point.

"I called to tell you that I'm in no mental state to lead this attack. Rear Admiral Turly, I am hereby relieving myself of command, effective immediately, and placing you in command of the fleet."

I've thought long and hard about this over the last several hours as we've closed the last of the distance to the sixth planet. I can't lead this fleet. Not when every fiber of my being—I never understood that stupid phrase until now—yearns to do the wrong thing and put my wife's life above that of every other person in the Corpus Christi Cluster. Even though Jacobs's deadline has passed, I want nothing more than to message him, begging him to let us change course now in return for Jess's coordinates.

"No."

I open my mouth to argue with Chris's one-word response, but I can't find the words.

"You tried to do this once already, Brad," he says with a small smile. "I said no then because you're a better commander than I am. My reasons haven't changed. Tell you what: you can hand command back over to me when this is all over. Then I'll throw you in the brig again for old times' sake. Now, if there's nothing else, Admiral Mendoza, I have a battleship to attend to."

He cuts the connection before I can even respond. So much for that. Insubordinate jerk.

Sighing, I get up from the desk and make my way through the hatch and onto the bridge. "Signal *Bainbridge*," I order the comm officer. "Tell the Marines to get pissed, and tell Hayley Uvalde to turn her hair white and let Lola out of her cage."

"Um . . . aye, sir?" the comm officer answers uncertainly, but she relays my orders word for word. Then I have her open a channel to the fleet.

"Officers and crew of the Promethean Royal Navy, Task Force 3.4, Corpus Christi Cluster," I say somberly and formally. "The time has come to do battle. Let's blow that SDF fleet out of space. Happy hunting."

There are no cheers around me on *Gunslinger*'s bridge, but there are several resolute nods. I wish I shared their conviction.

Except that suddenly, I realize I do. It may be too late to save my wife, but I vow now that I will make Nedrin Jacobs suffer and die for what he's done to her, and I'll do the same to every SDF spacer who decided to betray their star nation and throw their lot in with him, the Jutzens, and the traitorous King Chance.

"All ships," I order, "we start our deceleration burn in sixty seconds from my mark. Mark."

The deceleration burn is far too late to stop us from meeting Jacobs's fleet in battle. We'll still hit them at a high velocity. But it's necessary for us to have any kind of engagement envelope with them.

I just hope this all works, because if it doesn't, my wife will die for nothing.

## SEVENTY-SEVEN
# DRONES AND EXPLOSIVES

### JESSICA LIN MENDOZA

"How do you know this is going to work?" Gunter demands with significantly less vehemence than when addressing me two hours ago on the bridge.

"I don't, but I've got a good feeling about it," I tell him honestly. I know I sound way too cheerful delivering such an uninspiring response, but I'm almost giddy to at last be doing *something* that might have even the barest chance of saving us.

"Well, it had better work," he grumps. "I'm still stinging from those stun rounds in the cargo hold, saving your butt. And if I don't get back by next week's Constable Ball, my girlfriend is going to kill me."

The statement is so similar to what Brad might say in the same life-or-death situation that it makes me giggle involuntarily. I stifle it quickly, watching the feed from one of the drones on my implant as it approaches the exterior airlock door from inside the deserted cargo hold.

"Almost there," Jimmy says beside me, his eyes out of focus as he controls the drone from his implant, seated at the bridge's helm station.

"You've got this, ," Kimberly says from next to him, her hand on his shoulder.

Apparently, life-or-death situations make for quick friendships and even couplings—not that Brad and I would know *anything* about that. Sometime in the last few hours, Jimmy and Kimberly grew close. I've already heard Gunter call them 'Jimmerly'. He and Brad would *really* get along.

"Ready to fire on your order, Captain," Jimmy says solemnly as the virtual crosshairs in the vid feed line up on the housing for the bomb affixed to the airlock's outer door.

"Everyone's already moved to the safety areas?" I ask. "As far from the danger zones as they can get?"

"For the tenth time, yes," Gunter replies. By Hades, he's just a bigger version of my husband.

"Then brace yourselves. Jimmy, fire."

The vid feed goes blank the same instant the ship moves violently around us. Those not strapped into the limited bridge seating are braced against consoles and bulkheads, but several still fall over from the sudden movement.

I breathe a long sigh of relief after I get my wind back. If the painful jerk to the left was any indication, phase one of our plan worked. I wait five minutes to give all the air from the cargo hold and the surrounding compartments time to evacuate, adding its power to that of the explosion to push us a little off course to port.

"Get ready to blow the second charge," I order, and a new vid feed pops up in my mind's eye, this from the drone assigned to the port stern airlock. "Fire when ready, Mr. Nivens."

Jimmy repeats the performance, firing a stun round at this explosive charge's anti-tamper housing. Again, the feed goes dark, and the ship jerks and sways beneath us—or rather, around us—as the stern pushes to starboard this time, further angling our engines to push us to port.

"Well, it feels like that worked," Gunter says hopefully. But without sensors or even a visual fix on the asteroid, there's no way to know if it's enough, or too little too late.

As the final drone's vid feed pops up in my implant's view, its targeting reticle on the final set of explosives inside the starboard bow airlock, I breathe deeply. "Fire!"

This explosion nudges our nose further to port, adding to the new angle imparted by the previous two explosions. As with them, I wait for the air in that part of the ship, where we've literally wedged open the pressure bulkheads with clothing and a few broken panels from the cargo hold's lavatories. After a few minutes, I feel our yaw stop.

Despite the violence of the explosions, this is a big ship, and at best, we've only nudged it a few degrees off course. And in doing so, we've traded hopefully missing that asteroid now for less breathable air later.

It'll be enough; it *has* to be enough.

# SEVENTY-EIGHT
# ATTACK!

## BRAD MENDOZA

Space battles can be beautiful, like a delicate ballet, where every piece has a specific movement choreographed at a specific time, all working together to create something that's almost musical in nature.

This battle exemplifies that. The rotation of the third moon currently places Jacobs's weapons manufacturing station and his SDF fleet between the moon and its parent gas giant. Our ships are angled for a missile-range run farther on the inside, allowing us to enter the sixth planet's orbit after our pass and use its gravity to bring ourselves all the way around for another pass, then another, and so on, until we've destroyed Jacobs's fleet or our own.

Even with his bigger fleet, we have two advantages in this kind of engagement. First is our speed of approach. The shorter engagement timelines will make it harder for Jacobs to hit us with everything he has in each pass. Even if he places all his ships line abreast to us, we'll pass each one of them so quickly they'll only have time to launch a single volley. Of course, we face the same constraint, but it's a tradeoff that lands slightly in our favor given our lower punching weight.

Second, Jacobs and his SDF lackeys are convinced that only half our ships can fight. We're about to prove them very wrong on that count.

I have my fleet divided up into two parallel lines along our direction of travel. The starboard line contains all of our battleworthy ships, the two functional battleships anchoring the line, surrounded by smaller escorts and the battlecruisers filling the gaps in between. The port line, the one that will face the enemy as we pass, is made up of the drone ships, configured in similar manner.

All my ships are close to each other, and the distance between the two lines is small enough to make me sweat. Ironically, the very fact that the port line is made up exclusively of drones slaved to other ships' controls is the only thing that makes this small separation less dangerous. It's also an important part of our plan.

"Cut acceleration. Message Element to execute Sword Maneuver," I order.

Two things happen in quick sequence. First, every ship in both of my lines cuts their main drive. Second, every drone ship in the port line yaws to put its nose directed straight at the enemy. It's like opening a set of venetian blinds to reveal in the gaps between my battleworthy ships, their broadsides still facing Jacobs's fleet.

"Fire!"

On the plot, roughly four hundred missiles lance out from my battleworthy starboard line as every ship fires its broadside at the enemy. The missiles shoot through the gaps between the open venetian blinds of our drone line, their small green icons streaking at the SDF ships.

I try not to gasp when the enemy fleet returns fire, launching nearly double the missiles our way. It would be more, but for some reason, Jacobs is keeping that Hades-class behemoth of his just out of range, no doubt letting his SDF underlings risk their lives first to destroy us.

I watch the plot carefully, the seconds ticking down in my head as the two huge waves of red and green missile icons intermingle on the screen, some from each side interceptors that specifically seek out the other side's ship-killers. Just at the right moment, I call out my next orders.

"Message Drone Element to execute Shield Maneuver. Message Battle Line to turn head-on to enemy."

This time, all my ships yaw in one direction or another. The drone ships yaw back to starboard, presenting their broadsides to the incoming SDF missiles. Behind them, the rest of my ships turn perpendicular to the enemy, our bows pointed right at them, tucked in close behind the shields now formed by each drone.

It works beautifully, if not perfectly. The incoming missiles do their best, but the timing is against them. Wave after wave slam into the flanks of our drone ships, but few are able to change course in time to go around and hit my line of battle.

Two drone heavy cruisers explode in spectacular fashion, blown to so many atoms in the ether. Both drone battleships take heavy damage from the few enemy ship-killers that make it past our interceptors. One of them breaks into pieces, damaging one of our fully operational battlecruisers as a fragment flies into it too quickly for it to duck out of the way. The battlecruiser is damaged, with multiple decks out of space, but I exhale in relief when its drive continues burning bright.

Then, we lose our first battleworthy ship outright. The destroyer *Vancouver*, barely repaired from its ordeal at Huff, takes a hit from several heavy ship-to-ship missiles meant for *Liberator*, doing its job as the battleship's escort. The little destroyer breaks in half, and I wince at the far too few escape pods that launch from the remaining fragments. Seconds later, a battleworthy heavy cruiser follows her into the ether, a ship-killer obliterating it with all hands lost.

Just like that, we're out of range, though the enemy turns and tries to send a few missiles after us as we burn toward the gas giant's opposite horizon. Those desultory shots never reach us, the separation velocity too high for even their drives to overcome. It takes a while—the sixth planet is rather big—but we're soon over the horizon and burning around it to come back for another pass.

I survey the battle plot and smile grimly. We lost four of the thirteen drone ships assigned to be our shields, including one of the two drone battleships and one of the three battlecruisers. The rest are all damaged in some way, and as I watch, one of the drone heavy cruisers cuts acceleration, its drive sputtering out and putting it in an unstable orbit that will eventually result in it reaching crush depth in the gas giant's atmosphere.

But despite all that, I'm pleased to see that the enemy took far more damage than we did. Unlike them, who relied on their large number of missiles to target all of our ships, we focused our fire on their big boys. Three of their battlecruisers are out of the fight, but even more importantly, just as we went over the horizon, we were treated to the image of one of the two SDF battleships breaking apart and hemorrhaging escape pods. The other survived only because a light cruiser and two destroyers sacrificed themselves to block our missiles, as *Vancouver* did for *Liberator*.

The enemy still has double our offensive weight, after discounting our drones, so it's far from victory, but it's a start.

Unfortunately, they still have two operating battleships

with little-to-no damage, an SDF Olympus-class and Jacobs's deadly Hades-class, which never engaged during the first pass.

"Sir, message from *Bainbridge*. They are detaching and turning over now," the comm officer reports.

"Message them, 'Happy hunting'," I reply, and watch as my little destroyer fires its engines to decelerate and fall behind the fleet.

The rest of us follow a ballistic course around the gas giant while damage control parties rush to repair our ships and weapons crews reload and ready for our second pass.

# SEVENTY-NINE
# LIAISONS

## JESSICA LIN MENDOZA

When we blew up a large chunk of our ship with those airlock explosives, we damaged something critical. Less than ten minutes afterward, the freighter's drive stopped burning. A few minutes later, we lost artificial gravity and inertial compensators. I'm just glad it happened in that order, or we'd all be smashed against the bulkheads.

Now, I float through the ruins of our freighter, giving words of encouragement wherever I can to the three hundred plus former slaves turned crew on board with me. With roughly a third of the ship destroyed outright and another third open to space, they're crammed into the remaining spaces, finding handholds or chairs to strap into wherever they can.

Our cramped quarters and dire situation don't stop them

from looking at me with wide eyes and even clapping as I float in and out of the various compartments to check on them. I'm sure many of them have to know that we're far from rescued yet, but they don't seem to care. My heart breaks at the praise, especially since they also have to know that I doomed them all with my message to Brad.

These wide-eyed students don't seem to worry about any of that. A few even ask me about enlisting in Queen Anne's Navy when this is all over. I smile back at them and tell them the queen would be lucky to have them, and of course I'll sponsor them for officer training, assuming it even exists after the destruction of the Academy on Prometheus.

But all the while, I'm dying more and more inside, as if the hope they take from me draws down any I have left for myself.

I'm about finished with my rounds when I hear a clang from inside a storage closet in one of the intact corridors leading back toward the bridge. Confused and a little wary, I push off the bulkhead and float to it, grabbing the hatch wheel and unlocking it, then bracing myself against the hatchway's edge to pull the door open.

I stop with it half-open and gape. Fully clothed—thank goodness!—but entwined as they float in zero-g are Frank and Pauline, the computer science major who helped me hack the comms.

"Uh, hi Captain," Frank says sheepishly as they both stare at me like I've caught them . . . well, like I've caught them making out in a broom closet while we all wait around to die.

But all I can think to say is, "You two, really?" It's a valid question.

Pauline answers first. "I like cops. And Frank is sweet."

Frank blushes at the praise. "And I like gamer girls."

Stunned speechless, I simply close the hatch and move on,

suddenly sympathizing with Illian's fear of walking into any compartment where Brad and I have been alone. It's good to see something positive come out of our dire circumstances, even if I'm afraid Frank and Pauline won't have much time to enjoy their new relationship.

# EIGHTY
# DRAWING THE DEVIL OUT

## BRAD MENDOZA

"For this to work, we need to draw out *Vigilant Dagger*. If Jacobs's battleship stays near the station, *Bainbridge* won't stand a chance to board that factory and free those people."

There are nods all around in the quick virtual conference between my ship commanders as we near the horizon for our next pass. I outline the revisions to our plan, and everyone signs off to get ready to implement.

As soon as we peek over the horizon and get a clear view of the enemy still at the third moon, Jacobs hails us to once again taunt me. Perfect; it saves me the trouble of reaching out to him.

Unlike his previous messages, now that he isn't trying to hide his identity, this call has video. Sitting on a command chair in the middle of an expansive bridge trimmed in Promethean Blue and Gold, but wearing a black skinsuit, is the blond, muscled Adonis who so intimidated me when he first barged into my quarters on *Persephone* nearly a year ago.

"Nice try, Brad, but that little maneuver with your drones won't work again. You're done for."

"I'm sorry, Ned—can I call you Ned? Nedrin just sounds so pretentious, you know. I mean, I've always thought of you more as a Ned, kinda like an annoying little cousin. Your cousin, Queen Anne, is doing well by the way. I can't wait to tell her what you've been up to here. I think that's a family reunion you might want to miss."

There's a sputtering sound on the other end, and several of *Gunslinger*'s bridge crew turn to gape at me with expressions of either horror or sheer joy, depending.

"Shut up, Mendoza!" Jacobs snaps back, his voice rising a little. "Your stupid little jokes won't save you, your crews, or your wife."

"See, when you say stuff like that, Ned, it only makes me want to kill you more. Time to work on your people skills, buddy."

"You won't win, Brad," he growls.

"See, Ned, you already said that. You know, for a traitorous king's nephew, I'd expect more. You might want to ask for a refund on that fancy education. Turns out you're just slaver scum like any common pirate. I mean, how many times are you going to threaten me and my wife? It's really getting old. What if I started making 'your momma' jokes in the middle of battle? It would be inappropriate, wouldn't it? Even if your momma is so fat that I'm using her gravity to slow down my ships right now. See, a comment like that would be entirely inappropriate and uncalled for."

He tries to interject, but I just keep talking right over him. "Come on, Neddy boy, I know you're nothing more than a coward. Smart, I guess, if not a little wussy, to send your SDF buddies out to die while you relax out of range. But you've got a habit of making others do your work for you. Or maybe you haven't even figured out how to use that shiny new battleship of yours. You always were a terrible Navy man."

I motion to the comm officer to cut the comm while Jacobs is still sputtering his next threat

Quarrie shakes her head. "Do you often do your best to enrage your opponents like that?"

I smile over at her, though my insides are twisted up into knots. "Yep. It's kind of my thing."

"Well, let's hope you can back it up."

"Let's hope *we* can back it up," I correct her. "I think the odds are in our favor." They're not, but it helps to pretend they are.

"Admiral, *Vigilant Dagger* is joining the SDF fleet," the tactical officer reports a few minutes later, and I relax my shoulders a bit. Checking my own console, I see the battleship is slowly moving out of range from the station. I've done all I can for my friends on *Bainbridge*, and now it's time to turn my full attention to my fleet's next pass.

A little while later, the battle is upon us. This time, we burn our drives to leave orbit at an angle that will take us directly at the SDF fleet for a head-on pass. This will be a close-quarters fight, with missiles as well as lasers, and in every combat tactics manual, it's the last thing a less powerful force like ours should attempt. But I'm relying on the enemy to see that and on their inferior training to take it as a mistake on my end and not think too hard about why I'm changing tactics so soon.

"Captain Quarrie, is my flagship ready for another engagement with the enemy?"

There's a real sense of pride in her dark response. "Aye, Admiral. Just point us at whoever you want to kill next."

I can't help but smile a little in reply.

This engagement starts much like the first, with hundreds

of missiles launched from both sides streaking at each other. This time, I've had my fleet load 70 percent of our missile tubes with defensive interceptors, drastically reducing our offensive punch but allowing us to swat a large chunk of the enemy missiles out of space before they enter close range.

Our drone ships, this time, are no longer out in front but rather tucked in behind my battle line. Someone on the other side needs to be wondering why I would put them there, when they could hypothetically still shield my battleworthy ships. Instead, I've got my remaining light cruisers and destroyers in front, where they can play their escort roles and take out as many missiles as possible before they hit our larger ships.

Our escorts, along with our interceptors, do surprisingly well. Few enemy missiles get past our first lines of defense, and those that do mostly fall to the close-in defenses of our battleships and battlecruisers.

Then, something gets through, and I watch in horror as two ship-killers launched from *Vigilant Dagger* hit one of my fully operational battlecruisers in the bow, spaced out so that the first opens a hole and the second buries itself deep into the former mothballed ship's innards. The second explosion rips the battlecruiser apart, instantly killing every member of its three-hundred-strong skeleton crew.

As the two fleets near close range, ships punch and kick, switching primarily to lasers and carving at each other with invisible lines of coherent light that dig deep into hull plates and try to take out engine exhausts to hobble their opponents.

To the normal viewer, it would look like my fleet is about to lose badly, our few battleworthy ships no match at such close quarters with the destructive firepower of the SDF fleet. But at just the right moment, I call out the order that should change all that.

"Execute Ramshead Maneuver!"

With that order, the thrusters of every drone ship come alive, changing their aspects. Then their main drives fire at full power just as we near minimum engagement range. I know that, without inertial compensators, those rapid course changes might tear those drone ships apart at the seams, but we only need them to live a little while longer.

The SDF fleet is a little slow to realize what's happening. Up until this point, their targeting AIs have deprioritized the drones coming in behind my battle line, designating them as nonthreats due to their lack of weaponry. But now, I imagine alarms are screaming all over those SDF bridges as human and machine belatedly realize what the drones are doing. It's hard to blame them; no one's ever fought a battle quite like this one, at least in recorded Promethean history. Drone ships simply aren't a thing. The very thought of an AI having full control of a warship goes against so many interstellar laws—which is, in fact, why our AIs can't fire the weapons without a human on board to tell them it's okay.

That's alright. I don't need them to fire their lasers. I just need them to fly.

The enemy reacts, but too late as the SDF flagship, a Kronos-class battleship, is rammed head-on by our sole remaining drone battleship, *Excalibur*. The SDF captain makes a valiant effort to sidestep the hit, but *Excalibur* is closing too fast and the surprise is too great. When her bow impacts that of the SDF battleship, both monsters break apart in spectacular fashion.

All throughout the SDF fleet, similar deaths are occurring. The enemy loses two more battlecruisers as smaller but fast-moving light cruiser and destroyer drones hit them from offsetting angles. One of the SDF cruisers explodes just like its battleship sister, but the other manages to maneuver and take only a glancing blow, still enough to send it spinning out of control.

Unfortunately, *Vigilant Dagger,* at the back of the SDF formation, has more time to dodge the two drone battlecruisers we send her way. I grip my chair's arm so hard it hurts as Jacobs lives to fight another day.

All in all, however, the second engagement is another win for us. We end up losing three battleworthy ships, putting us down to only eight from our original thirteen. We also manage to lose the last of our drones, as those that missed their targets fly off on vectors that won't allow them to catch up to us again, even if they weren't too damaged to be of any help anyway.

But while the enemy still has fourteen operational ships, they're down to their last battleship, *Vigilant Dagger,* and only one battlecruiser plus assorted escorts. Whereas we still have two battleships, *Liberator* and *Adjudicator,* both with only minor damage, plus three battlecruisers, including my own *Gunslinger,* damaged but still ready to fight.

In other words, they outnumber us, but we have far more mass. It's nearly a miracle.

There's a muted cheer across *Gunslinger*'s bridge as the tactical officer reports these outcomes—muted because of the comrades we have lost, but still exuberant as our David has somehow managed to thwart Goliath thus far.

But despite the numbers now being in our favor, I don't join even the light celebration, because I know that *Vigilant Dagger* alone is still a force to be reckoned with. Unlike the rest of my underlings, my implant has that monster's full specs, added to it in an automatic intel update when Annie made me a vice admiral. And even with our two surviving battleships, we're simply no match for it.

Once again, we enter the gas giant's orbit, preparing for our third and likely final pass at the enemy, and I say a silent prayer for the lone friendly ship we leave in our wake.

# EIGHTY-ONE
# THE PROBLEM WITH SUPER-SECRET STATIONS AND VACUUM CLEANERS

## BRAD MENDOZA

The problem with having your secret slaver fortress orbiting the moon of a gas giant is that gas giants tend to be the vacuum cleaners of a star system.

Ever wonder why your home planet isn't destroyed every Tuesday by a killer asteroid? Thank your local gas giant. These massive planetary bodies circle your star system using their big old gravity wells to suck up all sorts of dangerous objects that would otherwise make it into the inner system and kill your nice little slice of paradise.

Don't believe me? Look it up. I'll wait.

Okay, now that we've cleared that up, let me explain why it's such a bad thing for a super-special slaver base. Because, as we've established, Linford Commons' sixth planet is a gas giant—with me so far?—and it's been a good vacuum cleaner for millions of years.

That means it's surrounded by a few dozen moons of various sizes, a bunch of asteroids of various smaller sizes, and a ring system that's a mix of asteroids, chunks of ice, and maybe the odd wrecked spaceship, even. Who knows—it's a lot of junk.

That junk is perfect for a small attacking ship to use to sneak up on your super-secret slaver base. Which is exactly what *Bainbridge* does. She comes behind my battle fleet, using the distraction of our charge through the enemy lines and the various moons and pieces of junk to get nearly all the way to Jacobs's station before the station's sensors or any of the SDF sensors pick her up. By then, it's too late, as multiple scramblers from my little destroyer disable the station's defensive weaponry and systems. Shortly thereafter, *Bainbridge* does a crash docking maneuver, having shed just enough of its velocity in two orbits of the gas giant to make it a nonsuicidal affair.

Do you know what happens when over two hundred angry Marines led into battle by a short, psychotic Latina with a penchant for sharp objects storm a base full of slavers holding two thousand captives as 'bargaining tools'? It ain't pretty for the slavers.

Of course, I can only imagine all this because I'm not there, but my imagination is really good, and I've seen Hayley—Lola, really—enough in action to know what to expect.

The Marines are there too, but in my mind, they don't have a whole lot to do except clean up the leftovers after Lola.

This time, as my fleet goes around the sixth planet for our next pass, we launch comm buoys in our wake, keeping our lines of communication back to *Vigilant Dagger* open.

"Mendoza!" Jacobs screams over the comm shortly after *Bainbridge* disgorges its angry Latina and Marines onto the station. "You'll pay for storming my station. I'm ordering my ships to destroy it with your people on it!" You know, I never realized on *Persephone* just how much he really sounds like a petulant toddler.

"You can do that, Ned," I tell him soberly, "but if you do, you can also tell your SDF goons that I'll view them as slavers themselves and destroy every escape pod they launch."

"They can't hear you, they . . ." He trails off, probably just now figuring out that I'm transmitting my response in the clear for everyone to hear. He swears loudly, confirming it for me.

And with that, I know I've won this round. Nothing terrifies a spacer more than the thought of being cooked alive by a missile or laser fire inside a helpless escape pod. I'll be surprised if any of those SDF crews have the guts to try me on this one.

Plus, they all need to be thinking hard now. Their so-called ally/boss just promised to let them kill his slave overseers on the station. Betrayal of one's own really makes your other friends stop and think. And now Jacobs himself can't even launch the attack from his battleship, or he'll risk alienating his only support in the system.

At least, I *hope* all of that is true. It's part of what makes our assault plan so insane, but there's nothing to be done about it now.

# EIGHTY-TWO
# THE THIRD PASS

## BRAD MENDOZA

Our latest orbit around the gas giant brings us right back to the same point for a third pass against Jacobs's fleet. This time, they're understandably more wary of us, especially given our advantage in overall firepower after the success of the last two passes.

Unfortunately, with all their other battleships destroyed or floating as disabled hulks, Jacobs now has no choice but to get *Vigilant Dagger* more involved in the fight, and the Hades-class monster now sits front and center, anchoring his line of battle as we streak toward them.

"*Liberator, Adjudicator,*" I order my two surviving battleships, "concentrate all fire on *Vigilant Dagger. Fleetfoot, Sprinter*"—these are my two surviving destroyers—"move into cover position and keep those battleships safe."

Once again, I immerse myself into the battle using my

implant, and I'm now a giant standing next to the sixth planet, though it still fills one entire half of my view. But all my focus is on the three battleships charging at each other.

Quarrie takes *Gunslinger*, *Guardian*, and *Sapper*, our three surviving battlecruisers, and attacks the enemy escorts. My hope is that, with the SDF's smaller ships busy defending themselves, we might just even up the odds between our two battleships and *Vigilant Dagger*, but that it's a vain hope becomes apparent in the opening seconds of the battle.

Jacobs and the SDF may no longer have many heavy hitters, but they do have six surviving destroyers, and those fling themselves into the fray, heedless of the fire from my battlecruisers. They valiantly block most of the fire from *Liberator* and *Adjudicator* aimed at Jacobs's battleship. Those few missiles that get through are mostly taken out by *Vigilant Dagger*'s own defensive weaponry, as it opens up with more lasers and Gatling guns than I've ever seen on a Promethean warship.

With the rapidity of our third pass, there's little I can do to change the outcome, and I watch helplessly as three ship-killers slam into *Adjudicator*'s bow in quick succession. At first, I think she might survive, as none of the missiles hit the same place, impacting the outer hull rather than burrowing deep inside the battleship. But one of them must find a hole from prior battle damage, and I cry out in anger as it damages enough of her systems in the aft for her reactor to go critical.

As designed, the battleship attempts to eject the reactor before it blows up, but it doesn't do it fast enough, and the back half of *Adjudicator* disintegrates. The only thing that gives me some solace are the dozens of escape pods that launch from the remaining bow sections, far fewer than I'd like but at least something.

*Liberator* flies by *Vigilant Dagger*, turning over as it passes to keep its thick bow armor toward Jacobs's ship rather than its vulnerable exhaust ports. It launches missile after missile at the enemy behemoth, and a few actually manage to get through, but none of them do more than take a few chunks out of *Dagger*'s hull before the two battleships are out of each other's range.

Our battlecruisers fare only somewhat better. We destroy the last remaining SDF battlecruiser and two of their three heavy cruisers and a few smaller escorts, but doing so costs us *Sapper*, leaving only *Gunslinger* and *Guardian* behind. To add insult to injury, we also lost our two destroyers.

We don't, thankfully, lose *Bainbridge,* though I watch in concern as my little destroyer undocks from the station and weaves back and forth in front of it, darting in and out of weapons range. She launches a few ineffectual shots at the enemy as Illian seems to fly it in a random pattern to do no more, perhaps, than distract Jacobs and the SDF fleet from their true targets, with little success.

As the opposing fleets pass each other and move out of weapons range, I'm down to only four operational ships, including *Bainbridge,* which dances again out of range, back to the relative safety of the station; Jacobs has seven, and from what I've just watched, *Vigilant Dagger* counts for two or three on its own.

We likely can't win this fight, but to leave now would be disastrous, abandoning not just the two thousand slaves on that station, but also my crew on *Bainbridge* and the full complement of our Marine companies. It's not a sacrifice any of us are willing to make, so as we enter what is to be our final orbit of the gas giant, we prepare ourselves for the disaster to come.

# EIGHTY-THREE
# DESPERATE MEASURES

## BRAD MENDOZA

"Brad, you've come up with a lot of crazy plans in the short time I've known you. But this one is the worst."

I smirk at Chris on the ready room console. He doesn't return the expression, glaring at me from hooded eyes rimmed with shadows that have nothing to do with fatigue.

"Sorry," I tell him bluntly, "but I can make it a direct order if it helps."

"I'll show you exactly where to put that direct order," he snaps back. "There has to be another way."

I hold both hands out, palms up. "If there is, I can't wait to hear it. You and I both know we can't survive another pass against the monster. *Vigilant Dagger* will rip *Liberator* to shreds with plenty left over to take out *Gunslinger* and *Guardian*, and there are still those cruisers and destroyers to worry about. This really is the only way, and you know it."

His mouth opens and closes for a moment, but no words issue forth, as if he's thinking of and discarding a thousand alternatives to my latest plan but can't find a single one worth voicing. It's hard to blame him for feeling the way he does; if an admiral had ever presented this plan to me when I was a ship's captain, I would have called the medical staff to evaluate them for insanity and remove them from command.

As it is, our medical staff is too busy treating the wounded from the beatings our ships have taken. Thousands of good spacers are already dead, but that doesn't stop the valiant doctors and nurses across the fleet from doing their best to save those who remain.

"Do you think he'll actually go for it?" Chris finally says in a tone that tells me he's done arguing, even if he's still incredibly upset.

"Only one way to find out," I admit.

Things start moving very quickly after that. Our three remaining ships turn over and burn hard to slow our speed before what is to be our fourth and definitely final pass. And I use the extra time to hail *Vigilant Dagger* through our trail of comm buoys, broadcasting in the clear once again for Jacobs and all his people to hear.

"Earl Jacobs," I say, using his proper royal title for the first time. "This is Vice Admiral Mendoza. I'd like to negotiate the terms of my surrender."

"Power down your fleet and strike the colors," he snarls over the camera feed. "No guarantees until you do."

"I'm not talking about my fleet's surrender," I shoot back, resisting the urge to add a few choice words to the response. "I'm talking about my personal surrender. My life for Captain Lin's. Send me the coordinates, and I'll surrender myself to you."

He cackles, an unhinged sound that reminds me of a cartoon hyena in an animated film that gave me nightmares as a child. "Brad, your piddling collection of ships can't win this fight. What possible motivation would I have for letting you dictate any terms to me? We'll fight this to the end, and I'll have the pleasure of killing you and Jessica either way."

The hatch to *Gunslinger*'s bridge opens behind me, and I turn to see two armed enlisted men roughly escorting Terry Galpin onto the bridge. She glares at me and then looks at the forward viewscreen, where Jacobs sits on *Vigilant Dagger*'s command chair like it's his dead uncle's throne. For the barest of instants, I see her eyes go wide, but then she returns her glare to me as if nothing happened. Luckily, it's all the confirmation I need.

The two men bring Terry to stand by my side. I reach out to one of them and nod toward his pistol. Confused, the spacer hands me the weapon, which I immediately point at Terry's head.

She's a cool customer, I'll give her that. The look of terror in her eyes and her gasp of surprise are almost believable, but behind them, she barely flinches, and there's a cold calculation in the set of her jaw.

"Tell you what, Earl Jacobs," I say to the man on the viewscreen, his title tasting foul in my mouth. "If you're not willing to trade my life for Jessica's, then how about this? You let everyone go—the surviving Navy crews, the Marines on that station, and the rescued slaves. Then you give us Jessica's coordinates, and you'll get me *and* your little sister."

Around me on *Gunslinger*'s bridge, there are whispers of surprise, but I ignore all of them, keeping the gun pointed at the woman who's called herself Terry, my eyes firmly locked on her older brother. Nedrin Jacobs goes through multiple emotions in seconds, from disbelief to acceptance to calculation to rage and back to calculation. The man enjoys the suffering of others, and there is a very real risk that he'll call my bluff and accept the possibility of his dear sister dying in the battle to come. I might have overplayed my hand.

But unlike those early days on *Persephone,* I've actually read his file now. There were some very interesting tidbits buried in his psych profile, breadcrumbs left there by a Navy psychologist obviously too afraid of the royal family to come out and say Jacobs has strong sociopathic tendencies, but too professional not to hint at it. He also implied Jacobs may have a classic Oedipal complex, which I take to mean severe mommy issues.

I continue to meet Jacobs's angry gaze. Worried that I might have read him wrong despite all I studied in his file, I play my final card. "Think of what your mother, Lady Jacobs, would say if you let your little sister die when I offered you the way to save her at such a low cost?"

For an instant, his nostrils flare, and I worry he might reject my offer just to salve his wounded pride, but the emotion dissipates quickly, and he smirks at me. "Very well, Brad, have it your way. Get in a shuttle and come over to my flagship—with my sister. Once I have you both over here and my gun in your mouth, I'll let your underlings run away with their tails between their legs."

I shake my head emphatically. "I wasn't born yesterday, Jacobs. You're going to let *Liberator* dock with that station and take off all those rescued slaves and our Marines. You so much as twitch in their direction, and I'll put a bullet in Jasmine's head." Next to me, she flinches at the sound of her real name, which I also found in Jacobs's file. "Your sister and I will be on that station to keep you honest. Only after everyone else is off the station will I let you send over a shuttle to pick us both up. Are we clear?"

Holding my breath, I watch him process things. He knows I'm up to something, but he can't seem to figure out what. Still, I think he's about to agree until another man dressed in a similar black skinsuit steps up next to him and whispers something in his ear. For the first time, I think I'm seeing the battleship's true commander, probably pretending to be Jacobs's XO to assuage his ego but likely the man responsible for actually directing and fighting the battle.

Unfortunately, this man is smarter than Jacobs, and emboldened by his lackey's advice, my old nemesis calls my bluff. "Sorry, Brad. Nice try, but no deal."

I stare at him in disbelief. "But your sister!" I scream, motioning with the pistol still at her head.

He smiles, showing his teeth. "Kill her if you must, but I don't think you will. You're far too much of a Boy Scout."

The vid feed cuts off before I can say anything else, but *Vigilant Dagger* keeps transmitting for another two minutes, sending us nothing but its own sensor feed, so we can watch it power up its drive and start to move toward the station.

My fleet can do nothing about it. We're out of position, still on the backside of the sixth planet, and moving far slower than before. We're at least two hours from weapons range; our three ships can't possibly arrive in time to stop Jacobs from killing the thousands of people on that station, along with all my crew and friends on *Bainbridge*.

# EIGHTY-FOUR
# CARBON DIOXIDE

## JESSICA LIN MENDOZA

"Really, only fifteen hours left?"

Kimberly nods with a frown. She's not telling me anything new. My implant did the revised math after we lost two-thirds of our atmo to help us maneuver off our collision course with the asteroid. But I was hoping no one else would figure it out and panic.

"Thanks for letting me know," I tell her. "Keep it yourself, if you will. No need to cause a panic."

By the look on her face, it's already too late for that. She no doubt told others before she brought it to me. I suppose this is what happens when your crew is a bunch of untrained college kids.

"It's okay, Kimberly," I reassure her. "The fleet will come. Trust in the fleet."

The words taste like ash on my mouth. With the ship's systems all knocked out, including comms, I can't call Brad, and he can't call me. I have no way of knowing if he even has a clue where we are. I have to assume he doesn't, which means we're out of options.

I've thought long and hard to the point of banging my head against a bulkhead in frustration. We're on a dead ship, with our air rapidly deteriorating, and we don't even know our own location, nor can we call for help or signal with our running lights.

All we can do is pray. I was never religious growing up. My mother was a casual observer, though she changed churches like some people change clothes. When I was little, she'd drag me along now and again, but she stopped doing that when I became old enough to stay home alone.

So I've never believed much in God or divine help. But there's an old saying that there are no atheists in foxholes, and I start praying like crazy, unsure who I'm even praying to. It can't hurt, at least.

# EIGHTY-FIVE
# NO HOPE

## BRAD MENDOZA

Seven years ago, when I was put in the unfortunate position of liberating the Jalisco system from the traitorous forces of Duchess Charlotte Garrison, I stopped a nuclear bombardment of the inhabited planet by appealing to the humanity and conscience of her battleship's flag captain. It was a long shot, even by my standards, but it worked.

With nothing else to lose, I try it again. Once again using our comm buoys and transmitting in the clear, I beg the surviving SDF forces not to kill the innocents on that station. It's even possible my pleas might reach someone on *Vigilant Dagger* who still has a shred of conscience. It's a long shot, but it's all I have.

Unfortunately, I don't hear any responses, even from my attempts to call Illian and O'Malley on *Bainbridge*. Either *Vigilant Dagger* is jamming them, or they're purposefully staying quiet for some reason. Either way, I know it wouldn't matter. They would refuse to run, even if it means taking on the entirety of Jacobs's surviving fleet in their one small ship.

Idiots. Those wonderful, brave idiots.

The hours pass in agonizing slowness. Six different times, I consider commanding the three surviving ships of my little fleet to burn their engines on full power, the better to get back to the station and the battlefield faster, but I can't. We need to be going slower this time when we engage the enemy. We have one last shot at destroying them. We won't get another.

# EIGHTY-SIX
# A GLIMMER

## BRAD MENDOZA

"Admiral, we're getting our first sensor view over the horizon!"

I grip the arms of my chair so hard my fingers hurt. "Is the station still there? Are we too late?" I'm not exactly the picture of calm, cool professionalism right now.

There's a long pause, and I look over at the sensor officer, expecting to see her stunned into silence, unable to come to grips with the deaths of thousands of people while we were helplessly out of range. But instead, I see her staring down at her console with a quizzical expression, head cocked to one side and nose wrinkled.

"What's going on, Lieutenant?" Quarrie asks before I can say anything. "Tell us!" It's the most excited I've ever seen her.

The sensor officer shakes herself out of her fugue state and looks up at us, surprise writ large on her features. "I don't understand, sirs. The station . . . it's intact. But . . ." She shakes her head and makes a flicking motion on her console that throws the sensor image onto the main forward viewscreen.

There's a sharp intake of breath all around as we take in the sight. She's right: the station is still there. As is *Vigilant Dagger*, but its escorts are gone. And on closer inspection, the enormous Hades-class battleship is heavily damaged, venting atmosphere through a dozen hull breaches, sitting dead in space just inside laser range of the station, but not firing on it at all.

"What happened?" I ask no one in particular.

Not surprisingly, no one speaks up. As we leave the sixth planet's low orbit to head up to where the third moon, the station, and the damaged enemy battleship await us, we start to see more details.

*Bainbridge* is alive! She's holding position defiantly between *Vigilant Dagger* and the station. Every so often, she lets loose a laser blast at the giant ship, carving a little deeper into its hull with her underpowered weaponry.

"How?" Captain Quarrie breathes. "A destroyer, taking out a battleship?"

I shake my head. "There's no way."

The overhead bridge speakers crackle to life, and a familiar voice fills the compartment. "Admiral Mendoza, are we glad to see you," Francis Illian says happily. "Reporting in that we've neutralized the threat. All enemy escorts destroyed, and *Vigilant Dagger* has been disabled. Awaiting orders."

"Guns," I say in awe, defaulting to the nickname as my brain goes mostly blank. "What did you do?"

"Well, sir. We sort of remembered that this station was a munitions factory. Specifically, a munitions factory that makes mines. Tiny buggers—hard to see unless you're looking for them—but they pack quite a punch. Earl Jacobs found that out when he tried to approach the station with his fleet." Suddenly, I realize what *Bainbridge* was really doing when Illian was dancing the ship in and out of the enemy's range during the third pass. He wasn't just trying to distract them by firing a few missiles; he was laying mines, small enough that Jacobs couldn't see them because he wasn't looking.

There's a whoop of triumph from next to me, and I look over in surprise to see Quarrie, her fist in the air. "Commander Illian, drinks are on me!"

"He's mine, chica," another voice intrudes, and we turn in shock to see Hayley seated at one of the auxiliary consoles on *Gunslinger's* bridge, grinning at us.

"Hayley! You're supposed to be on that station," I say, my voice rising an octave.

She shrugs. "Sure, boss, but someone needed to stay here and keep you safe. SDF had a few sympathizers still on this ship—a few tried to storm the bridge during the last pass. They're all dead now. You're welcome."

"Illian?" I ask, somehow needing the man's confirmation of what I can see with my own eyes.

"Sorry for the subterfuge, Admiral," my underling says, not sounding apologetic at all. "But Hayley and I both thought she'd be needed more there with you than with us."

I can't find words, but Hayley, of course, can. "Capitana," she says to Quarrie, "Illy is mine, but if you wanna buy us both drinks, go ahead."

We're drawing closer to the battlefield now, and the sensor picture continues to resolve. We still can't see the mines, but we can see the debris field from where they took out Jacobs's smaller ships entirely. It's a testament to the designers and builders of *Vigilant Dagger* that the battleship is even still in one piece.

"Admiral," the comm officer reports, "we're getting a distress call from the enemy battleship."

I nod, and she plays it on the bridge speakers. A voice I've never heard before frantically speaks. "Navy ships. We're disabled, and our reactor is in danger of going critical. Requesting immediate assistance. Power is out all over the ship!" As if to punctuate his call, several escape pods launch from all over *Vigilant Dagger*. "We don't have enough pods for everyone. We can hold the reactor for an hour, maybe two, so help us. Please help us!"

I trade a look with Quarrie and nod again. As much as I may hate Jacobs and everything he stands for, and by extension those who've willingly helped him, we're not the monsters they are. A distress call must be responded to.

"*Bainbridge*, keep your distance," I order. "You're too small to help with the evacuation anyway. *Guardian*, provide overwatch in case the SDF has any other ships still around. *Liberator*, follow us in. You dock on *Dagger*'s starboard, we'll take port."

All our ships acknowledge my orders, and *Gunslinger* and *Liberator* cautiously approach *Vigilant Dagger*. The same voice that called for help speaks to us several more times, giving status updates on their reactor, which he claims they've been able to keep from going critical, but he's not sure how long they can hold it. Our scans corroborate the story, showing some minor radiation leaking from the ship's aft flank, but luckily nothing that signifies a reactor about to blow.

Time passes, and we finish our approach, *Bainbridge* transmitting us a map of the minefield so we can avoid falling prey to the same trap that caught our enemies. We come into close range of the derelict battleship so we can dock and offload the survivors, all the while watching it closely but seeing no signs of duplicity, not even the power signature of charging lasers or—

"Captain, incoming!" the tactical officer cries at the same moment klaxons sound and the ugly images of three massive missiles appear from *Vigilant Dagger*'s port flank, streaking straight at *Gunslinger*.

"All hands, brace for—" Captain Quarrie shouts, but it's too late.

*Gunslinger*'s defensive systems do surprisingly well, and the tactical officer thinks fast on his feet, authorizing the AI to fire even without the direct order from me or Quarrie. Point defense lasers take out two of the three missiles as they come toward us so fast they might as well be lasers. But they miss the third.

Idly, when I was at the Academy, I wondered what it might be like to be on board a ship hit by a ship-killer nuclear missile. There are rumors that the Sol Fed has come up with even more powerful antimatter weapons, but in most of human space, nothing beats the destructive power of nuclear weapons. And for the first time in my life, I have the misfortune to experience that firsthand.

In the end, it's anticlimactic, really. One second, Quarrie is shouting for us to brace for impact; the next, the ship bucks underneath us and spins like a top. Then everything goes black as the violent g-forces knock me out cold.

# EIGHTY-SEVEN
# DEVIL'S OWN

## BRAD MENDOZA

The sound of the klaxons is the first thing I become conscious of when I wake up. They seem muted and distant, like they're not really there, but maybe part of a movie someone is watching in the next room. For a moment, I'm tempted to tell them to turn down the volume.

Then, reality comes rushing back, and I suck in a deep, gasping breath as my eyes fly open to see nothing but diffuse light and clouds around me. There's a moment of panic—an instant only—before old training kicks in and I recognize the inside of a crash cocoon. The muscles in my arm protest as I reach up and find the emergency release lever to one side of my bridge chair, pulling it and watching as the cocoon retracts and deflates around me.

Around me, *Gunslinger*'s bridge is deathly still, lit only by the dimmest of red emergency lamps. Every seat is covered by a cocoon similar to the one that saved my life. A couple of them twitch and move as their occupants wake up. I carefully unstrap myself and stand, relieved to find that I'm sore but nothing appears broken. The pain will be unbearable later, but for now it just feels like I've completed a particularly strenuous workout. I imagine that without the still-functioning gravity and inertial compensators, we'd all be dead.

I move to the closest cocoon, the one encapsulating Quarrie's command chair. Finding the external release, I make it deflate and retract as mine did. I stop. Captain Risa Quarrie is dead, her eyes open wide but her neck at an unnatural angle. I swear loudly.

"Who's there?" a frantic voice asks, and I stumble my way in the wan lighting to the comm station, opening the cocoon there to find the frantic comm officer. She looks at me with wide eyes. "Sir? Admiral? I can't move!" She starts sobbing uncontrollably.

A quick survey shows me that her cocoon only retracted halfway, and the reason is apparent: there's a jagged piece of metal, part of another console by the look of it, that pierced the back of the cocoon and embedded itself in her spine.

"Don't try to move," I try to tell her, but she's too frantic to listen. Stumbling away to the emergency locker at the back of the bridge, I return a moment later with a med kit, and I hit her with a hard dose of sedatives.

To my relief, she stops weeping and her head slumps forward, but not before I tighten her seat's restraints so she hopefully won't be able to move and make the damage to her spine worse.

Around me, three others have emerged from their cocoons. The tactical officer has a bloody gash on his head but is at least upright and coherent. The helmswoman seems the least damaged of all of us. And Hayley looks up at me with wide eyes, cradling an arm but otherwise unhurt.

I quickly set them to work, opening the other cocoons. We find one more officer, the navigator, unconscious and with a broken leg—we hit her with a dose of sedatives as well to keep her under until help can arrive.

Everyone else is dead. Of the fifteen officers and enlisted crew on the bridge, only six of us are still alive, and one of those is on death's door.

"They lied to us," the tactical officer says, voice rising in near panic. "Sir, they told us they needed help. They . . . they . . ."

I put a hand on his shoulder and squeeze hard, forcing him to look at me. "They did, Commander. And it hurt us bad, but right now, we need to figure out what's going on with the rest of the ship. Then we need to get a view of the battlefield and see what's happening."

"Sir?" a small voice says, and I turn to see the helmswoman. Her console is still lit up, the only one that appears to be, and she's pointing at the screen.

We all crowd around and see that she's managed to pull up both the internal damage reports and the view from our few operating sensors. Neither story is good. *Gunslinger* is missing most of her front half. In fact, the only thing surviving of our bow, where the missile hit, is what looks to be a jagged piece of the keel, the giant central support girder—our literal spine. It sticks out from the damaged area like the bowsprit of an old sailing vessel.

But it's the external sensors that really grab my attention. The story they show is obvious: *Vigilant Dagger* didn't just hit us, they hit *Liberator* hard as well. She's still in one piece, but there are multiple decks open to space, and she's floating dead under no power, her engineering compartment breached and her reactor shut down completely, probably to prevent it from blowing.

"Sir, look!" the tactical officer says, pointing to a readout on the console. "*Vigilant Dagger* is charging laser capacitors and preparing to fire."

I see immediately what he means. The enemy battleship, playing possum up until now, is coming alive, its laser capacitors showing steadily building charges as she prepares to finish killing us and *Liberator*. Thousands are about to die, followed by everyone on *Bainbridge* and that station, unless I do something in the next thirty seconds.

A strange happens to me in this moment. Before, when faced with the first fleet engagement at Huff, I froze, unable to shoulder the responsibility of command, desperately wishing someone else would take it from me.

Here, I don't have that option, and suddenly, my brain sharpens its focus, and the sound of the klaxons and the shouts from my fellow survivors fade into the background. In an instant, I know what I have to do.

Pushing the helmswoman out of her seat, I take her place. "Everyone, find a cocoon, now!"

Stunned, they hesitate. Hayley shouts, "Now, idiotas! Move!", and it's like a starter's pistol. Each survivor runs back to their station or, in the case of the helmswoman, to my chair. There, they strap in and use the manual overrides to reinflate their cocoons around them. On the way to her seat, Hayley reinflates what's left of the comm officer's cocoon.

All of this I'm barely conscious of, as I input the commands into the helm station to goose *Gunslinger*'s remaining thrusters and stop her rotation, bringing her bow to face *Vigilant Dagger*'s port flank head-on. I hit another command that should sound a collision alarm throughout the ship, but I have no idea if anyone outside the bridge hears the warning, nor do I have time to find out. Taking a deep breath, I shove the throttles forward with a prayer, and almost cry out in exultation when the battlecruiser starts gaining speed, accelerating straight at the enemy battleship.

I wait one more second to ensure we're on course, ignoring a pop-up notification warning me that laser fire from the battleship is imminent, and then I seal my cocoon around me and prepare to die.

When *Gunslinger*'s hundreds of thousands of metric tons —those remaining with most of her front half missing—slam into *Vigilant Dagger*'s *millions* of tons, they do so with the full force of her powerful and largely undamaged main drive pushing her forward. At first, I feel a severe jolt that sends my face careening into the front of my cocoon. There's a sound of tortured metal followed by what I imagine all the groans of the damned in Tartarus must sound like. The ship bucks and shudders so hard underneath me that I'm expecting her to explode at any second.

But our main drive keeps pushing from there, and there's a new sound, like the universe's largest can being opened with a dull knife, the sound so grating that I instinctively squeeze my eyes shut hard and try to put my hands to my ears, though the cocoon stops me. The sound seems to go on forever, and I think that I must have already died and this is part of my well-deserved eternal torture, but then it stops, and everything goes deathly silent.

# EIGHTY-EIGHT
# DEAD . . . AGAIN

## BRAD MENDOZA

There's no way any of us should have survived that. But at the end of the day, the only new casualty on the bridge is the injured comm officer, whose pierced cocoon couldn't save her from the jagged piece of metal already impaling her.

The tactical officer weeps over her, and it makes me wonder if there was more there than simple professional respect between them.

Either way, and not counting the still passed-out navigator, there are four of us alive and functional. Unfortunately, the same can't be said of our ship. Just looking around the bridge, with its twisted and deformed bulkheads and a rear hatch that thankfully popped open under the stress instead of getting bent shut so badly we'd never be able to open it, I imagine that the entire battlecruiser is now more a twisted piece of broken metal than anything resembling a queen's warship.

"Did we do it?" the helmswoman asks. "Did we save *Liberator*?"

"Only one way to make sure," I tell her soberly. The gravity is out. That it and the inertial compensators in this part of the ship gave out only just *after* we rammed that battleship is the only thing that kept us alive. I float to the back of the bridge and force open an emergency locker painted red. Inside are a dozen assault rifles and other assorted weapons, and the locker next to it holds vacsuits in various sizes. I give everyone instructions, and a few minutes later, we've all donned vacsuits, helmets, and air bladders.

I hand a rifle to the tactical officer and another to the helmswoman. At last, I look to Hayley. Her right arm floats uselessly at her side in the zero gravity, but she looks as pissed as I've ever seen her. "You can stay here," I tell her, knowing her answer before the words leave my lips.

Glaring at me, she reaches into the locker with her gloved left hand. She jams a few grenades into her vacsuit's pockets along with several extra pistol clips, and then grips one of the pistols, ready for action.

"Okay, people," I tell them all through our helmet comms. "There's no guarantee we damaged that monster enough to keep it from killing *Liberator,* then the rest of our ships, and that station. But we definitely hurt them badly. My assumption"—it's more a hope, really, but I need to keep morale up—"is that we're currently embedded into the side of *Vigilant Dagger* like a giant tick. We're going to head forward and find a way onto that ship. Then we're going to kill everyone who so much as breathes in our direction in a hostile manner. Our destination is the enemy bridge. Got it?"

Hayley nods, holsters her pistol, and uses bulkhead handholds, even with only one functional arm, to pull herself off the bridge and into the corridor beyond. The other two officers eye me skeptically but follow, and I take up the rear before moving past them to float down the corridor next to Hayley.

The next twenty minutes are some of the worst of my life. We pass few survivors but a lot of bodies. The bridge of a warship like *Gunslinger* is at the heart of the ship, literally attached to the spine and encircled by nearly as much armor as the ship's outer hull. In addition, Promethean warship bridges all have a very light netting of indestructible stellarium that crisscrosses through the bridge's armor, so expensive that its lines are thinner than a spider's web, but enough to provide some additional protection. Even with all that, the bridge was twisted and nearly destroyed. So you can imagine what happened to the rest of the ship. Most of our twenty-minute journey is spent simply trying to find ways through the ship that aren't blocked by collapsed bulkheads or warped hatches jammed shut.

For a while, we float, push, and pull our way through corridors still pressured. On the way, we find two groups of survivors. Reluctantly, I leave first the helmswoman, then the tactical officer behind to minister to the wounded crewmembers. I don't even try to suggest that Hayley, injured as she is, stay behind instead—I already know her answer.

Finally, we arrive at part of the ship that's in vacuum. Sealing a hatch behind us, we open the one between us and the airless corridor ahead, holding tight to it as the little trapped air with us escapes through it. We proceed cautiously, our suits' shoulder lamps throwing light that's all hard edges without atmo to diffuse it.

It's another few minutes, which includes two aborted paths, before we arrive at the place where *Gunslinger* simply stops. Peering out of the end of a twisted corridor completely open to space, I can see similarly peeled-open corridors on

*Vigilant Dagger* about thirty meters away. Apparently, after we rammed her and our engines finally died, we drifted back from her until part of our ship got hung up on part of her structure, keeping us together but not flush.

While I'm still analyzing the angles and having nightmarish thoughts of impaling myself on jagged girders on the other side of that gap, I hear a cry like a child going down a slide, and Hayley flies right by me and out of the opening. She's trailing something, a hose, taken from a nearby fire panel. It unspools behind her like a rope as she sails across the gap. For a second, it looks like she's going to slam right into one of the jagged ends I was afraid of, but she manages to bring her knees to her chest and kick off of it lightly with one foot, changing her course a little and landing right in the open end of one of the battleship's corridors.

"Your turn, boss," she says over the helmet comms, and I take the easy way, using the extended hose, which she's looped around a girder on the other end, to pull my way across, the assault rifle floating free on the end of its sling.

Smiling grimly, I pull myself into the battleship corridor next to Hayley and . . . fall flat on my face when I cross into the battleship's still-functioning gravity. I lift my head to see, gratefully, that no one was around to see that. When I tell this story, assuming I live long enough to do so, I'll be sure to leave that part out.

Now on board the enemy ship, all Hayley and I have to do is do the reverse of what we just did, making our way to the damaged battleship's bridge so we can seize control, only with something close to two thousand hostiles between us and there.

No sweat.

# EIGHTY-NINE
# THINNING AIR

## JESSICA LIN MENDOZA

"Make sure everyone moves as little as possible. We need to reduce our CO2 output as much as we can," I relay to the small group I've chosen to be runners. "If we're careful, we can stretch our supply by another few hours."

"Will that really make a difference?" one of the girls asks. She's young enough that she must have been a freshman at Poe's university.

"Maybe, maybe not," I tell her honestly. "But every hour we can buy is one more hour for the Navy to find us."

They all nod in desultory fashion, but then depart to carry my message to the rest of the huddled crew packed in the freighter's few remaining habitable spaces.

# NINETY
# BOARDING PARTY

## BRAD MENDOZA

We're inside Jacobs's ship now, though this part of it is nearly as twisted and gutted as what's left of *Gunslinger*. The corridor ahead of us is navigable, barely, and Hayley and I make our way carefully along it, guns at the ready as we scan ahead.

We don't see the first sign of the slave ship's crew until I'm about fifty meters down the corridor. The man, at least I think it's a man, looks a lot more like a pancake these days. Too bad for him. I'm sure he was a wonderful guy, as far as men who serve with rapist slavers go.

The next crewman we encounter is alive, though barely. I put him out of his misery before he can call to warn anyone that we're on the ship.

We kill six more men and women over the next ten minutes. None of them seems to suspect we're coming, as I suppose that after a ship rams you, you typically don't worry about any survivors from said ship boarding you as well. Their loss, our gain. And I don't feel the slightest remorse at ending their lives. They forfeited those by every interstellar law the moment they chose to be slavers, and again when they committed an act of piracy by luring us in with their false distress calls.

Hayley and I haven't taken our helmets off; there's smoke and all sorts of noxious gases spouting everywhere, but that doesn't stop me from hearing the klaxons and the call to abandon ship. I swear out loud inside the bubble helmet, drawing a sharp look from Hayley. Jacobs, unlike most ship commanders, is likely to be among the first to find an escape pod. If I'm particularly unlucky, he's already gone, and with him, Jess's coordinates. But there's nothing to do but forge ahead.

Except, maybe there is something more we can do. Why do I keep forgetting I'm an admiral? I reach out with my implant to the ship's AI. It's still there, though it's a little overtaxed right now. So it doesn't put up a fight when I enter my admiral's command codes and gain full access to its systems. I breathe a sigh of relief to see that Jacobs never thought to change the access codes—probably assuming there'd never be a member of the Promethean admiralty on board his personal battleship. Well, I never thought the guy was the brightest crayon in the box, and this proves it. The AI, still otherwise mostly ignoring me, gives me access to *everything*.

It takes my implant five seconds to locate Nedrin Jacobs, and with a grin, I lead Hayley on a hard right down an intersecting corridor. We no longer need to go to the bridge. Jacobs is already headed to the escape pods, and if we run, we can get there first.

I won't bore you with the details of how we heroically cut down several dozen more slavers on my way—slavers wearing the same plain black uniforms that seem to be the style for Jacobs's private little death squad. Let's just say I'm super heroic and leave it at that; Hayley helps a little, too. It also makes it easier that none of them are armed, and I override any warnings they try to send via the ship's systems. Not exactly a fair fight, but I'll take it.

Finally, we arrive at another junction of two corridors, just in time to see a familiar figure stumble by in the intersecting hallway, helped in his travels by a crewman under each arm and completely oblivious to the two intruders on his ship. As Jacobs passes, I catch a glimpse of blood caked on the side of his head and several scorch marks on his uniform, which gives me a measure of happiness at the thought that he might be in a lot of pain.

I turn down the intersection to follow him and his two helpers. At the other end, they stop at an escape pod. Just as one of the crewmen opens its hatch, I shoot him in the head. His friend soon follows.

Nedrin Jacobs cries out in alarm as he slumps to the deck without their support. Looking at me with wide, frantic eyes, he scrambles backward, desperately trying to reach the safety of the pod before we can close the remaining distance. One of his legs isn't working right, and he doesn't make it. I easily avoid the kick he sends my way with his good leg as his butt finally clears the hatchway's sill and lands inside the pod.

"Where is she?" I demand, pointing the assault rifle at his face.

For a second, he looks terrified. Then his face hardens into a foul and belligerent grin. "Let me go and I'll tell you where to find your—"

I lower the rifle and shoot him in the kneecap before he can finish. His attempt to negotiate disappears in a scream of agony, and for just a second, the usually deep-voiced Jacobs sings soprano.

"Try again," I growl when his wails of pain subside enough for him to hear me. When he doesn't answer, I move the gun up and fire it again, the bullet flying right by his face and slamming into the base of a console behind him.

"Ok, okay!" he screams, holding up both hands to ward me off like I'm a monster from his nightmares.

My implant pings, and I accept the coordinates. Then I switch the gun to stun rounds and shoot him again, right in his stupid face.

That's gonna leave a mark.

# PART FIVE
# AFTERMATH

# NINETY-ONE
# FRESH AIR

## JESSICA LIN MENDOZA

I stir when there's an unexpected but highly welcome noise: the clank of a hatch's locking mechanism opening.

Even the emergency lights on the bridge died hours ago when their dedicated power sources failed. We're just lucky the reactor itself never exploded after all the stress we put this freighter through. But less than an hour ago, the CO2 got to be too much, and one by one, we started to get groggy. I'm just about to close my eyes for the last time when the wonderful noise of the bridge hatch opening brings me back, despite my pounding head.

"Captain!" a voice calls—a familiar voice. Illian?

"She's over here!" I hear him yell. "O'Malley, did you rig up those air scrubbers yet? Hurry it up, man! You, get those emergency air bladders in here. On the double, Marine!"

I close my eyes, trying to fall asleep to stop the thudding

pain in my skull, wondering idly why in Hades' name Brad didn't come on board himself to get me. I'll have words with him later. He's so . . .

# NINETY-TWO
# FINDING EACH OTHER

## JESSICA LIN MENDOZA

"Captain Lin, that's the last of the escape pods, ma'am. I'm sorry."

I look at the despondent visage of Commander Jonathan Smith, acting CO of *Guardian,* the last surviving battlecruiser of Brad's fleet, which has been searching the wreckage of *Gunslinger* and *Vigilant Dagger* for the last sixteen hours while Illian and O'Malley took *Bainbridge* to a set of coordinates provided by Brad to rescue me and the people of Poe.

That was the last message Brad sent to anyone, coming from one of *Vigilant Dagger*'s escape pods before it went mysteriously dark.

"You're sure?" I ask Smith in a small voice, desperately trying to hold myself together. I'm on *Bainbridge,* still an hour out from the debris field and the floating conjoined hulks of the two large ships that were once a Hades-class battleship and a Hermes-class battlecruiser.

He nods somberly on the screen. "We've picked up every transmitting escape pod from our ships and from Bollen's—excuse me, Nedrin Jacobs's—battleship. No sign of Admiral Mendoza. Our Marines have also searched both ships top to bottom. We found a lot of survivors, ma'am, but no sign of Admiral Mendoza or Nedrin Jacobs."

Or Hayley, who was last seen leading Brad on a suicide leap to *Vigilant Dagger*.

Apparently, Nedrin Jacobs has succeeded in ruining my life once again, taking from me the only man I've ever truly loved. It's entirely no comfort that the king's cursed nephew must have also died in the process.

"Search again," I tell Smith, though I have no right to order him about. Brad's death charge at *Vigilant Dagger* gave *Liberator* the time to get her critical systems back online. The battleship is tremendously damaged, but still somehow spaceworthy, and Admiral Turly is alive and now technically in command of what remains of our fleet.

But Smith doesn't argue. "Aye, Captain." The screen goes dark.

Tears well up in my eyes as I regard the blank console screen in front of me in *Bainbridge*'s ready room. Before I know what I'm doing, I scream at the top of my lungs and bash both fists into it, like I've seen Brad do a few times when he's extremely frustrated. It doesn't make me feel an iota better.

The hatch to the bridge opens, and a face peers in. "Jess, you okay?" Harris asks timidly.

I shake my head, and next thing I know, he's kneeling next to my chair, holding me as I cry into his shoulder like I did back in Carter's System so many months ago, when I thought I'd lost Brad the first time.

Ten minutes later, my tears exhausted, I'm back on my destroyer's bridge. On the forward viewscreen, Laia has helpfully displayed our sensor feed, with every passive and active sensor we have trained on the debris field still the better part of forty-five minutes away from us, as Kelly ekes every spare ounce of power out of our drive.

I try my best not to cry again in front of everyone as I study the feed, searching hard for any sign of a missed escape pod in the debris field and the space surrounding it. My knees grow weak, and I'm about to collapse to the deck when a strong arm snakes under mine and catches me.

"I've got you, Captain," Gunny rumbles as I sag into him.

"He's gone, Quinn," I say in a near whisper, as if I don't want the universe to hear me.

"No way," he says. "The admiral's too stubborn to die. You'll see. He'll show up for dinner and ask why we started eating without him."

I choke a half sob, half laugh at the mental image, just as a shout comes from across the bridge.

"Captain! *Guardian* reports they've found something in the debris field. Looks like flash code!"

# NINETY-THREE
# REPEAT SALVATION

## BRAD MENDOZA

This is the second time in the last year that I've found myself drifting in a damaged escape pod with little chance of rescue. Turns out shooting a gun inside a pod can damage some of the delicate circuitry. Who knew? Anyway, the last time this happened, after Richard Ingbar dragged me into the pod on *Persephone* before he valiantly blew up the ship to take out a Koratan destroyer, I was unconscious until Jess found my pod.

This time, I'm awake for the entire nerve-racking, terribly boring wait. In fact, it takes so long that I have to keep shooting Jacobs with new stun rounds every time the big imbecile wakes up, cursing and promising to tell his mommy how mean I've been to him. Hayley seems to get a kick out of that. After a while, we start taking turns.

The waiting sucks, but shooting Nedrin over and over

again *is* pretty cathartic. I wonder if, assuming we get rescued, the Navy will let me keep him in the brig of whatever ship I'm commanding so I can pop on down whenever I'm stressed or weary and shoot him a couple of times to lift my spirits.

I'm not kidding—this is the most fun I've had since my wedding night. Don't tell Jess.

This time, my first clue that she's coming to save me again isn't hearing her voice over my nonfunctioning comm. Instead, it's when I see the lights of a large battlecruiser approaching and I sag in relief, finally dropping the two bare wires I've been mashing together to create flash code with the pod's external lights until my fingers bled.

Hayley, typically, never even tried to help with that little task. I mean, she only has one functioning arm, but the least she could have done was offer.

# NINETY-FOUR
# REUNIONS

## JESSICA LIN MENDOZA

"I love you."

Those are the three most wonderful words any human being can hear. Hearing them now from my husband of one month, after he and I both somehow successfully cheated death again, has to be in the top five of the greatest events in human history, and there's absolutely no way you can convince me otherwise.

"I love you too, Brad."

The hatch to our quarters on *Bainbridge* opens after a short knock, and a familiar head pokes into the gap, though we can't see the man's face because he's holding a hand over his eyes. "Admiral, Captain, you decent?"

"Shut up and come in, Francis," I say with an involuntary giggle. I blame the CO2 poisoning.

He enters as directed and smiles widely at me and Brad sitting practically on top of each other on the room's small couch. I scramble off my husband's lap when, behind him, enters Rear Admiral Christoph Turly.

"Don't move on my account, Captain Lin," the redheaded admiral says with a smile almost as big as Francis's. "I'd say if two people ever earned the right to show a little PDA, it's you two."

Nevertheless, I take a new seat *next* to my husband, though still very, very close to him, my hand holding his in a death grip. I'm not letting go of Brad for at least the next year. Every time I do, one or both of us have to go and get killed. By now, we've died so many times that even cats would envy us.

"How's our guest?" Brad asks Turly as he and Francis shut the hatch door behind them.

"Singing like a canary now that he's realized his fancy title means nothing," Turly says, taking one of the room's folding chairs from its stowage on the nearest bulkhead and handing it to Francis before grabbing one for himself. The two of them set the chairs up and sit across from us. "Actually, I think he's hoping that if he talks, we'll protect him from Admiral Mendoza. Did you really shoot him over a dozen times in that escape pod?"

Brad smiles. "Only a dozen? Seems I still owe him a few hundred."

"Anyway, it's amazing how much the man hates you," Turly continues, ignoring my husband's good humor. "He and his mother sided with Fuller—no surprise there; for all their supposed loyalty to Charles, they were always snakes—and they convinced the false king to put Jacobs in charge of subduing this sector with the SDF forces already in position here and that monster Hades-class battleship."

"And the whole Bollen thing?" I ask, though I'm fairly certain I already know the answer.

"Well," Turly says, opening up a folding chair normally

stowed against one bulkhead and sitting across from us as Francis does the same with another. "Like I said, he *really* hates the two of you. When he found out you were investigating his slaving operations, he saw an opportunity to lure you in and exact his revenge." The admiral huffs a laugh. "Undid his whole operation is what it did. Like grabbing a tiger by the tail. Remind me sometime why I ever thought I could mess with the two of you."

Brad gives him a warm smile. "And what about his sister?"

Turly sobers up a little. "Dead. The brig on *Gunslinger* was in the bow, the part that blew up when *Vigilant Dagger* launched its surprise attack. Tell me, how did you figure out who she really was?"

I find it hard to be upset that Jasmine Jacobs died in the battle. There's a certain poetic justice to her own brother pulling the trigger that killed her.

"I figured out her identity as soon as I determined Andre Bollen was Nedrin Jacobs," Brad replies. "They have the same dead blue eyes. I'm guessing he took those slaves from Poe just to make us follow him after it looked like we'd hit a dead end, and he sent his little sister along to fake saving us and make *sure* that we followed him to the natural conclusion of his trap."

"What about Gregor?" I ask, surprised. "She almost got me killed there."

Brad nods. "I think she went off script, maybe believing we were a distraction for her dear older brother and that if she could kill you off and then maybe me later, it would get Nedrin focused back on the important task of subduing the Corpus Christi Cluster."

Turly glares at Brad. "You're no fun. That's exactly what happened, at least the way Jacobs tells it. He's blaming her for her own death, believe it or not. All too happy to tell us how she screwed things up. Plus, my interrogators can be very persuasive."

"I'm sure," Brad says dryly, still smiling. "I'm just glad they both failed to kill us."

Turly shakes his head again. "Seriously, is there anyone in this galaxy who *doesn't* hate you?"

"My mom," Brad says back with an even wider grin.

"Wonders never cease," the other man says, returning a measure of his smile. "I doubt King Chance knew all that Jacobs was doing here, but I also imagine Jacobs thought that delivering you to Chance would gain him even more favor with his new master and the Jutzens. Either way, it was pretty elaborate, using the reality of his slave raids around the Cluster to invent the fiction of Andre Bollen and lure you in. His sister really did mess the whole thing up by forcing you to take that detour to Huff, though."

"I want to see him. I want to see Jacobs."

Everyone turns to stare at me in shock, and I'm just as surprised as they are that the words came out of my mouth.

"Jess, I don't think that's such a—" Brad starts to protest, but I cut him off.

"I need to see him. I need to talk to him. Alone."

He studies me, frowning, for a long time. Finally, he nods. "Okay, but I'll be right outside with Gunny and Hayley. Even with one arm, she's more than a match for Ned."

An hour later, after cleaning up and a brief shuttle ride, I'm standing in an interrogation room on *Liberator,* looking across a metal table at the seated and handcuffed form of Nedrin Jacobs. He sneers at me across the table, though the effect is partially ruined by the fact that half his face is swollen black and blue from where Brad shot him with a stun round at point-blank range.

"So the tramp finally comes to see her better," he says, slurring his words a little through the swelling.

I don't reply, not giving him the satisfaction of a rejoinder. I just stand there, staring at him, my face expressionless as I look at him and feel . . . nothing. No trauma response, no near panic. Simply nothing.

"You ruined my life, you . . ." He calls me another foul name, but it gains no purchase in my brain, washing over me like a sprinkle of rain, annoying, but not enough to bother with. I don't even feel the urge to point out how he really ruined his *own* life, how each of us has the agency to make our own decisions, and he chose poorly time and time again.

"If you and your self-righteous husband hadn't sent those lies to the press at Gerson, it would be *me* running the government now instead of Chance Fuller."

I resist the urge to laugh. I can't tell if he's being serious or not, but I also can't imagine even the Jutzens not recognizing the severe imbalance of the man sitting across from me. If he wants to delude himself otherwise, that's fine with me.

He starts to fidget, shifting in his seat, obviously unsettled by my refusal to engage him. Up until now, I haven't said a word, and I can see it's driving him crazy. I smile a little, and it makes his face scrunch up in confusion.

"Y-you haven't won," he stutters. "*He* won't let you. He's coming for you and Brad, and he'll get you both when you least expect it."

"King Chance has tried to get us before," I finally reply. "Hasn't gone well for anyone who's tried."

He attempts to laugh, but it comes out more as a rasping cough. "Chance is a figurehead. I'm talking about the real power behind the throne. And not that daft Jutzen Führer either. The real boss. He's one you'll never see coming until his knife slices your throat."

I frown a little at that. I've listened to the recordings of Jacobs's taunts toward Brad, and this is now the second time he's mentioned a mysterious boss. I can only wonder who it is. I imagine Turly's interrogators will eventually get it out of him, and I won't be surprised if we find it's the same person who was behind Hernandez, Duchess Charlotte, and Hornsby.

I turn my mind back to Jacobs now, studying him. I truly expected that, upon seeing my old abuser again, my chest would constrict with fear and my knees would go weak. But looking at him now, sitting there chained to the table, a broken man with no authority left over anyone else, ranting like a lunatic, I realize something: it's been a long time since he's had any real power over me. And for the first time in this conversation, I feel an emotion: pity. Oh, I don't sympathize with the man, but I do pity him, the same way I might pity an ant on the sidewalk who gets trampled by an unseeing pedestrian.

"How does it feel," he growls, though the slurring ruins the effect, "when you're with your husband, to think of the times you and I were together before you even met him?"

I smile again, born of finally understanding. "Actually, Nedrin, I wouldn't know. Since Gerson, I've rarely thought of you at all."

His face goes slack, and he stares at me through wide, red-rimmed eyes. I turn and walk out of the room, never looking back, closing the book entirely on any chapter of my life that ever included Nedrin Jacobs.

I'm free.

An hour later, Turly informs us that an explosive implant triggered in Jacobs's brain and killed him instantly. I feel nothing other than disappointment that we won't be able to force him to give up the name of his mysterious employer. Turly is convinced Jacobs triggered the implant himself, but I have to wonder if maybe someone else did it for him. He wouldn't have been that brave.

# NINETY-FIVE
# FINAL DECISIONS

## BRAD MENDOZA

"She thought you were the finest flag officer she ever served under, you know."

I look up in surprise from my temporary desk on Huff Naval Base, where I've just finished signing off on the strategic acquisition of five thousand boxes of Girl Scout cookies for what's left of the fleet. Turns out Troop 486 on Cillian Heights was willing to match the offer from Troop 1326 on Linford Commons. Now if I could only get the Cub Scouts to give us a similar deal on that popcorn of theirs, I'd be a real hero.

Commander Jonathan Smith is standing at my hatch. Sorry, *Captain* Jonathan Smith; what good is being an admiral if I can't hand out field promotions? I motion for him to come in and take a seat. It's been three weeks since the battle at Linford Commons, and I've been here helping Chris Turly deal with the myriad tasks to prepare his few surviving ships to hold this sector until I can convince Annie to send him reinforcements.

"Who?" I ask Smith, though I already know of whom he speaks.

"Captain Quarrie. She said it wasn't even close. She would have followed you into the pits of Tartarus, sir."

"She did," I say sadly. "I just wish she'd come out the other side with us. Or that I could have saved more of her crew."

He smiles, a surprisingly warm expression on his face. "You didn't kill anyone on *Gunslinger*'s crew, sir. Jacobs did when he invited us in under a false distress call and took the coward's path. When you charged his ship afterward, you did so to save thousands more. You did the right thing, Admiral. And I'm certain, sir, that if we could ask Captain Quarrie now if she regretted a thing about it, she'd tell us to stop talking nonsense and get on with the task of saving the Federation."

I return his smile, just a little, surprised to find that I agree with him. I've had a lot of time to think about it since the battle, and as pained as I am for the lives lost on *Gunslinger*, it really was the only way. And every time I start to get down on myself for it, I stop, mainly because I won't dishonor the brave men and women—including Risa Quarrie—who died on that battlecruiser to stop a tyrant and a slaver by even suggesting that their sacrifice wasn't necessary.

It's an odd feeling. I've talked long into the night a few times with Chris about it, and even more with Jess. And somehow, I've made my peace with it all. Beyond that, and strangely enough, in Jacobs's psychotic attempt to make me relive Bellerophon, I might have even made a little peace with that as well. The nightmares, at least, have mostly stopped for the time being.

Odd that I would have such a terrible man to thank for that. I wish he'd survived so I could go down to the brig and show my thanks by shooting him in the face again.

"I think you're probably right, Captain," I tell Smith. "I think Risa would tell us exactly what."

We sit there, both of our minds dwelling on the indomitable battlecruiser captain we'll all miss, until Smith clears his throat again. "Admiral, begging your pardon, but what will you do?"

"Excuse me?"

"About the war, sir. Scuttlebutt gets around, Admiral. We all know you tried to hand off command a few times to Rear Admiral Turly. And Commander Lund looked in the map room after you were in there last month. Said you'd been studying the Bellerophon system. I know it's not my place, sir, but we all want to know if you're still intent on forging your own path"—he's diplomatic enough not to say 'running away'—"or if you'll go back to the queen and take command of part of the fleet, like she wants you to."

I frown at him now. "Captain, that is an incredibly brash and inappropriate question."

"Sorry, sir." He doesn't look the least bit apologetic.

It's hard to be mad at him. I couldn't see *Guardian* on the sensor screen when I was doing my suicide charge in *Gunslinger* at Jacobs's battleship, but I learned later that Smith threw his battlecruiser in between *Vigilant Dagger* and the station, preventing Jacobs from destroying it with a last-ditch barrage out of revenge for me slamming my ship into his. *Bainbridge* had a part in that desperate defense as well, but without the larger and better-armed *Guardian,* Illian told me that at least several missiles would have gotten through.

Still, I give Smith my best stern admiral's glare. "Talk like that, Captain Smith, might make me rethink recommending you for the Queen's Star when I get back to Her Majesty's fleet."

He smiles once more, a wide grin that mingles happiness and relief. "Well, sir, we certainly wouldn't want that, would we?"

# EPILOGUE

## BRAD MENDOZA

"We *must* retake Hecate, Your Majesty. If we fail to regain that system, we forever lose our only staging point for the battle to liberate Prometheus!"

"I disagree. Your Majesty, we must consolidate our forces here in Kipling and cede outlying territories to concentrate our defenses in the worlds we can hope to hold."

"Both of you are wrong. With all due respect . . ."

I listen with only half an ear as the myriad of stuffy admirals in the large conference room in Kipling's ducal palace argue with each other while Annie regards them from the head of the table with a permanent frown. Her senior admirals have been squabbling for the better part of two incredibly long hours, and none can seem to agree with a single thing that any of the others has said.

"Silence," Annie finally says, not raising her voice but

achieving instant obedience nonetheless. "Admiral Mendoza, you've been quiet. What are your thoughts?"

"Huh?" I pretend to be surprised. "About what?" I know what she's asking, but I'm playing for time. Because I also know my answer, but it's very much not one I want to give, despite thinking long and hard about it on the long journey here to Kipling on *Bainbridge*, which is still in orbit above our heads with a good chunk of Annie's fleet. I wish desperately that I were up there with Jess and our crew, not down here in this room full of flag officers.

"About what our next strategic move should be," my queen clarifies in a long-suffering tone. "Do you agree with Admiral Barringer about retaking Hecate, or do you favor Vice Admiral Carmichael's take on consolidating our forces at Kipling?"

I look at Barringer, an octogenarian whom Annie plucked up from retirement to be the senior admiral in her fleet. He glares at me from across the table. Never did like the old guy, not ever since he spoke to us at the Academy and was so boring I fell asleep and got screamed at by the instructors afterward. On the same side as me, but two seats down, Vice Admiral Carmichael leans forward and spears me with her own icy gaze. Never met her before today, but I already don't like her.

"Neither," I finally say, ignoring the indignant grunts from both admirals.

"Then what do you suggest?" Annie presses, one corner of her mouth quirking upward in what might be the beginning of an amused smile.

I plead with her silently not to make me say it, but she stares back just as defiantly.

In the end, she's a queen, and I'm a mere admiral, so I fold first. "We need to go to Admiral Oliphant at Gerson, force him to choose sides, and make him bring his fleet back here to stand with you, Your Majesty."

"But the stellarium!" Admiral Barringer protests. "Your Majesty, we can't ask our fleet there to leave it undefended; that would be—"

Annie holds up a hand again to cut him off. "Go on," she prompts me.

"We've been thinking about the stellarium at Gerson all wrong," I say, gaining steam. "We assumed it was the reason the Jutzens invaded, but they've clearly been planning this long before we ever found the deposit. Sure, it may have moved their timetable up, but the events in Koratas and at Hudson confirm they've been preparing to invade Prometheus probably for years."

I leave off the rest of the thought, which is that even the Jutzens don't seem to be the ones making all these plans. I agree with Jess's assessment from her brief interrogation of Jacobs, that he was telling the truth and someone else is pulling the strings, like a puppet master juggling a dozen marionettes across the Federation and Confederacy.

"But even if the Nazis get their hands on the stellarium," I continue, "it will take them *years* to mine and even more to build ships from it. There isn't a single operating shipyard in the Fringe that can work with stellarium at that scale—it requires too much specific infrastructure that's never been needed this far from any previously discovered deposits. We're talking four, maybe as many as six years before the Jutzens could get their first stellarium-hulled ships into service."

"I disagree," Carmichael starts, but Annie silences her with a glare.

"We need to give up Gerson," I continue, sitting up straighter now, "because it's always been our Achilles' heel. The Jutzens knew we were so intent on defending it that they used it as a distraction to take Prometheus itself and a third of the Federation along with it. So let's turn our weakness into theirs. Let them have Gerson, and they'll be the ones who have to devote half their fleet to holding it, while we can take what Oliphant has of first and second fleets and use them to beat back the Jutzens and King Chance's forces on all sides." I'm breathing hard by the end for some reason.

The table is silent, eerily so. Predictably, it's Admiral Barringer who speaks first. "I admit there's some merit to the plan, My Queen." His tone says he sees exactly *zero* merit. "But Fleet Admiral Oliphant seems content to sit out the war and see who wins before he chooses a side. He's ignored every envoy and message we've sent him, even those directly bearing your royal seal. So while *Vice* Admiral Mendoza may be right in some ways, it's a moot point if we cannot count on Oliphant to even talk to us." It's the perfect diplomatic answer. He's managed to discredit my plan without directly discrediting *me*. He badly wants to do that as well but lacks the guts, given that it's clear Annie has a soft spot for me. A well-planned, very political move on his part.

I can see Annie is about to answer him, but I jump in and do it first. "He'll talk to *me*."

All eyes turn back my way, and I continue. "His daughter —my ex-wife—likely died in the bombardment of Prometheus." It's surprising how hard those words are for me to say. "And knowing Terrence Oliphant, he somehow blames me. He'll talk to me, even if it's just to tell me that he *won't* help us."

"Then what good will it do?" Carmichael demands. "If you get him to talk to you but you're certain he'll say no, why go to all the effort and risk losing ships and spreading our forces thin to send you there?"

I look over at her and smile. "Because, Admiral Carmichael, if I can't talk Terrence Oliphant into doing the right thing and supporting his queen, then maybe I'll have better luck with his successor."

It takes a second for the import of my chosen wording to sink in. Carmichael gasps first, but it's Barringer who speaks up. "Are you seriously saying that you'll remove Oliphant from the chain of command if he refuses to side with Queen Anne? You're daft, man. He's a fleet admiral, and support from the queen or not, you're his subordinate, and one he hates with a particular passion. Not to mention that his fleet is far larger than ours."

I look across the table and smile at him now, showing my teeth. "You misunderstand, Admiral. If Terrence Oliphant refuses to side with Queen Anne, I don't intend to remove him from command. I intend to kill him."

He starts to sputter, as does nearly every other admiral at the table, even the ones previously silent, all shouting over each other and having a contest for the one who can find the most creative way to call me an idiot without drawing the queen's ire.

"Silence!" Annie says, louder this time, slamming her hand on the table for emphasis, immediately shutting up every flag officer in the room. "Brad, what do you need in order to make this happen?"

I ignore the expressions of utter shock around the table and look at her grimly. "I need a fleet, Your Majesty. Manned by commanders I personally select who won't be overawed by Oliphant's bad breath just because he's a fleet admiral." I cast a look at Admiral Barringer, who glares back at me. "Give me that, and I'll charge the fires of Hell with a bucket of water. I'll bring you Oliphant's fleets one way or another, because I have to—because it's quite literally the only chance we have to win this war."

The room is so silent I can practically hear Barrington's pacemaker hammering away in his chest across the table.

Annie studies me, and I study her. We exchange a flurry of short messages through our implant comms, mostly about a certain redheaded King's Cross agent, whom I want to come along with me for the mission. My queen relents on that point surprisingly quickly, if not on a few others.

When we're done with our silent negotiations, I scowl at her for good measure. She made *me* be the one to state the obvious: that my ex-father-in-law is the key to victory and no one else is as well suited to bring her that key—dead or alive—as I am. I may never forgive her for that, even though it had to be done. If the queen herself had been the first to suggest killing her star nation's senior admiral, it would have undermined her in the eyes of the other admirals at the table. This way, she can turn the majority of their anger onto me.

Finally, Annie nods for all to see, looking suitably and very royally reluctant to agree to such an outlandish and rakish plan. "Very well, Vice Admiral Mendoza," she says with proper solemnity. "Have your list of ships and commanders on my desk by 1600 tomorrow. You'll have your fleet, Brad, and you'll get to go back to Gerson. This time, please do try not to die."

THE END OF BOOK NINE

Don't ever miss a new release!

Sign up now for Skyler's newsletter and get access to new release updates, free content, and great deals.

Just go to
**www.skylerramirez.com**

# BOOKS BY SKYLER RAMIREZ

## DUMB LUCK AND DEAD HEROES

The Worst Ship in the Fleet

The Worst Spies in the Sector

The Worst Pirate Hunters in the Fringe

The Worst Rescuers in the Republic

The Worst Detectives in the Federation

The Worst Traitors in the Confederacy

The Worst Fugitives in the Star Nation

The Worst Mercenaries in the Border Systems

The Worst Admiral in the Star Cluster

The Worst Carrier in the Resistance (Coming Soon)

## A STAR NATION IN PERIL

*Set in the same universe as Dumb Luck and Dead Heroes*

Rogue Agent

Suicide Mission

Assassin's Flight

## THE GALAXY'S WORST MERCENARIES

*Set in the same universe as Dumb Luck and Dead Heroes*

The Kaelen Extraction: A Billy Firebrand Adventure

The Calypso Enigma: A Billy Firebrand Adventure (Coming Soon)

## THE BRAD MENDOZA CHRONICLES

*Short stories in the same universe as Dumb Luck and Dead Heroes*

Saving the Academy

Battle for Poe

Siege of Jalisco

Death Station

Bells and Bullets

---

## THE FOUR WORLDS

The Four Worlds: The Truth

The Four Worlds: Subversion

The Four Worlds: Wrath of Mars

Ascension (Working Title; Coming 2026)

Revolution: A Four Worlds Story

## BLACK SKY CLUB (WITH STEPHEN GAY)

Awakening

## STANDALONE SHORT STORIES

Serena

## TRANSLATIONS

Select books also available in:

German

French

Italian

Spanish

Japanese

Simplified Chinese

Hindi

Dutch

# ABOUT THE AUTHOR

I just love writing. My goal is to write books that my readers enjoy and that celebrate everyday imperfect heroes. I want to show that everyone, no matter how life has dealt with them or how they've dealt with life, deserves a second chance and can go on to do amazing things. Just look at Brad and Jessica in Dumb Luck and Dead Heroes or Jinny Ambrosa and Tyrus Tyne in The Four Worlds.

It's important to me that everyone be able to read my books, including my teenage children, so I purposefully leave out any swearing or graphic scenes, though I don't shy away from serious topics. In this, I follow a tradition set by many (far better) writers before me, most notably in my life, Louis L'Amour.

As for the personal side, I live in Texas with my wife and four children (and often a revolving door of exchange students), and I work for a major tech company in my spare time. But writing is my passion, and I often toil into the early hours of morning, especially on the weekends, and it's all worth it when I see people enjoy my books.

Thanks for reading!

Skyler Ramirez

Visit me at www.skylerramirez.com

amazon.com/stores/author/B0BLM4MML2
facebook.com/skylerramirezauthor
instagram.com/skyler.ramirez.author
tiktok.com/@skylerramirez_author

Made in United States
Orlando, FL
10 December 2025

74232642R00272